What readers are saying about previous books by

DIANNA CRAWFORD

"Your stories have been the refreshing oasis that I so often need but can never quite find."—Kathryn Soulier, Louisiana

"I could *not* put your books down! I have highly recommended them and passed them around to my friends."—Mary Lou Hess, Illinois

"So real, exciting, and funny. We have problems every day, and it's so much fun to see how God will help us. Your story shows this in a big and wonderful way."—Sherrie Sumner, Texas

"I used to laugh at my mom whenever I'd see her crying over something that happened in the book she was reading, but now I understand why she does. Now it's her turn to laugh at me, because I have been crying over your books."—Quimbly Walker, Texas

"I loved your book so much that I read it over and over. I thank you for writing such wonderful books that have to do with God, romance, and our nation's history."—Kim Hanson, Maine

"I can't begin to tell you how much I enjoyed your book. Please keep up the great work."—Jo An McNiel, Texas

"My seventeen-year-old daughter and I just finished 'devouring' your Freedom's Holy Light series. We both enjoyed them tremendously. Could hardly put them down."—Doy Groenenberg, Washington

"Definitely the best books I've ever read."—Jasmine Madson, Minnesota

"Your books have turned many a boring night into a wonderful evening and a trip back in time."—Stephanie Bastion, Illinois

"You don't just tell a story; you make it live. I look forward to each evening when, once again, I laugh with true enjoyment and get to know the oh-so-interesting family of characters you have created."—Deborah Jones, Maryland

HeartQuest brings you romantic fiction
with a foundation of biblical truth.
Adventure, mystery, intrigue, and suspense
mingle in these heartwarming stories of
men and women of faith striving to build
a love that will last a lifetime.

May HeartQuest books sweep you
into the arms of God, who longs for you
and pursues you always.

Freedom's Belle

Dianna Crawford

HEART
QUEST®

Romance fiction from
Tyndale House Publishers, Inc.
WHEATON, ILLINOIS

Visit Tyndale's exciting Web site at www.tyndale.com

Check out the latest about HeartQuest Books at www.heartquest-romances.com

HeartQuest is a registered trademark of Tyndale House Publishers, Inc.

Edited by Kathryn S. Olson

Designed by Jackie Noe

Scripture quotations are taken from the *Holy Bible,* King James Version.

Scripture quotation in the epigraph is taken from the *Holy Bible,* New Living Translation,
copyright © 1996. Used by permission of Tyndale House Publishers, Inc., Wheaton, Illinois 60189.
All rights reserved.

Library of Congress Cataloging-in-Publication Data

Crawford, Dianna, date
  Freedom's belle / Dianna Crawford.
    p. cm.
  ISBN 0-8423-1918-2 (SC)
  1. Frontier and pioneer life—Fiction. 2. Tennessee—Fiction.   I. Title.
PS3553.R27884 F72 2001
813'.54—dc21   00-046703

Printed in the United States

06 05 04 03 02 01
9 8 7 6 5 4 3 2 1

I dedicate this novel to Sally Laity and Sue Rich,
who gave selflessly of their time to take yet another long walk with me,
and to Kathy Olson,
who has been the thoughtful, gentle, and most gracious
editor of this trilogy.

How do you know what will happen tomorrow?
For your life is like the morning fog—
it's here a little while, then it's gone.
JAMES 4:14

1

Salem, North Carolina
June 1795

"This sure is livin'," Drew Reardon drawled as he lazed back in one of the barn-shaded chairs lining the front of Salem's livery. Stretching out his long legs in the sultry afternoon, he crossed one Indian-moccasined foot over the other. "Yessir, just sittin' here next to the road and watchin' all of North Carolina go by."

"What y'all means is, watchin' *me* go by, totin' water while you sits dere on yo' lazy behind." Drew's Negro hunting partner growled his displeasure in a fair imitation of his Indian name, Black Bear, as he trudged from the well with a bucket in each hand. But unlike the furry creature, sweat beads glistened across his wide brow.

Drew stifled a chuckle, but a one-sided smirk managed to slide upward. "Now, Joshua," he said, calling his partner by the name he'd gone by as a small child—before he and his family escaped the slavery of a Virginia plantation and found refuge with the Shawnee. "You knew you'd have to pretend to be my 'boy' if you wanted to come east of the mountains. And we got us a string of horses that need feedin' and waterin'."

1

Bear swerved toward Drew, stopping directly in front of him, his wide-set eyes turning to angry slits.

Sensing a dousing might be in the offing, Drew sat up straight.

"Are you sho' tomorrow is June third?"

Drew relaxed slightly. "Positive."

"Well, dat teacher fella better show up den, cuz I'm gettin' shed a dis place with or without him."

"Now that's gratitude," Drew quipped. Nonetheless, he prudently came to his feet—those buckets were mighty full. "Here I took the trouble of lettin' you come all this way with me to fetch back Reardon Valley's very first schoolteacher, and all you want to do is get outta here. Just cuz you gotta wear those raggedy ol' clothes and keep your mouth shut when we're out in public. Oh yes, and walk three paces behind me, keepin' your eyes lowered to the ground." His teasing grin spread wider.

Jaw muscles knotting, Bear took a chest-expanding breath that nearly popped the wooden buttons of his too-tight shirt. He plunked the oak buckets on the ground, sloshing water over the sides. "Wipe that smirk off yo' face, or I'll do it for you."

"Ah, but then you'd be settin' yourself up for a hangin' . . . a slave hittin' such a charmin', good-lookin' master. Folks round here got no sense of humor a'tall."

Nonetheless, when Bear's fists bunched, Drew knew he'd gone too far with his teasing. Besides, what he'd said was more true than even he, a white man, ever wanted to admit. He placed a hand on his friend's rock-solid shoulder. "I know it's hard, seein' all your kind bein' treated no better'n workhorses. But you knew that's how it was gonna be. Stick it out one more day; then we'll both head overmountain again." Drew glanced up the vacant street lined with mostly one-story tradesmen shops and stores shaded by an occasional tree. "If that teacher ain't late gettin' here from Richmond."

The tension drained from Bear, and his expressive dark eyes became pools of suffering as they had too often this past week since the two hunters had accompanied blacksmith and preacher, Brother Rolf Bremmer, overmountain. This was Bear's first trip this far east since he and his family escaped bondage when he was six years old. "I jus' don' understand. Folks round here's supposed to be Christians. All dem fancy churches we counted comin' down into here. Da good Lord ought'a rain a whole mountain a fire an' brimstone on dese hypocrites for what dey's doin'."

Now Drew really did feel guilty. "I know. But try not to lose sight of the fact that sooner or later everyone will face a reckonin'. I know it's of little comfort at the moment, but . . ." Drew shrugged. "Prayer. We'll just have to keep 'em in our prayers day and night . . . the slaves and the souls of their masters."

An unexpected grin eased across Bear's generous mouth. "An' jus' when did you take up prayin' day an' night?"

"Since we come on this trip with Brother Rolf. Thank heavens, he's visitin' with that minister friend of his till tomorrow. I'll swan, that man would pray over a weepin' willow."

A chuckle rumbled up from Bear's chest. "He's jus' practicin' up for all dem gals you go off an' leave a-weepin'."

Drew felt himself start to bristle. "Just cuz I don't want to get myself rooted down by one of them females Ma and Annie keep tryin' to foist off on me. Like I said before, there's too much wilderness left to explore. We've hardly scratched the ground on the far side of the Mississip'." He eased off, not wanting Bear to know how much his mother's matchmaking riled him. "It's not that I ain't interested in a purty face . . . so if one of you comes up with a gal who's willin' to run a trapline and don't mind sleepin' out in the snow, then I'll take a second look."

Bear snorted. "You ain't gettin' any younger, y'know. Seein' as how yo's nigh onto thirty." White teeth flashed a brilliant smile in contrast to his ebony face.

"Not for four more years. You're only two winters younger than me. Plumb old, I hear, for a bridegroom in the Shawnee towns."

"You know I made a solemn promise to my pa dat I'd waits till I finds me a God-fearin' woman like my mammy was. I didn't say nothin' about it before, but dat's da main reason I risked comin' east of da mountains. But now I sees da folly in dat. I ain't seen a solitary Negress—Christian or no—what was free to say yea or nay about nothin', let alone about jumpin' da broom wit' me." Bear's brief moment of good humor had disappeared. Reaching down, he retrieved the water buckets and started toward the wide barn opening.

As Drew settled into his chair again, he made one more attempt at levity. "I know you think you're a handsome devil, but even if you found one who could choose, I doubt she'd be any more likely to go traipsin' off into the savage wilds with you than them gals Ma and Annie parade in front of me ever' time I go home. And I know *I'm* irresistible."

Bear stopped just short of the entrance. But instead of the expected retort, his attention was on something up the sleepy main street of Salem.

Drew followed his gaze.

Two young women—one white and one black—came walking purposefully up the dusty rutted road from the direction of a traveler's inn, just as if they'd been ordered specially for the two frontiersmen. The Negress was keeping a prudent two steps behind as each shaded herself with a parasol. The white woman's parasol was, of course, much more lavish. Trimmed with lace and striped in pink and beige, it matched her voluminous skirts. Though Drew couldn't see her face beneath its deep shade, she had the promise of being a beautiful woman. Considering his own considerable height, he also liked the fact that she was taller than most women.

As the twosome neared, they veered toward Drew.

Grateful for a chance to see what was hidden under the lacy umbrella, Drew rose to his feet, wishing he'd taken the effort of putting on his town clothes rather than the usual belted overshirt, deerskin breeches, and moccasins.

"Pardon me," the young woman called, her full skirts swishing as she came closer. "Are you the proprietor of this establishment?" Her voice was soft and pleasurable, like a feather being drawn slowly across Drew's palm.

"No, but perhaps I can help you," he stalled as he strode toward her for a better look. If she knew that the liveryman was napping in his house next door, she'd most likely make a beeline toward the white clapboard dwelling.

She cast her parasol to the side. Haloed in the afternoon sun, her dark auburn tresses seemed to catch fire. She was as beautiful as her voice had promised. Her eyes, a few shades lighter than her hair, smoldered in the shadows, and her complexion was flawless, her thick lashes . . .

"I was told at the inn down the road that this is the only livery in Salem. Perchance, has a Reverend Bremmer left his stock in your care? I am to rendezvous with him here tomorrow."

"Bremmer? Rolf Bremmer?"

"I suppose Rolf could be his Christian name. Am I to presume he has arrived, then, from Tennessee?" Gold flecks sparked in her chestnut eyes as she smoothed a hand over the striped day gown.

"Aye."

The young woman whirled to her servant. "Did you hear that, Josie? Reverend Bremmer's here to fetch us. See, I told you there was nothing to worry about."

Drew stepped up behind the lovely woman, who gave off a mind-stealing mix of exotic spices and blooms. Skimming his gaze across the top of her head, he trained his attention on her servant. Shorter and more curvaceous, the young woman probably would have an infectious smile. But at the moment she wore an exceedingly solemn expression.

The servant, Josie, glanced furtively behind her.

5

Drew followed her gaze but saw no one else on the street in the wilting afternoon heat. "The name's Drew Reardon, ma'am," he said to the lady, remembering belatedly to sweep his beat-up hat from his head. "I accompanied Brother Bremmer here. Am I to presume you're with Professor Hazlett?"

"More or less. Are you the Reardon the valley in Tennessee is named after?"

"More or less," he repeated with a teasing smile. He wasn't yet ready to tell her that, in reality, it was his two older brothers who'd founded the township while he'd spent most of his time trading with the native tribes and exploring. "We weren't aware that the professor was bringin' along a wife—not that we won't be mighty pleased to escort a lovely lady such as yourself to our valley."

"Is that your slave?" Bear had moved up behind Drew unnoticed. He didn't sound pleased.

"Why, yes," the lady said, a small frown marring a spot just above her perfect nose. She obviously was not accustomed to being questioned by a Negro. Her attention returned to Drew. "I'm afraid there's been a slight misunderstanding. Professor Hazlett has indeed married, but not to me. He's gone to take up residence with his new wife's family. I am here as his replacement."

"You? But you're a woman."

That perfect nose hiked a notch. "Am I to assume you believe females are incapable of higher learning? or of imparting that knowledge to others?"

Drew threw up a hand as if to ward off the accusation. "Not me. I wouldn't dream of assumin' anything when it comes to females, even though I never heard of a woman hired on to teach a mob of boys before. But then, I can't think of a single thing I'd like better than to have you for a teacher." This trip overmountain had suddenly become a whole lot more interesting.

The last hint of pleasantness fled her lovely features as she arched a censuring brow. "I'm sure you can't."

But it didn't damper Drew's own high spirits in the least . . . until he remembered the big German. "Brother Rolf—now he might be a tougher nut to crack." But not too tough, Drew hoped. "I'm afraid he'll have the last say about whether or not you can come with us. He's not one to take real quick to newfangled notions."

Her chin shot up another notch. Her spine straightened. "Lead me to him."

2

"Not so tight," Crystabelle Amherst gasped over her shoulder the following morning as her personal servant and dearest friend tied the back laces of Crysta's forest green hunting skirt. Fear that she wouldn't be able to convince the Tennessee minister to hire her already threatened to cut off all breath. Both her and Josie's very futures were at stake. "Having to wait all night for Reverend Bremmer to return to town has me on pins and needles."

"Well, dat's where you oughts to be right now," her servant reprimanded, "sittin' on yo' mama's pincushion for what you done, draggin' me way off like dis."

Josie still hadn't forgiven Crysta for not divulging their true destination until they'd left Miss Soulier's Young Ladies' Academy far behind. But it couldn't be helped, Crysta thought as the two stood in a sparsely furnished room at Rigby's Coaching Inn, easily two hundred miles from Richmond, Virginia. A far distance, but not nearly far enough. Her father had the money to hire ten—even twenty—trackers.

Josie gave another cutting tug on the strings.

"Please, not so tight. If Reverend Bremmer agrees to take us over the mountain—and he must, he really *must*—I'll need extra breathing room. From what that Reardon fellow said, we won't have a wagon from here on out. We'll both be riding sidesaddle."

"*Me, too?* Y'all never said nothin' about *me* goin' horseback." Josie whirled from behind to face Crysta, her expression warring between fear and resurging anger at her mistress. "I ain't never rid on a horse in my life. I's skeert of 'em." Her fists embedded themselves into her hips. "Yo's just set on gettin' me kilt one way or t'other."

Josie had been threatening to bolt on Crysta from the first moment she learned they weren't on their way home but headed for some town in the hill country of North Carolina. Would the girl indeed run away, desert Crysta in her most harrowing hour? She again presented her back to her servant. "For months now, you've been reminding me to trust in the Lord—ever since Papa accepted Mr. Chastain's offer for me. Well, I feel this is the Lord's answer to my prayers. For both of us," she added with conviction. "So I say, perhaps it's time you took some of your own advice."

Josie, a mere three years Crysta's senior, was always bent on acting as if she were decades older. She snatched up the ties again and gave them another fierce tug. "If it was da Lord's will, missy, why didn't you tells me afore I had to figures it out on my own? No, I say it's time you start thinkin' a somethin' 'sides yo' own self. I'll bet you never give a minute's thought to what'll happen to me when we gets caught. And dey *will* catch us. You, dey'll probably just send to yo' room for a few days. Me? I'll have da skin stripped offen my back. Then da masta, he'll sells me off to heaven knows what evil kind a devil."

"If they do catch us—which they *won't*—I'll tell Papa the truth, that when we left the academy, I led you to believe we were going home. And if you think back, you'll see I never once actually lied to you. I told you I'd gotten a letter from Mama saying the wedding date had been moved forward, and that was absolutely true. And when I said we had to leave school before the term was over, I never once said we were going home."

Josie pursed her lips, making her cheeks seem all the rounder. "Y'all didn't say da words, but you knowed what I believed was a lie. Miz Amherst is gonna have my hide, fo' sure. You knows I's supposed to send word to her if you ever did any li'l ol' thing to embarrass da family. If you start actin' like a tomboy agin or takin' up with some young fella. And dis is about da worse thing you could do . . . 'cept maybe run off with Professor Hazlett like dat foolhardy Miz Marty done."

"Foolhardy she may be, but at least she took matters into her own hands, just as I have. You know I can't allow us to end up under Harland Chastain's thumb, no matter how much Mama brags on him. She absolutely will not believe he has a mean bone in his body." Taking a labored breath, Crysta attempted to shake off the remembrance of her betrothed wielding that whip. "Besides, I refuse to be told whom I shall or shall not marry. I wish you could read, Josie. I'd loan you my volume of Mary Wollstonecraft's *A Vindication of the Rights of Woman.*"

Josie's expression went flat. "You knows it's agin da law for slaves to read."

Those devastatingly true words took the starch out of Crysta's new argument. How could she talk about the rights of women to someone who didn't have a hope of ever enjoying even the most basic of human rights? The injustice Crysta had been feeling since she'd been promised to Harland Chastain against her wishes was like the injustice Josie had lived with her entire life. Crysta reached down to fetch her own riding boots. "I do apologize," she said, as she stepped back to sit on the lumpy straw-ticked bed. "That was thoughtless of me. If you truly wish to go back to Amherst Farms, I'll find you a ride with someone going north. As long as I don't marry Mr. Chastain, I'm sure you'll be able to remain with the family. But first, help me get these boots on?"

"Even if I could show up home wit'out y'all, you knows a slave cain't be out on da road on dey own. I wouldn't get ten miles."

"And I can't go home, for *both* our sakes. *Please,* Josie, have faith. Why else would Reverend Bremmer's letter to Professor Hazlett arrive, complete with the date and place of their rendezvous, the *very day* we needed to escape? Why else would I have been in the office that very moment to overhear the instructors discussing it? Fate. It has to be fate, pure and simple."

"Well, missy, you best be right, cuz *my* fate depends on it."

Crysta caught Josie's hand. "Trust me. I won't let anything happen to you. Please, instead of going over this again, I really need to concentrate on exactly the right words that will convince the minister to accept a female teacher. I do wish he'd been in town yesterday. I hardly slept last night, praying and worrying over it."

"Y'all shouldn't have no problem convincin' dat preacher man. Just show him dat big crate o' books you brung. La, you got books 'bout ever'thing, even da one you said was 'bout all da stars." Josie shook her head as she stooped to help Crysta with her footwear. "I still cain't figure out why anyone would take da time to give names to ever' single star in da sky. Dat man must have three, four slaves doin' nothin' but lookin' after him to have dat much free time on his hands."

Fortunately Josie was preoccupied with working a boot onto Crysta's foot, because Crysta couldn't stop the smile that skipped across her lips. She schooled her thoughts to the topic at hand. "You're right. Showing the reverend all my books should help. You see, God does work in mysterious ways. If I hadn't been trying to stump my brothers with tricky questions since I was banished to that awful school, I wouldn't have collected nearly so many." Suddenly a great sadness swamped Crysta. "Oh, Josie, I'll never be able to write Hank and Monty again . . . or get a letter from them . . . or go riding with them, or . . ."

"Dat's what got you sent away to school in da first place, missy . . . you tryin' to outrun and outwrestle dem two yahoos. Shove yo' foot in. Y'all ain't helpin' a'tall."

Crysta pushed down on her heel and worked her foot into the second boot. "Thank you." Standing up, she rearranged her riding skirt over the tall boots. "Well, there's no turning back now. I refuse to marry that supposed *gentleman*. Besides, he's almost twice my age and already has three children. I don't care *how* rich Mama says he is."

"Dere ain't nothin' unseemly about a widow man takin' hisself another wife. When a woman dies bornin' babes, her husband just naturally goes out an' finds hisself another one to run his house and mother his young'uns. Happens all da time."

"Well, I thought you didn't want to go to his plantation any more than I did. You saw how hard he whipped that poor horse he was racing against Papa's last fall? A man's true character shows through in how he treats his animals, and I know you believe that just as much as I do."

"I believe yo's let yo' 'magination run off willy-nilly. Now I know dere was talk 'bout him treatin' his slaves bad, but dat was pro'bly just da usual kitchen whispers. You know how cookhouse folks likes to make things out to be worse dan dey is."

"That's not what you were saying just last week. And, Josie, I just know Mr. Chastain won't treat a *wife* any better than a—than his horse . . . no matter how much he tried to sweet-talk me at Christmastide."

"Speakin' of sweet talkin'," Josie said with a measuring tilt of her head, "I seen how dat tall hunter was a-lookin' at you yesterday. Smilin' wi' dat devilish crooked smile o' his. Y'all best steer clear o' dat one."

"For goodness sake, Josie, I scarcely noticed the man. Besides, he's nothing but an uncouth backwoodsman." Snatching up her drawstring purse, Crystabelle swung toward the door, not about to admit now or ever that she'd found his ruffled blond hair falling across his tanned brow or that lopsided grin or the accompanying dimple *mildly* attractive. "Come along. Let's head down to the livery and see if Reverend Bremmer has arrived yet."

Drew strode out of the livery barn, where he and Bear had been bedding down for the past few days since they arrived in Salem. Before reaching the water well, he stopped and filled his lungs with morning air. There'd been a light shower during the night, and the air had a freshness to it, heady with the blossoms of June. Even the tree leaves had an extra sparkle to them in the early morning light.

And the day had yet another treat to offer—he'd have more time to feast his eyes on the gorgeous Eastern belle. He glanced up the shaded street toward the inn where she was staying. A couple of wagons and a lone horseman were rolling into town, but as yet, not a single young lady strolled out onto the street.

Cranking up the bucket, Drew's lips slanted into a habitual one-sided grin. He sure hoped Brother Rolf took his sweet time riding in from Reverend Urich's place. Brother Rolf was Reardon Valley's spiritual leader and emissary of the people, and Drew was almost certain the good man wouldn't betray the settlers' trust by bringing back a woman to teach their boys history and the sciences. It was unheard of.

His grin broadened, though, as he envisioned her doing just that . . . hickory stick in hand, and that delicate chin hiked so high she'd get a crick in her neck.

With the bucket rope wound to the top, he unhooked a dipper from the well post and quenched his thirst . . . and had a sobering thought. What a waste of time it would be if he and his companions had made the long ride overmountain only to go back home empty-handed. They'd be hard-pressed to find another qualified teacher willing to uproot and come with them on such short notice.

The aroma of coffee drifted across the stable yard, initiating a morning craving. The pot must have come to a boil. He turned to cut through the big barn, which led to the rear where Bear had built a small cook fire. But before Drew reached the yawning door-way, he heard the almost musical lilt of a woman's voice. He turned back.

Dressed in a simple white blouse and a dark green skirt minus the hooped skirts of the afternoon before, Miss Amherst hurried in his direction. Hanging on to the loose ties of a small pert bonnet with one hand, she waved at him with the other. Her expectant expression only added to her auburn loveliness.

Her slave lagged behind, not nearly so enthusiastic.

"Mr. Reardon," the beauty called as she closed the gap, "has your Reverend Bremmer returned to town yet?"

"Nope. Not yet."

Her eagerness dimmed as it had yesterday when she'd learned that Brother Rolf wouldn't be available until today. This one was in an inordinate hurry to plead her cause, even though it was a hopeless one.

"But you might as well wait here," Drew added, wanting to enjoy her company. "He should be along anytime now. Take a seat in one of the chairs lining the front, and I'll fetch you a cup o' coffee. It should be ready by now."

Miss Amherst glanced up the dirt road. "How far out of town did you say the reverend was staying?"

"Only a coupla miles."

"Very well. Come along, Josie," she ordered to her servant, who had just now caught up. Settling her velvet skirt folds into the near-est chair, the belle glanced up at Drew again. "I take cream and sugar in my coffee."

She sure was used to being pampered. Drew quirked a smile. "Afraid all we got is sugar."

But those gorgeous gold-and-ginger eyes weren't looking at him any longer.

Drew turned to see Bear coming, carrying two crockery cups filled with steaming brew. He, too, was looking elsewhere. Bear's dark-eyed gaze and a hint of a smile were reserved for the slave girl. He walked straight to her and held out one of the cups.

The servant's eyes widened with amazement as she took it.

The sound of Miss Amherst's sudden intake of breath was also unmistakable. *A slave being served first?* But to her credit, she said nothing; she merely came to her feet and stared woodenly at Bear as he handed her the second cup.

"Where's mine?" Drew asked with mock disappointment.

"You has to wait," Bear said. "We only gots two cups."

"Something we'll need to remedy," Miss Amherst inserted. "In the future, I would prefer that we each have our own drinking vessels." She turned to her servant. "Josie, as soon as the store across the road opens, I want you to go buy us two." She turned back to Drew. "Is there anything else we should purchase for the trip? I have my own horse, and I've rented an extra sidesaddle for Josie and three more pack animals to help carry our chests. You did say you brought two extra horses, didn't you?"

"*Six horses* just for the *two* of you?" Eastern women sure must travel with a lot of truck. "Just how many trunks do you have?"

That chin hiked. "Ladies do have to make themselves present-able, you know. And then there's my crate of books. As a teacher, I wouldn't dream of leaving them behind."

"A whole crate of books?" Bear asked, forgetting that slaves weren't supposed to include themselves in white folks' conversations.

This time, Miss Amherst shot her disapproving glower at Drew. Not quite sure what to say, he merely shrugged.

Then she surprised Drew. Looking at him instead of Bear, she answered the question. "I have books on all subjects. You'll find I am as well versed in the arts and sciences as Professor Hazlett. Maybe more so. I know I have a larger personal library than the good teacher has. You see, for the past four years I've spent most of my monthly allowance on books because my brothers and I have had an ongoing contest since I was sent away to finishing school. Through correspondence we try to stump one another with academic questions."

"Do you have books on India and China?" Bear would *not* keep his mouth shut.

"Yes." She still didn't address Bear directly. "I've tried to obtain information on all the continents and nations of the world."

"Even Africa?" Bear stepped closer.

Drew prudently stepped between them. "Perhaps if you're allowed to come along, you might loan us a book or two to read of an evening. We'd be mighty . . ."

Seeing the big burly German come riding down the wooded rise and into town, Drew lost his train of thought. Resigned to the inevitable loss of the belle's enchanting company, he raised a hand to beckon the pastor, then turned back to take one last look at the lovely Crystabelle Amherst . . . a last look at that stubborn little chin and those gingersnap eyes before Brother Rolf dashed her hopes.

3

When Crystabelle saw the rusticly handsome frontiersman wave to someone up the road, her heart leapt and her breathing became painful despite her looser clothing. Filled with desperate eagerness, she followed the direction of Mr. Reardon's gaze, sighting the man she would have to convince of her worthiness. Her fear heightened and her heart pounded all the harder.

Except for a plain white cravat, only the severest black covered the overly large rider coming their way. Even his thick-boned horse plodded darkly, grimly, toward them. As the formidable man neared, she realized he was older, perhaps in his fifties, yet his bulk was still more muscle than fat. Heavy jowled, he had flushed cheeks and a gaze so piercing, she was sure he could see past any deception, spoken or not.

Crystabelle took an involuntary step backward . . . and bumped into the frontiersman.

Steadying her with a hand at each shoulder, he whispered, "Brother Rolf don't bite. I promise."

Mr. Reardon had sensed her fear. How mortifying. Immediately she stepped out of his grasp and moved toward the horseman as he brought his massive steed to a stop.

The minister swung to the ground, his complaining saddle groaning, and he now became an even more imposing figure. Almost as tall as Mr. Reardon, who was several inches over six feet, he was almost twice as broad. *"Guten morgen,"* he greeted in German. "Has da teacher come?"

Mr. Reardon stepped alongside Crysta. "More or less."

Though she didn't glance up at his face, she knew by the woodsy one's tone that an amused smile accompanied those words. Why on earth had she thought she could simply replace Professor Hazlett as Reardon Valley's teacher? *Almighty God,* she implored silently. *Give me courage, I beg of thee.* Fervently hoping that God truly was with her in this, she straightened to what she'd always considered a rather imperious five feet seven inches, which now seemed rather insignificant sandwiched between these two giants. Nonetheless, she sallied forth. "Good sir, I am here to replace Professor Hazlett. I come to you all the way from Richmond, Virginia, with an entire crate of educational books, a ream of writing paper, and a dozen slates. I am well versed in all the arts and sciences. You'll find I am eminently qualified to fill the position the professor has vacated."

Her words had been spoken with all the confidence and purpose she could muster, yet the minister remained as silent as a dark looming mountain, his sharp blue eyes staring down at her. Finally, he pushed back his straight-brimmed hat and turned to Mr. Reardon. "Drew, you make da joke, *nein?"* His deep, thunderous voice matched the rest of him.

"'Fraid not. This is Miss Crystabelle Amherst, and she seems mighty determined to be the school's teacher."

The heavy-featured man swung his attention back to her, his scowl more rejecting than words.

"Like she says," Reardon continued, "she *has* come all the way from Virginia with teachin' in mind."

A deeper frown puckered the minister's wide brow. "All dat vay . . . ?"

Crysta willed her knees not to shake under the weight of his assessment. She simply had to convince him to hire her. She had no other plan, nowhere else to go.

"Da folks in da valley, dey pay goot money for a real teacher. Vat dey say if I bring back dis young voman instead?"

"They'd be more unhappy if we came back empty-handed."

Mr. Reardon was actually pleading her cause!

Reverend Bremmer shook his head. "I t'ink ve speak *mit* da storekeeper. Maybe he know of someone . . . *nein*. I write him ven ve first start to look for a teacher. Young men here, dey have no desire to teach. Dey all read for da law now. Everybody vant to be da next president," he huffed with a note of sarcasm.

"She did come all this way. That shows the girl's got grit."

Crysta had never thought of herself as being anything quite so masculine sounding, but . . . "Yes, and with your permission, I shall train up for you young gentlemen who can go on to read for the law or become ordained ministers or engineers or pursue any other dream they wish. Young ladies would be most welcome too. I have texts on every subject. You and your neighbors would surely get your money's worth from me."

"But you are a *voman*."

"A very capable, educated woman," she amended. "And I'm sure you will agree that my gender doesn't change the fact that two and two are four, or that Johannes Gutenberg invented the movable-type printing press in 1439, or that Martin Luther, the great religious reformer, lived from 1483 to 1546." She'd deliberately used two world-changing Germans as examples.

The minister's gaze wavered, giving her hope.

"What can it hurt?" The blond hunter came to her aid again.

"At least you'd have a teacher while you send out more letters in search of another one."

The older man's jowls went slack as he returned his full attention to Crysta. "You are villing to come *mit* us, even if it is chust until ve find da suitable man teacher?"

What choice did she have? She had to be far from this town very soon. Her father would be able to trace her here once the driver she'd hired returned to Richmond with the wagon. She had a week's head start, ten days at the most. And though she'd ever-so-casually asked the livery man how far it was to Savannah, Georgia, they still might discover her true destination. But even if they did, she'd at least have more time in which to come up with an alternative plan. "All I ask is that you give me a fair chance."

Reverend Bremmer regarded her steadily. Then with some reluctance, he nodded his head. "Very vell. But I do not promise anyt'ing."

"I gladly accept that," she said, trying to imply a confidence she did not feel.

"Ve leave in one hour."

"It's settled then," the frontiersman, just behind her, added with much more enthusiasm than either of them had mustered. "I'll start loadin' up our gear. And didn't you say you needed some cups, Miss Amherst?"

"Cups?" She turned to him questioningly, then remembered she still held his mug in her hand. "Ah, yes," she said, handing back the remaining beverage. "And thank you." Her last words she expressed with a sincerity she hoped would convey her gratitude for far more than a mere cup of coffee.

The warm smile the flaxen-haired frontiersman returned told her he understood. Even his dingy, fringed hunting shirt and crude leather leggings couldn't diminish the glorious white gleam of his teeth against his tanned, statue-crisp features. And that disarming dimple . . .

Her heart gave a strange little kick.

Josie was doing it again. As she walked out of the rustic traveler's inn, she searched the road coming into Salem like a hunted animal.

Crysta sidled close as they strode across the gravel drive with their satchels in hand. "Stop acting like a frightened rabbit," she whispered. "We don't want Reverend Bremmer to think we're being followed. He might change his mind." She led the way to the trio of men and the string of loaded horses waiting at the edge of the road.

"But we *are* being followed," Josie returned, her own husky whisper edged with hysteria.

"Trust me, Josie. I won't let anything happen to you." Crysta eagerly stepped ahead. Any second now they would mount and be on their way into the Blue Ridge Mountains. Reaching the waiting party, she assessed the horse with a sidesaddle for Josie. The liveryman had said the roan gelding was his gentlest mount, and it did appear much more placid than her own white-stockinged bay mare. "Josie, you take the smaller one."

Josie stopped in her tracks. "I cain't! I cain't!" she railed. "I don' know how to steers it. I'll fall off. It'll rear up an' buck me off."

Crysta rushed back to Josie and wrapped her free arm around the frightened woman. "It won't do any such thing," she assured her servant as she herded her forward. "Boy!" Crysta called to the Reardon slave. "Come. Help my girl up on the roan."

Bear swung toward her, his features darkening, the muscles in his square jaw bunching. That disturbing rebellion Crysta had seen yesterday reigned in his eyes again.

"Bear—*Joshua,*" Mr. Reardon rebuked from where he was tightening the straps around one of Crysta's crates. "Don't forget

where you are." Dropping the ropes, the frontiersman hurried to
the women. "Here, Miss Amherst, allow me to give you a hand up
while Joshua helps your girl." Before Crysta could protest, he
ushered her toward the bay. "How's your own horsemanship?"

"I've ridden since I was a tot. I'm as capable a horsewoman as I
am a teacher," she expounded rather loudly, hoping Reverend
Bremmer, several yards away, would overhear. But the older man
was preoccupied, checking a packhorse's mouth. She lowered her
voice then, for Mr. Reardon's ears only. "But Josie's not all that
experienced. She's a mite nervous."

"Aye, I can see that. She's shakin' like a leaf in a hurricane."
Clasping his fingers together just below the left stirrup, he gave
Crysta a quick hand up, then left her for Josie and his slave, who
were speaking in urgent whispers beside the patient gelding.

Crysta nudged Sheba, her Arabian, closer.

"What's the problem?" she overheard Mr. Reardon ask his
slave.

"The li'l missy won' lets me hoist her up. Says da horse is too
big."

"He's smaller than the others." Reardon nodded down to Josie.
"He's a surefooted animal. I promise, he won't stumble with you."

Josie wasn't appeased. "How can you know dat?" Desperation
still showed in her dark eyes, and her face turned ashen as she
clutched the slave's sleeve. "Why cain'ts we just take a wagon?"

"Cuz there ain't no wagon trail betwixt Boone-town up the road
and the Watauga settlements," Mr. Reardon answered for him.
"It's either ride horseback or walk."

"I'll walk then," she cried in a relieved rush. "I sho will. I'm a
fast walker, Masta Reardon. An' I don't gets tired. No, sir."

"Josie," Crysta interjected, glancing nervously at Reverend
Bremmer. "That simply won't do. You'd never be able to keep
up." Her gaze locked with Josie's. "And I know you don't want to
be left behind."

Josie took on the look of a trapped animal, and for the first time Crysta's own resolve faltered. Could she really force her bosom companion, her only confidante, to do something that terrified her as much as being caught did?

"I'll take Miz Josie up with me," Reardon's man said. "Till she gets comfortable enough to ride her own mount." Without waiting for his master's permission, he took the girl by the elbow and escorted her to his own horse as if she were a fine lady and he her gentleman—this upstart who had been so surly with Crysta.

However, all the terror and fight seemed to go out of Josie as she walked along with a gentle grace Crysta had never seen in her before. Crysta strongly suspected that Josie was smitten with the proud slave. And after the girl had accused Crysta of admiring his master!

The slave mounted, and Crysta couldn't help smiling as Mr. Reardon lifted Josie up into Joshua's waiting arms. Then Crysta noticed how very unflattering Josie's drab linen day gown was. Something would have to be done to improve her appearance—tonight. This was the first time a man had shown an interest in Josie these past four years since they'd been sent away from the plantation. At the academy there'd been only two male slaves, and both were married. It had been as lonely a time for Josie as it had been for Crysta.

Another rather amusing thought struck Crysta. Their roles had just reversed. For a change, she'd be keeping an eagle eye on Josie, making sure her "watchdog" of a servant didn't do anything fool-hardy.

But then Crysta really didn't have anything to worry about. Reverend Bremmer had noticed the two on the one horse and strode over to them, shaking a thick finger at them. "Bear, dere is to be no extra business *mit* da hands. I be vatching you all da time. You hear?"

For once, the slave tempered his demeanor. Shaking his head, he raised a hand to ward off the censure. "No, sir, Brother Rolf. I wouldn't do nothin' to bring shame on dis fine young missy. Nothin' a'tall."

Crysta felt eyes on her now. She swiveled in her saddle and saw that the hunter had mounted and was beholding her. And from his droll grin, she wondered just how honorable he'd be when it came to a young lady.

4

Reverend Bremmer took the lead, setting a lively pace as they rode out of Salem and into the surrounding patchwork of fields and meadows, dotted with farmhouses and outbuildings. Spring flowers edged the wagon road in profusion.

Crysta trotted along beside the reverend, her spirits high. She reveled in the unrestricted view of the mountains that lay ahead of them, the soft morning breeze feathering her cheeks, the giddy sense of freedom that she hadn't felt since the last time she'd been riding with her brothers. Not since last Christmas. Less than six months ago, yet it seemed like years since she'd last seen them. And years it may very well be before she rode with them again, racing down the back roads of their lands, laughing wildly. Her pleasure began to flag.

That sacrifice, she reminded herself, had to be more thinkable than marrying the mean-spirited Harland Chastain and being trapped in the suffocating binds of matronhood. To him she'd have been just one more acquisition, a fancy ornament to decorate his house and his arm, to order about at his will, a broodmare to bear him many sons. A possession to be shelved and retrieved at his whim.

Considering her own possession, Crysta glanced back to see how Josie was faring.

Mr. Reardon was preoccupied with the string of packhorses as she looked beyond him to Josie riding a good distance behind. The girl seemed quite comfortable seated in front of the other slave. In time, maybe Josie, too, would see that this move was better for both of them. Once she was answerable to no one but Crysta, she'd never again have to fear the lash of a whip or worry about being forced into an unwanted union herself.

Yes, this was best for both of them.

And more exciting, they were traveling into the unknown! A thrill shot through Crysta as they neared a river crossing. On the other side, they would be heading into an ever-narrowing river valley with thickly wooded hills rising on each side. Into the wilds where she'd heard that wolves and bears still roamed free.

Of course, she'd have to keep that bit of information from Josie if she didn't want a real revolt on her hands.

As they covered the next few miles, Crysta continually felt the presence of Mr. Reardon riding close behind her. She'd made a point of not glancing back even to check on Josie because she didn't want him to think she was aware of his nearness. But once they'd guided their animals down to a ferry landing and the hulking reverend helped Crysta dismount from her sidesaddle, she knew she wouldn't be able to completely ignore Reardon—it would take several minutes for the rope-hauled flatboat to cross the wide, rather swift, fork to reach their side.

Walking as stately as possible, she swept past the moccasin-shod man and the packhorses to reach Josie and the other slave, both still mounted on his sturdy, intelligent-looking Spanish dun. Crysta was pleased to see that Josie seemed quite relaxed now. Not waiting for one of the men to come help Josie down, Crysta raised her hands to the girl. "You did really well. I'm very proud of you."

Once Josie's feet touched the ground, she gazed back up at Reardon's slave with something bordering on adoration. "Black Bear, he kept his horse a-walkin' extra smooth jus' for me."

Talk about someone being smitten. Then Crysta's amusement slid into curiosity. Black Bear? Crysta glanced up at the efficiently built man as he dismounted. "I thought his name was Joshua."

"It is," Josie hurriedly supplied. "But he likes bein' called by da name da Indians give him. Him an' Masta Reardon spend most o' der time in da far country, huntin' and tradin' with da Indians. Black Bear say he gots hisself a whole poke o' coins he been savin' up for years. All his very own."

Small wonder he was so uppity, Crysta thought as the Negro strode purposefully past her without so much as a by-your-leave. And, of course, Josie watched after him as if he were the very reason the sun and moon rose and set.

"Come along." Crysta snatched Josie's hand and started down to the landing in long sure strides of her own. She'd purely love to put that *boy* in his place. But with her own position here tentative at best, she'd better hold her tongue—for now.

Five passengers and ten horses proved too many for the flatboat. Reardon's slave remained behind with the pack animals to await the ferry's second trip.

After helping to off-load the first horses, Reverend Bremmer lumbered up the muddy bank to where Crysta and Josie waited beside the road on a willow-shaded patch of grass. He'd removed his frock coat by this time and no longer looked so severe with much of his white shirt exposed. Taking a large kerchief from his vest pocket, he wiped his hands, then settled his sharp blue gaze on Crystabelle before softening his expression somewhat. "I am vanting to ask you a few questions to see how you vould answer da *kinder* in da school. Ve are strict beliefers in chust vat is written in da Bible."

"I welcome any question," Crysta answered with a confidence she suddenly didn't feel. She sensed the minister was embarking on a bit of an "inquisition," and serious apprehension began to curl her insides. To a theologian, these answers would be far more vital than her knowledge of math, history, or science. How well did she really know her Scriptures? She hadn't concerned herself so much with the basic precepts as she had with looking up remote names and places to stump her brothers. Most of what she really knew, she'd heard at morning chapel . . . when she'd been listening.

"You know da Ten Commandments, for sure."

"Of course, and I try to abide by each and every one of them."

"Dis is goot. *Und* about dis one, 'Thou shalt not kill.' Vat does our Lord Jesus say about dat?"

Such a simple question. "He agrees, of course." She began to breathe more freely.

"*Und . . . ?*"

"And? And . . ." The preacher wanted more. Details. Didn't Jesus say something about killing in the Sermon on the Mount? Adjusting her small riding bonnet to buy time, she recalled the second part of the verse. "Jesus said the killer is in danger of the Judgment."

"*Und . . . ?*" The minister was being overly insistent about details.

"And . . ." Finally she remembered—just as she caught sight of Mr. Reardon off to the side, wearing an amused expression. He'd obviously been listening. "Jesus said that if anyone is angry at his brother without cause, he'll also be in danger of judgment."

The reverend's pinning gaze softened, and he nodded. "Is goot."

Crysta relaxed somewhat and, with a smug expression of her

own, glanced back at Reardon. She'd successfully cleared another hurdle.

"Now, Miss Amherst," the minister continued—he wasn't through. "Vat do you say to da child if he ask you vat must he do to be saved?"

The way he queried her, one would think he was trying to trap her. But, thank goodness, that question was incredibly easy. She'd certainly heard her instructors spouting that admonition often enough. "As his teacher, I would tell him that he needs to study hard and obey my orders, because God has blessed him with the opportunity to go to school."

Tucking his sagging chin, Reverend Bremmer frowned. Obviously, he was not pleased.

"Well, I mean . . ." She backtracked, but to where? What exactly did he want to hear?

Mr. Reardon came forward, his expression as waggish as ever. "I think Brother Rolf is more interested in the child's eternal salvation than if he's mindin' his p's and q's."

"Oh yes, how shortsighted of me." But what exactly did this Baptist minister want? She'd never been to a church of that particular persuasion. Her own family had been Anglican for as long as there'd been a Church of England. Her mind raced through the Lord's Prayer then, providentially, landed on John 3:16. "One must believe in our Lord Jesus or perish."

"Aye," Reardon readily supported. "And, as the apostle Paul said to the church at Ephesus, 'For by grace are ye saved through faith; and that not of yourselves: it is the gift of God: Not of works, lest any man should boast.'"

When he finished, Crystabelle discovered that her mouth had fallen open. This man who didn't seem to have a serious thought in his head was quoting an entire passage of Scripture.

It must have surprised Reverend Bremmer, too. With a big

smile, he clapped the younger man on the shoulder. "You make me da happy man, Drew. I never know if you are listening to me."

"I wouldn't start boastin', if I was you," Reardon teased the minister. "I taught Bear to read by using my New Testament."

"Vatever make you to read it, dis is goot."

At that moment, Crysta realized how very little she knew about the hunter. It would seem that her premature assumptions about him had been all wrong. He merely liked to tease as her older brother, Hank, did. Mr. Reardon had not only come to her rescue, he'd diverted the pastor's attention away from her ignorance.

Josie, who'd been standing quietly beside her, sprang forward. "Black Bear. He's comin'."

Josie traipsed down the bank to the landing. No doubt remained—the girl was completely taken with Reardon's man . . . this slave, who not only seemed to do exactly as he pleased, but one whom his master had freely admitted to teaching to read—breaking a cardinal rule.

Had a different set of slave laws been drawn up for Tennessee? Crysta doubted that very much.

"Ve go now," the minister ordered, interrupting her troubling deductions.

As Reverend Bremmer lumbered by her to fetch his tethered mount, Crysta glanced beyond him to Reardon's man unloading the last of the livestock, and she had an amazing realization—that slave would know far more answers to the biblical questions the Baptist preacher might ask than she, who owned a trunkful of books. Particularly since he'd been taught by another Baptist.

Mr. Reardon caught her elbow. "Shall we go?"

Still pondering this revelation, she allowed him to escort her in the direction of her mare.

"Brother Rolf will not be fooled for long," he warned in a low quiet voice. "I'd start honin' my Bible facts, if I was you."

She nodded. Good advice. But there were so many. Which ones would a Baptist be most interested in?

As Mr. Reardon clasped his hands and bent beside Sheba's stirrup to form a step for Crysta, she raised her foot, then hesitated. "Is there a private place where we might be alone later?"

He turned rock-still and tilted his face up to her for the longest moment before remembering to hoist her atop her saddle, which he did much too swiftly. Then, for the first time since she'd met him, his chiseled features became unreadable as he looked at her much longer than any gentleman ought. "We'll be spending the night at a little inn in Wilkesboro. After everyone's abed, I'll meet you behind the woodshed."

Drew could hardly believe what he'd heard. Not once had Crystabelle Amherst passed him a glance that could remotely be called flirtatious. Even now as she rode just ahead of him, she sat her horse as proper and demure as any well-bred maiden should. Everything about the young woman had bespoken genteelness . . . up until she said those last words to him. Words that weren't remotely subtle.

Until this moment, he'd thought her stubborn and determined, and almost certainly she was on the run from someone, but not once had he thought of her as wanton.

And he still couldn't make himself see her that way. There must have been more to her suggestion. There had to be. Mayhap, she was trying to trap him into a compromising position so he'd be obliged to wed her. Did she assume that marrying him would save her from whatever, whomever, she was running from?

Drew eyed her again, but for the life of him, all he could concentrate on was how well she sat a horse. He shifted his gaze to the cool shadowy woods they were passing through, the ruffled carpet of ferns.

The main problem, as he saw it, was that a man could never be sure of anything when it came to women. Except one thing. He hadn't met a maiden yet who didn't have matrimony on her mind. And, as his mother was forever reminding him, he was considered somewhat of a catch. He was a landholder and had a sizable savings—not that he'd deliberately set about to obtain either. His older brothers had deeded him the land as his share of the Reardons' grant. And as far as his poke went, he simply hadn't seen that much in the way of goods he wanted to tote with him into the backcountry. He preferred to travel light . . . something this woman knew nothing about.

Drew glanced back at the four packhorses burdened down with her trunks. The girl probably had a gown and a bonnet for every day of the week and two for Sunday.

Involuntarily, he shifted his gaze ahead again to the elegantly straight posture of the young woman and the green scarf flowing out behind her small-brimmed bonnet. No matter how his better sense warned him that she was dangerous, all he wanted to see were those wide autumn eyes smiling up at him.

He glanced skyward. It was nowhere near noon. Tonight was a long way off.

5

"That's the last of 'em," Drew said, looking past Black Bear to scan the center aisle of the Brushy Mountain Inn stable. All ten horses had been rubbed down, and now their heads were deep into feeding troughs.

"Looks datta way," Bear drawled. He nodded his curly head toward the pile of goods they'd just pulled off the animals. "I hates to think we gotta load dem trunks back on again come sunup. Dat brown one feels like it gots rocks in it."

"That's probably the one with the books."

A glimmer sparked in Bear's deep brown eyes. "You think she'd mind if I takes a peek or two at 'em?"

"We got sidetracked when I asked her this mornin'. I'll find out at supper. We're all supposed to meet in the common room at dusk." *And somewhere alone after that,* he was tempted to add.

"You privileged white folks, dat is. I'll be takin' my meal in the kitchen." Then Bear's bitter tone softened. "With my Josie. Did y'all notice her name's a match fer mine? Josie an' Joshua. Don't that sound fine?"

Drew started to remind Bear that the object of his affection belonged to someone else—Miss Amherst. But both he and Bear were in too good a mood. He blew out the lantern, casting the stable in near darkness. "Aye, let's go wash up."

Bear continued his praises of Josie on the way to the washstand that stood next to the split-log inn's kitchen door. "She looks plumb sweet when she smiles. An' she's a fine Christian, too. I pretended I didn't know much, you know, askin' her lots o' questions. An' she knew all da answers. Yessir, she's just da kind o' female my pappy said I should find. An' ain't she da purtiest li'l thing you ever did see? An' light . . . she ain't no heavier'n a handful o' feathers."

In all the years since Drew had met Black Bear out in Shawnee country, he'd never seen him so animated about anything. Or anyone. Respecting his father's wishes, Bear had never considered marrying any of the Indian maidens. Not that some of them hadn't given the handsome fellow that "come hither" look. But none had been willing to give up their pagan superstitions even for a man with hair like the mighty buffalo.

"Nice to know your Josie passed her test with flyin' colors," Drew said on a chuckle. "Her mistress wasn't farin' so well with Brother Rolf's questions. But I helped her out a mite, since she's so dead-set on comin' overmountain with us. By any chance, has Josie mentioned what they're on the run from?"

"Not yet. But it sho gots her watchin' her back."

Drew dried his hands on a clean section of an already smudged towel. "I'll be goin' on in now. See you in the mornin'." Leaving Bear behind, he headed for the side entrance to the common room. Just before he opened the door, he remembered his hair. Removing his hat, he untied the leather thong holding his mane at the nape of his neck and quickly jerked a comb through his hair—something he forgot to do often as not.

After retying the thong, he strolled into a long room, which was illuminated by two ironwork chandeliers, along with several wall sconces and table lamps. The savory aromas of meat broth and fresh bread greeted him. A dozen or so men sat eating on benches at a quartet of cloth-covered trestle tables, but Brother Rolf and Crystabelle Amherst sat in straight-backed chairs across from each other at a smaller table near a front window. Their food, too, was sitting before them; an extra plate and cup waited that he reckoned were for him. Had the thoughtfulness been Crystabelle's? Most likely. She knew as well as he did that the sooner they ate, the sooner they could have that private meeting. He plunked his hat on the nearest empty wall peg and hurried across the room to join them.

"Good evenin'," Drew offered and received the same brief greeting from both as he took his seat between the two. As he did, he caught a whiff of Crystabelle's perfume, more enticing than any flower he'd ever smelled; the aroma of food no longer mattered. And, he noted, she'd changed from her riding clothes into a summery creamy coral frock that had small white flowers trailing hither and yon. Pristine ribbons held her auburn locks aloft . . . exposing her slender neck. Her name suited her perfectly. She purely was as pretty as a crystal bell.

"I vas chust telling Miss Amherst about mine Baptist fore-fadders. Dey vas calling us Anabaptists back den. *Und* dey vas helping dat Martin Luther fellow ven he vas persecuted by da Roman church. If not for mine people, dere might not be da great Reformation!" the minister ended exuberantly. Given the opportunity to expound on his favorite subject, his spirits seemed almost as high as Bear's. And Drew's own.

Still, Drew couldn't resist bringing Rolf down a tad. "I think God probably had a little something to do with the Reformation."

"*Ja, ja,*" the good preacher hastily agreed. "God *und* da Baptists."

Drew caught a smile flicker across Crystabelle's generous lips. Just the response he now realized he'd hoped for all along. After saying a quick silent blessing, he spooned in a mouthful of food before he'd even noticed what lay before him—chicken pie topped with spoon biscuits. Another treat to savor.

"*Und* vat is your opinion about da teachings of Calvin?" Brother Rolf asked their lovely companion before taking a swallow of spring-cooled cider. His aggressive assessment of her knowledge and beliefs was ongoing.

Before answering, she glanced at Drew, uncertainty in her eyes. And such long lashes. "Wherever his teachings agree with the Bible, I agree with him."

Carefully evasive, but it sounded good.

But not good enough. Brother Rolf leaned forward. "*Und* vere do you disagree?"

"Let the poor lass eat in peace," Drew pleaded for her.

"You're right," the minister deferred, but his reluctance to desist was obvious.

But Drew's intrusion was worth it. Miss Crystabelle offered him a grateful smile that lingered as she brought a crust of bread to her lips.

Drew spooned in another mouthful. This had the promise of a very pleasant evening.

Crysta could have kicked herself for not having the foresight to don a darker color. The lantern hanging beside the back door out of which she slipped made the white flowers on her frock virtually sparkle. Meeting a man privately during the day would have been damaging enough to one's reputation, but at night? In the dark, behind some outbuilding?

But it was a risk she had to take.

She hurried away from the glow as swiftly as she dared, considering she had nothing to light her path but a rising moon and sporadic flashes of light made by fireflies.

Aside from the larger stable, she noted the silhouette of three smaller structures. Surely the woodshed would be the one closest to the kitchen door. When she narrowly escaped slamming into an axe buried in a tree stump, she knew she'd been correct and hurried toward the far side of the low shed.

Rounding the corner, she was abruptly seized. Strong hands caught hold of her upper arms. Her feet left the ground as she was whirled around. She touched ground again only when her back was flattened against the rough wood of the structure. She started to scream in outrage, but a hand covered her mouth.

She ripped it away and kicked the interloper hard in the shin with the pointed toe of her shoe. He let out a yelp and stumbled back, then bent down to rub the spot. A vulnerable position. She took full advantage and gave a mighty shove.

The interloper toppled onto his side. *"Hey!* What's the matter with you?" he flung in a sharp whisper. It was Reardon.

"Me?" Her own whisper was just as fierce. "How *dare* you put your hands on me!"

He sprang up from the ground, towering over her. "It was *your* idea!" The words came out in full force.

"Shh! Do you want to wake the whole town? And just when did I say you could manhandle me?"

He lowered his voice, but his words were no less angry. "All I was doin' was pullin' you into the shadow. Them flowers on your dress catch the light like they was mirrors. 'Sides, it was *you* who wanted to meet *me* all private-like."

"Aye," she flung back with equal fervor, "to ask you what Bible facts Reverend Bremmer will be likely to ask me about."

Reardon fell back a step. "You asked me out here to talk theology?"

"Considering your outrageous behavior just now, you could use more than a little discussion on the subject," she huffed as she straightened her shawl collar.

He stiffened again, his shoulders growing all the broader. "I'm the one with the throbbing shin. Knocked in the dirt." Then he visibly relaxed. "Put in my place by a slip of a girl." He flashed a grin—a grin that reflected a sudden new source of light. A lantern had flamed to life in the stable.

"What's going on out there?" came a deep voice at the entrance, one Crysta assumed was the stableman's.

"Nothin'," Reardon returned. "Just took a wrong turn."

The man grunted something Crysta couldn't make out. But, thank heavens, he didn't come to investigate. He returned inside, and within seconds the lamp was extinguished.

"You certainly took a wrong turn, all right," Crysta reprimanded in a low voice as soon as she thought it was safe. "And so did I, thinking that you were a man with some semblance of honor."

"Well, no real *lady* asks a man to meet her in the dark of the night."

"The *hour* was not my choice."

"You win." He threw up his hands. "I concede." With his next words, his tone changed to his usual teasing one. "But it sure does make a fella feel good to be asked any ol' time."

The bounder needed a serious upbraiding. But she'd risked her own reputation, coming out here in the dark, and all they were doing was arguing. She could ill afford to waste this opportunity. Drawing a deep breath, she composed herself and softened her tone. "Mr. Reardon, I do apologize for leading you on, albeit unintentionally, and for kicking you in the shin. Now, please, will you indulge me with some much needed answers?"

"My poor abused shin could sure use a kiss to make it better."

The man simply would not take anything seriously. *"Mr. Reardon,* do you know how the Baptist views differ from Calvinism?"

He exhaled. "If you insist. But you have to understand I ain't the scholar of the family."

She would have agreed wholeheartedly but again thought better

of giving her tongue sway—not when he held some of the answers
she desperately needed.

"But I've sat in on enough of Noah and Brother Rolf's discussions to know that, unlike the Calvinists, Baptists have always
wanted the liberty to worship without interference from some state
church's laws. Fact is, I've heard Brother Rolf lay claim to comin'
up with the idea of the First Amendment of our Constitution. Not
personally, but for the Baptists."

"Ah yes. 'Congress shall make no law respecting an establishment of religion, or prohibiting the free exercise thereof.'"

"More or less," he drawled with that infernal grin in his voice.

"Not more or less—*exactly*. I've memorized verbatim the entire
Bill of Rights."

"I'll bet you have." The tease was still there.

She ignored him. "I have a history text with a chapter on Calvin.
I'll fetch it first thing in the morning and reread it. But I have nothing that I know of on the Baptists. Does anything else come to
mind?"

"I'm surprised a thorough young lady such as yourself isn't
better prepared. Didn't Professor Hazlett inform you that you
would be expected to follow the Baptist doctrine in your Bible
teaching?"

"Actually, no, he didn't." *Not on that topic or any other*, she could
have added. So far she hadn't actually lied, but what she'd left out
created a total misrepresentation. But was it the same as bearing false
witness against her neighbor? Regardless, she still felt dishonest.

"If I were you," Reardon was saying more seriously now, "I'd get
Brother Rolf to talkin' about how the Baptists have been persecuted
down through the centuries. He can drone on about that for hours.
An' I'm sure when he does, you'll learn all you need to know."

In her appreciation for this tidbit, she softened a touch toward
the bounder. "Thank you for telling me that. And for the help

you've already rendered in assisting me in my endeavor to accompany you on this journey."

"I might be more helpful if I knew why goin' to Tennessee is so all-fired important to you. Like, what you're runnin' from."

Crysta swung away. "Thank you again, Mr. Reardon. Until tomorrow."

He snagged her arm. "Not so fast."

Panic shot through her. Would he hold her until she confessed? Or did he have something more carnal in mind? Had he just been fooling her till he caught her off guard?

"Miss Amherst," he said, releasing her as abruptly as he'd grabbed her, "I was wondering if me an' Joshua could borrow a book or two of an evenin'. It'd be a real treat for him."

After her initial relief, she was again reminded of Reardon's willful disregard for the law concerning slaves, but at this point, a hasty retreat was a wiser course. "You may," she agreed tartly. "Just make sure your hands are clean. Both of you."

That said, she quickly left him for the inn before any more questions were asked . . . before he cornered her into admitting she was on the run from two rich and powerful men. That would surely be the end of her trip overmountain.

Or would it? She touched her fingers to lips the frontiersman had silenced with his hand. This was a man who seemed to enjoy taking risks. Wasn't that what he did in the wilds on a daily basis? Perhaps she could trust him. Perhaps . . .

Safely within the glow lighting the entrance to the inn, she looked back, knowing he was somewhere out there in the shadows, probably watching her. An uneasy feeling overtook her. She needed to bring this whole thing to the Lord. She needed some clear answers. Had she really gone off on her own, as Josie thought, or was this, in truth, the escape for which she'd so fervently prayed?

6

Drew smoothed wrinkles from the beige sleeve of a city shirt he had bought before leaving Wilkesboro that morning. From his reflection in the small cracked mirror above his commode, he decided he looked quite presentable. That particular shade of creamy brown blended well with his hair and sunned face.

Now perhaps he'd be a more welcome dinner companion. He'd felt like a leper all day, mostly because of Miss Amherst.

Leaving the cramped room he shared with Brother Rolf and two other men, he walked down the narrow stairs to the open-beamed common room of Boone's only ordinary. A body would've thought he'd kicked her, instead of the other way around. His shin still had a bump the size of a chicken egg on it. One thing she'd made clear—she was a proper lady through and through.

Drew spotted Brother Rolf and Crystabelle Amherst sitting across from each other at the end of one of the long uncovered tables, chatting as amiably as the two had all day. Of course, they hadn't been nearly as amiable as Bear had been with Josie. Bear still hadn't put the lass on her own horse, keeping her on his lap practically the livelong day. And the girl hadn't looked like she minded one bit. Bear's thinly veiled excuse that she was still too inexperienced to handle her own mount was getting old.

Drew started between the tables in the tallow-lit room that had only three other patrons—a coarsely attired elderly couple and what looked like a merchant, wearing tailored clothes. Deeper into the mountains now, this inn was plainer than the one they'd stayed at last night, with few of the niceties. Studying Miss Amherst, who'd dressed for dinner in yet a different outfit than the one she'd worn yester's eve, he doubted she'd ever even dined at a bare table before. He couldn't even imagine her eating deep in the woods by some campfire with a log for a seat.

But the woods sure would've been cooler on this balmy evening. The afternoon's heat was still trapped in the room, relieved only slightly by the air coming through the windows that had been flung wide.

A soft pine-scented breeze swept across the long room as he reached his companions. It ruffled the hem of Crystabelle's blue-and-green-plaid gown. This latest costume was liberally adorned with ruffles and lace, making her look all the prettier. He swung his leg over her bench. If she still insisted on ignoring him, he'd at least enjoy the scent of her perfume, listen to the sound of her breathing. "Good evening to you both." He added his most disarming grin.

"*Ja*, you too," Brother Rolf answered with a wholehearted smile of his own. Obviously, he had not been informed of Drew's impetuous behavior with Miss Amherst last night. But as far as Drew was concerned, she was as much to blame as he. More so.

Crystabelle's acknowledgment of his presence, Drew noted, was no more than a polite nod. He grinned all the more. He wasn't about to let her snub affect him one smidgen.

She turned his way and spoke directly to him for the first time today. "I noticed one of your packhorses was beginning to favor his left back leg this afternoon. I do trust you've checked it properly." Her haughty nose looked poised for flight.

Drew made sure his own posture was relaxed as he let his expression settle into one of bemusement. She wasn't about to make him feel either inferior or incompetent. "You must mean poor old Job . . . the one who drew the back-swayin' chore of totin' your heaviest trunks all day."

"One of da horses is going lame?" Brother Rolf frowned with concern.

"Nay," Drew reassured. "Just picked up a stone." He smiled back at Miss Stiff Neck. "Tell me, have you and Brother Rolf discussed every jot and tittle of Calvinism today and where it differs from the Baptist doctrine?"

Her gold-flecked eyes widened ever so slightly in an otherwise frozen face. "I wonder what's taking so long for our food to arrive." She was obviously trying to change the subject.

Brother Rolf wasn't redirected though. As a blacksmith by trade, his already flushed face fairly beamed—his favorite subject had been brought up. "I t'ink ven I leaf Reverend Urich's company, I am no longer hafing dese goot talks. I am proud of you, Drew-boy, for dis new interest you take. You haf not come to me *mit* da questions since you vas teaching Black Bear to read."

An almost imperceptible, but definitely disparaging, *harrumph* came from the judgmental one next to Drew.

Drew turned to her again and pleasantly drawled, "Speakin' of questions, I'm curious, Miss Amherst. Do you believe that the prosperity of a man is a testament to his faith?"

She stared hard at him.

He could almost see her brain churning away behind her lovely brittle gaze, looking for the right answer.

"Actually, Mr. Reardon," she finally said with a smug raise of a brow, "although our salvation is not earned by our good works, I strongly believe they are a testament of our faith in God. What kind of a testament do you think your misguided notions of the past twenty-four hours have been? Do you believe they've all been pleasing to the Lord?"

Where was that food? Drew looked toward the kitchen door.

"I do know one t'ing," Brother Rolf added. "It is time da lad stop dis infernal vandering out in da vilderness and find hisself a goot vife. Take up his responsibilities on da land God sees fit to gif him."

The kitchen door opened none too soon, and out came the server, bearing a tray of food and drink. The woman of middle years headed in their direction.

"Smells like beef. Good." Drew turned forward and picked up his fork. "I hope there's plenty," he added, feigning a great hunger, especially since he'd just lost his appetite for talking.

After Brother Rolf gave the blessing, the supper of roast beef and new vegetables was a silent affair. He did what little talking there was. Drew merely wanted it to end so he could leave for the barn, where even the horses were friendlier.

Stuffing the last of the corn bread into his mouth, he untangled his long legs from the bench and rose at long last. "If you'll excuse me, I need to go check on the stock."

Miss Amherst swiveled toward him with the stiffest of smiles. "Would you be so kind as to tell Josie to come to my room. I need her to help me undress now."

Drew knew he shouldn't, but he couldn't resist. "For a young woman who plans to take up the position of teaching, don't you think it's time you learned something as basic as taking off your own clothes?"

Her aghast drop of the jaw was all he'd hoped for.

Before she had a chance to retort, he spun away for the back exit.

Outside, Drew spotted Black Bear and Josie across the clearing. They sat in front of a small cabin with another Negro on logs that

faced a small campfire. Perched next to Bear, Josie had changed for
supper just as her mistress had. She wore a becoming plaid gown of
red, blue, and black; the lace of her mobcap matched that which
adorned her bodice and sleeves. Mighty fancy for a slave.

Pleased to see that Josie's mistress provided her with attractive
wear, Drew found his opinion of Crystabelle softening. Perusing
Bear's raggedy attire, Drew grinned. Bear had always taken such
pride in his appearance . . . beaded buckskins and feathers galore.
And here he was, having to do his courting dressed in those
tattered clothes.

The older man, a silver-haired slave, had been talking, but
seeing Drew approach, he stopped and stood up.

So did Josie.

But not Bear. Surly as ever about this slavery business, he eyed
the other two with a hard disapproving glower.

"Sorry to intrude," Drew said pleasantly, "but I'm afraid, Josie,
your mistress has need of your services in her room."

"I better be goin' den." Immediately the object of Bear's affection hurried off toward the inn. Then, just as abruptly, she swung
back, her plaid skirts flying up enough to show off her ruffled
petticoats. "I be back," she said, looking directly at Bear with a
dimpled smile, "quick as a flash."

The anger melted from his expression. "An' I be right here
a-waitin'."

As Drew dropped down beside his friend, the older man said,
"I 'spect I best be gettin' on in now. 'Lessen," he amended, "y'all
wants somethin', sir."

"No, thank you, I just come out for some fresh air." Drew
turned to Bear. "Your Miss Josie looks mighty fetchin' this
evenin', wouldn't you say?"

"You seed da new dress she gots on. I figure it ain't nothin' but a
bribe. Her mistress didn't come out and say da words, but Josie

know it's just cuz she wants to keep Josie quiet. Don' want her tellin' Brother Rolf the truth about why dey's here with us."

"Ah, then Josie's let you in on their secret, has she?"

"Yessir. An' it's just like we reckoned. Dey's on da run."

"I knew it!" Drew slapped Bear on the back. Then his thoughts turned more serious. "She's not runnin' from the law, is she?"

"No, nothin' like dat."

"Then she's runnin' from her pa. Or a husband. Which is it?" For some unaccountable reason, Drew hoped she wasn't married.

"From da way Josie tells it, it's both. Only it's a pappy and da man she's set to marry. And from what Josie says, Miz Amherst's menfolk won't never give up till dey catches up to her. Dey's both rich enough to hire all da trackers and hunters dey need to find 'em. Dis Mr. Amherst, he gots a big cabinet," Bear said, spreading his arms, "stocked chock full wi' nothin' but long rifles and pistols and such. An' Josie's sure he'll bring 'em all. And his bullwhip. She's plumb sure o' dat."

Although Drew was pleased to learn that Crystabelle was still untaken, it sounded as if her people would be coming with a small army. He sighed. "Reckon I'd better tell Brother Rolf right away. We don't want to tangle with no heavily armed party alone up in the mountains. Specially over somethin' that ain't none of our business in the first place. Did Josie say how much of a head start she and her mistress have?"

"She ain't sure. Miz Amherst keeps tellin' her dey gots maybe ten days, but Josie don' think it's dat long. Da two o' dem was supposed to be goin' from da school to dey's plantation. Miz Amherst was a-goin' home to get ready for da weddin'. Josie say it takes two days by wagon. An' even dough Miz Amherst tricked poor Josie, it's Josie dat'll be takin' da whippin' when dey catches up to 'em, iffen dey don' try an' kill her on da spot. You see, it be Josie's job to tell da school boss iffen Miz Amherst was up to any mischief." Bear stood up, his fists clenched, as he stared at the upstairs windows of the inn. Then he heaved a heavy sigh and his hands went slack. "Drew, is y'all sure you gots to tell Brother Rolf? He'll leave 'em behind, and Josie'll get catched, for sure."

"I'll have to, and before we leave tomorrow. This is the last settlement before we head into the high mountains." He patted the log beside him. "Sit down. Relax. Crystabelle Amherst is a clever lass. She won't let 'em get caught so easy. And if they do, she won't suffer no harm to come to Josie. If nothin' else, she'll see to that. You go ahead and enjoy your last evening. I promise I won't spill the beans till mornin'." Drew's lips lifted in a smile. "Perhaps over breakfast. It'll be a pure pleasure, seein' Miss Amherst's face when I break the news."

7

A tapping sounded at Crysta's door.

Finally. Last night Josie could hardly wait to finish her evening chores so she could run back to that arrogant Bear. Now this morning Crysta had been waiting for a good half hour for Josie to come help her finish dressing for the day. Clutching the back of her dress together as best she could, Crysta hurried to the entrance of her very small but, thankfully, private room.

Her toe caught in her sagging petticoats, and she practically tripped as she reached the door. She kicked them aside and pulled it open. "What took you so—"

In front of her stood not Josie but the lad she'd hailed from her window and sent to fetch the girl.

"Sorry, it's just me, ma'am." The straw-haired lad belatedly doffed his hat. "I couldn't find your gal nowheres."

"Did you check in the kitchen as well as the servants' quarters?" This was not like Josie.

"Aye. I told cook to send her soon as she comes in." He took a backward step. "If there ain't nothin' else, ma'am, I gotta get back to my chores."

"Josie needs to get to hers, too," Crysta groused as she closed the door. Tonight she'd see that Josie slept in her room. From now on, she'd be chaperoning her chaperone.

It was getting late. Reaching behind her neck, she started fumbling with the first of at least two dozen tiny buttons that would close her formfitting bodice—if she could manage them all.

Her skirts slipped down farther. More for her to contend with. But she couldn't tighten the laces at her waist until she mastered the buttons and tucked in the blouse.

The skirts fell into a pool around her feet.

Forgetting the buttons for the moment, Crysta gathered up the many yards of fabric and strode to the window to survey the back-yard below. Nothing. Then she searched around the other build-ings of the inn. Still nothing. She extended her gaze to the gardens and fields and on to the surrounding tree-covered hills. Where *was* that girl? This simply was not like Josie. Was she so smitten with that uppity slave she'd forgotten how vital it was not to dally and keep Reverend Bremmer waiting? He couldn't be given the slight-est cause to leave them behind.

Growing more angry by the second, Crysta grabbed one of her boots from beneath the lumpy straw mattress. She'd track Josie down herself, and when she did, that girl was in for a good tongue-lashing, at the very least.

When Crysta had done her best to stomp her way into her boots, she fastened enough buttons to hold her blouse closed and hastily laced and tied the two sets of skirts behind her waist—not as tight as she'd like, but they would have to do for now.

Then came her long mass of wavy hair. She didn't take the time to brush it at the mirror above the commode—the glass was much too small anyway. Instead, she caught up her tresses in a hasty knot, rammed in a few pins and set her scant riding bonnet on top, wishing it covered more. Not bothering with the ties, she dug into her satchel sitting on the floor and looked for her matching riding jacket that would hide the sloppiness at her back.

But she couldn't find it. She dumped the contents of the bag on the bed. It wasn't there.

Then she remembered she'd had Josie pack the cropped coat in one of the trunks because of the warm weather. And the trunks were out in the barn. She'd have to go downstairs as she was.

Crysta practically stomped to the door. How dare Josie do this to her—especially the very next morning after that rude Mr. Reardon accused her of not even being able to undress herself.

The remembrance made her all the angrier. That bumbling woodsy didn't know the first thing about what it took for a young lady to become properly attired. Flinging the door open, she strode out and swiftly descended the dark narrow stairs.

Her steps slowed, however, when she reached the bottom. She'd forgotten that the stairwell landed her directly in the eating area. The other overnight guests were already dining. She was later than she'd thought. Along with the minister and Reardon, four men and one woman were occupied with their breakfasts.

Not wanting them to see her partially fastened blouse, she couldn't turn her back on them to go out the door. And to walk out backward would only draw unwanted attention to her person. She'd never been in such an awkward position in her life. Only one option remained.

She sidled between the two long tables toward her companions. She'd send Reardon out to find Josie, then scurry upstairs to wait.

Just as she reached the two men, an entire section of her hair started sliding down her cheek. She shot a hand up, catching most of it. When she reached over with her other hand, her bodice rode up and her riding skirt began to slip. She had no choice but to forego the hair and hitch up the waistband.

All while the frontiersman stared at her with that insolent smile of his.

Then it came to her. The brute had deliberately kept Josie from her. He was playing an outrageous joke on her.

Crysta marched up beside his bench and leveled her most condemning glower at him. *"Mr. Reardon,* I expect you to produce my servant this *instant."*

Drew had thought Miss Amherst had delayed coming down for breakfast because she'd somehow learned he'd be waiting for her—waiting for her to appear before he informed Brother Rolf that she was a runaway bride from a rich and powerful family. But here she finally stood, not as the accused, but as the accuser, despite the fact that she'd obviously overslept. She was a disheveled mess, especially her hair. One side had spilled down and over her shoulder like a mountain waterfall. And still she was spouting orders!

She was the most audacious lass he'd ever met. And adorably funny. "Your servant is missing, you say. Hmmm . . . that's plain to see."

Her cheeks flamed, and her lips tightened to a thin line. She swung toward Brother Rolf. "Sir, would you kindly order this . . . this . . . man to produce my girl and send her to my room this instant."

Strangely, she didn't turn around to walk away. Instead she backed away to the stairs as swiftly as her sagging skirts would allow. When she bumped into the first step, she whirled around and ran up, but not before Drew saw the pitiful job she'd done with her buttons. Some of the few she'd managed to fasten weren't even in the right holes.

Chuckling, he turned back to the table to find Brother Rolf scowling at him.

"Dat is not da funny joke. Now, you go. Tell dat girl to come."

"Sure. Right away." Rising, Drew attempted to restrain his grin as he placed a defending hand on his chest. "But I haven't done a thing. Leastways, not yet."

Brother Rolf waved him off. "Go. Fetch da girl."

Upon reaching the barn, the horses they'd boarded for the night set up a racket, whinnying and neighing, while the other stock happily munched on their morning rations of hay. Even though Black Bear had been quartered in the barn for the night, he'd neglected to feed them. Odd. Very odd.

And where was Bear's dun? Before Drew counted heads, he knew. Two horses were missing.

Bear was gone, and he'd taken Josie with him.

Of course. Bear had become too enamored of her to go off and leave her to the mercy of slaveholders.

Last night he'd offered Bear no choice. Yet Drew had been so caught up in his own little game, he'd not given it a thought.

Bear would know he and Josie couldn't risk being seen till they crossed the Ohio River. He'd stay off the main trails all the way back to Shawnee country. Still . . . "Keep an eye on 'em, Lord."

Drew turned to the complaining horses. "Well, let's hope his Josie is all he ever dreamed of." With a shrug, he grabbed the pitchfork leaning against the ladder and tossed it up to the hayloft. Better get the animals fed and watered before delivering the news to Crystabelle.

This was not going to be one of Miss High-and-Mighty's better days. Left stranded here in a small hill village without a single slave to dress her.

Soon, though, Drew's smile began to fade. Pitching hay down from the loft, he realized that the spoiled young miss was only trying to do what he'd been doing for years—run away from an unwanted marriage. A marriage to a rich man, he reminded himself. The fool girl was fleeing the dream of every other young maiden. After all, what else was there for a pampered young miss but an advantageous marriage? Unless she preferred spinsterhood and living at the sufferance of one of her kin.

Ah, but this one thought she could get by on her own—take on a man's job, support herself.

After tossing the last forkful to the ground below, he let the tool drop onto the pile, then started down the ladder. A woman might succeed at taking care of herself if she were like his sister-in-law Annie. Annie was a hard worker and almost as capable as a man with hammer or axe. But this one? She couldn't even dress herself.

Crysta's arms ached as she surveyed herself in the mirror, but most of her buttons were now fastened and the full length of her hair was brushed smooth and knot-free. It fell all about her like a shiny russet veil. Josie still hadn't arrived.

And when she did, there wouldn't be time to do anything but get Crysta properly buttoned and laced. Reverend Bremmer must be pacing the floor with impatience by now. One long braid pinned up beneath her riding bonnet would have to do.

While separating her hair into three parts, Crysta heard footsteps. She rushed to the door and flung it wide . . . to dismal disappointment. Again, no Josie.

Mr. Reardon stood there, taking up the entire opening, and again he stared at her hair, every bit of which was hanging down this time.

All patience gone, Crysta pushed past him and looked both ways down the miserably empty hall.

"She's gone," he said from behind.

"What do you mean?"

"Just what I said. Your Josie is gone. She's run off with Black Bear."

"That's impossible." Josie would never willingly leave her.

"Well, it's happened just the same. I should've guessed he'd do it, once he learned she was in danger. He was that taken with her, you know."

"You're saying he stole off with her? Oh, my poor Josie." Crysta shoved him toward the stairs. "Go get the authorities. We have to save her from him."

"He'd never do anything to harm her. His intentions toward her are completely honorable."

"*Honorable.* Have you completely lost your senses? Your slave has absconded with mine. I don't know what kind of laws you have in Tennessee, but on this side of the mountains, that's a hanging offense."

"Don't worry about that. He'd never let himself get caught."

Crysta stared at him in disbelief. The man's slave had run off, and it didn't seem to bother him one whit. Did *anything* bother him? Ever? She whipped all her hair over one shoulder and turned her back to him. "Finish buttoning me. I'll go fetch the authorities myself."

At least he did as she bid—or tried to. "These sure are tiny little buttons," he grumbled, fumbling with those last stubborn two in the middle. Then his voice slipped into a lazy drawl. "By the by, I don't think I'd be in such an all-fired hurry to have the dogs set on Bear. You might wanna ponder, instead, on a little exchange I have in mind."

"I doubt there's anything you now possess or ever will that means remotely as much to me as Josie." She jerked away from him and hastily started coiling her hair—a braid would take much too long.

The man followed her into the room. *Her private room.*

She swung around, outraged.

He stopped in his tracks, then quickly backtracked to the threshold. "Sorry about that. I wouldn't dream of takin' any liberties with you. Ever again. 'Specially when you got your boots on." A hint of a smile returned. "But I think you'll be real interested in my little bargain. My silence for yours. You see, I now know who you're runnin' from—your father and your betrothed. And I don't think you'd want to have that tidbit bandied about, 'specially not to a certain German minister we both know."

A sudden chill coursed through Crysta. "Why, that's—that's blackmail!"

"Personally, I'd rather think of it as a favor for a favor. Have we got a deal?"

8

Crysta practically had to stand on her head as she dug deeper into a used-clothes barrel at Boone's only mercantile—a store with few provisions in its sacks, kegs, or on its shelves. Less, even, than the pantry at the academy. She knew she was creating yet another delay this morning, but she was determined to find a simple front-laced outfit that required no help whatsoever in donning. She refused to be thought of as some silly useless child ever again. Even by the blackmailing likes of Drew Reardon.

Her fingers caught hold of a rather coarse piece of fabric that looked like part of a skirt. She pulled it to the top. A heavy linen garment, its color somewhere between beige and gray, it looked as if it had never seen an ounce of dye. Not only was it ugly, but it was a castoff, something she never dreamt she'd be obliged to wear. But the overdress fit the necessary requirement—it laced up the front.

Tossing it over her shoulder, Crysta rooted again in search of a simple drawstring blouse like those Josie usually wore.

"Miss . . . Miss," the elderly storekeeper called from behind.

Crysta kept searching. "Yes?"

"Your menfolk are calling for you to hurry along."

The last thing she wanted was to have anyone thinking those men outside were *her* menfolk—in particular Mr. Reardon—but she couldn't afford to be left behind. She lifted her head from the barrel and smiled politely at the balding merchant. "Thank you. Would you be so kind as to tell them I'll be no more than another minute?"

The narrow-faced man glanced at the garment draped over her shoulder, and his mouth fell open. "Surely you'll want something of better quality than that."

"Please, I beg thee, do as I bid." Unwilling to justify her choice to this stranger, she returned to her search. She'd already swallowed down more pride and contempt because of an extorting scoundrel than she cared to in one day.

Just then she found the exact item she was looking for, a simple peasant blouse. Shaking out the wrinkles, she saw what looked like a tea stain streaking down the front, but it would do. Surely she wouldn't be seeing anyone of import during the next few days of travel through the mountains.

At least she hoped not.

Her red-haired father's aristocratically English face flashed before her. And the deep disappointment in his light green eyes. Not anger, never anger. If it had been solely up to him, Crysta knew she could have talked him out of the wedding. But not Mother. That woman had an unbendable will when it came to her children—demonstrated when she sent Crysta away to school to keep her from, as she called it, running wild with her brothers.

Yes, Simone Angelique Amherst had unshakable plans for her children. Especially her daughter. Crystabelle was to marry someone as far removed as possible from her mother's humble origins. Although she wasn't supposed to know the closely kept family secret, Crysta had learned that her grandfather had been a common-born sea captain who'd gained his wealth in the shipping trade; and her grandmother, a lowly French Creole.

And, of course, Harland Chastain, Crysta's betrothed, was everything her mother could hope for. He actually had a cousin who was first cousin to the king of England. And as her mother loved to remind Crysta, no revolution, American or French, could erase *that* heritage.

Well, Crystabelle was as determined as her mother ever was. She'd manage this morning's setbacks—and any others that came her way. She refused to be deeded over like a tract of land, to be used or misused as her new owner saw fit. For as the apostle Paul said in Galatians 3:28, "There is neither Jew nor Greek, there is neither bond nor free, there is neither male nor female: for ye are all one in Christ Jesus."

Aye, she'd tossed down her own gauntlet, was waging her own private revolution. And it was time, as that eminently enlightened British thinker, Mary Wollstonecraft, wrote, "to restore women to their lost dignity and to make them a part of the human species." And that, Crystabelle Amherst surely intended to do.

With this banner for womanhood waving boldly in her mind, she carried the two garments to a simple counter made from a board placed on two barrels. "How much for these?" Then she noticed several firearms racked on the wall behind him. They were mostly long rifles, but one was a shorter musket like the weapon her brothers had taught her to shoot. If she truly was going to be venturing into the wilds of the West as an independent woman, she would need one . . . even if it cost her the last of the money she'd gotten in exchange for her sapphire earbobs. "I'll take that Brown Bess, too. And all the fixings."

When she walked outside with her new purchases, Reverend Bremmer, saddled and waiting, frowned. "Vat you vant *mit* a gun? Ve take care of you. *Und* more clothes?" He pointed toward her trunks strapped to the packhorses. "You already got more dan you need."

Reardon stood beside her mount.

She turned away, not wanting to view his mocking insolence. "I don't wish to ruin my good ones on the trip."

"*Ja,* I see. Vell, da little time vasted is not so bad. Ve go faster today, I t'ink, now dat Black Bear takes your Josie to meet his papa. You are good girl to gif your slave her freedom. I vas bond servant myself. Seven years. I know vat is like."

"Where did you hear—?" Her gaze shot to the hunter.

He stared back, his face surprisingly bland. She didn't know exactly what he'd told the minister, but she'd have to hold her tongue until she found out. And that she would be doing as soon as possible.

She just wished she didn't have to accept his help to mount the bay mare. But it was fitted with that blasted sidesaddle—another invention by some man meant to perpetuate women's helplessness.

"Milady?" His infernal smile was back as he nodded toward the horse. "Time's a-wastin'."

Oh yes, he was smug. He may have won this morning's battle, but they were a long way from finished with the matter of Josie and her abductor. Crysta eyed him straight on as she strode to her horse. Ignoring the waiting miscreant, she rolled and stuffed her clothes into a saddlebag and lashed her new weapon and bullet pouch on top. All before she deigned to place her boot into his laced hands.

He merely chuckled.

Nothing ever seemed to bother him. Not even his own slave running away.

And just why was that?

Another thing she intended to find out as soon as they were on their way.

Still, as they rode out of the rustic hamlet nestled in a small cove above the Watauga River gorge, she felt alone for the first time. Josie was gone. From Crysta's first memories, Josie had been with her, always, even when her own parents were not. Almost like an older sister. Especially these past few years when Crysta had been banished from her brothers. Her deepest longings and fears she'd shared with Josie. She'd shared everything. Always.

Except the true destination of this trip.

And now Josie had done the same to her. No, worse . . . she'd left Crysta behind to go off into the unknown without so much as a word. Out of fear for her life, Drew Reardon insisted. But he was mistaken. Josie's life was in far more danger now than before. Two lone Negroes were obvious prey for any bounty hunter roaming the countryside.

Riding along with these two men, Crystabelle climbed out of the valley along a narrow, densely shadowed trail crowded by brush and trees. Visibility was limited to only a few feet into the under-growth on each side, and only glimpses of the blue sky could be seen overhead. The birds seemed quite happy in the seclusion. Their chirps filled the air, along with the occasional chattering of squirrels. The only other sounds came from the clop of horse hooves and the groan of leather. That conversation she wanted to have with Reardon was not feasible, since there was only room for them to travel single file.

Finally, her opportunity to speak to him presented itself as the trees gave way to a meadow blanketed with wildflowers and alive with butterflies.

She reined in her arch-necked mare and waited for Mr. Reardon's surefooted but rather homely gray gelding to come alongside. A man with his blond good looks should be astride a more stylish animal, such as one of the great warhorses of yore or her own Arabian.

She'd let her thoughts drift for the merest of seconds, and Reardon stole the stage. "I see you bought yourself a musket. Plan to be shootin' it anytime soon?" The usual teasing condescension was in his voice.

"One never knows when an opportunity might present itself, now, does one?" she replied, her own voice and smile lethal as she aimed her gaze, if not her gun barrel, straight at the blackmailer.

He lazed back in his saddle, seemingly unconcerned. "Well, if you're thinkin' on baggin' yourself some of our more dangerous game, I'm afraid the pickin's are mighty slim this far east. Ain't heard o' no bears or wolves in these parts for quite a spell. But if you'd like, this evenin' I could teach you how to load and shoot. Don't want you blowin' your purty li'l head off, now, do we?"

"I'll take my chances." For all his affable grinning, he was even more uppity than his slave. "Now, if you don't mind, I'd appreciate knowing why you refused to send the law after your own valuable property. Is it because you knew all along exactly where he was going, as you so blithely informed Reverend Bremmer? Joshua—or Bear, as you like to call him—hasn't really run away, has he? Not from you, a paragon of truth and virtue. You schemed with him to deprive me of my servant. My original assessment was the correct one, after all. You did it just to make me look foolish and helpless. Anything for a laugh."

"Aye, that would make for a whopper. Too bad it didn't occur to me. I merely told Brother Rolf where I think Bear headed—to his pa's lodge. Bear has great respect for his father and would never 'jump the broom' with Josie without his blessing."

"So what you're really saying is, when we get to your valley, they'll be there waiting for us. Now, let me tell you. If your man has harmed her in any way whatsoever, I'll show you just how good I am at loading a musket."

"You don't say?" At least there was a hint of surprise in his teasing tone this time. "Well, I'm afraid you're not gonna get your gal back quite so easy. Bear's pa doesn't live in Reardon Valley. He lives in an Indian village two weeks' ride to the northwest, deep in the Ohio wilderness. And for the record, I never once said Bear was my slave. Another of your assumptions. He and his pa are both honored Shawnee braves. The only difference from them an' any other Shawnee is that Moses raised Bear to be a Bible-believin' Christian. And that's why there's no need to fret over your gal. He'd never do nothin' to harm her—her person or her spirit. Or make her go anywhere she doesn't want to." A seriousness had, at last, diminished his humor. "Joshua Black Bear took her for the noblest of reasons . . . to keep her safe from the wrath of your people."

"*Safe?* Hardly. He ripped her from my protection to carry her into a hostile and heathen land." Crysta swallowed down her mounting fear. "My poor Josie, what will become of her?"

Reardon guided his horse closer and ground out a defiant retort. "She'll be free. Just like you say you want to be."

Crysta wasn't intimidated by his irrational stance. "What good will that do her? She'll be hunted wherever she goes—if the Indians don't kill her first."

He relaxed into his saddle again, but the cocky smile was long gone. "I reckon she's willin' to take her chances, just like she was takin' with you. Only this time it's her choice and her own self she's freeing."

He was beginning to sound like one of those Northern crusaders who wanted all the slaves emancipated, set adrift without a single thought as to how these penniless souls would survive.

But now that she had a taste of her own freedom, it was easy to see how even the most destitute would want it, hang the cost. An equally great sadness, though, was that so many of her own gender didn't even know they were just as trapped and enslaved as the slaves—first as daughters, then as wives. Down through the centuries, countless women had chafed at their bonds, thinking their only recourse would have been to be born a boy.

But the brilliant Mary Wollstonecraft had defined in print the long-hidden yet dire injustice. And Crystabelle Amherst would not fail in her own crusade to impart this truth, given the spark of a chance.

Beside her, though, rode the one man who could thwart her mission before it began. "Speaking of freedom, now that we've left behind the authorities who would see that Black Bear is arrested, what's to stop you from telling Reverend Bremmer about me?"

"I gave you my word. But I want you to know, if he comes straight out and asks, I won't lie for you." Reardon reined his horse closer. "Now tell me, what really makes a pampered rich miss like you decide to leave your fancy life behind? I can't picture you in some backwoods settlement, teaching a bunch o' boys who're rougher'n dry cobs."

She ignored his latest barb. "I do hope the families will send their daughters as well. If their minds are enriched, they shall be more pleasant company for their husbands . . ."

That irritating smirk was back. Again, he was finding her a source of amusement.

Undeterred, she continued, " . . . and more instructive mothers to their children. I'm sure the reverend would be pleased to hear that women would gain a much deeper spiritual understanding if they're able to read the Bible for themselves. Isn't that what you Baptists believe in, that it is the right of each and every person to read and interpret for themselves the Word of God?"

"Ah, then you do know something about us Baptists."

"I know that many down through the centuries have died for this precious right. Women as well as men. It's mentioned in my volume of church history."

"So you've been doing some studying by the dim glow of a candle, have you?"

He did love to make light of her every effort. "Getting back to the subject of young ladies attending class—"

"Before you start harpin' on that, better spend your time worryin' about whether the folks in the valley are even gonna be willin' to take on a woman teacher."

"I'm sure if your minister, their spiritual leader, accepts me, they will too."

A chuckle rumbled up from his chest. "You still have a lot to learn about us Baptists. We're a contrary bunch. Each of us thinkin' we got a say in how everything's run."

"Even the women?"

He snorted. "Specially the women. Baptist women are the bossiest bunch you ever want to meet. An' meddlesome, too. In my family, they're always tryin' to marry us poor men off. Tie us down. I've had to keep on my toes to stay ahead of them matchmakers."

"And well you should. I pity the poor woman saddled with anyone as unwilling to be a loving, caring husband as you say you are."

Her insult didn't faze him. "I like the way you think."

"I'll take that as a compliment. Aside from the fact that you revel in making sport of me—*and that you're blackmailing me*—I do have to admit, you've proven to be more helpful with Reverend Bremmer than most men would've been."

His sun-bleached brows raised above his light gray eyes. "Now there you go again. I wouldn't call our agreement blackmail. A good horse trade is more like it. Josie's freedom for yours."

Crysta glanced behind her, forgetting her brave pose. "Neither of us is assured of that just yet."

"I wouldn't worry overmuch." He'd read her weak moment. He reached across as if to touch her hand; then he must have thought better of such a comforting action and retrieved it. Instead, he smoothed a mussed section of his gray horse's mane. "You both had a good head start. Even if they do track you to Salem and learn you left with us, they'll be askin' about a party of five, and now we're three."

"I hadn't thought of that." She stroked her bay mare's sleek neck. "I should've traded off Sheba. Being Arabian and with four white stockings, she's quite noticeable."

"I'm surprised you didn't. You're always such a busy thinker. But gettin' back to this teachin' business you plan to take up. I was wonderin', have you ever heard of this writer fella Shakespeare?"

"Of course," she retorted with a roll of her eyes. "His plays are considered the world's best."

"Well, my brother has some of them plays, and he was tellin' me about one I'll bet your students would sure find interestin'."

Crysta reined in her chin and took a second look at the woodsy. "You, a man with no social graces whatsoever, have a brother who reads Shakespeare?"

Reardon burst out laughing. "We tried to put a stop to it, but he's just as stubborn about keepin' his nose in some dandyish book as I am about riskin' life itself to explore the great unknown. I like to think of myself as Columbus on a horse."

"Columbus, you say." The man certainly was full of himself. "I think perhaps you're more of a Don Quixote."

His sun-bronzed forehead crimped above his nose. "I don't recall that name."

"Ask your brother. I'm sure he'd be pleased to tell you all about him." For once it was Reardon's turn to be unsure, giving Crysta a surge of satisfaction.

Absently he tucked a blond strand into the thong-tied queue at the nape of his neck. "I'll be sure and do that. Now," he said, regaining his smug grin, "let's get back to my brother and Shakespeare. The play he likes to talk about is called *The Taming of the Shrew*. Somehow, talkin' to you brings it fresh to mind."

The Taming of the Shrew. Ha! With a man like this, could it have been any other play? "And might I add, talking to you makes me want to rewrite the ending." Clucking her tongue, Crysta slapped the reins across Sheba's neck. The mare lunged into a trot, speeding away from the woodsy boor. Too bad such good looks were wasted on one such as he.

9

As Reverend Bremmer had promised, a faster pace had been set, even though the terrain grew increasingly more rugged. As the morning edged toward noon, Crysta was slapped and snagged by more vines and branches than she could count. Yanking her emerald gabardine riding skirt from yet another bramble bush, she wished she'd taken the time to change into the used clothing she'd bought earlier.

Still, her excitement mounted, knowing she was riding into mountains taller than she'd ever seen. She sensed more than saw their immensity as she rode through thickly vegetated gorges or along the sides of pine-covered ridges.

But as the hours wore on, the trail they followed began to look more like a deer path than anything else. Ofttimes it was scarcely visible. Staying seated became increasingly difficult and uncomfortable as her mount lurched up and down rises.

Though she refused to complain, she prayed they would stop soon for a rest.

Her poor Sheba stumbled over a root, wrenching Crysta forward, inflicting a sharp pain to the ache already gnawing at her right hip.

It was at that moment a niggling thought started to take form. Thousands of people had traveled to Tennessee before her. There was even talk of granting it statehood. This couldn't possibly be the road over the mountain—the Wilderness Road she'd read about.

A sudden wave of fear swept over her. Here she was, deep in the mountains with all her worldly possessions, and what did she really know about these two men who were supposedly escorting her to Reardon Valley? Were they even who they said they were?

She surveyed the hulking German riding a few yards ahead of her, truly studied him. He wore no rings or fancy boots one might expect to find on a successful thief . . . even his musket looked old and abused. And absolutely nothing in his speech or manner had given her cause to suspect him of treachery. He had to be as he said—a simple man of the cloth. He just had to.

Yet after riding for hours, they had not passed a single person or dwelling, no eating establishment where they might take a much-needed respite. Her stomach began to knot, and not from hunger. She glanced skyward. The sun had passed the midday mark, streaming down through scattered holes in an umbrella of the otherwise deeply shaded forest. Something was very much amiss. She was trapped between two strangers . . . and her musket wasn't even loaded.

Father in heaven, what have I gotten myself into?

Reminding herself that she wasn't alone, that God was always with her, Crysta shoved down her fear. Still, answers to her questions were in order. Knowing she'd never get satisfaction from the hunter, she nudged Sheba forward toward Reverend Bremmer.

It was a tight squeeze, with her horse traveling on a slant. Her mare had to trample through some ferns and dodge around a couple of birch trees, but Crysta managed to come alongside him.

The beefy minister glanced over at her with what anyone would take for a guileless smile.

"Kind sir," she began, attempting her own pleasant expression, "how much farther before we reach a place to dine?"

"I vas vanting to climb to da top of yon ridge before ve stop." His coarsely sleeved arm pointed ahead of them. "Ve be dere soon. You vill like very much, I t'ink."

He sounded most sincere. Still, she probed further. "Sir, I find it most curious that we haven't encountered any other people along the way."

In a shocking move, he grabbed her horse's reins. He pulled her mount close to his. "Look out! A hole," he warned, nodding down to the edge of the path.

She saw where a slice of black earth had broken away on the downhill side. Had Sheba stepped into it, they would have gone crashing down the mountainside.

"You stay behind me, ride in center of trace. Ve be dere soon."

As Crysta reined in, she felt foolish. She'd let her overactive imagination cause her to become careless.

But her questions were valid and still unanswered.

Worse, she felt the eyes of Mr. Reardon boring into her. The last thing she wanted was to look less than capable in front of the blackguard.

As they climbed, the pines became increasingly gnarled and stunted. Moments later, they gave way to a sun-bathed knob of stone. And all other thoughts swept away.

Stopping at the edge of a sheer drop-off, Crysta saw ridge after mountain ridge spread before her, eventually fading into the horizon. Consumed by the immensity of the panorama, she seemed insignificant, yet at the same time she felt as if she'd conquered the world, since she was surely at its top. Even the soft breeze smelled fresher, sweeter.

"You think this is somethin'?" came from beside her. "It's just the beginnin'. There's sights out there most folks never even thought of."

She glanced at the frontiersman, who'd halted his mottled gray horse beside hers. He, too, gazed into the vast beyond, a light shining in his eyes she'd never seen before . . . that same desire she felt . . . to see what lay beyond the horizon. Columbus on a horse, he'd called himself.

In her own way, she planned to be a Columbus, too, stretching the boundaries for womankind. And she liked the idea of bringing these new ideas to a virgin land that had no boundaries. Here anything was possible.

He dismounted, breaking the spell. "Let me help you down; then we can see about noonin'."

"Where?" Crysta swiveled in her saddle. She saw no travelers' inn.

"Right here," he said, pulling her off and setting her feet on the solid surface. "Have Brother Rolf show you where the coffee fixin's is. And, by the way, I like mine strong."

"Coffee? Me, make coffee?"

"Yep. I don't think you'll find any slaves up here waitin' to do it for ya."

"And neither will you," she flung back. He never missed a chance to bait her. "Make your own coffee."

"Suit yourself." He shrugged in that nonchalant way of his and sauntered off. "Just thought you might wanna eat with us."

What exactly did he mean by that?

Stretching out the kinks in her stiff legs, she strode to the minister.

He was unhooking a large sack that hung from one of the packhorses. Setting it on the ground, he spread open the drawstring neck

74

and pulled out a blackened pot. "Here," he said, handing it to her.
"You fill from dat pool over dere. Da ground-up coffee beans are in
here, too. You make ready. I get out da food *und* da cups. *Ja?*"

He obviously hadn't heard her exchange with Reardon. Holding
the sooty pot away from her skirt, she stared from it to the big man
still rummaging through the bag. "But I . . ."

He looked up at her. *"Ja?"*

"But I don't know how."

"To vat? Make da coffee?"

Despite her years of schooling, she suddenly felt incredibly
inadequate. "I'm afraid not."

He rose to his feet, staring at her in disbelief. Then he shoved
something into her hand. A small cinched bag. "You learn. *Now.*"

Crysta couldn't fathom why he was so shocked. He seemed
more upset about this minor inadequacy than when she'd told him
she was the new teacher.

She whirled away, knowing she'd better do his bidding, and
walked across the stone surface to a catchment that wasn't much
larger than a washtub. To her surprise, it looked as if water had
just been poured into it from a crystal-clear stream, yet she knew it
had to be runoff from some past rain or snow.

After dipping the pot in and filling it, she turned back toward
the minister. She had no choice but to ask what she was supposed
to do with the ground coffee beans and how she was expected to get
it hot. Although she'd consumed very little coffee in her lifetime—tea, naturally, was preferred in civilized circles—she did
know coffee was always served steaming hot.

Out of the corner of her eye she saw the lanky hunter returning,
his arms loaded with sticks. He hadn't merely walked away like
some woodsy lord and master, as she'd thought. He'd been tending
a chore, just as Reverend Bremmer was, and just as they expected
her to. Everyone pitching in and doing a share. There was a fairness to that.

Planting a pleasant expression on her face, she walked to Reverend Bremmer, trying to ignore the fact that she knew Reardon would probably watch her every step.

The minister scowled up at her from where he was setting wooden plates and pewter cups on a slab of raised stone, their makeshift table.

She still couldn't believe her acceptance or rejection by him had more to do with her ability to make coffee than her teaching. "I do beg your indulgence, sir. My training has not been in the domestic arts. But I'm very quick. Just explain how the coffee's made, and it shall be done."

Shaking his black-hatted head, the man sat down on the table of stone and spread his calloused hands. "*Fräulein,* tell me da trut'. You haf never pluck a chicken in your life or vash da clothes or plant a garden, haf you?"

"But, sir, that's not what you hired me to do."

"Even teachers, dey got to eat. Who do you t'ink is going to cook *und* clean for you ven ve get to da valley? Everyone dere already haf plenty work of dere own to do."

Much too close by, Reardon dropped his armload of wood, and Crysta knew without looking that he was reveling in her downfall.

She bristled at the position into which Reardon and that black Indian had put her. She gritted out her answer to the minister's question. "I had expected my servant to take care of those details."

"I see. *Und* now she is gone. Dis is not goot. I t'ink maybe ve take you back to Boone. Get you escort from dere on back to Salem."

"Back?" Crysta swung around to Reardon. "I can't go back."

Panic. The spirited beauty's autumn eyes were shouting pure panic. Thundering at Drew's conscience. What could he do but come to her rescue? "Brother Rolf, I think we should at least give the lass a chance to prove herself. I'll teach her what I can between here and Knoxville. And if she don't work out by then, she can hire someone from there to take her back to Virginy."

Brother Rolf rubbed the stubble on his jaw. "I vonder." Then he riveted his sharp blue gaze to Miss Amherst. "Vat you say, *fräulein?*"

"Give me this chance. I promise I won't let you down."

The older man took the coffeepot from her and handed it to Drew. "Here. You vant to teach her? Is big job. Dis one, she cannot even make da coffee." Head wagging, he walked away, mumbling, "I chust glad mine Inga is not here to see dis."

She can't even make coffee. Laughter threatened to bubble up from Drew's chest. He caught Miss Crysta by the arm and led her toward the pile of wood. "I reckon it's useless to ask if you can get a fire goin'."

"*I reckon it is,*" she repeated through clenched teeth. Her fighting spirit was back.

Reaching into his pocket, Drew withdrew a jag of stone. "Let me introduce you to this. It's a piece of flint. We're gonna be havin' a lot of fun with it . . . and pots 'n' pans an' . . ."

Although the breeze was cool at this lofty altitude, the sun beat down from above and reflected off the stone bald. Beads of perspiration moistened Crysta's neck and brow as she sat on the jutting slab of rock to eat the almost tasteless offering of dried meat and hard biscuits and the blasted coffee. Not even the simple comfort of a soothing cup of tea.

But, she noted, the two men didn't seem the least bothered by the heat, much less the meager fare. They crowded onto the slab on each side of her.

After Brother Rolf asked God's blessing, both men relaxed and chatted as if they were on a summer picnic.

Brother Rolf reminisced a few moments about his first trip across the mountains; then his rumbly voice took on a serious tone. "Now dat I haf you away from Black Bear, Drew, I vant to ask, vat is really happening up nort' in Indian country? Do you t'ink da Shawnee is going to rise up again? Go on da varpath against da settlers?"

"It's hard to say. Mostly, they've been movin' their towns farther west into Frenchy country. As you know, there's a lot of bad feelin's between them and us Americans. And the Indians know they're outnumbered."

Bad feelings? Uprisings? Crysta spoke up. "Are you saying that Josie could be caught in the middle of a war? Does that black savage she ran—"

Reardon, sitting beside her, had the audacity to elbow her in the ribs . . . along with sending her a silent scowl of warning.

She'd almost blurted out the truth. Almost broke their hateful bargain.

"Bear's village," Reardon continued, "is quite aways southwest of the tribes that was raidin' along the frontier. And like I told you, Bear would never do anything to put Josie in danger."

Crysta could hardly keep a hold on her tongue. Not only was Josie in danger of being caught by vicious slavers or hostile Indians, the frontier settlers might take a notion to shoot at her too, as long as she was with a Shawnee brave—whatever his color.

Sipping on the cooling coffee, Crysta chose to send her thoughts elsewhere rather than listen to another word Reardon said. Pulling a kerchief from her pocket, she wiped her moist brow, then bit off a piece of stringy dried meat and stared glumly off into the distance. To keep her mind occupied, she'd count the number of ridges she could see in each direction.

"Miss Amherst," Brother Rolf said, reeling in her attention again, "I know dis is rough trail for a lady *und* for da packhorses.

But I t'ink you vill be pleased to know dat because ve take da short-cut over da steep mountain, ve safe two veeks' travel."

So they were taking the quickest but roughest route. That put her mind at ease about that matter, anyway. Then another thought surfaced. "We save two weeks? Just how far is it to Reardon Valley?"

"Dis vay is only . . . from here, vat you t'ink, Drew? Nine, ten days?"

"Aye, as long as none of the animals don't come up lame, totin' all the lady's truck."

Crysta bristled. Every chance the man got he made a disparaging remark about her possessions.

"Ve pray for da horses. *Und,* Drew, you *und* Miss Amherst, don't you forget to keep praying t'rough da day."

Drew glanced back at their mounts and pack animals, mercifully left in the shade of the scrawny pines. "The ones packin' would probably appreciate it more if we lightened their loads."

"Are you saying that we don't have enough packhorses to make it over the mountains?" Crysta said. "You should have thought of that before we left Salem."

"Oh, they'll pro'bly make it," he drawled complacently. "Pro'bly."

The man was infuriating. Crysta picked up her cup again and gazed off in the opposite direction.

"Don't vorry." Kind Brother Rolf made an attempt to appease her. "By tomorrow noon, ve are down among da settlements again."

"That's right," Reardon agreed with an out-of-place cheeriness. "And even tonight, we'll have a roof over our heads—an abandoned trapper's old shack."

Even if her meal had been far more tasty, Crysta still would have lost what little appetite she had. An abandoned shack.

Unfazed, the other two wolfed down their food as if it were

roasted goose. Reardon lounged off to one side, and between bites he bragged at length about some bear he'd allegedly outsmarted up in Cumberland country.

Then abruptly he tossed away the dregs of his coffee and stood up. "Reckon it's time we get a move on. Miss Crysta, you'll need to water your horse before we leave."

"*My* horse?" She caught herself and lowered her voice. "Am I to assume that when you watered every other horse, including Reverend Bremmer's, you overlooked mine?"

"Oh, I saw her, all right. I just didn't water her."

It was going to be like that, was it? Help her with one hand, hinder her with the other. He was a worse tormentor than either of her brothers had ever thought of being. Rising from her hard seat to meet his challenge, she wished she were taller. "Henceforth, Mr. Reardon, I would appreciate being informed of any duty I'm expected to perform. I hate the thought of my Sheba suffering because you couldn't find the words to tell me—especially since you're usually so glib."

Reverend Bremmer eyed Reardon, and for a second Crysta thought he would come to her defense, if not for her sake, for her mare's. But he just shook that oversized head. "Be quick about it. I see dis is going to be a very long trip."

For the rest of the day there was scarcely a moment when Crysta found herself riding on even ground. They were either struggling up a ridge or dropping in a jarring descent, if not crossing some swift rocky stream. She was bone weary by the time the crude log shelter came into view. It huddled low in a small clearing, pines towering all around it. Moss clung to the north side, and as she rode closer, she saw a spiderweb spanning an entire upper corner of the doorjamb.

The hefty German eased down from his saddle and lumbered up

to a door that was hinged by only a few strips of leather. He pushed it open and ducked beneath the web, disappearing inside.

Though she'd been having reservations about sharing a room with two men for the night, she was now more distressed about what else would be lurking in there. She'd rather take her chances outside under a tree.

Reardon drew his big-footed horse to a stop beside her much more elegant Arabian. "Don't look real invitin', does it? I'd rather spend the night outside, except it's beginnin' to smell like rain." He tilted his nose skyward.

Riding in a densely forested hollow for the past half hour, Crysta hadn't noticed the dark clouds rolling in. Her disappointment thickened into a self-pitying lump in her throat—an ominous prelude to tears. Could nothing go right on this miserable day?

"You up to a little huntin' party?" Reardon asked as he eased down from his saddle.

"For more suitable lodging?" she asked, hoping against hope as he sauntered around his gelding to reach her side.

"Nope." He raised his arms to retrieve her from her mount. "For critters of the eight-legged kind. Looks like we're gonna hafta do a little house cleanin'."

As Reardon set her feet on the ground, Crysta closed her eyes against this latest demand. And though she would have liked to accuse him of planning this latest skin-crawling chore, she knew for once she couldn't blame him.

Still, she refused to let him use this opportunity to torment her again. She took the initiative. "We'll need some kind of a broom. As an experienced frontiersman, I'm sure you can easily fashion one."

"Aye, that I can." Then he just stood there in silence.

She'd stolen his thunder.

But not for long. "I'll make a couple soon as you an' me unload the horses."

"Surely you jest. That's men's work."

"So's teachin'. And since most of the truck on them poor pack animals belongs to you, it's time you learned a little about the feeding and care of the stock."

Whirling back to her mount, she refused to waste one more ounce of her flagging energy on this lout . . . at least not until Reverend Bremmer came out and witnessed how he was mistreating her. She was certain the minister would come to her rescue. She caught hold of the end of Sheba's saddle cinch.

As she wrestled with the buckle, Brother Rolf strode out of the cabin. And as she'd expected, he walked straight up to her and placed a hand on her shoulder. "Is goot," he said, giving her shoulder a squeeze. "Dis is goot, you pitching in." With no further comment on the subject, the reverend began unsaddling his own horse.

She couldn't believe it. Surely, even in the dankest backcountry, a woman wasn't expected to become a stablehand and a beast of burden.

"Drew, boy, ve haf to put ever't'ing inside tonight because of da rain. But ve got mouses in da cabin. Ve need to fix it so dey don't get into da oats, *ja?*"

Spiders *and* mice? An unstoppable shiver skittered up Crysta's spine. Praying that Reardon hadn't seen it, she shot a glance at him . . . just in time to catch that disgusting grin cocking upward.

"Don't worry about them mice," he drawled, letting his gaze slide slowly from her to the preacher. "The lady's volunteered to take care of all them li'l creepin' critters. Ain't that right, Miz Amherst?"

10

There's one very large creeping critter I'd like to take care of, Crysta ranted to herself as she slid Sheba's saddle from the mare's back. It was heavier than she expected, but she kept a firm hold, then glanced around for a fence rail on which to put it.

Of course there wasn't one.

Reardon toted his saddle to a fallen tree a good twenty yards away, his own shoulders scarcely taut beneath his coarse linen shirt.

Struggling after him, her anger mounted. If she'd known how far she'd have to carry the blasted saddle, she would've taken Sheba to the log, then removed it.

Reardon passed her on his way back to the horses, and he was most fortunate he wasn't smirking, or he would've had the saddle's tall pommel smack in his midsection.

Returning, Crysta ripped the damp blanket from her mare and slung the smelly thing over the nearest oak branch, then started for Sheba's bridle . . . but didn't quite know where to begin. Several connecting straps bound the mare's lovely shaped head. Then there was the saliva-slickened bit in her mouth.

"We'll figure it out, pretty girl." Crysta patted Sheba's neck.

"It's not as if I'm brainless." But at home the stableboy had always seen to that sort of thing. Trying to avoid thinking about the nastiness that might get on her hands, she peered past the horse and saw Reverend Bremmer returning from placing his saddle with the others. She'd better get to work—she couldn't afford to give him cause to send her back to Salem.

Seeing a buckle below Sheba's ear, Crysta went for it.

"Don't unbridle her now," Reardon ordered as he unlashed a rope on a packhorse. "'Lessen you wanna take a chance on chasin' her halfway back to Boone."

She glanced at his smoky gray mount and observed that the animal's reins were still dragging the ground.

"Wait till we're through unloadin' 'em," he said matter-of-factly. "Then you can rig a hobble for her."

Rig a hobble? He no doubt knew she didn't have the slightest idea how to do that either.

Leaving Sheba, Crysta stalked over to where Reardon worked on the pack ropes. If she'd thought her saddle heavy, it had been light as goose down compared to her trunks—which he expected her to help unload.

"*Nein,* Miss Amherst," Reverend Bremmer called from where he was straightening his saddle's stirrups. "You fetch da moss. Rub da horses dry. Me *und* Drew, ve do da unloading."

She caught a grin sliding across Reardon's face at her sigh of relief. He was really enjoying himself. Wondering what he'd come up with next, Crysta began to question whether her agreement with this insufferable lout was worth enduring his little games— or his entire smug self.

Drew had already hobbled the livestock and just finished securing the tips of pine boughs to two hickory sticks when he glanced up from his broom-making. The lass still had three more horses to rub down. It was either go help her finish with the stock or go inside the hut and start cleaning without her.

Before he could decide what to do, Brother Rolf beat him to it. A clump of moss in each hand, the stout man lumbered over to Crystabelle. "I finish *mit* da horses, missy. You go *mit* Drew. Chase out da varmints so ve can bring in all dis truck. Da rain, it is starting soon."

Looking forward to sharing the task with the lovely lass, Drew held out one of the makeshift brooms and waited for her to come fetch it.

As she did, he saw that her finely woven bodice was no longer remotely white—more like horse-sweat buff, from reaching across the animals' backs. Strands of her hair streamed down in her face, one of which she blew out of her eyes. Most likely she didn't want to dull that fiery auburn with her not-so-clean hands.

Drew doubted she'd ever been so dirty in her entire life . . . and cabin cleaning was yet to come.

Crystabelle snatched one of the brooms and kept on walking— or stalking, depending on one's point of view.

Not wanting to miss a second, Drew hurried to catch up with her just as she swung the broom up and knocked down the web in the doorway.

She strode across the threshold, turning the broom as she went, and started banging the handle against the log walls, the single-slat table, a castaway box . . . anything that made a noise. She used the stick end to pick up a dusty, holey old blanket, and a mouse scurried from beneath it.

Drew expected her to scream, run into his arms.

She didn't. As if she'd been chasing mice her entire life, the lass flipped the broom around again and madly chased the poor zigzagging creature out the door.

Then she turned back to Drew with determined fury.

He backed up a step. The woman looked dangerous.

"Well?" she asked, whisking past him. "Are you going to just stand there?" Without waiting for an answer, she started sweeping cobwebs from the cracks between the logs, unmindful of the dust that billowed out with them. Any spider that had the misfortune to hit the packed earth she stomped.

Really feeling like a slacker now, Drew went to work brushing down the ceiling.

Within the whirlwind space of ten minutes, they'd rid the small cabin of anything that even resembled a living creature as well as years of accumulated dust. Drew felt as if half of the dust clung to him, and the other half, he knew, had landed on Crystabelle.

He also knew she'd never go to bed without bathing first. Women were like that.

She continued to bang at the ceiling and walls. Nothing would be crawling on her in the middle of the night.

But enough was enough. "Miss Amherst, you go out and bring in some loads of pine needles for your bed while I rig a rope across the room to give you some privacy."

Her flurry of activity ceased, and she turned to stare at him. "Did you say I'd have some privacy?"

Her voice was quiet, tremulous, poignant, and Drew felt a pang of guilt. He covered it with, "You will if you got an extra sheet or blanket we can use."

"Why, yes." Wiping her hands on an already black kerchief, she tucked a long hank of hair back into her knot. "I'll fetch one from my linen chest."

She hurried out, looking as if he'd just handed her a bunch of flowers.

Now he really did feel guilty.

A humbling experience, crawling on one's knees beneath low-slung branches to claw out pine needles with one's fingers. But eventually, Crysta had gathered and delivered several skirtloads.

Enough to make a passably comfortable cushion. And like everything else she'd touched today, they were covered with dirt. By the
time she had bedding tucked around the thickness, Reardon had
hung the sheet she gave him, and along with Reverend Bremmer,
had brought in all of her trunks. They now lined the earthen floor
beneath the sheet, creating an even more substantial barrier
between her private space and the rest of the cabin . . . this kind act
on Reardon's part of which she hadn't thought him capable.

Or had he merely wanted to rid himself of her for the night? She
had no doubt she looked a fright.

Whatever, she owed him for this gesture. Plumping her pillow and
placing it at the head of the first bed she'd ever made—one of several
firsts today—she rose from her knees. She started to brush the dirt
from her skirt, but upon viewing her fresh bed, thought better of it.

She stepped around the sheet just as the men came in carrying
their crate of supplies. "Reverend, Mr. Reardon. I thank you for
my little . . . room." She ended on a sigh. She hadn't realized the
extent of her exhaustion. "And in return, I would be pleased to
fetch in the needles for your beds as well."

Reardon's smirk was gone for the moment as he tilted his head
slightly and eyed her.

Not waiting for him to come up with one of his snide remarks,
she hastened out the door.

The wind was growing ever stronger, she noted as she started for
a pine tree she had yet to scavenge beneath. They were in for a real
rainstorm tonight—a fitting end to this horror of a day.

"The harder you pour on us, the better!" she raged back at the
wind. If nothing else, she could stand out in it, wash off all the
horse sweat and grime and humiliation.

But first she had more dusty pine branches to crawl beneath,
more prickly needles to gather, more dirt to get under her nails.

"Josie," she wailed, "how could you do this to me? Leave me to
face this alone."

During these last trips outside to gather needles, Crysta permitted herself to indulge in some justified self-pity . . . aching muscles, broken nails, stringy hair, filthy clothes, obnoxious men—man. But as she bundled in the loads, she never allowed her eyes to even contemplate tears. As smudged as her face surely was, they would make telltale streaks. And never would she allow that bully to think she was a crybaby.

Both men were so much larger than she that sufficient padding for their beds required several more trips than her own had—trips she made into the cabin in silence, since she was in no mood for pleasant civilities.

Thankfully, both were also occupied with other chores—the minister with meal preparations at a small, rather smoky, fireplace, and Reardon out feeding the stock measures of grain from his hat.

Rising after spreading a load of needles along a side wall, she figured one more skirtful would do it. Then hopefully she could rest—if Mr. Reardon didn't come up with something else for her to do. Whirling away toward the entrance, she practically ran into the man himself.

"Whoa, there," he said, holding up a staying hand. "That's plenty padding for me. Supper'll be ready in a few minutes. Why don't you go—"

"*What now?*" she flung back, her teeth clenched. "What delightful chore have you saved just for me?"

"Uh . . . I . . . it'd be my pleasure to help, ma'am. But I really thought you'd prefer bathing alone." Reardon lifted back the curtain to her quarters, and there between her trunks and the bed sat two large kettles of water, one with steam wafting up.

She glanced back at him, utterly surprised and unabashedly pleased . . . so pleased her throat began to clog, and she barely managed, "Thank you," before she fled behind the drape . . . before he witnessed her tears.

11

Returning from checking on the hobbled horses, Drew stepped just inside the cabin door and shook the moisture from his wide-brimmed hat and clothes. It had rained steadily all night and didn't act like it was going to stop anytime soon. But not traveling this morning shouldn't matter since no precise date of their arrival in the valley had been set.

The bulky German, stirring a pot of porridge at the small hearth, put a finger to his lips, signaling for silence when Drew started tromping the water from the boots he'd donned instead of the more comfortable moccasins.

Crystabelle was obviously still asleep. Drew glanced in the direction of her "quarters" at the far end where, just above her stacked trunks, a ruffle-trimmed sheet hung from the rope he'd suspended to give her privacy.

Brother Rolf nodded him toward a steaming cup of coffee that sat on the narrow tabletop made of a single board.

Leaving the front door open for extra light, Drew grabbed the earthenware cup and went to stand with his back to the flames. Though the morning was not particularly chilly, his fringed home-spun shirt had soaked up quite a bit of the downpour. Taking a sip of his brew, he listened to the crackling of the fire mingling with the gentle patter of rain. Sounds he'd always found pleasurable.

Within seconds, his gaze naturally gravitated to the sparkling white sheet. Raising his cup, he saluted it as if it were a flag. And it was—in a sense—a banner to her spunk. She'd been a real Rogers' Ranger yester's eve, wielding her broom of fir fronds until they'd evicted all the wildlife from the cabin. Smiling at the remembrance of the determined set of her mouth, Drew took another sip. Not a single frightened squeal or complaint had passed her lush lips.

But her expressive eyes had told another story when she'd learned that he was rigging a private room for her. They'd turned doelike in her gratitude. And later, he'd thought she was actually going to cry when she spied Brother Rolf's largest kettles full of heated water for her own personal use.

A private room and warm water for bathing—two of life's nice-ties that she'd probably never given a second thought to until yesterday.

"Da porridge is ready." Brother Rolf pulled a rag from his pocket and removed the pot off the coals. He carried it to the rough-grained table, where wooden bowls and spoons had been left stacked since last night.

Holding the cup aloft, Drew gingerly settled his weight on one of the two moaning benches flanking the trestled board as the older man scooped them each a portion of oatmeal.

Another moan sounded. From behind the fabric partition this time. Crystabelle Amherst was beginning to stir.

Drew smiled, wondering how she'd fared sleeping on an earth floor with only a layer of pine needles for a mattress.

Rolf sat down across from Drew and handed him the cone of sugar.

Drew broke off a chunk and dropped it into his oatmeal. Watching the sweetness melt into the bland breakfast, he wished he had a dab of butter too. But no matter. The rain was bound to stop within the next couple of hours, and by this evening they'd be down along the Nolichucky, where they could easily find some settler family to put them up for the night.

Brother Rolf bowed his head in silent prayer.

Drew did the same, asking the Lord not only for a safe journey this day but for a farm tonight where the cook liked to slather everything with butter. Butter and spring-chilled buttermilk were two things he really missed during the months he was off trekking in Indian country.

"Oh, la."

Drew glanced up and saw Crystabelle peeking around the side of the strung sheet, her exceptionally long night braid swinging free. He had a sudden desire to see her hair let loose, as he'd seen yesterday morning in that brief moment before she learned Josie wouldn't be coming to dress it.

"I must've overslept," she said in a rush. "I do apologize. You should have awakened me."

"Da rain," Rolf said, pointing with his spoon to the open doorway. "Ve don't go till da rain stop."

She glanced nervously out the door. "But I don't mind riding in the rain," she assured him. The lass was obviously thinking about the men who were most likely following her.

"Have you forgotten your books?" Drew teased, knowing they were the last thing on her mind. "No sense takin' a chance on ruinin' 'em. 'Sides, the mountain creeks will all be runnin' full and fast. Too dangerous for even an experienced trailblazer to ford."

"Oh, I see." She seemed to relax as her gaze gravitated to the table. "Coffee smells good."

"Dere is porridge, too," Brother Rolf said. "Is goot *und* hot."

"Fine. I'll get dressed and join you in a few minutes." With those words, her head disappeared behind the cloth wall.

And it was just as well. At her mention of getting dressed, Drew remembered her attempts yesterday, and he had to stifle a chuckle. He sure was going to miss the young woman when he dropped her off at Reardon Valley. She amused him more than anyone else he'd ever met.

Without all the grunts and groans he'd expected, Crystabelle strolled around the curtain a few moments later in the simple country clothes she'd bought in Boone the day before. And her long hair braid was now in a halolike crown at the top of her head. "Good morning," she said in an almost musical lilt.

"Come. Sit," Rolf invited. "Your breakfast, it vaits for you."

Again, Drew wished she'd let her hair fall loose, all swirling and wavy past her waist. There was something special about a woman's hair . . . the way it framed the face of a beautiful woman. And even in those simple clothes, this one moved with the grace of a queen.

Avoiding him, Crysta walked around to Rolf's side of the table and held out a rather thin book. "Since we'll be whiling away a few hours, I thought you might enjoy reading this. I do believe there's mention of Baptists in it."

Drew squelched his persistent amusement as Brother Rolf took the brown leather volume. By now, she'd probably marked every page of every book that mentioned the Baptists.

The flush-faced German studied the print etched on the front. "Ah, *ja,* is da *Book of Martyrs.*" He tucked it against his chest and smiled. "I read dis once. But it vas long time ago. I t'ank you."

"And I thank you for preparing my breakfast," she countered as she took her place beside him.

"No book for me?" Drew asked across from her, pretending to be slighted. "And after I braved the raging storm outside to feed and water your horse."

Curling a slender finger through the thick handle of her cup, she slowly lifted her gaze to him. "I told you the other day that you were welcome to borrow any that interested you during our travels."

"You got anything on explorin' the West? I'm a whole lot more interested in what's out there ahead of us than in some musty ol' past."

"I'm sorry, no. The only account of western adventures I've ever read was by that Rogers fellow when he wrote about his experiences during the French and Indian War. It appears it'll be up to a *great explorer* such as yourself to enlighten the rest of us. I have a plentiful supply of ink and paper if you'd like to start this morning."

The lass always had a comeback. Drew picked up his own cup and raised it to her. "Not this morning. I'd hate to get all set up and started, only to have to quit because the rain stopped. I'll just rummage through the sum total of your knowledge you keep boxed up in one li'l ol' trunk."

That got her. Any pretense at a pleasant smile turned to tightly clamped lips. She snatched up the sugar cone and a knife and stabbed off a chunk.

If Crystabelle had been upset earlier when Drew teased her about her lack of any practical knowledge, it was child's play compared to the agitation she displayed now. From where Drew sat on the dirt floor braced against the doorjamb with a book in hand, he had a perfect view of her foot pumping away. But this time he'd done nothing deliberate to cause her discomposure. Not exactly anyway.

It was she who'd made the mistake of letting him choose whatever book he wished. But when he'd sauntered out of her private little haven with the blue clothbound book, she'd turned white as the sheet that was draped over the rope. She'd bolted up from the bench, then, glancing back at Brother Rolf, dropped back down and suggested that Drew might find another topic of more interest. . . .

Which had only tweaked his curiosity all the more. He kept it.

Thereafter, as Drew read, every few seconds she nervously glanced up at him. The lass was in absolute torture.

But what a whopper he'd dug out of the bottom of the trunk. Not that it was a particularly large volume. But such an intriguing title: *A Vindication of the Rights of Woman: With Strictures on Political and Moral Subjects.* Pretty weighty stuff to be written by a female author. More than merely controversial, it was downright revolutionary.

It started off with a bang. The writer had dedicated it with a lengthy introduction to some male legislative adversary—not a friend, a foe. And almost from the first sentence, this Mary Wollstonecraft made powerful and provocative statements—statements that gave Drew a new insight into Miss Amherst and her own attitude and motivation. One quote in particular caught his attention.

> If children are to be educated to understand the true principle of patriotism, their mother must be a patriot; and the love of mankind, from which an orderly train of virtues spring, can only be produced by considering the moral and civil interest of mankind; but the education and situation of woman at present, shuts her out from such investigations.

And later the woman wrote:

> Consider, I address you as a legislator, whether when men contend for their freedom, and to be allowed to judge for themselves respecting their own happiness, it be not inconsistent and unjust to subjugate women, even though you firmly believe that you are acting in the manner best calculated to promote their happiness?

Drew became even more interested when the author equated women's lot with slavery. "They may be convenient slaves, but slavery will have its constant effect, degrading the master and the abject dependent." Then a bit further she wrote, "Tyranny, in whatever part of society it rears its brazen front, will ever undermine morality."

He had yet to finish the introductory pages and already knew that in his hands he had a book that would be more explosive than gunpowder . . . one destined to blow Crystabelle Amherst out of her tenuous position as teacher in Reardon Valley if the men there ever caught wind that she owned such a mutinous volume. He slid a glance over to the stiffly prim young woman and began to understand why she'd become so rebellious, despite all the advantages she'd enjoyed—advantages most young women only dreamed of having.

But as he read further, he began to realize that women truly were born into slavery if one were to consider the letter of the law. At home with her family or married, a female owned nothing—not her dowry, not the land or wealth she might inherit, not any money she might earn. Legally, her husband took possession of all and had the right to rule over her in any way he saw fit. And if a woman fled from a tyrant's abuse, she would have to do so with merely the clothes on her back. If she took anything else, her husband could set the law on her, for not only did the children belong to her husband but even her very wardrobe.

And for Crystabelle, her family had not even given her the choice of which husband would become sole owner of her person, her dowry, and her worldly possessions.

Wait a minute here. Most men weren't tyrants. The Bible instructed husbands to love their wives as Christ loved the church and gave himself up for her. True, it said she was to be subject to her husband, but only as the church was subject to Christ, her leader and servant, her sacrificial lamb.

Drew laid the book in his lap. These words painted the worst possible picture of a woman's lot in life.

Yet he couldn't deny the truth in them. The law definitely favored men. That was the way of things since, as the book pointed out, men were the makers of laws as well as the voters.

Why was he even wasting his time thinking about this? It was none of his concern. None of it. He doubted if he'd ever be in a settlement long enough to vote on anything. Resting back against the doorjamb, he looked out to the woods, washed clean and fresh. He breathed deeply of the fragrant peace that always came after a rain. The forest never failed to attract him, as did all of God's wondrous creation. Traveling through nature was a simple pleasure that never needed to be chewed over or argued about. It simply was.

Unlike this radical book. He glanced up and caught Crystabelle staring at him.

Quickly she looked away.

As she should. Drew knew for a fact that his brothers loved their wives more than life itself. And were loved the same in return. Neither woman thought she was being misused. In fact, anytime Drew rode into Reardon Valley, he clearly saw the hard work, the sacrifices all the men made for the comfort of their wives and children. And their wives understood and were grateful, helping wherever they could. The couples were of one accord and much too busy trying to build a better future for their children to worry about who was bossing whom.

But what did he really know about Crystabelle's world? Among the wealthy and privileged, life could be very different. At least this author and evidently the young woman at the table with the pumping foot thought so.

Drew expelled a sigh. All this deep thought on the subject when the clouds were starting to break up and patches of sunlight brightened the sky. The rain would stop soon, and one thing he knew for sure—he'd much rather be out looking for a rainbow than have his nose stuck in some musty old book any day of the week.

He sprang to his feet and walked toward Crystabelle.

With a foreboding gaze, she watched him approach with the book and shot a quick glance at Brother Rolf.

The minister, so engrossed in the book she'd loaned him, never even looked up when Drew stopped beside her.

Without a word, he handed her the radical treatise, then gathered up the pile of bridles by the door and strode out into the diminishing mist. The sooner he got these two people delivered to the valley, the sooner he could go off hunting and trading again, and maybe check on Bear and Josie while he was at it. Find out if they made it home safely and if he'd lost his hunting partner to a woman. Contrary to what Crystabelle's book said, men were the ones who got trapped, tied down, when they fell beneath the spell of some female's smile—not the other way around.

He heard the muffled patter of footsteps coming fast across the wet pine needles after him. He didn't look back, but dropped a bridle over the nearest horse's ears and started working the bit into its mouth. He knew it was Crysta.

She came up directly beside him, hampering his efforts. "Mr. Reardon," she said with an edge of anger . . . or was it false bravado? "No sense dragging it out. Do you plan to tattle to Reverend Bremmer about the book or blackmail me with it, just as you're doing about the other matter?"

He didn't say anything until he'd finished buckling the bridle. He turned around just in time to see the sun come out directly overhead. It set her burnished halo of braids alight as if she were a true angel. Albeit a feisty one.

It took a second for him to regather his thoughts. When he did, he stooped down to untie the horse's hobbled front legs, then glanced back up at her with a smile. "Now there you go," he drawled, "callin' me a blackmailer again. It ain't Christian to go about name-callin', you know."

Impatiently, she filled her lungs, straining her bodice laces considerably . . . not that he minded. "Is there ever going to come a time when you'll simply give me a straight answer?"

"Ah, it's a straight answer you want," he said, coming up with the rope. "Interesting as that book was, it's your own private affair—unlike a party of armed men who could come riding down on us any day now, guns a-blazin'. But I do think a book with such enlightening ideas would've served a far better purpose if it had been slanted in a slightly different direction and had another title. What do you think of *A Vindication of the Rights of the African Slave*? I dare you to read your book again, only this time every time you find the word *woman*, replace it with *slave*. After that, we can talk about blackmail or anything else that might pop into that comely head of yours."

12

Crysta couldn't forget the inflammatory book in her pocket even if she wanted to. A corner of it rubbed against her leg with every step Sheba took on the narrow trail—a constant reminder of why she was again unrelentingly irritated with Mr. Reardon.

Just as she refused to give him the satisfaction of seeing her fish the book from her pocket to compare its content against that of slavery, she also refused to so much as glance over her shoulder at him. For someone who practically bragged that he had given little weight to the knowledge and enlightenment contained in books, he certainly had the ability to turn her most treasured volume back on her.

Reverend Bremmer, just ahead of her, descended an eroded bank into a stream no more than a few yards wide, but rocky and white-water swift from last night's runoff.

Crysta watched as his big-footed horse picked its way across, and for once she wished she had a similarly built mount instead of her dainty, highly bred Arabian.

"Your mare'll do just fine." Reardon was now stopped beside her. "She's as sprightly as she looks."

Determined not to give him the satisfaction of seeing her fear, she kneed Sheba into the swirl. And, as Reardon predicted, the sleek bay made her way across without the slightest stumble, leaping up the bank on the other side.

Crysta purposefully refrained from checking to see if Reardon and his pack train made it safely. He'd just have to holler if he needed help.

Reaching the top of the bank, she resettled herself around her sidesaddle for the miles that still lay ahead of them that day. Her hand swept across the book again, and as if she'd already pulled it out and opened it, an entire passage came to mind.

> It is then an affection for the whole human race that makes my pen dart rapidly along to support what I believe to be the cause of virtue: and the same motive leads me earnestly to wish to see woman—

Not *woman,* Crysta remembered, and replaced the word with *slaves.*

> . . . to see *slaves* placed in a station in which they would advance, instead of retarding—

Retarding . . . Josie, retarded.

Despite the laws, Mr. Reardon had taught Black Bear to read. He hadn't hindered his friend's learning, no matter what the law or the conventions of the day dictated. Mr. Reardon was his own man, determining his values, the first truly free man she'd ever met. No one else's opinion swayed him in the least—except, maybe Brother Rolf's when the minister reminded Reardon of some biblical truth.

Catching herself starting to peek back at him, Crysta slapped at a bothersome mosquito instead.

Another sentence from the book spilled forth. "They may be convenient slaves, but slavery will have its constant effect, degrading the master and the abject dependent." With those words, she didn't even have to substitute *slave* for *woman*. Why hadn't she noticed the unmistakable parallel? A slave and her mistress. The more abject the slavery, the more the mistress was degraded too. Both trapped by it. And both subject to the mercy of their common master.

Reardon had been right. Everything she'd wanted for herself, she'd been taught from her earliest remembrance to deprive the servants . . . as if slaves weren't as much a part of the human race as she . . . nor she as much a part as any man. It was all such false vanity . . . such perversion.

She'd read that in the United States Congress some men had argued that without freedom for all, there would never truly be freedom for any. Why had she merely brushed past those vital words?

The answer was clear to anyone who cared to look. Her family needed their slaves for plantation society to survive. Without slaves, their entire way of life, and that of all their friends, would come crashing down like a house of cards. . . . All the genteel parties and balls . . . who would dress them, serve refreshments . . . build the mansions, grow the food—all the while the privileged few kept their hands lily-white? Like the useless royalty the Americans had grown to despise.

Shame washed over her. Her people had become so vain that they regarded the performing of everyday labors as tantamount to a fall from grace.

Cleaning out that filthy cabin last night hadn't degraded her in the least. Fact was, she'd felt a real sense of accomplishment knowing she herself had done it. And just how unsightly could a few calluses on her hands look? God gave her hands to use.

A grin skipped across her lips. She could even dress herself now.

Reardon was right. Only after Josie became free, could she be free herself.

Josie's dimpled smile came to mind, and Crysta hoped the girl didn't find herself locked in fear of the unknown, but truly understood the gift she'd been given. Crysta glanced up to the light peeking through the boughs. "Lord, I pray thee, keep a loving watch over Josie. She deserves to be happy after putting up with me all these years."

Crysta breathed deeply of the fresh pine scent. Out here in the forest with all the expectations of family and society stripped away, the truth was so much easier to see.

Of course, she wasn't about to tell Mr. Reardon, let him know he'd been right all along. If she did, she'd never hear the last of it.

Her mare broke out of the shadows and trotted into a muddy marsh past a stand of canes as tall as the animal's withers.

A cloud of mosquitoes swarmed, and by mutual consent, the horses all broke into a gallop. Within seconds, the horses were all back in the trees again with Crysta madly swatting at the insects that still clung to her.

The next clearing they came to was man-made. A few large stumps dotted a wide piece of bottomland, where row upon row of young corn sprouted in the dark rich clods. At the far end stood a cabin and a couple of outbuildings, a fenced meadow with three cows and a few sheep.

It was a glorious sight. Crysta slapped the reins across Sheba's neck, urging her mare forward. "Reverend Bremmer," she called as she came abreast of the big German. "Is this the western side? Is this Tennessee? Have we arrived?"

"*Ja.* Is Tennessee. But, no, ve are not near our home. Reardon Valley is still eight or nine days to da vest."

"That far?" She pushed down her momentary disappointment—the farther from Virginia they traveled, the better. Then in an instant of panic she looked over her shoulder for her father's men.

The only one behind her was Reardon and the pack animals. And of course, he smiled and nodded in that smug, relaxed way of his. He really was insufferable.

The farther down the narrow river valley they rode, the more homesteads were tucked in anyplace that had a few level acres to be tilled. Nothing like the miles of unbroken farmland in Virginia but welcome sights, nonetheless. Although Mr. Reardon called these homesteads a desecration of his precious wilderness, the butterflies and birds seemed to revel in the sunlight of the cleared patches. They swooped and danced among the green-leafed corn and twining beanstalks.

"Miss Amherst." The reverend had halted his plodding horse. "I t'ink ve see if da family up ahead can feed us."

Crysta looked past an oak to where he pointed to a cabin much the same as the others they'd passed that day.

Reverend Bremmer turned his mount onto the settler's path, and within a couple of minutes they were being raucously announced by a yellow dog and half a dozen squawking chickens.

As they stopped, the dog ran up and started nipping at the horses' legs, while a small towheaded boy stood near the house, bouncing up and down in all the excitement.

A lean sun-browned woman came out the door, rifle in hand. Dressed as plain as any field slave, she wiped her hands on her apron. "How-do," she called, but the greeting seemed cautious. She eyed each of them and the pack animals.

"Goot afternoon," Reverend Bremmer returned above the yip of the dog. "Ve are on our vay from Salem-town 'cross da mountain. *Und* I vas vondering if ve might buy a meal from you. Hard cash."

"Cash money, you say." She took a few steps forward on feet as bare and dirty as her young son's; then she kicked the dog in the ribs. "Shut yer yappin'."

The dog did as ordered, though he continued to watch with alert eyes.

At that moment, the ragged little boy stopped bouncing up and down and ran to his mother.

She shoved him behind her and returned her no-nonsense attention to Reverend Bremmer. "We'll be noonin' in 'bout a half hour. You can water your horses at our well and put 'em in the pen."

"Where's your menfolk?" Reardon had dismounted and now stood beside Crysta's horse.

The woman shaded a hand over her eyes to get a better look at the fringe-shirted hunter. "Oh, they'll be along directly," she said almost as if it was a warning, then started for the cabin. "I'd best get to peelin' some more taters and turnips."

Then, without so much as a by-your-leave, Reardon swept Crysta from her horse.

Refusing to show him how much his presumptive rudeness bothered her, Crysta concentrated on these first folks they'd spoken to since leaving Boone yesterday morning. She saw another, smaller boy standing just inside the door and dressed as shabbily as the others. If all the folks this side of the mountain were this poor, how would they be able to pay for her teaching services?

At the door the woman turned back. "Ma'am, you're welcome to come in outta the sun if you've a mind to."

"Go on," Drew said, pushing Crysta from behind. "Offer to help with the meal."

Now the boor was pushing her. And wanting her to go in and help a total stranger—when she didn't have the foggiest notion what the woman would expect from her.

"Offer to peel potatoes," Drew whispered, giving her another shove.

Crysta walked into suffocating heat that blasted from the cook fire. As her eyes adjusted to the dimmer light inside the cabin, she saw that the floor was dirt, the walls logs, and what looked like bunches of weeds hung down from the rafters. Light streamed in only through the open doorway and a small cutout window. In the cramped hovel—not as big as the cookhouse at home—this entire family ate, slept, and cooked. The only added space was a loft suspended above one-half of the room.

She started to introduce herself, then thought better of it—the less anyone along the trail knew about her, the harder it would be for her father's men to track her. "If you'll loan me a knife, I'd be glad to peel potatoes for you."

"'Tain't necessary," the woman said, stepping to a worktable under the window and plucking a potato from one of the sacks below.

Crysta figured she'd better try again. She didn't want Reardon adding *slacker* to the list of failings he'd already accused her of. "It'd be my pleasure."

"Good 'nough." The woman put the brown-skinned vegetable down beside a knife and moved to the hearth.

Her young boys followed close behind, and the little ones' eyes never left Crysta. It was obvious they weren't used to seeing strangers.

Removing her riding bonnet, Crysta hooked it on a spike beside the window and took her place at the table. The knife felt awkward in her hand, but no more so than the potato. She experimented holding each a variety of ways as she hacked away the thin skin. And no matter which hold she used, she seemed to be peeling away more potato than skin.

The settler wife stirred a blackened cauldron with a long wooden spoon. The wafting aroma of meat juices reminded Crysta that she hadn't had a decent meal in two days. "Where'bouts do you folks hail from?" the woman asked without looking up.

"Virginia, mostly," Crysta answered evasively. "Reverend Bremmer hails from Germany."

"Which way you headed?" She never used extra words.

And neither would Crysta. "West."

"West?"

Crysta wiped the sweat beading her brow with the rough-cloth sleeve of her homespun bodice. "From what I understand, toward some town called Nashville."

"La, that is a fer piece."

"I suppose," Crysta answered politely as she surveyed her first finished potato. It looked more like it'd been shot by a blunderbuss. Quickly, Crysta dipped the mangled mess into a bowl of water sitting on the table, then chopped it into several pieces. She then reached into the potato sack and pulled out another.

The two little boys, leaning against a bench, continued to watch her.

By the time Crysta had dispensed with three more of the tubers, Reverend Bremmer and Reardon came tromping in with two other men, filling up the cabin with their booming voices.

"Aye, corn's comin' up good," one of the young men said. He and what looked like a brother were several inches shorter than Reardon, both lean and wiry. "The rain last night, praise God, come at just the right time. Course we still depend on huntin' and fishin' fer most our meat."

The other man, with the same lank brown hair and crowded front teeth, shifted his attention to Crysta.

Not wanting him to notice her potato mess, she quickly scooped the pieces into her skirt and carried them to the large charred pot in the hearth and dumped them in.

As she turned back, she noticed that the other men had stopped talking, and all of them were watching her.

Had she handled the potatoes wrong?

"Crystabelle," Drew said, breaking the silence, "this here's Logan Ivers." He nodded toward the one who'd been talking.

She wiped her hands on her skirt and bobbed into a quick curtsy. "How do you do?"

"And this here's his brother Ned."

She turned to the one who'd been staring. "It's a pleasure."

As she started to dip into a curtsy, he caught her hand in his rough callused one. "Pleasure's all mine, Miz Reardon," he drawled, his close-set eyes holding hers as he kissed her hand.

Miz Reardon.

"I'm absolutely no relation of Mr. Reardon's," she said, correcting this most unpleasant misconception. "My name is Amherst, *Miss* Amherst." She pulled her hand from the farmer's, realizing she'd just foolishly given her name.

"I'm real pleased to hear that." His sunburned face brightened even more. "And you say you're headed down to Knoxville? I get down thataway now an' then."

"You'll have to go a mite farther than that," the woman of the house said. "Set yourselves down," she ordered as she came to the large raw wood table in the center of the room, the fingers of one hand strung with cups and a coffeepot in the other. "They're on their way to Nashville."

Crysta felt the heat of Drew's disapproving scowl as the other detail she'd given came back to slap her in the face.

"Just west of Knoxville," he corrected. "On the road to Nashville."

What he said didn't seem all that different to Crysta, but it made Ned Ivers happy. He stepped closer to Crysta. "Amherst . . . when I get to Knoxville, do I ask the way to the Amherst farm?"

"No." What a mess she'd made of things. "I'll be in the employ of Reverend Bremmer."

"*Ja,*" the German said pleasantly, unaware of her plight. He'd taken his seat on one of the long benches bordering the table. "Mine Inga vill be keeping da close eye on her. *Very close.*"

"Sit down, y'all," the woman repeated with more force. "I cain't get the food on with y'all millin' about."

Reardon caught Crysta by the hand and pulled her down beside him.

Without protest this time, she did as he bade. Even if they walked out the door at this very second, the folks here wouldn't forget her or her name—she'd certainly seen to that. Feeling Drew's gaze boring into her, she looked up at him and gave him an apologetic shrug.

He returned a faint quirk of a smile, but it didn't come close to reaching his eyes.

She'd placed him and Reverend Bremmer in further danger—bit the hand that was feeding her, so to speak, or worse, bit off her own nose to spite her face . . . and all because she didn't want these complete, never-to-be-seen-again strangers to think she was Reardon's wife.

And, truly, just how awful could that be?

13

Traveling behind Crystabelle Amherst several days beyond Knox-ville, Drew saw her withdraw the musket from the bedroll tied down behind her. Silently, she commenced sprinkling gunpowder in its flashpan.

Drew searched past the trees and up the hollow to a sun-splashed sprawl of berry vines. He saw nothing at first, then caught sight of movement. A black bear sat among the prickly vines, stuffing juicy berries into its long-snouted mouth, oblivious of all else. Grateful the bear was downwind of the horses, Drew patted his mount Smoky's neck and let the gelding continue on none the wiser.

Her weapon at the ready, the lass kept a silent watch until they were well away from the bear.

Drew nudged Smoky into a faster pace until he'd caught up with her. She'd been an apt student and had taken care about unneces-sary talk since her first foolish encounter this side of the mountain. She was due a compliment.

Her musket still rested in her arms as he came abreast, but she seemed exceedingly calm for an Eastern female who'd just seen a bear. Uppity as usual, she eyed Drew.

"Just want to say that I'm proud of the way you've taken hold," he began. "Knowin' when to keep your mouth shut out here on the trail and wherever we've put up at a settler's cabin for the night. You might make a frontier woman yet."

"A frontier *teacher,*" she reminded flatly—her fighting spirit still as fiery as the highlights in her auburn hair.

"Why is it someone as beautiful as you prides herself only in doin' manly things like ridin' and shootin' an' book learnin'?"

She flashed him a raised brow. "I never considered those pursuits solely masculine. Living out in the country on a planta-tion, I had only my brothers for companions, and"— a smile broke out—"I couldn't let Hank or Monty get the best of me now, could I? I could out-horse race, outrun, and outwrestle both of them. Most of the time, anyway. And after Mama banished me to Miss Soulier's Academy, I found more facts in books than the boys did—to stump them."

At the picture of her as a half-pint tomboy, Drew chuckled. "You could outwrestle your brothers, you say? I would've thought all those ruffled petticoats would get in your way."

That pert nose of hers hiked. "Of course, one such as you would think about that. I wore my brothers' breeches every chance I got."

"I see." He couldn't help grinning.

"You find that humorous? I thought an intrepid explorer such as you would be more of a freethinker. That you would understand that to be truly free, one must be allowed to move about unencum-bered by the strictures of female attire."

"Does that mean you plan to teach in men's breeches?" he teased.

"Would that be so shocking?" she huffed, always going for the last word.

"Have you laid this latest bit of news on the reverend yet?"

"No, of course not. I was just letting you know that women teaching is only the beginning in our bid for equality."

Drew nodded in mock agreement. "Seems to me what you need is a flag. One you and all your cohorts like that Mary Wollstonecraft can rally round. Maybe it could show a bonfire where all the women come to burn those freedom-thwarting petticoats and corsets and . . . whatever."

Her gingersnap eyes narrowed. "No, I think our flag should display a big platter, and sitting on it would be the heads of all the men who made sport of us."

No matter how closemouthed she'd become of late, her rebellious nature always rode barely below the surface, just waiting to be scratched. And scratching it never ceased to entertain Drew. He framed his jaw with a hand. "Do you think this would make a good head for your platter?"

Her eyes widened; then she sputtered into laughter. "Aye, the best. I'd put yours right in the middle."

And he liked the sound of her laughter best of all. Only a couple more days to the valley and they'd be parting ways. He was going to miss her more than he ever thought he would miss any woman. But miss her he would, for he would never give up exploring the West, even for someone as fascinating and—face it—downright fetching as Crystabelle Amherst.

Nine days after reaching the Tennessee side of the mountain, Drew reined Smoky to a halt on the crest overlooking Reardon Valley. As he watched the late-afternoon shadows slant across the long valley, he never ceased to be surprised by the latest changes. With his every return, he saw that more fields had been cleared until now what had all been woodland down in the flat was more planted patches than trees. More cabins had been raised, more civilization spreading its tentacles. At the rate folks were coming over the mountain, every cove and vale of the great Tennessee River Basin would soon be overrun, all the way to the Mississippi, where, thank God, the mighty river would put a stop to them. It had to.

His attention was again caught by the woman who rode ahead of him. Her emerald-green riding bonnet perched atop her head with such regal flare. He let his gaze slide down to the simple homespun dress. Whatever she wore, she'd been a feast for the eyes all these long summer days . . . and their little differences of opinion entertaining enough to vanquish the tedium of the miles.

All the more reason he should be glad to reach their destination. Best he drop off Rolf and Crystabelle and not look back. Women brought with them this insidious creeping civilization, forever clipping, training, taming. The territory to the west was the only freedom remaining, real freedom, unlike that which Crystabelle and her fellow females imagined.

Interrupting his musings, Crystabelle looked at him and smiled. "So after crossing a thousand hills, a thousand streams, this is your valley. Hidden away in the forest like a green gem. It truly is lovely. The spread of it reminds me of our plantation back home."

"*Ja,*" Brother Rolf agreed at her other side. "Da promise land. A place of hope. Tomorrow is da Sabbath. You come *mit* us to church, and ve gif t'anks."

"Yes," she murmured wistfully, "a place for new beginnings." The girl sounded as if she couldn't wait to put her own mark on the valley.

And she undoubtedly would, too, Drew surmised with mixed feelings. The lass had come a long way from being the pampered belle to the quiet, self-reliant, young woman she was turning into. She could now start a fire with a piece of flint, saddle and load the animals, even make a fair cup of coffee. And Rolf had shown her how to make hoecakes. A good start toward her independence.

"Aye," Drew agreed. "I think you'll be able to make a new beginning for yourself here. And we've put a lot of miles between us and what we left behind in Salem," he added with special meaning for her understanding only. "Traveled many a different trail."

She didn't reply, just looked at him with those incredible autumn eyes.

Brother Rolf's horse began to whinny and strain against its reins. Rumbling into laughter, the minister gave him his head, and the big black horse trotted down the slope with vigor, then broke into a gallop. The animal knew he was almost home.

Even the hired animals sensed the excitement, and the entire train began to gallop pell-mell after them down to the flat.

By the time they cut through the last thicket to reach the bottom, Crystabelle was hanging on to her bonnet and laughing right along with Brother Rolf and Drew . . . a merry, airy laugh that went so well with her name. Drew was going to miss that most of all.

Crysta's enthusiasm continued to build as the trail widened to a wagon road that cut through open farmland, planted on one side with squash and on the other with rows of staked beans. The plants all looked strong and healthy—a wonderful, rich plantation. But no slaves labored in the fields here. Crysta saw two white men only, one easily in his fifties or sixties with a scraggly gray beard and a younger man, most likely his grown son.

The farmworkers spotted Crysta's group, and one yelled, "Hold up there," as both hopped across the plowed rows to intercept them.

Reverend Bremmer raised a hand for the pack train to stop, then greeted the two rawboned men. "Goot to see you, Steven, Dillard. Is ever't'ing going vell vile I am avay?"

"Aye." The older, grizzled man propped a foot on his hoe blade and leaned on the handle. "Been watchin' for ya fer the last coupla days now." He eyed Crysta with a deeply etched scowl. "Seems you didn't have no success fetchin' back a teacher."

Reverend Bremmer's saddle groaned as he shifted uneasily. "It seems dat most folks vat take up da teaching vant to stay in da Eastern cities vere da books is. Professor Hazlett, he marry up *mit* a rich miss *und* decide not to come. He send dis here teacher in his place."

"Who?" the younger bony-faced farmer asked. "You don't mean Drew Reardon?"

"*Nein.* Da voman. She comes *mit* a crate of books."

The men swung their deep-set eyes on Crysta. She could hardly contain herself from squirming in her seat.

"The *woman!*" they chorused in roared disbelief.

"She's fully qualified, men." Drew Reardon came to her defense with a forthrightness that surprised her. He reined his rough-coated gray between her and the two farmers. "Miss Amherst is well versed in every subject."

The younger of the two spat on the ground in what Crysta hoped was not his opinion of her ability, then stepped to the front of the horses and grabbed her mare's bridle. He looked squarely into Crysta's eyes.

She made every effort not to so much as blink as she stared back.

Abruptly the man released her horse and swung back to Reardon. "And how would a backwoodsman like you know enough about book learnin' to judge? All you been lookin' at is a purty face."

Crysta didn't appreciate her ability being questioned. "I assure you—"

Reverend Bremmer warded off any further words with his upraised hand. "Ve meet after services tomorrow. Talk about it den. Decide if ve vant to try her out."

"It'd just be a waste o' time," the older man said, looking up through wiry brows. "She's about as threatenin' as a butterfly. I agreed to pay hard cash for a man who could whip my grandsons into shape, not turn 'em into moon-eyed simpletons unfit fer learnin' or anything else. An' I'm sure the rest o' the men will feel the same."

The minister jerked a nod. "Steven, Dillard, tomorrow. I vant to get home to mine Inga. Ve talk it out tomorrow." Kneeing his mount into a walk, he gestured with his head for Crysta and Reardon to follow and started on down the path, his back rigid.

Their first encounter with men in the valley had not gone well. Not well at all. She was pretty sure she'd won over the pastor, but he didn't have the authority over his flock she'd expected him to have. She had imagined if she could just get to this valley, she'd be safely hidden from her father's men, be able to do her teaching unhindered, and live within the protection of the Bremmer household. How very naive she was. If the other men reacted as these farmers did, there would be no place for her here in this lovely valley.

Where could she go from here?

A band of fear began to tighten around Crysta's chest as they rode south into the heart of the valley.

Others along the way heard them approach and stopped their labors or ran out of cabins to investigate. But the minister never slowed the pace again. He merely waved in answer to their shouted greetings and yelled, "See you at church tomorrow."

Tomorrow. Her fate in the valley would be decided tomorrow. May the Lord have mercy on her.

14

The wide trail pretty much bisected the length of the valley, and from what Crysta could tell, the river ran along the western edge. She caught only an occasional glimpse of the water, which was thickly lined with willows and sycamores. Shortly before the sun dropped behind the western hills, she and the others rode into what appeared to be the center of the community. A small store, a blacksmith shop, and a church faced an open parade ground that spread out in front of a stockade—a grim reminder of the possibility of Indian attack, though Crysta hadn't seen a single one during her fortnight on the trail.

The tribes had all moved farther west, Drew Reardon had told her. They weren't anymore interested in living alongside the white man than the white man was with them. Drew always spoke about the Indians as if they were equals, just as he had urged her to think of the African slaves. Everyone free and equal.

Reverend Bremmer reined in at a log house next to the smithy, and Crysta remembered he wasn't merely the pastor but also the valley's blacksmith.

A woman burst out the door. Sturdy, Germanic, like the minister, she wore her graying flaxen hair in a coronet of braids. "Rolf! You are home. T'ank da goot Lord." On her faded gingham apron she wiped flour dust from her hands, then held them out to her man.

"Inga." Smiling wider than Crysta had seen before, the beefy man dismounted and pulled his wife into a big bear hug.

Uncomfortable watching their display of affection, Crysta looked about her. She caught a surprising flash of color above the covered porch. Flower boxes just below three glass-paned windows held bright pink flowers. Petunias. They dressed up the front, making the rustic dwelling seem permanent, homey.

Drew had dismounted. His hat kicked back, he walked over to Crysta and raised his arms for her to slide down into. "We're here." His voice was quiet, almost as if he were sad they'd arrived . . . as if he weren't happy he was now free to go his own way again. Off to his beloved exploring.

Crysta unhooked her knee from the saddle horn and slipped down into his arms, realizing how strange it would seem not having him around to argue with anymore.

His silver gray eyes locked with hers as he lowered her to the ground. He continued to hold her longer than necessary.

Crysta's breath ceased. Still, she couldn't bring herself to look away.

Then, in an abrupt change, he chuckled and let go. "You got a fight on your hands tomorrow."

Tomorrow.

"I'll get them to accept me. I have to."

He caught a loose strand of her hair with his thumb and tucked it behind her ear. Then, expelling a breath, he swung away and untied the packhorses from his saddle's ring and remounted.

Crysta caught his horse's bridle. "You're leaving the valley? This minute?"

"No, I'm just gonna mosey on down to my family's place. I'll stay till after tomorrow." He reached down and gave her bonnet tie a tug. "I wouldn't miss the meetin' after church for nothin'. Most excitement this staid ol' valley's had for some time." With one last look, he removed her hand from his horse's bridle and rode down the road.

Watching him go, Crysta felt as if her protection were being stripped away—protection she'd taken for granted. She felt suddenly and incredibly vulnerable.

"Crystabelle. Come here," Reverend Bremmer called. "I vant you to meet mine Inga."

Crysta tore her gaze from the disappearing hunter and plastered on a smile.

In the last glow of a balmy day, Drew rode onto the Reardon place. He knew he should take more pride at the sight of the one hundred and fifty acres planted in either pasture or crops. The years of diligent labor had paid off. The two adjoining farmsteads, along with his older brothers' gristmill, were prospering.

Yet Drew remembered almost grimly the backbreaking chore of helping to clear the first fifty of those acres . . . before he'd managed to run off with Ethan Yarnell—God rest the long hunter's soul. Farming would never be Drew's dream. It was Ike's and Noah's.

Candlelight shone brightly from all three cabins—two of which seemed to grow in size with each new baby. Ike and Annie now had four children, and Noah and Jessica had three, with another on the way . . . and each new babe rooted Drew's brothers ever deeper to this one spot. Of course, the cabin he shared with his mother had remained as small and simple as when it was first raised—much to his mother's dismay. The woman was bent on seeing all three of her sons married and settled round about her. But then, she was a typical woman.

Whenever Drew had questioned his brothers about being such

sticks-in-the-mud, they'd both said the years they'd spent fighting the Revolution had been more than enough adventure for their lifetimes, and then some. How anyone could have enough adventure, Drew would never know, but a godly home, hearth, and family were all either of them wanted now.

Annie's shaggy old dog shot out of her and Ike's open doorway, barking his announcement of Drew's arrival. With Cap around, no one ever sneaked up on the place.

"It's just me, ol' boy," Drew called to the dog, whose long-haired tail wagged with every bark. "Settle down."

But it was not to be. Family poured out of the two larger cabins, laughing and shouting and talking all at once.

Ike's eight-year-old, Jacob, reached Drew first. The skinny kid who seemed to grow a foot between each of Drew's visits grabbed Smoky's reins. "Did'ya bring me anything? I'll put up your horse for ya. Did'ya run into any land pirates or Injuns?"

"Give him a chance to climb down first," the boy's father reprimanded. Ike was sounding more like their own late father all the time. Like Noah and Drew, he favored their Norse mother, but the easy authority with which Ike spoke was all Pa.

Before both of Drew's moccasined feet hit the ground, he had three cuddly little girls and a three-year-old boy hanging off him— all clamoring to know what he'd brought back from Salem-town, as he'd promised.

"Did you bring me a doll with a satin dress?"

"A top!" shouted three-year-old Spencer above the rest. "A shiny red top!"

Not until the playthings were disbursed did the children settle down on the cropped grass to entertain themselves. Below a candlelit windowsill they all happily admired their new toys. Children were so much easier to please than adults.

Chairs were toted outside for the adults so they might enjoy the cool soft breeze and firefly show while Drew caught them up on the latest from the East.

Dark-haired Jessica, Noah's petite but noticeably pregnant wife, brought a plate of food out for Drew as the chairs were circled around. "We've already partaken," she said in that modulated diction that sounded even more aristocratic than Crystabelle Amherst's. "I do pray these remains will suffice."

The big crockery plate was heaped with steaming vegetables from the garden, pork and poultry, and three fluffy biscuits dripping in butter. Drew's stomach growled with anticipation at the aroma. "More than enough, Jessie girl." He perched on the nearest ladder-back chair and picked up his fork as the others began to settle around him. "God bless this food," he murmured, "our home, and all who dwell within." His *amen* was scarcely said before he had a piece of succulent chicken in his mouth.

His mother, seated directly across from him, scooted her chair closer. "Drew," she said in a tone that always set his teeth on edge—she would be expecting something from him. "Drew, you were back only two days when you insisted on taking off again with Brother Rolf. We had to cancel your homecoming dinner and everything."

The woman wasn't even going to let his mouth settle comfortably around the first bite.

"Aye," his brother Noah said with a sly grin. "You ruined all Ma's matchmaking schemes. Again."

His mother's rather long features looked even sterner in the candlelight as she turned to Noah, who sat between her and his wife. "Introducing your younger brother to some of our local maidens is not scheming." She turned her attention back to Drew. "I want your promise that you'll stay long enough for the newcomers in the valley to get to know the third Reardon brother, at least by sight."

"Where's Black Bear?" Ike, standing behind his wife's chair, asked. "Don't usually see one of you without the other."

Swallowing the bite of poultry, Drew was grateful to his oldest brother for changing the subject. "Bear took off a coupl'a days into the return trip. Took a fancy to the schoolteacher's servant girl and ran off with her."

"He did what?" Drew's mother came to her feet. She looked to the east. "Are you sayin' Black Bear stole off with a female slave? Surely you got her back . . . or there'll be the devil to pay."

Drew waved her down again with his fork. "It's all right, Ma. I convinced the schoolteacher to let the girl go in peace. Ain't no one out lookin' for 'em."

"By George," Noah inserted, "this teacher must be a very magnanimous fellow."

"You mean generous?" Drew teased. His brother did love to use big words. "Aye, she's learnin' to be generous—slowly but surely."

"*She?*" Ma plummeted into her seat, her pale blue eyes wide. "Did I hear right? The teacher's a *woman?*"

Drew eased back in his chair and took a bite of buttered squash. He would have fun with this tidbit. "You heard right. And it's been a pure surprise to everyone we tell."

Ike didn't seem amused. He strode from behind Annie's chair and stopped in front of Drew, the planes of his face reflecting his displeasure. "We sent you men all the way to Salem to fetch back a Professor Hazlett from Virginy as we bargained for. And you brought back a *woman?*"

"Seems this Hazlett fellow up an' married hisself some rich young heiress. Miss Amherst came from Richmond in his stead."

"To teach the valley's boys?" Noah leaned around Ike. "That's ridiculous!"

Annie, sitting to Drew's right, came to her feet. "And what's ridiculous about a woman teaching?" she demanded of Noah.

"Your Jessica has taught you a thing or two, whether you'd care to admit it or not."

Noah glanced at his fragile-looking wife beside him. "Yes, but that was in the privacy of our home. A sharing between a husband and his wife."

Now Jessica's back stiffened—Noah was in for it. "You don't believe I could impart the philosophical tales of Voltaire or the patriotic writings of Thomas Paine to anyone other than you?"

Noah reached over and caught one of her small hands. "I didn't say that, dear."

"Nor should you ever," the much taller Annie concurred, her green-and-gold eyes flashing. If there was ever an independent-minded woman, it was Ike's wife. She had her own dairy and a honeybee business on the side.

But Ike was by no means henpecked by his wife. "That's all well and good, Annie, but I paid hard cash for a *man*. Someone who will keep my son in line, along with the rest of the boys in the valley."

"I don't think you have cause for alarm where Jacob is concerned," Noah assured Ike, then smiled. "But Brother Rolf's youngest is more than a handful. At fourteen, Otto's big as a bull and twice as willful. And those Dagget twins are always getting themselves into trouble."

Chuckling, Ike sat down in Annie's chair, pulling her down on his lap. "Drew, you should'a heard it. Last Sunday while services were goin' on, the Dagget twins tied the tails of two cats together and tossed 'em under the church house. I never heard such caterwaulin'."

Annie swung a mutinous expression on her husband. "And who dragged those two young'uns home by their ears? Their ma. She took care of them boys good and proper."

"Now, sweetheart." Ike was having a hard time holding his own. He pulled Annie close again. "We're all gettin' ourselves worked up over nothin'. Eleven families put up money to bring a teacher here. I'm sure when they learn Brother Rolf brought back a woman, they'll all have somethin' to say about it."

"Aye," Drew said. "Brother Rolf is callin' for a meetin' after church tomorrow."

"I would think so," Ma said in a huff. "I can't imagine what he was thinkin', bringin' back a woman in the first place."

"It ain't like schoolteachers is growin' on trees, Ma," Drew argued in Brother Rolf's defense. "Besides, Miss Amherst is a real persuasive lady." He took another bite of a meal that was rapidly growing cold.

"Is that true, Son?"

Drew glanced up and saw the dreaded gleam in his mother's eye.

"What manner of young woman is she?" The matchmaking tone was back. "Does she present herself well?"

Drew couldn't believe that, with the many questions his mother could've asked about Crystabelle Amherst's ability, she was back to the subject Drew most adamantly wanted to avoid. "Miss Amherst presented herself along with a full crate of books. Now, if you want to know more about her, you can ask her yourself at church tomorrow. My supper's gettin' cold." That said, he stuffed half a biscuit into his mouth.

Once Inga Bremmer got over the shock that her husband had returned with a woman instead of a man, the sturdy woman had been most gracious. She'd seen to it that Crysta was well fed, then brought out a big tub for what she called a Saturday night soaking before offering Crysta what had been her daughters' room before the two girls had wed and left the family home. The big feather bed had been pure heaven with its fresh-smelling linens and crisply starched pillowcases—a luxury Crysta hadn't had since she'd left the academy.

It had all been so inviting that Crysta slept the night through, despite the "inquisition" that awaited. She didn't stir until the birds awakened her on a gloriously sunny morning.

Crysta threw back the covers and rose from her bed in the unpainted but cheerful log-walled room. Ruffled calico fluttered at the upstairs window, and a patchwork of flowers and trees adorned the bed. Simple but cheerful, like the mistress of the house.

In her batiste nightdress, Crysta padded on bare feet across a rag rug to the open window and looked out on the valley she hoped would be her new home. The dew-kissed leaves of the trees sparkled along with the petals of the flowers in Mistress Bremmer's window boxes. Just beyond lay the parade ground surrounded by structures. But it was the simple church that interested her most. With a spire that was no more than framework, it held an unimpressive bell—the same bell she would ring mornings to call her children to class if she were given half a chance.

She took in a deep breath. "Lord, please let this be the place you have for me. Please let me make my future here. I'll do my best to be worthy of this opportunity."

Hearing the loud clomp of feet racing up the stairs, she scarcely had time to whirl around before someone banged through her door without so much as knocking.

Towering over her was a lad who stood a good six feet tall with hair white as a cotton boll, a stark contrast to a husky berry-brown face. "Thought I heard you get up," he said with an unabashed smile.

Crysta snatched the counterpane from the bed to cover her nightgown.

His face reddened, a little anyway. "Sorry, ma'am," he said backing toward the door. "I plumb forgot to knock first, but I just couldn't wait to see what a female teacher would look like. I'm Otto. The only son left to home. Papa brung you here for me."

"And," she added with authority, "for the rest of the children of the valley."

"I ain't no child."

"No, you certainly aren't. So, if you would be so kind, would you go down and ask your mother if she'd mind coming up to assist me for a moment?" Crysta wanted to be dressed in her finest on this very important day.

"Whatever you want done, I can do."

He certainly was eager to please her—a good sign. But of course, his offer was totally unacceptable. "I thank you for your eagerness to be of service, but I'm afraid this is a matter concerning women only."

"Oh, I see," he said, though his bright blue eyes seemed confused. "I'll go fetch her right away." He swung toward the door but turned back and grinned. "I sure am gonna like goin' to school. You sure are the purtiest teacher I ever did see."

And, she'd wager, the only teacher he'd ever seen. "We didn't meet when I arrived yester's eve. I take it you were away from home."

"*Ja.* I was over to the Dagget place. Wait till the twins get a look at you." With that, he ran out and down the stairs as fast as he'd arrived, yelling at the top of his lungs, "Mama, Mama, the purty lady wants you!"

Crysta relaxed a bit as she walked to her largest clothing trunk and opened it. Retrieving her corset and petticoats, she knew if the other folks were even a tenth as pleased with her as Otto Bremmer was, she'd have no problem securing her position.

By the time Crysta had her choice of day gown laid out on the bed, Mistress Bremmer was at her door, wearing a serviceable black gabardine that laced conveniently in the front with a generous shawl collar overlaying it. Even dressed in her Sunday best, the woman looked as self-sufficient as the other folks Crysta had seen along the trail. "Mine son says you need somet'ing?"

"Yes." Crysta pointed to her own gown of pink flowers woven across yellow stripes and trimmed with ruffles and lace. "I'm afraid it and my corset require another person to lace and button them from behind."

"*Ja.* I can see dat. But if you are planning to be independent voman, ve vill need to fix dat. Turn around," she said in her no-nonsense German accent. She picked up the corset with its many ties.

Lifting her long hair, Crysta did as she was told but turned back. "Do you really think we could? Alter the gowns so I could put them on by myself?"

"*Ja.* Sure t'ing. *Mit* all dese clothes you got, ve find all da extra material ve need. I never see a lass *mit* so many clothes. You must be very rich."

Crysta swung around and gave the dear woman a hug. "With you as a friend, I shall be rich indeed."

Inga Bremmer seemed embarrassed. She quickly turned Crysta away again. "*Ja, ja,* dere is not'ing to it. Now, let us get you dressed. Ve haf big day ahead of us if ve are going to confince dem men you are da teacher for da boys."

"*And* girls," Crysta couldn't resist adding. "And girls."

15

Grudgingly, Drew sat atop the big wagon, where his mother had coerced him into being, and she rode alongside him, dressed in her primly elegant pearl gray silk summer gown. He'd wanted to ride Smoky to the Sunday service, which would give him the freedom to leave whenever he chose, but here he perched in moss-colored breeches and a frock coat she'd sewn for him, with the fancy brass buttons that had once adorned his father's coat—not to mention the matching buckles on the shoes his mother had the local cobbler make for him. The woman had even seen to it that he had one of those round-crowned, wide-brimmed plantation hats that he was sure she thought made him seem more gentlemanly and prosperous. The hat, a light buff felt, matched his stockings and ruffled cravat. He'd never in his life felt so much like some stupid strutting turkey about to end up in the cook pot.

And of course, Ma had him driving his inheritance from his father—the freight wagon with two giant Clydesdales. The woman might as well put a sign on his back that read Bachelor Son for Sale.

The rest of the Reardon clan rode in the back on hay-cushioned blankets. In record time, every last one of them had dressed in his or her Sunday best. They all knew today was destined to be exciting, considering the debate that was bound to take place over the advisability of hiring a female teacher, and they wanted to be there for every heady minute. The Reardon women had been cooking and baking since before dawn, making sure they'd have plenty of tasty food to share for the noon meal. And no doubt, every other woman in the valley had done the same. No one had to announce there'd be an impromptu dinner at the church today.

As they neared the settlement, Drew was not surprised to see most of the wagons and horses of the valley already parked beside the church house while folks milled about on the central parade ground. A few men were setting up barrel-and-board tables on the grassy spread, but most of the adults clustered in groups, talking, while their children ran and played.

Drew scanned the entire crowd and didn't find Rolf or Inga Bremmer . . . or Crystabelle Amherst. Only Otto helping to set up tables.

Noah's five-year-old, Hope—a miniature of her mother, with dark silky hair and almost colorless eyes—grabbed Drew's neck from behind and flung herself around until their noses almost touched. "Hurry up! Hurry up, Uncle Drew!" she cried. "Over there's Lorry. He loves me."

"I will," he assured her, "if you don't strangle me first."

"Sorry." She unwrapped her calico-checked self from around him. "There's a good spot to park."

"Thank you," Drew said, though he'd already guided the Clydesdales in the direction she pointed, between a cart and a hay wagon. Before he had the giant geldings pulled to a halt, every one of the children had clambered off the back and were running, screaming, for the other youngsters.

"Andrew, dear," his mother said as he wrapped the two sets of reins around the brake stick, "would you please help me down, then fetch the pot of ham and potatoes I baked this morning. Then I'd like you to introduce me to . . . Miss Amherst? Isn't that what you called her?"

"Yes, Ma. But she and the Bremmers haven't come out yet."

"Perhaps they're already in the church. Brother Rolf always spends some quiet time there before services. Hurry up, and go check. Then I want you to meet the storekeeper's daughter, Mary Ann Bailey. Lovely girl, and her father's willin' to give the young man who weds her enough cottonseed for one hundred acres. Mr. Bailey says that with the invention of the cotton gin, it's the cash crop of the future."

Drew could easily see why Brother Rolf would need to get away from his house for some quiet time. And for the life of him, Drew couldn't figure out why Crystabelle thought women were ruled over by men. From six to sixty, females had been telling him what to do this livelong morning. And now his mother wanted to introduce him to a young miss who would come with a hundred acres worth of seed. Seed that would need to be planted and hoed and picked and seeded and bundled and floated downriver to New Orleans, then shipped to some Eastern textile mill, all so the overworked farmer might see a pitifully small profit.

Cringing at the thought, Drew hopped off the high wagon and strode around to the other side to help his mother down.

Following her orders, Drew delivered the ham and potatoes to an already overburdened table that was set up under a sprawling oak. Then his brother Ike called him to where several men stood in front of the church, saving Drew from the remainder of his mother's plans. Gratefully, he joined them.

"I'd like to introduce you to Mike Hatfield," Ike said, indicating a short stocky man beside him. "He and his brother moved here this summer and are running the new saddlery between the store and the church." He nodded toward the west side of the square.

"Aye," the heavy-jowled man said after a hearty handshake. "Me'n my brother, Jonathon, was plannin' on headin' up north of the Ohio, but it don't seem the trouble with the Indians is ever gonna be settled."

That news disturbed Drew. "Has there been a new uprising I don't know about? Since the battle at Fallen Timbers last summer?" The fighting hadn't affected Black Bear's adopted tribe, but braves from several of the northern Shawnee towns had been involved, egged on by the British at Fort Miami.

"Nay," the saddler said, "but until a treaty is signed, we were advised not to venture between the Ohio and Lake Erie. I was wonderin', did you hear anything about the treaty while you were in North Carolina? Anything about the northwest opening up?"

"No, not yet." And Drew didn't want to hear anything either. It would mean more land to be gobbled up by settlers, more taming of his beloved wilds. He excused himself from any further discussion on the distasteful subject. "Ma wants me to go check on the Bremmers, so if you'll pardon me. . . ." He tapped the stiff brim of his hat and gave a parting nod.

"Speaking of the Bremmers," Auburn, one of the first settlers to come to Reardon Valley, interjected, "what got into Brother Rolf that he'd bring back a woman to teach our boys?" The slight-built man stared steadily at Drew as did the other three waiting men.

Drew couldn't escape without answering. "We didn't learn that Professor Hazlett wasn't comin' back with us until the day before we were to return. And surely you know qualified teachers willin' to trek out to some raw backwoods settlement for the pittance you can pay are few and far between."

"We're adding a bonus of twenty acres along the river to the first year's stipend," Ike said. "A quarter mile north of the gristmill. It's a nice piece. Almost level."

Drew wondered if the offer of the land would still stand if they accepted Crystabelle. He doubted it. They'd probably act like they

were doing her a big favor, just letting her teach. "I'm sure Miss
Amherst will be pleased to hear that."

Hatfield snorted. "She'll have to be as strong and steady as a
plow horse to get my vote."

"Well, at least you're willin' to think about havin' her," Drew
said. "Ike and Noah ain't so willin'."

"Is that right?" Hatfield asked Ike.

Ike shifted his weight from one foot to the other and looked from
Drew to the stocky saddler. "I reckon I can reserve judgment until
the meetin', if other folks can. Me an' Noah don't wanna be hard-
headed about it. Our wives sure ain't."

Hatfield snorted again, only in laughter this time. "Neither is
mine. She says she'll donate one of my new bullwhips if the lass
thinks she'll need it to keep order."

At the mental picture of Crystabelle standing on a chair and
snapping a whip above the ornery boys' heads, Drew couldn't stop
the grin.

Auburn pulled a watch from his pocket. "Time for church
service. I better go ring the bell."

As the thin man sauntered off to do his Sunday chore, Drew
glanced back at the porch-fronted, two-story Bremmer house.
Crystabelle had yet to emerge.

Within seconds, the bell suspended from the rough-wood frame
above the church door began to clang. The voices of the congregation grew louder, trying to outtalk the gongs, as they began to
converge on the large log building.

Still no Crystabelle.

Then Drew realized that when it came right down to it, she
must be frightened to expose herself to all the curious gawkers.
Especially since his mother had been right about Brother Rolf
always going to the church ahead of them. The minister now stood
in his black suit at the sanctuary entrance, greeting folks as they
streamed in.

Drew broke away from the others and strode toward the Bremmers' front door. Though he wasn't all that anxious to have Crystabelle see him in this city finery, he was pretty sure she'd be too nervous to notice.

After his knock, the plain iron-hinged door swung open, still held by Inga Bremmer.

She glanced behind her. "Now, dear," she called, "vill you come? It is Drew Reardon, here to take us over dere."

He'd been dead right. Dressed in her plantation-belle finest, Crystabelle lurked in the shadows, her usually creamy complexion white as a ghost's beneath a flower-bedecked straw bonnet. Seeing him, she stiffened, and that proudly stubborn, gorgeous chin hiked. "Good morning, Mr. Reardon. So nice of you to accompany us to church. For a moment, I thought we wouldn't have a proper escort." Though her words had a tremulous note to them and her first steps seemed awkward as she moved toward him in flounced and belled skirts, by the time she reached him and took his arm, he could hardly feel any trembling in her fingers at all.

"You look quite lovely this fine morn." Gazing into her golden brown eyes, he spoke the usual pleasantries as any gentleman might, then pressed his own hand over hers and guided her down the steps and toward the church . . .

. . . where everyone was staring at them. Even those who'd already entered were crowded at the entrance to get a look.

An unaccountable pride swelled within Drew, because he knew without a doubt he had the most beautiful woman this side of the mountains on his arm. "Don't be afraid," he whispered. "Smile. No one can resist your smile."

Squeezing his arm, she stepped forth with more confidence. "Not even you, Mr. Reardon?" The lass was actually flirting with him.

Yessir, the girl did have spunk. "Not that I'd ever admit it," he countered. It was best to always keep that part straight.

134

Brother Rolf banged a wooden mallet on the pulpit. "Order! Order! All you men take your seats. Everyone vill get a chance to speak."

Drew sat sideways at the outer edge of one of the two Reardon pews. Since he'd promised Crystabelle that he would do what he could on her behalf, he wanted a clear view of the entire proceeding, to know who said what.

And it was obvious a lot would be said. During the church service, there'd been more whispering back and forth than psalm singing or listening to Brother Rolf's sermon on the great day of Pentecost.

Now, as the men of the valley settled down for the meeting, Brother Rolf spoke with less booming force. "Now dat you all haf gotten a goot look at da voman in question, you haf seen dat she is young *und* healt'y *mit* plenty of vigor. Ain't dat right, Drew?"

Surprised that Brother Rolf was drawing him into the fray so quickly, Drew swung forward in his seat. "Aye. She handled herself and her horse real fine comin' over the mountain. We didn't have to slow up once for her."

"And I'm sure you didn't mind havin' a purty face to look at the whole way either, did you?" Shaggy-bearded Steven Underwood, the older of the first men they'd encountered yesterday, yelled out.

Ignoring the snickering of the others, Drew eyed Underwood across the room. "Are you saying we should condemn Miss Amherst on the grounds that God blessed her with a pleasing face?"

The man's mouth worked a minute before anything else came out. "All I'm sayin' is, it ain't fittin' for her to be teachin' half-growed boys."

As everyone started talking at once, Noah, seated closer to the center, scooted down the bench toward Drew. "The man has a point. You forgot to mention how pretty she is."

Brother Rolf banged his mallet again. "Men, I am not finished *mit* da talking yet. During da trip, I am studying da girl real goot. I ask her plenty questions about her knowledge of da Bible *und* da Baptists. *Und* she shows me da books she brings to da valley. Books on numbers *und* history. Maps *und* books about medicine *und* building bridges *und* animal husbandry. Such da variety of books I never see dis side of da mountain. *Und* she can talk about vat it say in all of dem. I say God is blessing us by bringing to us someone *mit* such a gift of knowledge. Ve vould be fools to send her *und* her books avay."

Big but gentle Ken Smith, one of the earliest settlers, stood up. "If we wanted a woman who reads a lot, we could'a hired Noah's wife, Jessica, to be our boys' teacher. Her an' Noah has quite a library of their own."

Noah quickly came to his feet. "That is not an option. My wife has more than she can handle taking care of our place and our children."

"And that brings up another point . . ." One of the newer settlers Drew didn't recognize stood up. He rubbed his sunburned nose with a freckled hand. "As purty as the teacher is, she'll be marryin' up with someone in no time; then we'll be without a teacher again."

With the exception of Brother Rolf's, there didn't seem to be a single argument in Crystabelle's favor. Drew stood up. "Kind sir, I'm afraid I don't know your name—"

"Wallace," the rusty-haired man said. "Davy Wallace."

"Well, Mr. Wallace, I can assure you Miss Amherst has no wish to marry. She turned down a very lucrative offer to come here— which I think speaks in her favor. As attractive as she is, I'm sure she had many offers for her hand, but she feels it is her calling to teach."

Ike, on the center aisle, turned a knowing grin on Drew. "She doesn't want to marry, you say. No wonder you find her so appealing."

The mallet was slammed down again. "Gentlemen, I vant to

propose a compromise. I vill again write to da towns of da East, inquiring after a teacher. In da meantime, I say ve give Miss Amherst da opportunity to prove herself."

Jessup, who'd settled south of the Reardon's, came to his feet. He had three boys of school age. "That still doesn't solve our problem. My boys won't be doin' nothin' but moonin' after that woman when they ain't fightin' over her. I ain't gonna sacrifice their labor in my fields for that kinda nonsense—and pay for the privilege, to boot."

If anyone was getting the boot, it was Crystabelle, Drew thought angrily. These men weren't even going to give her a chance. "If all you're worried about is gettin' your money's worth, I'll run roughshod over the boys. Till harvesttime, I'll sit in the schoolroom every day."

Both Noah and Ike swung around to stare at Drew in amazement. And rightly so.

What in the world had he just promised to do?

16

Although Crysta had hoped to make a good impression by looking her best, she was beginning to think that had been a mistake. Seated at one of the shaded outdoor eating tables with Mistress Bremmer, Crysta noticed several women fussing self-consciously with their unadorned bonnets and smoothing their simple day gowns. And worse, while she anxiously awaited her fate, the women stayed a cool distance away, though they repeatedly glanced at her as they spoke in low voices to one another.

Mistress Bremmer reached across the single-board table and patted her hand. "Da vomen, don't t'ink bad of dem. Dey is goot mamas *und* vifes. Dey chust don't know vat to say to a fine educated lady."

Though Crysta vowed she wouldn't, she glanced back at the door of the simple log church, inside of which were all the men. They would be even less receptive, since she was trying to usurp a male position.

"Goot. Here come da Reardon vomen. If dey take to you, it vill make it easier for da odders."

Three women, two quite tall and one much smaller, came strolling over from the serving table carrying extra cups containing some kind of drink. The younger women wore welcoming smiles.

"Howdy," greeted the tall golden-haired one in a simple green-and-white-checked day gown. "I'm Annie, Drew's sister-in-law, and this is his mother, Louvenia Reardon." She spread a hand toward a rather severe-looking matron in gray silk with a crisp white collar. The older woman was even taller than the blonde and Crysta herself. "And this is Noah's wife, Jessica."

Tiny and fragile-looking, with a noticeably round belly, she was dark-haired and had almost colorless eyes that gave her an other-worldly appearance. She seemed quite out of place, standing between the other two. Placing a cup on the table before Crysta, Jessica extended a hand and a charming smile. "I'm most pleased to meet another woman interested in books. We must get together and discuss our favorites."

Surprised and grateful, Crysta clung to the small hand. "Yes, I'd like that very much."

The tiny expectant mother became animated as she sat down on the bench beside Crysta. "Just last month I received three new books from my brother in Baltimore. One is a collection of poems by a Scotsman, Robert Burns. Have you read him?"

"That I have." Forgetting herself, Crysta recited, "'O, my love is like a red, red rose. . . .'"

Jessica's depthless eyes glowed from within as her smile widened. "'That's newly sprung in June,'" she said, continuing the verse. "'O, my love is like the melody that's sweetly played in tune.' La, yes, we will be the best of friends, I just know it. I'm so glad you've come."

Crysta already felt she had a soul mate . . . another young woman with a desire to broaden her world.

"Jessica," her mother-in-law reprimanded, "don't overwhelm the young lady."

"At least," inserted the other sister-in-law, "not until Miss Amherst learns if she's gonna be given the teaching chore." The sun-browned blonde in a plain straw bonnet set her extra cup before Inga Bremmer, then sat beside the minister's wife. She reached across the makeshift table to Crysta with a strong clasp of her hand. "Me an' Jessica are pullin' for you. Our menfolk know if they come outta that meetin' without doin' their best for you, they won't be gettin' any hot dinners for some time to come."

"I do thank you for that. But I don't think the other women feel the same."

Annie glanced over at a group standing so close to each other that their skirts were intermingling, as an old oak shaded them from the noonday sun. "They didn't have Drew to sing your praises."

Drew had sung her praises?

"Besides," Annie continued, "they're usually kinda standoffish at first. Most everyone in the valley's real nice folks. Ain't that so, Mother Reardon?"

The older woman had yet to sit down. She took a sip of what Crysta had noted was lemonade. "Folks just don't know how to talk to someone with all the advantages you've obviously had, considerin' all the tatted lace and ribbons you're sportin'—'nough trimmin's there to fancy up five Sunday dresses. Folks don't understand why a rich gal like you would want to settle in a valley with folks who don't have nearly as much."

The woman surely didn't mince words. Crysta elected to be just as forthright. "I cannot help that my parents lavished some of their riches on me. But I prize my freedom more than any amount of wealth. Here in Reardon Valley, I hope to be able to earn my own living, meager though it may be. And make my own choices. Not have anyone dictating who I shall or shall not marry or where I shall or shall not go. Those are the advantages I would not have had unless I came to Tennessee."

Annie, the taller of the two sisters-in-law, leaned closer. "If that's why you came, I'm behind you all the way. I came here to be on my own, too. If them dunderheaded men in there won't give you the teachin' job, you're welcome to come live with me an' my husband till you decide what you want to do."

"Yes," the older Mistress Reardon concurred, surprising Crysta. "We trust Andrew's opinion of you, and if he thinks so highly of you, you can come stay in my home with me. I could use the company with Andrew gone so much of the time. And mayhap, with a lovely young miss like you stayin' with us, he won't stay gone for such long stretches."

Crysta had a hard time controlling the smile trying to break free. This was quite a change of heart for a woman who'd been reluctant to even greet her just a moment ago. Drew had been absolutely correct about his mother's determination to see him wed and settled . . . even to the point that she would willingly invite a stranger into her home—someone whom she wasn't sure she even approved of.

"I don't t'ink ve haf to make odder plans chust yet," Inga Bremmer said. "Mine Rolf, he is speaking for Miss Amherst, too. If dey give her da job, she has her own cabin right next to ours."

Crysta noticed a sudden bustling about among the women at the serving table, lifting of cloths and lids from the food. She checked back toward the church and saw the door had opened and the men were walking out.

Not one was smiling.

Was that a good or a bad sign? Her heart plummeted to her feet.

"Time to eat," called one of the women at the food table.

The kids, who'd been in a big circle on the grassy parade ground playing a game of Drop the Hanky, came running.

Last out of the church came Brother Rolf and Drew Reardon, along with two other tall men. They were obviously Drew's older brothers, since both were close to the same height and build as

Drew, with light-colored hair and bronzed faces like their younger sibling. All stalwart-looking men. Any woman would be proud to have children with one of them.

Crysta was surprised by that strange thought, and it took her a moment to notice that, of all the men who had come down the church steps, only the two older Reardon brothers were smiling. What on earth could that mean?

"Come *mit* me, Miss Amherst," Inga said, rising from her bench. "I get you a plate *und* a fork. Time to eat."

Jessica struggled up from the table a bit awkwardly because of her condition. "Aye, then I want you to meet my husband. You'll like Noah. He has such a keen interest in books and good aptitude for learning that his father had intended to send him to college. But the Revolution interrupted their plans."

Crysta particularly wanted to stay close to Jessica Reardon, her one true female friend, until she was given the men's verdict. But three young children surrounded their mother, asking all at once for their plates and spoons. The smallest, a boy who looked about three, pulled on Jessica's fully gathered mauve cambric skirt.

Annie Reardon and her mother-in-law were surrounded by another bunch of youngsters, and Crysta felt as if she'd been thrust to the fringes of the family. She turned away and followed Inga Bremmer to a cloth-covered basket resting among surface roots of the big oak.

"Once ve all haf our food *und* are sitting," Mistress Bremmer said as she rummaged through the basket, "den I t'ink mine Rolf vill announce vat da men decide. Not before." She handed Crysta a plain earthen-colored plate and simple brass flatware along with a woven napkin of brown-and-black plaid.

Despite the butterflies fluttering around in Crysta's insides, she couldn't help noticing that, though the table service was plain, her hostess's choice of napkins complemented the rest quite nicely.

One didn't have to have the best, as her mother had always stressed, to have it pleasing to the eye.

Reverend Bremmer reached them, and as his wife handed him his table service, Crysta tried to unstick her tongue from her dry mouth to ask him the all-important question. Surely he would tell her, if not the others. She was so dependent on his answer.

But before she had a chance, their overgrown son, Otto, came barreling toward them at a big-footed run.

Crysta leapt to one side, or he surely would have crashed into her.

"Hurry, give me mine," Otto said, huffing for breath. "I want to get in line quick, while the best food is still there." He snatched the set his mother had in her hands and was gone again without so much as a thank-you.

"Alvays in such a hurry, dat one," his mother said with an indulgent laugh.

Crysta could hardly believe that such a sensible woman would allow such behavior. Her son was not only as big as a barn, but he was as spoiled as a baby. Crysta knew if she did get the teaching position, he could easily present a problem.

The teaching position.

She turned back to Reverend Bremmer . . . just in time to have him catch hold of her and Mistress Bremmer's elbows and, in great long strides, usher them toward the food table. With this bunch, food seemed to come before anything else.

For such a cumbersome-looking older man, Reverend Bremmer managed to beat out most of the younger men and had his wife and Crysta near the front of the line.

Crysta glanced over to where the older Mistress Reardon was handing Drew a plate. He still wasn't smiling. Fact was, he looked absolutely grim. Her insides began to cave in. Even with all his teasing, he'd always supported her efforts. No doubt he and Reverend Bremmer had failed to convince the valley's men.

The minister nudged her forward—she'd allowed a gap to develop between her and Mistress Bremmer.

A moment later they reached the loaded table, and Crysta forced herself to concentrate on the feast. Pork and chicken were prevalent, as would be expected, but so were several meat dishes she couldn't identify either by sight or smell. Wild game, she assumed. The kitchen gardens were producing well now, so the lineup of bowls heaped with a variety of vegetables—beans, peas, squash, and carrots—all floating in fresh herbs and butter. And, of course, ears of fresh corn, which were favorites with the children.

At a table to one side, desserts were on display—cakes and fruit pies. A grumpy stump of a woman stood over them with a switch in her hand. No children would be indulging in any sweets until after their main courses were consumed.

Just as Crysta reached for a serving spoon, Jessica Reardon wedged into line next to her. "Excuse me, Inga," she said, offering the older woman a sweet smile, "but I promised Miss Amherst that we would dine together." She turned and pointed to the table where they had been sitting. "Noah is saving us a place."

"Thank you." Grateful again to the tiny lady, Crysta returned Jessica's smile.

Side by side, the two filled their plates. Crysta took only a few small portions of food—nothing looked the least appetizing in this angst-filled moment, especially with all the adults taking turns staring at her.

Jessica, however, piled on the food, causing Crysta to wonder how she remained so petite.

"I love church dinners," the expectant mother said. "As a child I had very little variety in food, so these meals are always such a treat." When they reached the end of the serving table, Jessica said, "Follow me" and led the way back to the table.

Crysta looked neither to the right nor left as she tagged along. She only wished Jessica were tall enough to block her view of the folks who already had their meals and were settling down on benches at the other tables. All of them were, of course, still gaping at her. How she wished Reverend Bremmer would make the announcement so they could find something else upon which to concentrate. She'd been their prime target since she walked out of the Bremmers' home on Drew's arm. . . . Thank the good Lord, he'd shielded her from most of the gawking during the church service, but now he was keeping his distance.

But why? Why was he?

"Miss Amherst, I'm very pleased to present my husband, Noah, to you. Between the two of us, we have twenty-three books, don't we, dear?"

Standing there, tall and straight, Noah Reardon displayed a wide straight-toothed grin just like the one he'd sported when he came out of the church. "Aye. We had the most books of anyone in the valley. But Drew says you have more. I'm most interested in comparing titles."

"Go get your dinner first, dear," his wife urged. "I promise not to let her get away."

His grin grew wide again. "She's not the only one who's not getting away." Leaving them with that strange statement, he sauntered off, whistling a jaunty ditty Crysta didn't recognize.

With a tilted chin, Jessica watched him go. "Noah's got something up his sleeve, that's for sure."

Crysta scanned the crowd for the taller men and spotted the oldest Reardon male and saw that he was exchanging smirks with Noah. Yes, those two were finding something that had happened at the meeting quite amusing.

"Do sit down," Jessica urged. "As soon as we're all seated with our food, I know Brother Rolf will make the announcement." She grabbed Crysta's hand. "I just know it's going to be good news. Noah's such a good and gentle Christian man that he'd never laugh at your misfortune."

Crysta would have taken great comfort in that piece of information if it had not been for Drew. Like her, he scarcely had any food on his plate as he returned to the table the Reardons had staked out. And not once did he glance at Crysta as he sat at the far end. Not the least normal.

Jessica scooted down the cup of lemonade she'd given Crysta earlier—the drink Crysta had yet to sip. Something she did now. Taking a big gulp into her parched mouth, Crysta had a hard time forcing the liquid past her closing throat.

Reverend Bremmer returned with his wife and set his plate at the other end next to Drew's, then gave the younger man's shoulder a squeeze before walking to the head of the two long rows of tables.

The underlying drone of conversation ceased abruptly, and every head turned the minister's way.

Crysta held her breath.

"Folks, I know you are curious to know vat ve decide about da teacher *und* da school. I t'ink ve make ever'body happy. But first, ve give God da glory for dis fine day *und* da bounty he haf give to us. Let us pray."

His deep rumbling words rolled over Crysta unheard. Until she learned what her fate would be, she could concentrate on nothing else . . . except her own plea to the Almighty.

"Amen." Reverend Bremmer ended, then cleared his throat while the entire congregation remained silent and attentive. Not a single fork scraped against an earthenware plate. No child giggled.

Crysta ventured a glance across the table at Noah.

His grin had not dimmed one iota.

"For da next two months, between now *und* da harvest season, ve vill be giving Miss Amherst da chance to prove her teaching skills."

Jessica was right. It was good news! Crysta could hardly believe her ears.

From the sounds of the other women, they were as surprised as she. Their gasps and shocked expressions made the rounds.

"*Und* for dose of you," Reverend Bremmer continued after a slight pause, "vat haf vorries about leaving a purty young voman alone *mit* da boys, I put your minds at rest. Our own Andrew Reardon volunteers to be da sergeant at arms. He von't let dem boys get out of hand. School in da church house for two months, *und* ve see how t'ings go. *Ja?*"

Crysta swung her gaze to Drew. He had agreed to stay in the valley for two months to help her? Not escape to the wilderness, the untamed wilds he supposedly couldn't wait to get back to?

Drew Reardon didn't look up from his plate; he just stared at it like a condemned man.

His mother swung her long legs over the bench and rushed to him. Coming up behind her youngest son, she wrapped her arms around him and squeezed. "Why, Andrew, this is wonderful. Two months. Two whole months at home with us."

Drew did look up then. His gaze found Crysta—a steely, murderous gaze . . . as if his volunteering to stay here were all her fault.

17

"*Und* now I vould like to introduce our new teacher to you all."
Staring straight at Crysta, black-clad Reverend Bremmer beckoned
her to join him at the end of the tables.

Her heart stopped, then slammed hard against her ribs. She
hadn't prepared herself for anything except rejection. As she disen-
gaged herself from the bench and started between the rows of tables
with all eyes on her, her legs felt as weak as willow branches. The
weight of her layered petticoats seemed to double as they swam
around her feet, threatening to trip her. But, thank heavens, she
finally reached Reverend Bremmer without a single faltering step.
Her hands weren't quite so obedient; just as she stopped, they nervously straightened the yellow-striped flounces that swagged across
each hip.

"Come here, *fräulein,*" the reverend urged, holding out his huge
hand. He caught hers and pulled her to his side. "Ladies *und*
gentlemen, dis is Miss Crystabelle Amherst."

Down at the Reardon table, hands clapped resoundingly—all
except Drew's, of course. He still looked as if someone had hit him
in the head with an axe handle.

Less enthusiastic but polite clapping came from the other tables. Except for the Reardon family, folks still weren't ready to accept Crysta.

When the applause died away, Reverend Bremmer continued. "She comes to us from Miss Soulier's Academy for Young Ladies in Richmond, Virginia. She knows history *und* geography *und* all about da latest inventions, as vell as reading, vriting, *und* arit'metic. She comes *mit* a big crate of books dat I t'ink she vill borrow out to folks vat promise to take goot care of dem. Now, I am sure Miss Amherst is vanting to say a few vords." With that, he stepped back, leaving her alone to face what must have been a hundred pairs of staring eyes.

Her mouth had no moisture at all. It had all gone to the palms of her hands, which she clasped tightly together. Taking a calming breath, she cleared her throat. "First of all," she croaked, trying to remember Miss Soulier's standard speech on opening day of school each year. She mentally skipped the part about turning all the girls into young ladies who would not be ashamed to grace any court in Europe, and went to the next part of the speech. "I would like to thank you all for this wonderful opportunity to stretch your children's dreams to include every good and honorable possibility. And to give them the tools to make their dreams a reality."

From scanning the faces at the closest table, Crysta knew she wasn't impressing them as Miss Soulier had her mother and father. She needed to sound more practical. "I have the latest book on the caring and treatment of farm animals that I will share with the lads. I have a volume of church history for any who might feel called to go into the ministry. I also have two books on engineering. So many of the rivers and creeks I crossed on my journey here could use a good sturdy bridge. I also have a medical book and one that contains the laws of the Commonwealth of Virginia. I understand Tennessee has applied for statehood. As soon as it is granted, I will see that our school has a copy of its statutes as well. Your young men will be as ready as any in the other settlements to take up the law or run for the United States Congress if they so choose."

Honest applause erupted now. She must have said what they wanted to hear.

Crysta forced a smile to her lips as she shot an apprehensive glance at Drew. Even he seemed to have relaxed somewhat, giving her the courage to go on. "I was hired to teach your sons, and that I feel quite competent to do. During my first several years of schooling, I was taught alongside my two brothers. Our tutor made no concessions for the fact that I was a girl. And speaking of girls—I will gladly teach any who wish to come. I personally feel that it is a great advantage to have literate daughters as well as sons." Crysta took a breath while she formed in her mind reasons that would appeal to these people. "If a mother can read, she can tutor her children when the weather is too severe for them to make it to school. And here in Tennessee, you are all a great distance from your families in the East. I'm sure every young wife would find great comfort in taking quill in hand to write to the loved ones she left behind. So, please do send your daughters too. And as for any adults who would like to improve their own skills in reading and writing, I will gladly hold a class for you at a time that's convenient for you." Unable to think of another thing that would make her seem an asset to them, she ended with a simple "Thank you" and bobbed into a quick curtsy.

Suddenly the minister was at her side again, pulling her into a rib-crushing hug. "I tell you, she vill be goot teacher. On da outside, Miss Amherst may wear da fancy dress, but inside her head, she got da plain goot sense." Abruptly he released her and pointed at the congregation, giving his index finger a couple of stern shakes. "*Und* for all da young bucks vat haf a mind to come sniffing around—forget dat. Ve be keeping Crystabelle right in da house *mit* us, chust like she is our own daughter. Dere vill be no lurking about."

Laughter broke out, then enthusiastic clapping.

And, finally, Crysta truly felt that the people were willing to give her a chance. A relieved smile sprang forth.

Reverend Bremmer hushed the crowd again. "Tomorrow ve get da tables *und* all da books *und* supplies set up in da church. Den Tuesday, I vant to see every child seven years *und* older here by nine o'clock. Ready to sit *und* listen, chust like dey vas coming to da church. *Ja?*"

"*Ja!*" was called back from all six tables, with the children yelling the loudest.

The congregation's enthusiasm was building. And so was Crysta's. For the first time, she truly felt she wasn't merely running away from an unwanted marriage but that she was here to make a positive difference in the lives of these far-flung children. And she wasn't going to let Drew's glum expression dampen her joy one whit. After all, she didn't ask him to stay here and help her. That he'd volunteered to do of his own free will.

Even if Crysta hadn't been waking every few minutes for the last long hour before dawn on Tuesday morning, she would have been awakened by Otto Bremmer. The heavy-footed lad was bounding up and down the stairs and slamming in and out of the back door, racing around to get all his chores done before the first day of school. If anything, he was more excited than she.

The moment that the first rays of sunlight shafted through the trees on the eastern hills, Crysta's feet hit the floor, and she rushed to the washstand next to the window. Snatching an embroidery-edged washcloth from the hook beside the hanging mirror, she dipped it in the washbowl and began scrubbing her face while she looked past her ruffled calico curtains and out the open window. She couldn't miss Otto.

He was in the middle of the chicken pen, tossing feed from a bag to the flock with such wild abandon that he had them squawking and madly chasing in every direction, trying to keep up with their morning meal.

With a laugh, Crysta stuck out her head and shouted, "Good morning, Otto."

He looked up, a handful of chicken feed still clutched in a fist. His blue eyes sparked excitedly, brighter than the dew on the leaves of the nearby hickories. "Morning, Miss Crystabelle. I'm almost ready for school. How about you?"

"I'll be ready long before nine o'clock. Promise."

"When it's time, can I ring the bell?"

"Yes," she said as seriously as she could manage, "that would be a big help."

Turning back to her room, she spotted the green-and-brown-plaid day gown she and Inga had spent two evenings altering into something more sensible—a dress Crysta could don without help. In payment to the kind woman, Crysta had insisted on giving Inga the extra lace that had been removed, although the minister's wife had thought it much too generous a gift for her services.

And Crysta understood why she would think that. During the past two days, Inga had spoken a little about how she and her husband had come to live in Reardon Valley. They had been two of the thousands of poor Europeans who had sold themselves into bondage to pay for their and their two oldest children's passage to the New World. For seven years they had slaved for their American masters before they were free to make a life of their own. And only in Tennessee could they find land they could afford to purchase.

Having seen many of the other settlers' farmsteads on the trip here, Crysta couldn't help but admire this family's efforts. A two-story cabin with wood floors and filled with furniture, which though simple, was adorned with painted flowers and softened with colorful cushions and pillows. And there were so many other loving touches. Outside, the barn and sheds and fences were all built to last a lifetime. While Inga took care of the house and garden, her husband and their one remaining child at home had planted several acres of corn this spring while keeping up with the blacksmithing demands of the valley. Then on Sundays, Brother Rolf scrubbed the grime from his hands and dressed in his simple best to take his place behind the pulpit.

After years of watching her own family's vapid existence, any concerns they'd ever had seemed trivial in comparison to the Bremmers'. Crysta saw that the true joy of living was in the striving to make one's dreams a reality, rather than in waking each morning to a world where everything was either already accomplished or would be done for one. Small wonder ferreting out the latest scandal was the most interesting order of the day at Amherst Farms.

Her thoughts in Virginia now, Crysta was sure she'd given her neighborhood enough gossip to keep them entertained for the rest of the summer. Her mother had always liked being the center of attention, and Crysta had surely seen that she would be. And Papa— hopefully she'd left few true clues for his men to follow. They would give up soon.

But even if they didn't, there was nothing she could do about it here in Reardon Valley. Only today and this lovely spot were hers to deal with, God willing.

She inhaled deeply of the cool morning air, feeling more alive than she'd ever felt before. Today she would start her new life!

Without further delay, Crysta tossed off her nightshift and grabbed her undergarments from the trunk at the foot of her bed. If she hurried, she might get downstairs in time to help Inga with breakfast.

"Andrew, get your lazy hide outta that bed." Drew's mother stood over him, speaking to him as if he were still ten years old.

Against his will he opened his eyes. Looking around, he realized she'd actually climbed the ladder up to the loft to roust him out. For a woman past sixty, that was determination.

"Time to get up and go to the church and help that lovely Miss Crystabelle." His mother couldn't have been happier.

Stifling a groan, he rolled toward the wall, not wanting her to read his frustration. The last two days had been a nightmare. From the moment the valley found out he had agreed to assist Crystabelle, everyone had come to the identical conclusion: he was smitten with the new teacher and would give up the life that he'd always bragged was far and away better than the ones they led.

All for love of Crystabelle. He doubted a single man or lad over sixteen had bypassed the chance to thump him on the back Sunday while grinning like an idiot . . . the ones who weren't laughing out-right.

His mother was more convinced than anyone that her son was in love. No amount of denying it had changed her mind.

"Get dressed, Andrew. I'll have your breakfast on the table by the time you come down."

Drew heard the padding of her knit house slippers as she moved toward the ladder. He rolled to watch her leave. Too soon.

She turned back, flipping her graying night braid off her shoulder. "Wear that Sunday suit I made you. You want to put your best foot forward. 'Specially today. I'll wager every family in the valley will be deliverin' their young'uns to school personally. And you don't want any other bachelors outshinin' you in Miss Crystabelle's eyes."

They'll all be too busy laughin' at me to do much of anything else, he wanted to rail back. Instead, he swung his bare feet to the floor. On them he'd put his moccasins, right after he pulled on his deerskin leggings. He might be honor-bound to show up at the new school today, but he'd be hanged before he'd dress up for it.

Drew had misjudged the situation somewhat. As he rode up to the church house, no one paid him any mind at all—not one of the entire population of the valley. And everyone was dressed in their Sunday best. Even his brothers and their wives.

Crystabelle stood near the bottom of the steps, surrounded by mostly young bachelors, all smiling and talking at once despite the fact they were practically choking from the tightly buttoned and necktied shirts they all wore.

Deliberately nonchalant, Drew rode past without slowing on his way to the Bremmers' livestock pen, in case anyone glanced in his direction.

No one did.

Drew took his time unsaddling Smoky and turning him out to pasture. With all those people buttering up to Crystabelle, who knew when school would actually start. By the time he started back toward the church, someone started ringing the bell with such force, a body would think the whole blamed valley was on fire.

All this excitement just over the new teacher. How would he endure two months of all this nonsense?

As he reached the front of the church, most of the adults were already loaded in their wagons and heading home, yelling last-minute instructions to their children as they went.

Two of the young men remained with Crystabelle, both vying for her attention.

Drew was considering coming up behind and knocking their heads together when Crystabelle spoke to them in a firm tone. "Gentlemen, it was very nice of you to take time from your busy morning to wish the new school success. But I'm afraid we won't have a very successful start if I don't go in to my charges this minute. So if you'll excuse me . . ." Not waiting for a response, she whirled around in her sensible outfit of green-and-brown plaid.

Most of the frills she'd sported on Sunday were missing from this dress, and, Drew noted as he pushed passed the two young men, the dress had a front-laced bodice—the girl had been able to dress herself.

An unsummoned smile cracked his lips as he entered the large room.

Those same makeshift tables that they'd eaten on Sunday had been set up with the keg-and-board benches. They were set two across and three deep. Seated at them as if they'd been coming to school their whole lives were at least two dozen children, the smallest occupying the front tables and the oldest in the back, with the middle-sized children at the two tables in the center row. Their hands were folded on top of the slate boards Crysta had brought, and they waited silently, expectantly, for Crystabelle to make her way to the front.

The lass had everything under control before she'd even called the class to order. And she looked every bit the teacher, with her shiny auburn hair coiled into a sensible thick knot at the nape of her neck. She obviously did not need Drew.

Perhaps he wouldn't have to stay the full two months after all.

"Good morning, Mr. Reardon," Crystabelle said as she reached her place in front of the children. She held him in her golden brown gaze as the children also turned to stare. "Students, as you all probably know, Mr. Reardon will be sitting in on class each day. And since we're fortunate to have someone who's traveled extensively in the frontier regions of the West, perhaps he'll be kind enough to share some of his experiences with us from time to time."

That was an odd request. They were here to learn about reading and writing, not about his adventures. But he was expected to say something. "Sure, whenever there's extra time."

"Good. It's as important to learn about what lies ahead of us as what is behind us." The statement was made resoundingly, as if she meant it. "Take a seat anywhere you feel comfortable, Mr. Reardon."

Glancing around, Drew saw no chair anywhere. He would have to sit on one of the benches with the children. Feeling like some ungainly lad himself, he motioned for the big boys to move over on one of the back benches and sat on the end beside a sandy-headed Dagget twin. During recess, he'd be finding a lone chair, even if he had to hammer one together.

"I'm so glad to see girls as well as boys here today."

Drew scanned the children's heads and saw seven with hair braided into pigtails. Maybe not as many girls as Crystabelle would have liked, but it was a start.

"Now, children, raise your right hand if you already know how to read or write."

Four of the older boys raised theirs, Otto Bremmer among them. Only four.

Shocked, Drew slowly shook his head at such a travesty. He and Crystabelle sure had their work cut out for them. They surely did.

18

Crysta had done her utmost all morning not to show her astonishment. Her gratitude, though, she tried to convey with a nod here, a smile there. She still could not believe her good fortune. After she learned how few children even knew the alphabet, she'd felt completely overwhelmed. Fact was, unlike Drew Reardon, she'd never actually taught a single person to read. Coming to her rescue once again, Drew had left his place at the back and strode up to her. "While you find out how much them boys in the back know, I can introduce the others to the letter A." Then, as if it were the most natural thing in the world, he collected a slate board and a piece of chalk off the pulpit and drew the first letter, large and bold.

In that one short morning, while she assessed the educational level of Otto Bremmer and three other lads, Drew had all the children writing and sounding out their first five letters.

Crysta was working at a back table with Philip Clay, an unusually quiet boy, when she became aware of how overly warm the room had become despite the fact that every side window had been swung wide. Glancing outside, she saw that the shadow beneath a nearby oak indicated high noon.

She scooted off the end of the bench and rose to her feet. "Time to stop and eat." As the younger children turned to look at her with enlivened and mostly freckle-nosed faces, she finished instructing them. "Take your food baskets out under the big oak. Otto will draw up a bucket of water from his well for you to drink."

Before she could excuse them properly, they broke into a wild scramble, grabbing their baskets from under the tables and racing out the door, laughing and yelling—no longer the quiet first-day students.

Drew Reardon, who this morning looked as if he'd arrived under the threat of death, now gazed across the room at her, not with his usual smirk but with a surprisingly gentle smile.

Crysta's breath caught. Her heart skipped a beat. In that instant he was incredibly more handsome than ever before. She felt heat come into her cheeks before she glanced away. "Did you bring any food?"

The smile did turn into a smirk now. "Oh yes. Ma even sent enough for you."

"That was most considerate of her," Crysta said, surprised that his mother would go to the extra effort.

"It was more than that." Drew left the front of the room to saunter toward Crysta. "It's her subtle way of trying to get us to eat together. Ma thinks she's finally got me where she wants me." Reaching Crysta, his grin faded. "An' I reckon she does have me. For now."

Crysta did her best to return the conversation to a light note. "But," she said with a smile of her own, "think of the new vistas you'll open for these children. For the next two months you'll be guiding them into their own great adventures—which brings me to my next request."

Narrowing his silver gray eyes, he suspiciously cocked that blond head.

"When you finish eating, I was wondering if you'd tell the youngsters one of your wilderness adventure stories. Perhaps one about your times with the Shawnee when you taught Black Bear to read. Do the children know Black Bear?"

"A few. But as adventures go, that's a purty tame one. Not much excitement there."

"It might be for children just embarking on their own."

"And, to think just a few weeks ago, you were berating me because I taught Bear to read." One side of his smirk was back.

Her smile collapsed. "Much has changed for me since then."

"Good to hear that." He grabbed her hand. "Come on. We need to get outside before the little urchins set fire to each other."

Crysta knew his taking her hand meant nothing to him, but despite the fact that she considered him no more suitable for her than he thought any woman was for him, she enjoyed that he felt comfortable enough with her to be a couple—even if it was just for a few moments. The hand holding hers felt firm and strong and ever so friendly.

The next three school days progressed with equal success with Crysta splitting her teaching chores with Drew. His original purpose for being there—to keep order—had not been necessary. Surprisingly, the children seemed to be as glad to be at school as Crysta was to have them. Adding to the school's small staff, Brother Rolf walked over from his smithy each day at noon to give the blessing on the food and to impart a Bible promise or exhortation.

Crysta couldn't have been more pleased with everything . . . except for one family of children: Philip, Howie, and little Delia Clay. After the first morning, one of the three was missing each day, but never the same one, and they were all much too shy to offer a reason.

As she stood atop the porch landing on Friday afternoon, waving at the children as they left for home, she spotted the Clay boys, and her concern for them filled her thoughts again. The two rode bareback on an old dun workhorse, turning the plodding animal south onto the road that ran the length of the valley. She wondered what kind of home they were going to. Their clothes were in fairly good repair, but they still had an unkempt look about them.

Drew walked up beside her. "It's Friday. The sanctuary will need to be set up for church. What does Rolf want done with the tables?"

"I don't know. He never said."

"I'll go over to the smithy and find out." He started off the steps in that silent moccasin-footed saunter of his.

"Wait. I'll walk with you."

Glancing back, he grinned and offered a crooked arm. "You do know folks are talkin' about us like we're a pair."

Joining him, she quipped back, "For all the good it will do them." She knew that when his two months were up, he'd be gone, no matter how disappointed she'd be to see him go. She changed the subject. "I'm concerned about the Clay children. Have you noticed that they don't play with the others?"

"Hard to miss," he said, taking Crysta along the dirt track toward the blacksmith barn. "Woodsy shy. 'Specially little Delia and those big puppy-dog eyes she keeps hidden beneath her lashes."

"Personally, I'd like to get hold of her hair. It needs a good brushing." Crysta lifted her gray-and-black-checked skirts above the muddy remnants of last night's rain. "They go home down your way. Do they live near you?"

"I don't know. They must be some of the newer settlers. I don't

162

think I've met their ma and pa. But then I usually don't hang around the valley this much. Brother Rolf'll know all about 'em, though. Don't think much gets past him."

As they reached the smithy, Crysta perked up. Everything about blacksmith shops fascinated her, from the roaring furnaces—so fiery they could turn iron into liquid—to the smell of the molten metal mingling with horsey odors coming from the animals waiting to be shod. Then there was the sweat of the big-muscled men who pounded the cooling iron into shape, the hammering sounds, and the hiss of red-hot metal being cooled in the water barrel. She and her brothers had spent many an hour watching at their plantation's smithy. Now, as she and Drew walked through the wide doors, she had a sudden, intense longing to see them. Perhaps in a few months she could find a safe way to correspond with them again.

Brother Rolf, bare-armed and wearing only a leather apron over his breeches, was hanging his tools on wall pegs—his day of smithing done—when they walked in. A damp bandana kept the perspiration from dripping into a face that was red where it wasn't smudged with soot. When he saw Crysta, he quickly snatched a gray homespun shirt from a nearby hook.

Crysta turned her back, pretending interest in some new harness rings lying on a thick-wood table, until he was properly clothed.

"School is over, I see," Brother Rolf said, coming toward her and Drew. He'd removed the apron and was now buttoning his shirt. "It vas a goot veek, *ja?*"

"Oh yes. And Drew was wonderful with the children. I want you to pay him half my wage until he goes."

"Forget that," Drew protested. "No amount of money would be enough to keep me here."

Nonetheless, he was here. Because of her. A thrill tickled her heart.

"Drew haf talents he like to hide . . . even from hisself. But he comes around in da time. His ma *und* me, ve pray for him every day."

Drew didn't even try to stop his grunt of displeasure at the minister's last remark. "Aye, that's right. I'll be comin' round every day, Monday through Friday . . . for the next two months. Then I'm shed of this place for a long time to come."

The conversation was turning unpleasant. Crysta deftly moved between the two men. "Brother Rolf, although school has gone so well this week, I do have a concern—the Clay children. They're not mixing with the other youngsters. Plus, after the first day, only two of the three have come."

"Vell, dose *kinder* haf extra to do at home. Dey don't haf no mama. *Und* dey gots da little brodder to take care of."

"You mean they're takin' turns stayin' home to watch him?" Drew asked, his interest rekindled. "If that's the problem, maybe one of the women here at the settlement could keep an eye on him whilst the kids are in school? Inga, mayhap."

"*Ja*. But Baxter Clay is da proud man. He don't take help from no one since his vife die last year. He might t'ink of it as charity for da poor vidow man."

"We'll just need to be careful how we put it to him," Crysta said. "I could ride to his place tomorrow, with the excuse that I'm visiting all the children's families—which I do intend to do."

"I vill go *mit* you. Show you da vay. *Und* maybe Inga vill make dem a pie. Da first of our peaches is ripe."

"If there's gonna be peach pie, I'm goin' too," Drew piped in as if he'd go anywhere for the baked treat.

But Crysta wasn't fooled. For all his protesting about staying in the valley to teach, he was just as concerned about a certain pair of puppy-dog eyes as she was.

Drew was beginning to think he needed to have his mouth stitched shut. Every time he opened it, he was agreeing to do something that was absolutely no business of a man whose only interests were supposed to be on the frontier. But once again, here he sat astride Smoky, waiting in the scant shade of a half-dead hickory to rendezvous with Brother Rolf and that fine-looking Crystabelle Amherst.

At least he'd had the sense to tell them to meet him on the turn-off to the Clay place instead of at his own farm. His mother would have insisted Crysta come back there for supper. Anything to further her matchmaking plans. And even if Ma hadn't been able to make him wear his suit to go visiting today, she'd extracted a promise from him to ask Crystabelle to dinner after church tomorrow. If the young woman accepted, that would make for a very interesting day—so interesting he might decide to take sick.

At that moment, Rolf and Crysta rounded a tree-lined curve and came into full view. Seated on her stylish arch-necked bay, she looked as if she were floating toward him. She was wearing that same pink-and-beige day gown she'd worn the first time he laid eyes on her. As before, she held aloft the matching parasol. And he thought the sight no less enchanting today. Years from now, when his bones grew too stiff and achy for trekking the wilderness, mayhap he'd look for a wife just like her, back talk and all. It would be hateful to settle for less.

He rode Smoky out from under the branches and saw Crysta break into a smile at the sight of him. Another breath-stopping sight.

"Afternoon," Brother Rolf called as the two approached. Dressed properly for visiting, he wore his black Sunday suit. "Mine Inga makes two pies."

"Good," Drew called back, grateful for something other than Crysta to dwell on. Still, when the pair reached him, he let his horse go, easy as you please, right alongside hers instead of on the other side of Rolf's. As they rode up the woodland path toward the Clay farmstead, Drew slid into flirting with no trouble at all. "Crystabelle, you really shouldn't have gotten all dressed up just for me."

She shot him a really splendid withering glance. "Would you please try to be on your best behavior when we get to the Clays'?"

"I reckon that means you want me to keep my mouth shut."

"If that's what it takes."

"Brother Rolf, have you ever seen such a fussy gal?"

"She is right. You saf da teasing for ven ve start home."

These two always took everything much too seriously. But he would try to restrain himself . . . at least while they were at the farmstead.

As they broke out of the woods, Drew noticed that Mr. Clay had no more than ten acres of his land cleared and planted. But he did have a solid-looking dwelling with glass windows and squared-off logs and a large barn, plus another small house with pane windows. Drew wondered what Clay used the second one for.

After a quick survey of the grounds, it was obvious there was no woman on the place. The garden was overgrown with weeds, and garbage and debris were strewn about in front. As Drew's ma always said, no self-respecting woman would let a place go to pieces like this.

A thin, long-boned fellow came out of the smaller house, wiping his hands on a piece of deerskin. He raised one hand to shade his rather large brown eyes from the sun. "How-do," he said, as the threesome brought their mounts to a stop. "Come to be fitted for some shoes?"

"*Nein*, not today," Brother Rolf said as he dismounted his old black gelding. "Ve escort Miss Amherst around to meet da parents of da *kinder*. Oh, *und* ven mine Inga hears I come here, she bake da pies for you."

"*Pies?*" The word had come from the oldest boy, Philip. He stood at the door to the main house with his three siblings crowded up against him. None of them had run a comb through their fine brown hair today.

"Not so fast," his father said, warding off the boy's enthusiasm with a gesture. "I told you before, we don't take handouts."

"I know," Brother Rolf protested. "But I cannot carry dem back to Inga. I never hear da last of it if I do. You got to take dem from me."

Drew glanced at the kids. They weren't speaking, but those big brown eyes were. "Well, I, for one, hope you take 'em. I was countin' on talkin' you out of a real big piece."

"I was just hoping for a small slice myself," Crysta chimed in.

The man's mouth slid into a smile that softened his angular features. "I reckon we'll all be having pie then." He turned toward the house. "Philip, go in and make some fresh coffee while I assist your pretty young teacher down."

The man might be proud, but he sure wasn't blind. And though Drew knew it shouldn't, knowing that the man intended to put his hands around Crysta's waist bothered him a lot. That had always been Drew's chore—and pleasure—during their days on the trail.

Clay walked up beside Crysta and raised his arms to her. "So, Brother Rolf is introducing you to our valley. I do hope it meets with your approval." From the man's diction and choice of words, he sounded fairly educated—something Crysta would appreciate.

"So far," she said, dropping down to the man, "I think it's the loveliest spot I've seen since we started over the mountains. Such a large, level valley. It holds so much promise."

"That's how I felt about it, too. But I suppose Brother Rolf told you that my children and I had a great sadness befall us only a few months after we arrived. Since then it's been hard to remember what I saw about the valley that was good." He offered his arm to the lady. "It's nice to view it through fresh eyes again."

Drew dismounted with swift ease and joined the two as they strolled toward the house. He came along Crysta's right side. If Brother Rolf happened to have a problem fetching in the pies by himself, Drew was sure he'd holler.

"Good afternoon, Philip and Howie. Delia." Crysta, the impartial teacher, made a point of calling each of the older children by name.

They responded by mumbling something as they smiled shyly.

"And who is the fellow behind Delia?" Crysta asked. "I don't believe we've met."

There was a moment of silence, then Baxter Clay said, "That's my youngest, Samuel. But we usually call him Sammy."

"I'm four," the little one said with big serious eyes. "Papa says I can't go to school. I'm not old enough. But I wanna go." He'd just said more words at one time than any of his siblings had after several days at school.

"*Sammy,*" his father scolded. "We've been all through that. Now, children, move out of the way so Miss Amherst can get past the door."

As they scrambled aside, he added, "You'll have to forgive the state of our humble abode, particularly since it hasn't had a woman's touch in over a year."

First flattery, then two bids for Crystabelle's sympathy . . . for a supposedly grieving widower, the man sure wasn't wasting any time.

19

Walking inside the Clay home, Crysta gravitated to the parlor end
of the large common room; it was as messy as she'd expected after
viewing the untidy yard and unkempt children. But the quality
of the furniture amazed her. This humble abode housed an
assortment one might expect to find in a Virginia manor house.
A scallop-edged tea table in dusty but highly polished dark wood
was complemented by an array of other side tables. They lined the
walls, along with a writing desk, armchairs upholstered in red silk
damask, and a sofa in red-and-gold stripes. All in excellent condition, obviously not being used. In the center of the parlor end of
the common room, a pile of carved toys and pillows and blankets
lay on a much-trafficked floral rug. Undoubtedly, the children had
been forbidden to touch the furniture. Another surprise caught her
eye. On pavings of stone slate stood a small Franklin stove—the
first she'd seen since she left the East.

Crysta whirled in the opposite direction and saw, shoved against
that section of back wall, a large table and chairs shrouded in an old

blanket, but the lion-footed legs were mostly exposed. Next to the expertly crafted set stood an elegantly carved, cherrywood china cabinet, where etched-glass upper doors displayed fine dishes inside.

Mr. Clay, Crysta now observed, had a rather aristocratic nose. He stepped up beside her. "You might say I'm the poor cousin who insisted upon marrying for love rather than profit. My mother's furniture is the whole of my inheritance."

"It's better than inheriting a pair of workhorses," Drew inserted, "that are getting long in the tooth and are two gelded males so I can't even breed for more." There was the taste of sour grapes in Drew's statement. He seemed to have lost his good humor.

Mr. Clay turned to his taller neighbor. "I've seen your Clydesdales. And I've seen all the acreage they've helped your family clear. They may die in a few years, but the work they've accomplished shall benefit your family for generations to come."

Abruptly, Drew grinned. "You're right. I never thought about the boys that way. But it's my brothers' families they'll benefit. I'm the wanderer of the family. Who knows where I'll end up? Maybe all the way to the Pacific Ocean."

Brother Rolf, who'd come in and put the basket of pies on a homemade worktable near the hearth, moved up behind Drew and clapped him on the shoulder. "God knows. He knows vere you end up. No place is too far avay for him."

Drew shrugged out of the big German's clasp and headed for the worktable. "And no peach pie can get too far away from me." He tipped back one lid of the two-sided basket and gingerly lifted out the first pie, then glanced up at Philip, who stood next to the hearth. "How's that coffee comin', lad?"

"A few minutes more," the skinny boy said as he looked back at the tall blackened pot sitting on a layer of fiery coals.

Drew wasn't put off. "It'll take us that long to get the pie cut and put on plates. Isn't that right, Delia?"

Crysta had forgotten the three other children still standing just inside the door. Thank goodness, Drew hadn't.

The seven-year-old's only answer was a nod of her head. Crysta moved toward her. "Together we'll have that pie ready to serve in no time. Show me where your knife and plates are." Taking the child's painfully frail hand, she realized these motherless young-sters weren't getting extra desserts and snacks that would fatten them up. That was something she could remedy by having Inga teach her to bake cookies and pies. And the Clay children weren't the only thin ones she'd noticed at school. She'd better start check-ing all the children's food baskets and supplement wherever needed.

"Men, would you help me move the good dining set out into the middle of the floor?" Mr. Clay asked, getting into the spirit of the moment.

Soon they were all seated around the gleaming cherrywood table with fluted, flower-decorated china before them, along with pieces of ornate, silver table service placed neatly on pristine, lace-trimmed napkins.

Such elegance in a raw-wood-and-mud-chinked room.

Drew, who'd insisted on cutting the pieces, had merely quar-tered the two pies. Huge wedges of flaky crust and peaches smoth-ered in a thick golden syrup sat before each one, including the four-year-old.

From the way Sammy was looking at his serving, Crysta was pretty sure he planned to wolf it all down. The child sat to the side of his father on a pillow as much, Crysta was sure, to protect the cream brocade seat as to raise him up to the level of the others.

"Brother Rolf," Mr. Clay said, once Philip had poured the steaming coffee, "I would be honored if you'd ask the Lord's bless-ing over this heavenly repast your wife has so graciously prepared."

Brother Rolf, seated at one end of the table, was always at his best when asked to perform a religious function. He breathed in a vest-popping chestful of air. "I am happy to accept da honor."

Crysta, between Sammy and Howie, took one of each of their hands.

Across from her, Drew followed her lead and caught hold of Philip's hand and the hand of his little pet with the puppy-dog eyes . . . eyes that were looking solemnly up at him.

The sight caused a hitch in Crysta's heart. A tenderness that Drew usually kept hidden was laid bare as he smiled back at her. If Drew ever did come to his senses and settle down, he'd make a wonderful father.

"Almighty Got in heafen," Brother Rolf began, "ve t'ank you for da hospitality of dis household *und* for da fine peaches ve haf dis year. Lord, I t'ank you for bringing to us dis fine teacher, *und* for all da *kinder* vat come eager to learn. *Und* Andrew for his obedience to you . . . him staying here to help *mit* da school. In da name of our Lord Jesus. Amen."

As "amen" chorused around the table, forks and spoons were already digging into the delicacy.

Crysta glanced up at Drew, but he was too preoccupied with his pie to notice. So were the others. She was again reminded of the many luxuries she'd taken for granted her whole life. In all her growing-up years she'd never questioned the fact that there'd be dessert waiting in the kitchen.

Yes, she would definitely learn to bake for these children.

Though Crysta managed to eat only half her piece, she paced herself to finish about the time the others began to have that glutted look. Taking a sip of coffee from her delicate cup, she gently replaced it in its saucer and gazed at the youngest child seated between her and his father. "Sammy, you must get lonely for your brothers and sister when they're away at school all day."

His mouth crammed full, he could only nod. But that he did with force.

She switched her attention to his father. "I was wondering, Mr. Clay, why don't you send him along with your older children? He could play with the other little ones at the settlement while the students are studying, then spend time with them during the noon recess."

Mr. Clay frowned, his dark brows flared, making his nose seem all the more authoritative. "I can't allow Sammy to run free all day, getting into all manner of mischief."

"Oh, forgive me, no, Mr. Clay. I would never expect him to be left unsupervised." She shot a glance to Brother Rolf for support, both knowing this matter would have to be handled with finesse.

The older man nodded with understanding. "Mine Inga, she could not birt' any more *kinder* after Otto. *Und* he is almost growed. *Mit* Volfie blacksmit'ing in Nashville *und* da girls married *und* gone from da valley, taking dere own *kinder mit* dem, Inga misses hafing little ones around. You do her da big favor if you let her vatch Sammy."

"Say yes, Papa," the little boy cried, bobbing up to his knees. "I wanna go, too."

Clay's frown had not diminished. "Are you sure, Brother Rolf? That sounds like a tremendous imposition to me."

"Sammy is chust vat mine Inga needs to get her laughing again. If it gets him out from under your feet vile you make da shoes *und* boots in your cobbler's shop, I say, vy not? Inga is happy, da boy is happy, *und* you get your vork done faster. Everyone is happy, *nein?*"

"If you put it that way, I'd seem like a tyrant not to agree," he mused, then shifted his attention to his oldest son. "Philip, do you think you could handle all three on ol' Snowflake?"

The lad put down his fork. "As long as Sammy knows he has to mind me."

"I will! I will!" the tad promised, jumping up and down. "I'll be quiet as a church mouse."

"And just how quiet is that?" Drew quipped from across the table.

"Quiet as this!" Sammy immediately dropped back down on his chair and pressed his lips tightly together.

"Well, it looks like you have your answer, Clay," Drew remarked, directing his attention to the boy's father. "But I'll tell you what. I live off the road a short way up from you. And since I'm already going to the schoolhouse every morning, I'll ride along with them the first few days to see how things go."

Clay's fine-boned features relaxed. "Much obliged. That'd ease my mind considerably."

Crysta witnessed the exchange in silent amazement. Drew always managed to take her by surprise. He'd cleared away the last stumbling block as if it were nothing and did it so Mr. Clay could still keep his dignity.

Scooting back his chair, Drew patted his stomach. "That was good pie . . . and great coffee, Philip. But now that my belly's full, I'm gettin' real sleepy. I best ride on home before I fall asleep where I sit."

Bremmer lumbered to his feet. "Da time, it is getting late. Ve vill see you at church tomorrow, Baxter?"

Mr. Clay focused directly on Crysta. "Oh yes, we'll be there. You can count on it."

Crysta wasn't absolutely sure, but she sensed the widower had more in mind than simply fellowshiping with his Christian neighbors.

Drew, suddenly playing the gentleman, came around the table to Crysta. "And that reminds me, Miss Amherst," he said as he pulled back her chair, "my mother has invited you to our place for Sunday dinner tomorrow. And she says she won't take no for an answer."

Crysta had been right in her assumption about Baxter Clay. Not only did he and his children arrive at the Bremmers early Sunday morning to confirm that Inga would care for Sammy, the widower asked Crysta to accompany him to church service. And he did it attired in a suit of clothes more elegant than any she'd seen since she left Virginia. He looked quite dashing in a frock coat and breeches of bronze silk and a waistcoat made of gold-and-bronze brocade that complemented his deep brown eyes. When she'd hesitated to accept his invitation, Rolf and Inga had encouraged her to do so in front of him. She'd really had no choice.

Anyway, that's what she told herself when Drew strode into church in his own Sunday suit and found her sitting with Mr. Clay and his children. And though she knew Drew had no claim on her, she'd felt guilty during the entire service. The periodic glances from various other members of his family only made it worse— despite the fact that she hadn't agreed to anything more than Sunday dinner at the Reardons'.

When the last song was sung and the benediction finally given, Crysta was the first person on her feet.

Baxter Clay immediately stood up beside her, his expressive dark eyes warm and his finely etched lips forming a pleasant, even hopeful, smile.

That simply would not do. She held out a staying hand. "I do thank you . . . all of you," she added, including his plainly dressed children, who stared up at her with those same pleading eyes, "but I'm obliged to bid you adieu. As you already know, I have a dinner engagement with the Reardon family."

Delia, standing next to Crysta, didn't say anything, but her disappointment turned down the corners of her mouth.

Crysta's chest tightened with pity. The child's yearning— indeed, the need of her siblings as well—to be held and loved by a mother was keenly apparent. Crysta swallowed against her rising emotion and ran a hand along the child's delicate jawline. "I'll see you bright and early tomorrow morning."

Mr. Clay caught that same hand and in a gentlemanly bow,

raised it to his lips. "And this particular morning has been all the brighter because we were gifted with your company. . . . Till we meet again."

Why was it that the men most intent on courting her were widowers with a gaggle of children—not that Clay's weren't lovable. But still, she felt the man was probably more interested in finding someone to care for his house and children than anything else—a wifely slave.

Scooting past the children as best she could in her voluminous yards of summery yellow and white, Crysta was one of the first to reach the rear of the church. In her need to escape, she quickly complimented Brother Rolf on his sermon, then briskly walked down the steps and directly to Drew's mottled gray horse, tied to a hitching rail. She'd wait for him and his family here.

She'd scarcely reached Drew's unstylish gelding when she became surrounded by students and their mothers, all speaking at once.

A simply dressed woman with alert blue eyes spoke louder than the others. "My son, Tommy, says you're the best teacher a boy could have."

"Thank you, but I owe much to Mr. Reardon, who is assisting me, and, of course, to children who are all so well behaved."

The others crowded even closer and resumed talking all at once.

In the clamor, Crysta could do little else but smile and nod and say thank you. Someone stepped on her foot, and a child tugged at the fragile lawn of her skirt. She was beginning to feel in need of rescuing. Peering over a shorter woman's head, she searched for Drew. Repeatedly she glanced up at the church steps, where the townsfolk were still emerging, until he finally came out with his family.

The Reardon youngsters did as all the other children had done. Sighting her, they made a beeline for their new teacher, only adding more voices to the racket.

Drew, on the other hand, sauntered across the grass toward her as if there were all the time in the world, his expression unreadable.

But not to Crysta. Undoubtedly he was still miffed over her sitting with the Clays—as if he had some innate claim to her company. Or was he envious because she was getting all the attention?

When Drew reached the fringe of women and children, he stopped.

Now *she* was irritated. She'd have to save herself. She raised a hand, hoping for some semblance of quiet. "Thank you so much, kind people. I do appreciate your praise—praise that should be extended to Mr. Reardon as well. Now, if you'll excuse me, I have a dinner engagement."

She practically had to push her way through the gathering to reach Drew, then had to grasp him by the arm and pull him to a quiet spot away from the others.

Again, he was being no help whatsoever, as if she were taking him someplace against his will.

Crysta stared up at him, all trace of her own good humor gone. After all, it was he who'd asked her to dinner, not the other way around. And since he had yet to open his mouth to even speak to her, she wasn't going to mince words either. "Am I to ride in the wagon with your family, or shall I saddle my own horse?"

The aloof man finally leveled a steady gaze on her. "With this sudden new popularity of yours, are you sure you want to tear yourself away from all your admirers just to come visit with us?"

Oh yes, he was fuming. And she was sure it had much more to do with her sitting with Clay than her being the object of the women's and children's praise. It would serve him right if she walked away and left him standing here. Raising her chin, she glared back at him and gave him his one last chance. "Do I saddle my horse or ride in the wagon?"

"Neither." He stared at her a moment longer. "I invited you— *I'll* saddle your horse."

20

In the Bremmer horse corral, Drew ripped off his blast furnace of
a coat and vest, slinging them over a top rail, then went to saddle
Crystabelle's sleek mare. All the while he worked, he wanted to
kick himself for letting that female get his back hairs up. Whatever
she did was no business of his, he kept reminding himself.

Yet, despite the mental lecture, he was acutely aware of where
she stood and what she was doing, her every move. And at this
moment, she stood under a nearby beech, twirling a wildflower
between her finger and thumb . . . a daisylike bloom the color of
her pretty yellow-and-white lacy day gown. The hue heightened
the blush in her cheeks, and beneath the gauzy gathers of her
bonnet, the highlights in her dark hair seemed to flame. Was she
deliberately trying to look so beautiful?

Whether or not she was, he thought, giving the saddle cinch a
stout yank, shouldn't matter to him. Henceforth, he would not let
anything she did or said bother him. He would be his old easygoing
self again.

"She's ready to go," he called to Crysta as he led the mare out of the gate. "Get your buttercup self on over here, and I'll give you a hand up."

He didn't even attempt to keep from grinning at the hike of her chin or the flash of her golden eyes as she walked toward him. Yes, it was much nicer to have her hackles raised than his.

Walking alongside the mounted Crysta to retrieve his own horse, he noticed that most of the congregation had departed the church. His family, though, was all settled in the big wagon and waiting for the two of them. Watching as they approached.

His mother sat high up on the driver's seat along with Ike, and from the near scowl on her face, Drew didn't even want to know what thoughts were running through her head, though he knew she wasn't the least happy that he'd let some other fellow get to Crystabelle ahead of him this morning. But then he hadn't been exactly thrilled with himself either—which would *not* happen again. He and jealousy were not going to be walking the same road from this moment forth.

Gracie, Noah's flaxen-haired seven-year-old, sprang to her feet. "Miss Amherst, do you like Delia and her brothers more than us?"

Jealousy seemed to run in the family.

Crysta maneuvered her mare alongside the wagon. "Absolutely not. I hold all my students in the highest regard. The Clays merely happened by early and kindly asked me to sit with them. Just as I sat with your family last week."

"Well," her older cousin Jacob said, "we got you for dinner, and that's a whole lot better."

At the towhead's boasting statement, the adults in the wagon burst into laughter—all except Ma. To her this was serious business.

Drew was doubly glad he'd put Crysta on her horse. In the wagon she would've fallen prey to all manner of Ma's questions and maybe even some embarrassing tales about him.

He captured Crysta's attention by catching hold of her mare's reins, then nodded toward his horse that waited near the front of the church. "The road is too narrow for us to ride alongside the wagon. It'd be best if we ride on ahead, so we don't have to eat their dust."

Crysta regarded those in the wagon with what Drew was coming to recognize as her public smile. "We'll meet you all at your farm."

During the leisurely hour-long ride back to the Reardon properties, Drew pointed out the other homesteads along the mostly tree- and brush-lined way, informing Crysta of which schoolchildren lived down each cutoff. This gave the two of them a safe topic of conversation—the various children and their needs. By the time they reached the Reardon cutoff, Drew was quite pleased that they'd regained the relaxed companionship they'd enjoyed all week . . . before Clay had butted in.

"Isn't that your path up ahead?" Crysta asked. "Up next to the half-burnt hickory?"

"Aye, lightning struck that tree the first year I was here."

"And where exactly does your land start?"

"Noah's land started a mile back. On the other side of our road, Ike's starts and runs south till it boundaries mine. My brothers staked out three square miles along the river for our family."

"La, but that is a lot of farmland."

"They were bent on havin' enough to divide up amongst all their sons, not just the oldest. We know what not bein' firstborn can be like. Our oldest brother, Lazarus, inherited Pa's entire farm back in North Carolina. After Pa died, even Ma didn't feel comfortable stayin' there, since Lazarus was the son of Pa's first wife."

"Had I married Harland Chastain, that would have been the fate of my sons as well. Even though it's no longer the law, the big plantation owners in Virginia aren't any more inclined to split up their little kingdoms than the lords in England were. Oh, I'm sure

Mr. Chastain would have given each of my sons a sizable purse, but when money's spent, it's gone. The land is always here."

"You think like my brothers. They were off fightin' for our freedom when Pa died. And when they come back, they didn't even have a home. Oh, Lazarus never said they couldn't stay on, but if they had, they would've just been workin' for him, fillin' his coffers. So when they cashiered out of the army, they took the offer of land this side of the mountains instead of money. Stumbling on to such a big valley in this hilly country was a real boon for them. Parceling off what they didn't need has given 'em a real fine start."

"And you say your square mile is south of Ike's. What kind of crops are you growing there?"

"Me?" He burst out laughing. "Trees, my beauty. Untouched by a woodsman's axe. And my livestock is possums an' coons an' deer an' squirrels, and anything swimmin' in the river."

She looked at him as if he was the one who'd said something absurd. "Are you saying you haven't cleared any of it? Not even enough for a house and a barn?"

"I don't need one. Ma always insists I stay with her when I come home. We built her cabin straddlin' Ike's and Noah's land, with their houses on either side of her."

"That sounds nice. The women have someone close to visit with, and the cousins will always have playmates. On my father's plantation, our closest neighbors were a mile away."

"But you did have your slaves."

"And as you've made me painfully aware of, that's not the same." Crysta's gaze fled off into the distance. "Josie," she murmured. "I do hope she's happy. I pray for her every night." Her attention returned fully to him again. "You are absolutely sure Black Bear will take good care of her."

"The best. And to put your mind at ease, when I leave here, I'll ride on up to Shawnee country and look in on them." He patted the neck of his steady, strong-hearted steed.

"Alone? Isn't that terribly dangerous?"

He shrugged. "Usually when I travel north into Dan'el Boone's Kentucky, I run across a hunter or two what wants to ride along."

They broke out of the stand of trees into the huge clearing, planted in corn, wheat, and flax, with plenty of meadow grass to see the livestock through the winter. The fields ran all the way down to the willows and sycamores that edged the river. The only remaining trees shaded the three homes. The houses, along with two barns and an assortment of sheds, were all clearly visible.

"My," Crystabelle sighed, "this is nice. You should be very proud of what you've all accomplished. A very promising future your family has carved out for themselves."

Drew found himself seeing the place through new eyes . . . Crysta's. In its own orderly, civilized way, the farm really was quite beautiful. "It's good bottomland," he conceded. "But for pure beauty, on my land there's a small glen with a streamlet runnin' through it. I feel more at one with the Lord when I'm sittin' there than at any of Brother Bremmer's Sunday services. Whenever the hullabaloo at the farm gets to be too much, I ride over and spend a couple o' hours. Just me an' God's creation."

"That sounds lovely. Would you show it to me? After all the attention I received at church this morning, I have a feeling I'm going to need a quiet haven to escape to once in a while—if you don't mind my borrowing yours."

The problem was, there wasn't *anything* about her he minded. The thought of her in his secret place on nights when he bedded down with nothing but the stars for company? That just might dispel some of the loneliness that had a way of catching up to him at times like that. "If you like, we can ride over there after dinner. By then, you'll probably be just as anxious as me to get away—between Ma's questions and the kids climbin' all over you."

Drew had been wrong about Crysta feeling uncomfortable with the whole Reardon bunch. She didn't in the least. From the moment his clan pulled up in the wagon in their noisy, neighborly fashion, they made her feel as if they'd all been friends for years.

"Come inside with us," the older Mistress Reardon said, hooking her arm with Crysta's. "We can always use an extra pair of hands to help set the tables and bring out the food."

Already their dining tables and chairs had been moved outside under a couple of leafy sycamores, a shady spot Crysta felt certain had hosted many a gathering. She liked the idea of physically helping to serve the meal. It was so much more exhilarating being in the center of the hustle and bustle, rather than sitting to the side and being waited on. That boring, useless life she'd gladly given up. And the fact that these women wore the same, rather simple, day gowns they'd worn last Sunday made the occasion no less festive.

"The food smells marvelous," Crysta said as she walked into the log house with its savory mix of aromas.

"We've been cooking since yester's eve," Annie said with a lively lift of her golden brows. "Since Drew said you was comin'."

Jessica moved to Crysta's side. "We're that pleased to have you," she said with a sincerity that Crysta hoped she could live up to. "After we eat, you must come over to my house and look at our books."

"I'd love to." With this young mother so hungry for knowledge, Crysta was sure she'd be most interested in the book about women's rights . . . sometime when they were alone together. But right now, the others shouldn't be neglected. She turned to Annie. "I gather this must be your house then." It was a home filled with simple but sturdy furniture, befitting the woman and her husband. The spinning wheel pushed into the far corner was the only piece that looked remotely delicate with its spindle-turned legs. The only wall decorations were samplers with Bible verses embroidered within borders of flowers and butterflies. "Did you do the samplers yourself? They're really quite lovely."

Annie grinned. "No, I'm not much when it comes to feminine arts like needlework. I'm much better at milkin' cows and weedin' gardens. Choppin' wood. Mother Louvenia made them for me."

Louvenia Reardon walked to Crysta, carrying a tray loaded with white table linens and dishes. "I take great pleasure in doing stitcheries for all my daughters," she said with an overriding meaning. She handed the tray to Crysta. "Would you and Jessica mind setting the tables while Annie and I get the food ready to serve?"

Crysta managed to allay her smile until she stepped outside. Drew's mother wasn't the least bit subtle. Walking across the covered porch, Crysta's attention was drawn to loud screeching laughter.

The five younger children were lined up for Drew to toss them into the air. Even as Drew kept insisting, "This is the last time," the little ones jumped up and down, begging for "One more! One more!"

Crysta stopped to watch the happy sight.

Jessica paused beside her. "Poor Drew. They all know he can't say no to them. Small wonder he has to take refuge in the wilds to get any respite."

"The children at school all love him, too. Especially the little girls."

Jessica chuckled softly. "Ah yes, the girls are always partial to our Drew. Sometimes I perceive that to be the reason he's never married. Being the hunter he is, I don't believe he ascribes much value to anything that's just sitting there waiting for him. He needs to track it down himself. The land his brothers deeded to him is another example of his not wanting what comes too easily. Mother Louvenia would save herself a lot of grief if she ascertained that truth."

Crysta gazed into those faraway eyes of Jessica's and was again caught by how insightful the young woman was.

Yet Jessica spoke as if her words were mere toss-away thoughts. "Well, we'd best busy ourselves before they beat us out here with the food."

Still, as Crysta walked down the steps, she couldn't resist one last look at Drew in the midst of delighting his nieces and nephews.

"Come an' eat, everyone," Ma called, though they'd all already converged on the tables. "Andrew, you help Miss Amherst into her seat." Being her bossy self, she pointed to one of the better chairs. "Then take the one opposite her."

Anticipating her command, he'd already headed for Crystabelle. As their eyes met, she broke into a grin, prompting one of his own. At least she was still amused by his mother's matchmaking. Most likely, though, his mother would misinterpret the meaning of their exchange and think they were falling in love.

"Still having fun?" he whispered as he helped her and her billowing skirts into the seat.

"More than you, I daresay," she returned with a blithesome tilt of her head.

As Drew circled to the other side and took his place, Noah's Gracie stepped up between Jessica and Crystabelle and placed a jar of wildflowers on the table in front of their guest. Pinks, yellows, and purples looked all the prettier for being near Crysta. Crystabelle and flowers sure went well together.

"For you, teacher," the flaxen-haired child said as she looked adoringly at her.

"What a wonderful surprise!" Crysta pulled Gracie into a hug, then kissed the child's round cheek. "Thank you so much. I love flowers."

Gracie returned the embrace. "So do I."

"She keeps our house overrun with them," her father, Noah, said, taking his seat on the other side of Jessica. "Annie, our beekeeper, says her bees are going to starve if Gracie doesn't stop picking the flowers."

"Gracie, hurry up and get to the children's table," Ike ordered his niece from the head of the adult one. "Time to pray."

Ike thanked God for the family's many blessings, then expressed his pleasure in having the new teacher for a guest. As he did, Drew sneaked a peek at Crysta. No more beautiful portrait could ever be painted than of her sitting there with her slender neck bent and her long auburn lashes fanning her cheeks. It was hard to believe that this was the same snobbish belle he had met in Salem a few weeks ago. Despite her much fancier clothing, she seemed to fit right in . . . like one more pea in the Reardon pod.

His chest swelled with pride for her, knowing better than anyone all that she'd willingly given up to come here and teach. Too bad she hadn't set out to be a female long hunter instead of a teacher. He sure would have enjoyed the company.

"We was doubtful about havin' a woman teacher at first," his mother said.

Drew realized that not only had Ike finished saying grace, but his mother had claimed the chair right beside him—the better to torment him and Crystabelle.

"But with all the children loving you so, Miss Amherst, I can see we were wrong," Ma continued. "And I've been thinking what a brave soul you were to venture all this way. You've got the pioneer spirit, all right. The kind of woman we need in the valley. Don't you agree, Drew?"

She'd caught him off guard, but just for a second. "Absolutely, Ma." Picking up a bowl of honeyed squash, he handed it to Crysta. "And she eats like a pioneer, too."

Crysta's mouth fell open. "I do not."

"Well, you'd better eat enough for three today," Ike teased, jumping into the fray as he forked a chicken thigh off a platter. "Cuz there's no way we can eat all the food these women cooked."

"I can," shouted Ike's Jacob from the other table.

"Me, too," Noah's squirt, Spencer, piped in.

Ma craned her neck toward the children's table. "I don't want anyone showin' off by makin' pigs of themselves." She turned back to Crysta. "Miss Amherst, I hope you don't think we're raisin' a bunch of heathens out here."

"By no means. I grew up with two brothers." Crysta passed the bowl to Jessica. "I'm used to a lot of horseplay."

"I'm very pleased to hear that," the older woman replied. "My boys can be such bedevilers, 'specially Andrew. But underneath, he's all heart."

At the rate Ma was going, Drew was surprised she didn't have Brother Rolf standing by to marry the two of them this afternoon. He picked up a pitcher and Crysta's glass to pour her some cider. Escape was in order. "Did I mention I'm taking Crystabelle to see my land right after dinner?"

A body would have thought Ma's face was a lantern he'd just put fire to, her smile was so bright. "Why, that's a real fine idea. Now, don't you worry none about helpin' with the dishes, Miss Amherst. Just go and enjoy the cool of his woods while them trees is still standin'. And, by the by, did he tell you he owns the best team of workhorses in all of Tennessee? With them, we could have his land cleared in no time. No time a'tall."

21

Crysta began to feel quite comfortable with the Reardon family. Throughout the meal, the conversation shifted congenially back and forth between book talk with Jessica and Noah, the latest fabrics that had arrived at the store, the newest baby, and this year's corn. Then everything changed when Ike made mention of a cooper who had come to check out the settlement last month.

Drew's mother, her graying hair pulled into a braided knot, put down her fork and looked across the table at Crysta. "He came from a small town near Richmond, so I recall. Mayhap you know him, Miss Amherst. A Mr. Ford. Russell Ford, I believe."

Crysta tried to sound nonchalant, though she would've much preferred that the topic not shift to the vicinity from which she'd run away. "No, the name's not familiar. At the academy I attended, we were discouraged from socializing with the local folk."

"I would imagine havin' a school of young ladies would be quite a responsibility," the older woman said. "I'm sure your teachers was merely tryin' to keep close watch over you."

"So they never failed to remind us." Crysta hoped that would be the end of talk of Virginia. She started to pose a safer question of her own about Nashville to the west, but Mistress Reardon was quicker.

"I take it your family lives a distance from Richmond?"

"Yes. And how far is Nash—"

Mistress Reardon overrode her. "And what sort of business is your father in?"

"He farms." Crysta deliberately spooned in a big mouthful of berry cobbler. It was definitely time to finish her meal and take that ride Drew had promised.

"It must be a most successful farm, considering your fine wardrobe and that handsome mare you own."

Mistress Reardon's words closed in on Crysta's throat as she tried to swallow the bite of dessert. Crysta had hoped they would all get to know one another better before she was forced to divulge her situation, but from the determined look in those faded gray eyes, the woman wasn't giving up.

"Are you *ever* going to finish eatin' so we can go see my land?" Drew groused from across the table. Then he turned to Ike. "I told you she ate like a horse."

His mother's long face stiffened, and she targeted her youngest son. *"Andrew."*

But Crysta didn't mind his insult in the least. He'd come to her rescue. Again—in his rough but timely fashion.

"Ma," he cajoled, "I was just havin' a little fun. But I would like to ride over and check out my land while there's still plenty of daylight. I haven't been there since last fall."

Crysta shoved away her dessert plate. "And with all the bragging you've done about your property, I, too, can hardly wait to see it. *If* you can remember your manners long enough to help me out of my chair."

"Get up, Andrew," his mother demanded. "And you'd better be

on your best behavior. Miss Amherst," she said, looking across at her, "he will be a perfect gentleman, if he knows what's good for him."

Beside Crysta, Jessica caught her hand. "Yes, you two have a lovely ride. The peaceful solitude of Drew's woods always reminds me of what this valley was like before so many people settled here."

As Drew walked Crysta to where their horses waited, he patted her hand, which he'd placed in the crook of his arm. "You do know Ma's gonna be lecturin' me from now till Wednesday, just cuz I jumped into the fray to save your hide again."

"I suppose you do deserve to be thanked. I really would rather wait to tell people about my predicament until after we get better acquainted."

Drew nodded absently as if something else were on his mind. "I'd say we know each other purty well by now. After we get aways from here, I have a question or two of my own."

There was an uncustomary seriousness in Drew's tone. He was usually a man who liked to keep conversations light. Fortunately for Crysta, they headed straight south into Ike's furrowed fields, with her following directly behind him between rows of half-grown corn until they reached the far side of the clearing. Even then, with only a faint narrow trail to follow, she had the perfect excuse to keep Sheba to the rear of his horse.

Still, as they rode into a summer tangle of virgin woods, she didn't want to seem unsociable. "Let me know," she called out, "when we reach your property."

He swiveled in his saddle to look at her. She was suddenly stirred by the contrast of his sun-browned face against his blond hair and white shirt in the deep shades of the forest. So often his good looks caught her by surprise.

"Just up ahead," he said. "We'll be passin' between two pines with notches in 'em. That's the start of my land."

Soon they reached the marked trees, and for the first time Crysta took notice of the birds flitting about in the branches. They verily filled the air with song. The squirrels, too, seemed livelier as they raced in front of the horses' hooves to reach the safety of their tree nests. Perhaps it was just her imagination, but she doubted if people often wandered this deeply into his land.

From time to time, Crysta heard the rustle of something larger, but the creatures never exposed themselves. She felt as if she were up in the mountains again, scores of miles from the nearest settlement. Removing her liberally tucked and gathered bonnet, she let the piney breezes play through her loosely piled hair.

A shushing of water bubbling over rocks danced across her ears, gentler, more musical than a river rapids might make—the river, she knew, edged the Reardon lands somewhere farther to the west. Stretching high in her saddle, she couldn't locate the source of the sound through the dense brush.

Just then, Drew stopped ahead of her, dismounted, and tied his gray gelding to the lower branch of a young pine. "We'll have to walk the rest of the way," he informed her as he sauntered to her mare's side to help her down.

As he placed his hands around her waist and lifted her to the soft carpet of last year's leaves, she became aware that they were utterly alone. She felt the heat of his hands, his breath feathering through her hair.

He held her well past the proper span of time. Then abruptly he let go and stepped back, his gaze not quite meeting hers. "We'll have to climb down some boulders to reach the glen. With that dress you got on and them puny shoes, I'll have to help. Do you still want to go? You might snag that thin material."

"Don't fret about my skirts. I'm accustomed to getting wherever I have to in them."

And it really wasn't that difficult. He held her hand to steady her a few times as they made their way gingerly down a tumble of boulders; she had to slide off only two of the larger ones worn smooth by the ages. But she was so busy watching her step as they navigated through the rocks and roots, she'd looked no farther than a few feet ahead at any time . . . until they reached level ground.

Before her, like an emerald jewel, lay a shimmering pond a few yards in width, spreading from the bottom of a small cascade. On banks surrounding the pool, delicate flowers mingled with the brighter green hues of moss and water grass, which gave way to the darker shades of ruffled ferns. These crowded around the trunks of a stand of white-barked birches. At the lower end of the pond, water spilled gently over the giant roots of a great old oak. Above, on one of its gnarled branches, sat two young squirrels as still as the moment.

Crysta leaned back against the boulder she'd just slid down. "You didn't exaggerate, Drew. This is a fairyland. I wouldn't be surprised if an elf was peeking through the ferns at us this very second."

Drew, she now realized, had been watching her as she surveyed his glen. He smiled. "Ah, the little people . . . I'm afraid they don't come out this time of day." He held out his hand to her.

She no longer needed his assistance; nevertheless, she twined her fingers in his and let him lead her to a low flat rock.

"A throne for milady."

Such a gentleman he was being for a change. "I thank thee, kind sir," she replied, not letting him outdo her. Settling on the flat surface, she spread her lace-paneled yellow skirts about her, then positioned her palms on the cool stone and braced herself with them, breathing in the pungent smell of damp earth. "My brothers and I had a secret place we went to as children, but it couldn't hold a candle to yours."

That seemed to break the spell. He snorted. "And this can't hold a candle to so many other places I've seen."

She sat up straighter. "I doubt that. It couldn't be more perfect. I think you're just itchy footed to go exploring again. For me, this little piece of paradise will do just fine. I've done all the traveling I care to for one summer."

His face hardened into its strong Scandinavian angles. "You may not have a choice if your pa catches up to you."

Crysta's idyllic moment shattered as shivers chased up her spine. Clenching her hands together, she tried to vanquish her angst. "You said yourself that we traveled seldom-used trails coming to the valley. If they were able to track us, I'm sure they would've been here by now. I really do think they'll give up looking and go home."

"If you were my daughter, I'd never give up till I knew you were safe."

"Maybe so, but besides running the plantation and finding the best markets for his crop, my father has many other responsibilities that need his attention. There are my brothers to instruct and my parents' demanding social schedule. And then there's my mother. She takes a lot of pleasing."

"She does, does she? Like mother, like daughter." His grin was back. He propped a foot on the stone beside Crysta. "Well, I hope you're right about your pa, cuz I'm not always gonna be around to save that scrawny neck of yours."

Instinctively a hand flew to her exposed throat. "I've been led to believe I have a rather nicely shaped neck."

His gaze gravitated to the spot she touched . . . and stayed there.

The air around Crysta became suddenly very warm, and her pulse began to throb beneath her fingers. He was much too close. Could he see her racing heart? See how much his nearness affected her? Would he try to kiss her? Did she want him to?

Not waiting to find out, she shot to her feet. "I've yet to see more than distant glimpses of the river since we arrived. You did say it was called the Caney, didn't you?" she added breathlessly, her words spilling over themselves. "That it forks into the Cumberland? I would really enjoy riding down to take a look at it."

His gaze raised from her throat to meet her eyes, and he expelled the air from his lungs. "Aye. I think that would be a very wise idea."

22

Weary in mind and body, Drew walked to the table near the open window and blew out the lamplight, sending his loft bedroom into darkness. The glow of the moon pulled his gaze to it, then on to the silvery shimmer of the river.

The river.

It had saved him today. But what about tomorrow? What about the next time he found himself alone with Crystabelle Amherst? And it was bound to happen. Every morning he rode to the school to her, saw her, spoke to her. Listened to the soft music of her voice . . . when she wasn't hotly bandying words with him.

Grinning, he slowly shook his head. How he loved her quick wit. Even as beautiful as she was, it was her spunk that intrigued him most.

More with each passing day he was coming to count on watching that enchanting face come alive in her enthusiasm for teaching. But nothing matched the tender smile she shared with him when one of the youngsters did well . . . it warmed him through and through.

And this afternoon, wrapped in the stillness of the glen, all she had had to do was look up at him with those luminous autumn eyes. They seemed to reflect every emotion he felt. He'd very nearly scooped her up in his arms, said all those things a man says to the woman he wants to keep for his own.

Drew pivoted away from the window and started ripping at his shirt buttons. This kind of thinking, wanting, had to stop.

"Lord, you and I both know I can't have my cake and eat it too." He spoke out loud as he always did when alone and needing to talk with his God. "No rich plantation belle is gonna go trekkin' off into Indian country with me. And I sure don't wanna be tied down to this one spot. So why has she been placed before me like this to tempt me out of my good senses?"

He sat down on his narrow bed and freed a foot from one of those uncomfortable Sunday shoes. "Lord, I tell you, she's like Delilah to my Samson. But this one would cut off my walkin' legs 'stead of my hair."

Shrugging out of the rest of his Sunday outfit, he folded the clothing across his ladder-back chair, then dropped down on his bed again without bothering to get between the sheets—the room still held the heat of day . . . just as he did.

He propped his head on his hands and watched the shadows from the tree outside play across the pitched ceiling. If he were looking up at the stars somewhere far away from here, he knew he'd feel a whole lot safer.

Then Drew remembered his mother sleeping in the lean-to off the main room. He was such a disappointment to her. "Lord, I know Ma and Brother Rolf think I need to settle down, but I've never felt you wanted that from me. Fact is, I thought I was smack in the middle of your will, 'specially during those stretches of time I spent teachin' Black Bear to read. His pa said more'n once that I was a godsend. And when I took Bear to Salem-town last month, he found that Christian wife he wanted. That was a good thing.

And," Drew added for good measure, "as for me, someone has to go ahead of the others in this new country, checkin' it out, mappin' it an' such."

It was time he got back to it. Even if the Indians were to go on the warpath, it would be safer than staying here for the next two months.

But he'd promised.

Ah, folks wouldn't hold him to that. Crystabelle was doing just fine. Every kid at school had fallen in love with her. Even Otto and the Dagget twins did everything they could to please her. She'd be just fine. And besides, Brother Rolf was just two doors away at the smithy if she needed help from a firm hand.

Next Saturday. He'd be out of here by next Saturday.

His decision made, Drew punched up the fluff in his feather pillow and settled down to sleep.

But sleep didn't come. Every word Crysta had ever said to him kept running through his head. Her every glance . . . the hike of her chin when he teased her . . . the sound of her laughter . . .

I've had worse nights, Crysta told herself. Hurrying down the stairs from her bedroom, she evened the bow of the front-lace ties on her blue-and-gray-striped day gown—one of the three she and Inga had refashioned.

Just before reaching the bottom step, thoughts of Drew intruded again, and she slowed to a stop. How would she face him today? It had been painfully obvious yesterday that she'd given away her feelings about him. Every time she even thought about that moment in the glen, her cheeks turned to flame. When he'd said it would be *wise* to ride down to the river, she knew he'd seen the desire in her eyes . . . the desire to have him take her into her arms and kiss her. She was the very wanton he'd thought she was when they first met behind the woodshed. She'd given him a swift kick then, and now it was she who needed one. If she ever did fall in love, she lectured herself as she walked the rest of the way down the rustic stairs, it was not going to be with someone who couldn't wait to get away from her.

As usual, Inga had beaten her to the hearth. Not only was the coffee made and the biscuits out of the oven, the side pork had been fried and the older woman had eggs sizzling in the leftover grease. The delectable breakfast smells filled the room.

"Goot, you are here," Inga tossed over her shoulder as she pulled the skillet of eggs off the coals onto the hearthstones. "Holler up Rolf *und* Otto, den set da table, *bitte.*"

Being in the midst of the hustling activity in Inga's simple kitchen brushed aside Crysta's troubling thoughts. With Inga, life was always the work to be done today and the hope for tomorrow.

As Inga had bidden, Crysta stepped outside to a warm morning made more pleasant by the fragrance from a rosebush beside the back door. It was heavy laden with pink blooms. She spotted the menfolk, each toting two buckets of water to fill the trough for the family's horses, as well as for her own and the ones she'd rented in Salem—horses that would need to be returned by the next valley person going east. "Breakfast!"

She only had to shout for the men once. They both looked up with the interest of the hungry and grinned.

Returning inside, Crysta hurried to collect the plates and table-ware. As she did, Inga swung around with her spatula in hand, and Crysta noticed a marked difference in her this morning. The middle-aged woman's freckled complexion surrounded a wide youthful smile.

"Today is da day Sammy Clay comes to me."

"That's right." Crysta had completely forgotten Saturday's visit to the Clay place.

"It is many years now since I hear da laughter of a small boy in mine house every day. Not since Otto. He vas mine joy . . . *und,*" she added on a chuckle, "mine mischiefmaker, too. Da last *kind* Got gifs to me. I haf only da four *kinder* living, you know."

Not wanting to break the happy mood by asking how many children had not survived, Crysta returned to the original subject. "I'm so glad you truly want Sammy here. I think because we went out to the Clays, showed we care about the children, they'll be less shy now. Having Drew ride in with them for the first few days will help, too."

"All I got to say is, I do not see Baxter Clay dat cheerful since his vife die. Dressed up in da fine clothes like he vas yesterday. Dat one, he has his eye on you."

"Inga, I didn't come here looking for a husband. I want to teach. Pioneer men don't want their wives working with other people's children. They want them at home, minding their own."

"*Und* gardening," Inga added, still smiling as she brought the egg platter to the woven plaid tablecloth and nested it between the meat and biscuits. "*Und* for milking of da cows *und* making soap *und* da candles *und*—"

"*And,*" Crysta playfully finished in a singsong, "cooking and cleaning and raising chickens and sewing *and pulling the sun across the sky!*"

At that, they both broke into laughter.

"*Ja, ja,* being da farmer's vife *und* teaching school don't mix. But if you vant me to run off all da fellows vat vant to come calling, I vill need a bedder broom for dat—dat is for sure." Inga's expression lost its humor. "But vat about Drew Reardon? He is not interested in being da farmer, but he sure is interested in being *mit* you."

Crysta almost dropped the brass utensils in her hand. "You're mistaken. We're just friends. His true love is his freedom."

Inga grunted her disbelief. "Men alvays t'ink dey can't live wit'out dere freedom . . . until da right voman comes along. Did you haf nice time at his place yesterday?"

Just then Brother Rolf and Otto came tromping in for breakfast with cheery greetings, saving Crysta from having to respond to Inga's question.

Otto plopped down on his chair and took the fork Crysta was placing beside his plain earthenware plate. "Miss Crystabelle," he said, looking up at her with a gusty grin, "all last week you sat with the little squirts at noonin'. Me and the twins want you to eat with us this week."

"How about if I trade off days? Today I eat with you older kids and tomorrow with the squirts." Crysta loved the way everyone in the valley had become open and friendly and now vied for her company—a far cry from last week at this time. But what about Drew? What did he really want? He always talked about being off exploring, yet he'd taken time out to go east with Brother Rolf to fetch a teacher. Then when they returned and he was again free to leave, he'd volunteered to stay two more months.

Crysta glanced at Brother Rolf as he settled into his chair. She had so many questions for the minister. Both Brother Rolf and Drew's mother said they were praying for Drew to settle down and start a family. And at the academy she herself had been praying for God to save her from a loveless marriage. . . . Was this some plan of God's to bring her and Drew together? Which was it, God's true will for her or just wishful thinking?

"Everybody sit down now," Brother Rolf said, patting the table with his big square hand. "Ve pray."

Dropping into the seat across from Otto, Crysta stared at the minister. She was sorely tempted to ask him to seek God's clarity in this matter. But of course that was something one simply did not request at the breakfast table.

The entire day at school, Crysta and Drew taught and helped the children with the same dedication they'd had the prior week. But

Crysta could not deny that the smiles Drew sent across the room to her today were as forced as her own. And during the noon recess, no moment between them was spent in casual conversation. He filled the entire time talking and playing an Indian stick-and-ball game with the children. He was avoiding her. The man was clearly as disturbed as she by what had almost transpired in the glen.

At long last, the tension-filled school day came to an end. As the children filed out of the building, Crysta was again telling herself—as she'd done a dozen times today—that this estrangement was really for the best. He was not a good choice for her, no matter how much she enjoyed arguing with him, teasing him, being teased. No matter how much more alive she felt every time he was near, Andrew Reardon was not for her.

Crysta stood in the doorway waving good-bye to her students, while Drew lifted the younger ones onto their horses. The Reardon cousins, Jacob and Gracie, waved back at her as the boy turned their old brown horse southward. Two beautiful blond and tanned children, just like their uncle.

Soon the only children left were the Clays. As they clustered around Drew, he said something to them Crysta couldn't hear; then they raced to the Bremmers' house.

Going to fetch little Sammy, Crysta surmised, as Drew turned and started toward her, his expression grim. Something was surely amiss.

"Could we go back inside?" he asked as he came up the steps. "I need to speak to you. No sense puttin' it off."

This was more serious than yesterday's embarrassing moment. Had she done something wrong? Or been wrong about the valley people? Were they planning to reject her after all?

Leading the way inside, she stopped as soon as she was beyond the shaft of light streaming in the entrance and turned back to Drew, her chest beginning to tighten. "You look entirely too serious. What's the matter?"

"Nothing. Fact is, you're doin' so well, there's no need for me to keep hangin' round, gettin' underfoot."

"You're a tremendous help, and you know it."

"With me or without me, you would've done just fine. Kids just naturally know when folks care about 'em."

And how about you, Drew Reardon? she wanted to ask. *Do you know how much I care for you?* But of course she didn't. "And . . . ?" she prompted instead. Whatever was on his mind, he was taking his time getting to it.

He shifted his weight from one moccasined foot to the other and expelled a breath. "I sent the Clay kids to ask Inga if they could stay with her for a few minutes. I'm gonna speak to the men here at the settlement today, and I'll pay visits on the rest of the folks in the valley during the next couple of days."

"But why? I thought you just said—" She was thoroughly confused. "Do you want me to come with you?"

"Come with me?" Now, for some odd reason, he looked surprised.

"To see the children's parents, of course."

"Oh. No, that won't be necessary. You see, I'm merely going to tell them you're doin' a fine job and don't need me." He cleared his throat. "I'm leavin' for Shawnee country soon as school lets out on Friday."

"*What?*" He was leaving her? *Leaving her?* "But you said—"

"I know," he returned almost angrily. "But I can't stay here any longer. Like I said, I'm a man used to bein' on the move. 'Sides, I wanna see if Bear made it home safe with your Josie."

"Josie . . ." Crysta was so stunned, a moment passed before her servant's situation could crowd out the imminence of her abandonment. She schooled her features into what she hoped was a calm facade. "Pray, do send back word the moment you know anything about Josie. Now, if you'll excuse me, I need to straighten the room." Her eyes stung with tears. She swung away before her composure completely crumbled.

But he didn't leave as she expected. She could still feel his presence behind her as she moved down a row of tables, noisily piling one slate board on top of another.

As she stepped around to the middle row, he spoke in a low voice. "It really is for the best, you know."

Slowly, she turned to face him and saw the sadness in his eyes. He was hurting, too.

She sighed. "Yes, I know."

23

This had been the longest four days of Drew's life. And the shortest. But mercifully, the end was near. School had just let out. He stood in front of the church, helping the youngsters onto their horses, checking the saddle cinches, trying not to be affected by all the going-away gifts that now cluttered the steps—baked goods from the children's mothers, fruit from their orchards, favorite rocks and scraps of fur, even an albino lizard skin tacked to a scrap of wood. Even if there were no other reasons to feel guilty, leaving these sad-eyed kids with woeful, downturned mouths was plenty.

The teary good-byes were the worst . . . grasping hugs where he could feel every rib of their little bodies. And all the while, Crystabelle was probably watching the spectacle from the porch, though he wasn't brave enough to look back and check. Their own farewell would be upon him soon enough.

"Uncle Drew." Noah's Gracie, her big silver blue eyes swimming in tears, tugged on the fringe of his shirtsleeve. She and Jacob had hung back till the other children were on their way. She mumbled something else, but her words were too soft for him to hear.

Drew dropped down on his haunches and tugged on one of her flaxen braids. "I didn't hear you, sweet pea. What did you say?"

Her chin started trembling, and her gaze slid away.

He pulled her thin body close. "Tell me what it is."

Leaning into him, she moved near his ear. "Grandma said you was stayin' with us from now on. That you wouldn't never go away and leave us again." Her tiny frame shook with her ragged sigh. "Did we do somethin' wrong? Did I do somethin' bad? I'll be better, I promise."

"No. No." He rose from the ground, scooping her up with him. "You're my very own flower girl. The sweetest, purtiest one in the whole wide world. I'll be back. I always come back. And just so you know I'm always thinkin' about you, I'm gonna collect seeds from every new flower I see and bring them home to you."

"You will?" Leaning away to look up at him, she rubbed the wetness from her cheeks, the tentative gleam of hope in her eyes, making Drew feel all the more wretched. "But don't stay gone just to get me more flowers. You know I'm growin' so fast, you might not know me the next time you come."

"You could never grow too big that I wouldn't recognize you." He carried her to where old Brownie was tied and dropped her in the saddle. "How could I forget the very first niece I ever had?"

Sensing that Jacob had come along with them, Drew turned back and swung the eight-year-old up behind Gracie, then collected the reins for the boy.

All the while Jacob just stared at him dry-eyed. He was Ike's son, all right. Stoic as an Indian. This one wasn't about to betray his feelings.

Drew extended a hand to the boy.

For a second Jacob didn't seem to understand what was expected. Then he grasped Drew's much larger one and shook it.

"Jacob, some of the other kids ain't as quick as you when it comes to learnin'," Drew said, still hanging on to his nephew's hand. "I'm countin' on you to help 'em keep up with their readin' and sums. And I 'specially want you to be extra friendly to the shy ones. Will you do that for me?"

The boy sat a little straighter. "Aye, I'll make you proud."

"I already am, son." Feeling his own eyes starting to smart, Drew slapped the horse's rear, sending it into a fast walk. "Tell everyone at home I love 'em," he called, as Brownie took them away down the road.

Drew swiped any telltale sign from his eyes as he tried to work up his nerve to turn around toward the church and Crysta. This was proving to be the longest and the hardest good-bye of his life. It had started this morning with his very distraught mother. His brothers hadn't been much happier. Despite Drew's every denial, they'd all convinced themselves he was staying for good this time. That he'd stay because of Crysta, when, in all reality, she was the reason he had to go.

And the worst was yet to come. He had agreed to a farewell dinner at the Bremmers'. The Bremmers and Crysta. At that thought, he could hardly breathe—his chest felt as if it had been banded with iron wagon-wheel tires. Straining against the painful tightness, he forced in a lungful of air and turned to face her.

But she was not on the steps as he'd expected. She must've returned inside.

There was no way he was going in the church after her—get himself trapped in there alone with her. In the state he was in, no telling what he might say or do. What he might ask . . . or promise.

Ignoring the children's gifts lying on the lower step, he pivoted away from them—from her—and headed for the smithy's corral. His horse needed to be saddled and his gear loaded on. . . .

The last thing he wanted was to prolong his final farewell.

Crysta had escaped from school as soon as Drew had turned his back. She couldn't stand one more awkward silence. Still, she was no better off up here in her room. Her insides were wildly a-flutter, as if one of Inga's chicks were trapped inside. But she didn't dare let herself dwell on the oppressive heaviness in her spirit.

Moving to the washstand, she dipped a cloth into the water bowl and used it to cool her face. She simply had to get control of her feelings before Drew came in for supper. Brother Rolf's inviting him here on his last day in the valley would be much too difficult, too painful to bear. But somehow she must see it through.

To make matters worse, it had been one of those humid days, a day when her hair, the ruffles edging her dust cap, the very starch in her petticoats had all wilted. She pressed the damp cloth to both sides of her throat and to the back of her neck.

That helped. So did removing her gathered cloth cap.

Her hair, she noted from the reflection in the mirror above the commode, had not fared well either. Sighing, she began pulling out pins as she moved to the window, hoping to catch a breeze on such a still afternoon. Then a frightening thought came to her. Since she'd fled without so much as a word—left Drew to see the children off alone—perhaps he wouldn't come for supper. He'd brought all his gear with him when he arrived at school this morning. There was nothing to stop him from leaving the valley at any moment.

In a panic, she thrust her head out the window, tumbling mass of fallen hair and all. Her gaze instantly flew to the corral behind the blacksmith shop, where Drew's big-footed gray horse was kept during school sessions.

Drew was there! His bare blond head was unmistakable as he stood behind his mount.

Her knees went weak, and she had to lean into the windowsill for support.

He was saddling up! Was he leaving without so much as a fare-thee-well? How could he leave her so callously? so carelessly?

She pulled her head back inside before he saw her.

Was God punishing her for running away from her fiancé with no warning?

But this would be too great a punishment. Harland Chastain didn't love her. He scarcely knew her by sight. They'd actually spoken only a few times. And he'd always affected such a superior attitude, as if his mere presence were a gift in itself. A gift for which she—or any woman, for that matter—should be supremely grateful.

Drew Reardon, however, was not at all like that. He always enjoyed life too much to be bothered with such nonsense. And if nothing else was true, she knew he'd enjoyed her company. Until the past few days, anyway, when everything between them had changed. Had become unaccountably strained. Even charged. As if an approaching thunderstorm were now overhead.

She looked out the window again.

He was still there.

But what if he mounted his horse and started out? Would she call to him? run after him?

"Dear heavenly Father," she prayed quickly, fervently, "no matter how much his leaving hurts, please, please help me to restrain myself and maintain my dignity."

And a very important part of being dignified would be to have her hair dressed again as quickly as possible . . . and to be down near the kitchen door in the event she needed to dart outside.

But maybe she should change into something prettier than the brown-and-green plaid she'd worn today.

Now that was laughable. Getting dressed up for him? The only time Drew ever donned a suit of proper clothes was to go to church. And that he'd probably left behind with his mother.

She returned to the mirror and, taking her tortoiseshell brush, began to run the bristles rapidly through the length of her hair . . . as she returned to the window to check on Drew yet again.

He was now tying down his bedroll behind the saddle. Even from this distance, she could see his shoulder muscles—his very capable muscles—bulge as he pulled the thongs tight. He never shirked at doing the mundane chores, though he easily could have paid Otto to do this one for him.

But not Drew, Crysta conceded. He was a hardworking, practical man, whether he wanted to admit it or not.

Except for the first day she had met him, she recalled, and her lips slid into a smile. That day he was playing lord and master, with Black Bear relegated to the part of slave. Small wonder the African had looked as mean as his namesake.

But not Drew. That smirk was the first thing she saw. Even before she noticed he wore frontiersman's clothes. Normally, she would've dismissed any extra thoughts about a man dressed so crudely, but Drew wasn't a man to be dismissed so easily. Then or now.

A crazy vision flashed through her mind . . . a picture of the scene she'd cause if she brought him home to meet her mother and father, introduced him as her betrothed. Mama would fall into a faint, and Papa would run to get his pistols. But not Hank and Monty. Her brothers would like him almost as much as she did.

No, not nearly so much. That wouldn't be possible.

And this day Drew was leaving her. Her hands fell from her hair.

"Dear God, is this truly your will? To bring me here only to have me become more forlorn, more desolate than I would've been if I'd gone home and wed a man I cared less than nothing about?

"No, I mustn't lose faith. Here I have a purpose to my life. The children." And didn't the Bible say the fruit of the Spirit included love and peace and joy? With God's help she would find happiness again in her teaching.

Despite her attempt at bravado, she continued to gaze out the window.

Drew, walking around the rear of his horse, looked toward the house.

She stepped out of the light but still watched. She had to know where he was going. See if he actually might leave without saying good-bye.

He paused at the corral gate and rested his arms on it . . . all the while staring her way.

Would he come to her, or would he go? Perhaps he'd had second thoughts and wouldn't leave at all.

He shoved off the closed gate and strode, not toward the house but to the smithy.

"That's all right," she said, rushing back to the mirror. "That's good." Brother Rolf would make sure Drew came to supper and, the Lord willing, he might even convince him to stay.

"Please, God, let it be so. The children need him. *I* need him. If he leaves, my heart will surely break."

"Goot," Inga said as Crysta came down the stairs. "Everyt'ing is ready. But I need more budder. You run out to da springhouse vile I put da food on da table. And da men—you call dem in."

Crysta stared at her a moment as Inga wiped her damp brow with the bottom of her soiled muslin apron. Crysta wanted to slow things down for just a moment, talk to the older woman. But as motherly as Inga Bremmer was, Crysta couldn't tell her that she'd fallen in love with Drew Reardon, that every fiber of her being wanted to reach out to him, stop him from leaving—the two women had met a mere fortnight ago. Far too short a period to develop that level of confidentiality.

Taking a bowl and a spoon, Crysta hurried out the open door. She couldn't stop herself from glancing in the direction of the smithy. Drew, along with Brother Rolf and Otto, was crowding around a washstand next to the shop, cleaning up for supper.

They'd be here any second.

Not wanting to have to make pleasant conversation before she had to, she picked up her skirts and bolted for all she was worth down a side slope to the half-buried springhouse.

Crysta stepped inside the stone room with its water-filled trough running along three walls. It was always cool and quiet here. She breathed deeply of the refreshing air. And for just one panicky instant, she thought how preferable it would be to simply remain in here, to be spared from having to face Drew across the dinner table.

But that was just childish thinking. She scooped a portion of butter from a crock on the stone floor next to the milk pail, then hurried out the heavy wood door.

None too soon. As she raced across the side yard back to the kitchen, the men were walking past the big oak tree on their way from the shop.

Dashing inside, Crysta knew she had to calm herself. With slow deliberate steps, she walked to the table and placed the butter among the other food. And a very feastful table it was, with slices of ham drizzled with honey and a platter of fried chicken, plus sliced German sausages and two kinds of cheese. Pickled beets and cabbage joined the two bowls of fresh vegetables from the garden.

And Inga had done it all alone. Crysta felt very inadequate by comparison. What right did she have to think she'd ever make a fit pioneer wife?

"Inga," she said to the woman who was bringing a plate of sliced bread to the table, "this is wonderful. So much work. I should have helped you."

"Nonsense." Inga handed her the bread. "You teach all day—I cook. Here. Put dis on da table—dat is help enough—*und* I get da pitcher of cider."

"*No,*" Crysta countered, taking the plate from Inga. "Take off your apron and sit down. You rest. Anything else that needs to be done, just tell me."

Surprisingly, Inga smiled wearily and did as Crysta bade. "*Ja, mine feet, dey start to ache.*"

As Crysta retrieved the pitcher of cider from the window shelf, the door swung open and the men tromped in, filling the room with their oversized presence.

Her eyes locked with Drew's. Quickly, she glanced away. Heart pounding madly, she pretended that carrying the cider needed every bit of her attention. And the way her hands were beginning to shake all of a sudden, it just might.

But if she couldn't even look at him, how would she get through an entire meal? Or, heaven help her, the good-byes that would follow?

24

"You come chust in time," Inga said, looking up at the men from her place at the end of the table. "Everyt'ing is ready."

"Looks great, Mama!" Otto hurried to his chair, plopped down, and picked up his fork. "Come on, everyone. Food's getting cold."

Seeing that the extra place for Drew was next to her own, Crysta hung back, waiting for him to take his seat.

But he just stood there, behind his chair.

"Hurry up," Otto urged. "Papa needs to say the prayer so we can eat."

Drew pulled out the sturdy-legged chair but didn't sit down. He turned to Crysta, his usual teasing grin missing as it had been all week. "Well?" he asked.

Crysta squelched the sudden warmth threatening her cheeks. The chair—he was holding it out for her. She hurried forward and slipped into it.

While she settled her skirts around her, he sat down beside her . . . too close. How would she think? speak intelligently?

Thank goodness, she didn't have to. Brother Rolf cleared his throat and began in his deep rumbly voice. "Our Fadder, vich art in heaven. Ve t'ank you for anot'er fine veek. Nobody in da valley is sick. Ve haf chust enough rain for da crops. *Und* da new school is da great success. *Und* now ve humbly ask dat you vill continue to bless da school, even if Andrew Reardon is not staying—*as he promised.*"

Crysta heard the slight moan of Drew's chair as he must have moved slightly . . . or was that Drew himself moaning? Whatever, she just hoped Brother Rolf would make him feel too guilty to leave.

But would she really want him if he was staying only out of guilt?

"Almighty Got, ve don't alvays know vat your vill is for us," Brother Rolf continued, "but ve do know dat if ve luf you *und* are following you da best ve can, everyt'ing vill vork togedder for da goot. So for now, ve t'ank you for dis fine meal you provide *und* mine vife cook for Drew's last day *mit* us. In da name of our Lord Jesus. Amen."

"Pass the chicken" was out of Otto's mouth on the heels of Brother Rolf's last word.

For once, Crysta was very glad the Bremmers took eating so seriously. Busy filling their plates and forking in their first bites, they spoke few words. She especially tried to ignore her acute awareness of the person to whom she passed the serving bowls and platters. And the hand that accidentally brushed hers once. *Only once.* The shock of it shot right to her heart.

Too soon, all the plates were filled—except hers. She'd spooned on very little food, spreading it wide to appear as if there were more—she didn't want Drew, in particular, to know that swallowing would be next to impossible. She did fork a few green peas into her mouth, hoping to get them down.

The others were eating heartily, even Drew . . . the truest sign he had no abiding feelings for her.

Determined, then, to eat or die trying, she buttered her bread

and took a bite. She absolutely would not give away her own heart-
ache.

It wouldn't be long, though, before someone started a conversation. She prayed it would be about politics or the weather or even
religion—nothing that was personal . . . nothing that might link her
and Drew.

She tried to think of a safe comment, but with Drew sitting so
close, her thoughts had room for nothing else. He was too near. She
could actually hear him chew.

Could he hear her?

She stopped, then resumed much more quietly.

"Otto."

The suddenness of Drew's voice startled Crysta. She jumped as
if a door had slammed.

"Otto," he said in that pleasant baritone that she'd grown so
used to hearing, "with me leavin', I have something very important
to ask of you. I know Grady Jessup is older than you, but you're a
whole lot bigger, and the youngsters look up to you. Will you take
my place, be the man of the schoolhouse? Keep order for Miss
Crystabelle?"

Across the table, Otto actually put down his fork. His already
berry-brown complexion beamed as he sat up straighter. "I'd be
honored. And you don't need to fret, Drew. I'll take care of the
whole lot for you—the kids and Miss Crystabelle."

"I thank you for that, Otto. I can rest a lot easier about ridin' out
now."

Oh, so that was how he planned to assuage his guilt—pass the
banner to nothing but an overgrown kid. How convenient.

That fired up her ire, and she took a full-sized bite of spicy
sausage and didn't care who heard her chew. Never, not once, had
she ever said she couldn't handle the class by herself.

"Where'bouts you headed?" Otto asked. "Last I heard, your
Shawnee friends was on the warpath."

"That's farther north than where Black Bear's village is. 'Sides, there hasn't been no trouble for quite a spell now. I'm plannin' on fetchin' Bear and maybe headin' on over to that Frenchy town, St. Louie. There's a river they say's even bigger'n the Ohio that forks into the Mississippi there. Thought we'd canoe up it awhile, see what we see."

"I pray Got is *mit* you." By Rolf's grating tone, it was obvious he didn't think the Lord would be. "Sounds like you be going into da land of da heat'ens and da Cat'lics."

Crysta paused with a piece of chicken at her mouth. Maryland, a Catholic colony, had been just north of Virginia, and they'd always gotten along just fine. Then it came to her. In her text of church history she recalled reading that the Baptists in Europe had suffered tremendous persecution at the hands of the Catholics.

"Here in America it's not like in Germany, Brother Rolf," Drew argued. "On the frontier, we're all just hunters and traders, tryin' to help each other survive—when the white man's politics don't get in the way."

As so often before, Drew surprised Crysta with his store of knowledge, though he always seemed embarrassed if someone dared allude to the notion that he might be halfway intelligent.

He then mentioned something about the vast treeless plains that were supposed to lie farther to the west, comparing them to the steppes of Russia.

It was easy to see that Drew had already left her in his mind's eye. Already gone exploring with Black Bear. The breast meat in her mouth became very dry.

"If the land is flat and there ain't no trees," Otto reckoned enthusiastically, "then a fella could see in any direction for a hundred miles."

"That's what they say." Drew at least had the decency not to sound as thrilled.

"Soon as I'm old enough, I'm gonna get me a smart horse like Drew's and go take a look for myself."

Smart horse? There was something special about Drew's scruffy gray? That piqued Crysta's interest but not enough to speak out.

Otto's father had something else on his mind. Clearing his throat, Brother Rolf leveled a piercing glower at the lad. He was obviously not pleased with his son's intent. He turned back to Drew. "One t'ing I vant from you ven you are out dere chust chasing around. You make sure Black Bear *und* Crystabelle's Josie haf da proper Christian vedding. *Before God.* No heat'en mumbo jumbo is goot enough."

"If they're already married, I'm sure Bear's pa has seen to that," Drew assured Rolf. "It's as important to him as it is to you."

"*Und* you, Andrew. Marriage is da sacred business to you too?"

"Aye, Brother Rolf, just as sacred." A weariness had crept into Drew's tone.

Yes, Crysta thought bitterly. *Marriage is too sacred for him to ever consider.*

Drew swung his attention past her to his hostess. "And how have things gone with little Sammy this week?" he asked of Inga.

Blessedly the conversation reverted to the schoolchildren after that, giving Crysta the opportunity to regain her temper. She even managed to comment when asked her opinion about their social or scholastic progress. Finally the dreadful meal was over. Now Drew would be allowed to make the escape he so clearly desired.

Crysta rose from the table and spoke in carefully modulated tones, so as not to betray her mercurial emotions. "Inga, you've been working in a hot kitchen all day. Go sit outside while I clean up."

"*Nein.* You haf da guest leafing. I know you vant to be alone to say da farevells and vish him Gotspeed."

"Yes," Drew agreed quietly. "I have a couple of things I'd like to speak to her about before I go."

"Walk with me back to the corral," Drew suggested to Crysta as he stepped outside behind her. He was surprised to see that there was still an hour or so left before sundown. The meal had seemed to drag on forever. But no, he would be able to start on his journey this eve, as planned.

He noticed Crysta didn't respond as she strode off the front porch. Nor did she speak as they started for the smithy. He was pretty sure she was angry, but for the life of him, he couldn't think of a single thing he'd said at supper that would have set her off.

Another reason not to hang around here. Women's moods simply could not be outguessed.

Nonetheless, Drew had a private piece of business with her that he couldn't ride away and leave unattended.

"Hey, Drew!" came a yell from behind.

Drew glanced back to see Newcomb, Jesse Auburn's oldest, standing in front of the saddlery with Hatfield's grown son.

"Are ya leavin' now?" Tricorn pushed back to show the same straight brown hair as his pa's, Newcomb looked as if he'd reached manhood since the last time Drew had taken notice. Dressed in a clean white shirt and his Sunday breeches, the young man sounded as if he were eagerly awaiting Drew's departure.

"Purty soon," Drew hedged, eyeing the other lad now. With his brassy gold hair all slicked back, Danny Hatfield looked just as interested. The minute Drew rode out of sight, they'd be up on Crysta's front porch hoping to take his place.

But I have no place for anyone to take, Drew sternly reminded himself. Crystabelle was free to take up with anyone she wanted. But surely she'd pick someone with more to offer than those two young squirts.

When he started forward again, he saw Crysta had not slowed, but had gone on ahead of him. He lengthened his pace to catch up, which he did just as they reached the corral at the rear of the smithy.

There she stopped and turned toward him, her expression suspiciously bland. "Well, Mr. Reardon? What is it you wish to say to me?"

She wasn't going to make it easy. Yet he sensed her ire and didn't want to leave her like this, with her angry at him. "Crysta, please, I thought we'd become friends. Maybe even good friends."

She stared up at him a moment, and the hardness left her countenance, leaving him with those soulful golden brown eyes that so eloquently bespoke her pain.

This was the Crysta he wanted so badly . . . the one he was running away from.

He had to shift his gaze just to regain his thoughts, to recall the purpose he asked to see her alone. He took a deep breath and plunged on. "I purty much believe as you do that your pa would've found you by now if he was goin' to. But somethin' could go wrong at the school or . . . I don't know. But I have to be sure you'll be all right." He reached inside his homespun shirt and pulled out a small drawstring bag that had been resting just above his waist. "I want you to have this. It's enough money to get you by for a spell."

She arched her dark brows and slowly raised her lashes to meet his gaze. But she did not hold out a hand to accept his offering. "You owe me nothing. Our bargain was your silence about my circumstance for mine concerning Bear taking Josie."

She was being stubborn again.

He caught her hand and slapped the purse into it. "This has nothing to do with that. That's water long since under the bridge. Now listen to me. If for any reason you have to leave here, you ride back outta the valley the way we came in, and when you reach the main trail, go west to Nashville. Once you get there, ask anyone where the Thompson family lives. They'll put you up till I can come to fetch you."

"Fetch me? Why would you want to do that?"

"That's a silly question. To get you settled safe and proper again."

"That's very important to you, isn't it?"

"Of course."

"Fixing it so you don't ever have to think about me again." She shoved the money back into his hand. "Well, thank you very much, but I'm not yours to worry about."

"I can see why you might feel that way, but sayin' it won't make it so." He tossed the money toward the old oak tree. On this she would not be allowed to defy him. "I'm not gonna argue with you. Pick up the purse on your way back to the Bremmers'." He grabbed her by the shoulders, deliberately steeling himself against their fragility. "And don't forget the name Thompson."

She stared defiantly up at him, so incredibly close. Too close.

"Say it. Thompson." He refused to let her go until she complied.

She glowered a moment longer, then looked away. "Thompson. The Thompsons in Nashville."

"And there's still one more thing," he said more gently now, not quite ready to take his hands from her. He attempted a lighthearted grin. "If you promise not to kick me in the shin, I'd like your permission to kiss you good-bye."

Where did that come from? he asked himself as he heard her breath catch. He couldn't believe the words had fallen from his mouth. And her eyes, why had they grown so pulse-racingly dark and luminous?

After a moment her shoulders beneath his palms relaxed, and she tilted her mouth up to him. "I don't make promises to cowards. You'll just have to take your chances."

25

Before Crysta had the chance to recant her foolhardy dare, Drew's hands moved to the sides of her face, and his lips came down to capture hers. Full on the mouth . . . and her entire being began to melt around her pounding heart. She started to sag.

He caught hold of her waist, held her close, and deepened the kiss.

The dizzying sensation of his nearness overwhelmed her. Her eyes fell shut, and her arms found themselves around his neck. This was beyond imagination.

From deep within his chest, he groaned. . . .

Then, without warning, he broke away from her. "I'm sorry. I shouldn't have done that. I have to go." Abruptly, brashly, he vaulted over the four-foot rail fence and practically ran to his horse.

As she stood there trying to regain her senses, he caught up the reins, swung up into his saddle, and was already at the back gate unlooping the rope latch before he looked back at her.

Then he was gone.

And still, no words, nothing could get past what had just happened. Her legs wobbling, lips tingling . . . heart breaking . . . she watched him ride away and out of her life.

He was leaving her, actually leaving her.

It was a long time before she could gather the energy or ambition to leave the spot where she'd been thoroughly, unforgettably kissed. *And abandoned.* Not up to facing anyone on the road, she cut across the grass toward the Bremmers' and the safety of her room.

Just before Crysta reached the oak tree, she spotted the small deerskin pouch on the ground.

The money.

Her first instinct was to walk on by, leave his guilt offering in the dirt. But whether she wanted to admit it or not, she might very well need it, just as he'd said. She'd spent most of what she'd received from the sale of her sapphire earbobs to get this far. Bending down, she retrieved the pouch, pocketed it in her plaid skirt, then looked beyond to the house.

The parlor candles had been lit. She would not be able to walk into the front or the back without encountering someone. And the thought of speaking to any of the Bremmers, especially Otto or Rolf, was unbearable.

Giving the back of the house a wide berth, she walked on shaky legs to the side door of the church. The school supplies needed to be put away, she told herself, and the windows closed. Because of Drew, she'd run off as soon as school adjourned, leaving everything scattered about.

Though the sun had yet to set, the interior was growing dark in the shade of the surrounding trees. Under normal circumstances, she would've put flame to a lamp wick or two, but she really didn't want anyone to know she was in here. She needed time to gather

her emotions . . . if that were possible. Tears, great racking sobs, were trying to push their way out.

With the utmost concentration on the mundane task, Crysta soon had all the chores finished. As the last ink jar had been placed in the cupboard near the side door, her choking torment returned full force. She slumped down on the nearest bench, where her stinging eyes gravitated to the simple iron cross gracing the wall behind the pulpit . . . the symbol that Jesus had died for her. "For God so loved the world, that he gave his only begotten Son. . . ."

"But, Lord God, I don't feel loved," she moaned. "I don't." And, as if she were a jar shattering, all her emotions suddenly exploded from her.

Hearing her own wail, she pressed her hands hard across her mouth to muffle the sound. Even though she'd closed the windows, the Bremmers were no more than half an acre from the church on one side, and Hatfield's Saddlery was on the other.

"I didn't know I could feel so alone," she said in a high tight voice as she looked up at the cross. "So rejected. My heart is being ripped apart. Why did Drew leave like that? And why, Lord, did you make loving someone hurt so much? You always tell us to love. In everything . . ."

Words that Jesus spoke just before he was arrested came from a stillness outside herself: *My soul is exceedingly sorrowful, even unto death: tarry ye here, and watch with me.*

Jesus had known suffering, too. On the cross, he'd lived the very depths of it, of sorrow. And even knowing it would befall him, he still waited for the soldiers to come and take him away. But only after he'd called out, pleaded, "O my Father, if it be possible, let this cup pass from me."

But Jesus had been so much stronger than Crysta felt at this moment when he'd added, "Nevertheless not as I will, but as thou wilt."

"Lord God," she cried in a choked voice, "how can I surrender my will to you when I'm never sure what or where your will for me is? Oh, I pretend to know. I say I know. But if I truly am following your will, why am I feeling such pain?"

Isaiah. There was something in those Bible passages Brother Rolf had been reading to them the last few evenings. Had God known she'd need that particular comfort?

Wiping the tears from her eyes, she rose and walked to the pulpit, where Brother Rolf kept his good Bible, not the worn and dog-eared copy he read at home. She took it to the window for more light. Opening it to the fifty-fourth chapter of Isaiah, she began searching for the specific verses. When she found them, they almost jumped out at her:

> Fear not; for thou shalt not be ashamed: neither be thou confounded; for thou shalt not be put to shame: for thou shalt forget the shame of thy youth, and shalt not remember the reproach of thy widowhood any more. For thy Maker is thine husband; the Lord of hosts is his name; and thy Redeemer the Holy One of Israel; The God of the whole earth shall he be called. For the Lord hath called thee as a woman forsaken and grieved in spirit, and a wife of youth, when thou wast refused, saith thy God. For a small moment have I forsaken thee; but with great mercies will I gather thee.

"For a small moment have I forsaken thee; but with great mercies will I gather thee." . . . *Lord, please gather me. I need to be gathered.*

Any further words on the page blurred as Crysta's eyes pooled and tears rained down her face again. Though the promise eased her wretchedness somewhat, she could not yet relinquish her travail.

After a while, she did manage to repair her ravaged face enough to return to the house and escape to her room, but it wasn't until she awoke in the middle of the night that the full awareness came—an awareness of what God was trying to tell her . . . what it meant in the New Testament for Jesus to be called the bridegroom and the church his bride.

At the realization, she sat straight up. God was gifting her with a new understanding. And she was even more amazed because she hadn't worked it out on her own.

When Drew left her, she'd been forced to come face-to-face with the depth of her desire for him and the despair of her loss. For the first time she began to understand just how full and deep and powerful love could be.

This was how much her Lord loved her, and this was that same deep love he hoped for in return. Being a good Christian was not merely going to church or reading and studying the Bible, or thinking things through logically. It was taking Jesus' hand and saying, as Ruth said to her mother-in-law, Naomi, "Whither thou goest, I will go; and where thou lodgest, I will lodge: thy people shall be my people, and thy God my God." It was passionate, abiding love . . . the kind she'd seen glowing within Brother Rolf . . . the kind of love Jesus had waiting for her if she'd just reach out and embrace it.

As enlightening as Crysta's night watch had been, she awakened before dawn the next morning with more new knowledge . . . disturbing knowledge. As the rooster's crow brought her from her slumber, she knew she could not give herself to Jesus until she was completely truthful with him, confessed the sins she'd been pretending she wasn't committing. Sliding out of bed, she dropped to her knees and bowed her head.

"Lord Jesus," she whispered. "I know I'm not honoring my father and mother. I should have gone home and faced them with the fact that I could not marry Harland Chastain. That I could not give myself to a bridegroom I neither loved nor trusted. Instead, I left them to worry and wonder where I am, whether I'm dead or alive."

From the room across the hall, Crysta heard someone cough.

Inga. She and Brother Rolf were probably rising for the day . . . rising with the misconception that the young woman they had taken in and loved had been honest and forthright with them.

Although Crysta had never actually borne false witness against the Bremmers, she had received their hospitality under false pretenses. It wouldn't be enough for her to ask only God's forgiveness; the wrongs to these good people must be righted, too.

With the unpleasant decision made, Crysta came to her feet . . . a sense of well-being, of love, swelled within her as nothing else she'd ever felt.

The Spirit of God filled her to overflowing.

Now, instead of dreading her imminent confession to the Bremmers, she grabbed her summer robe from off the bedpost and practically ran for the door. If she hurried, she might even have coffee waiting for them by the time they came downstairs.

"Is dat coffee I smell?" Inga came into the big kitchen with Brother Rolf lumbering behind her, still looking half asleep. Her blue German eyes glowed with pleasure.

Crysta returned Inga's happy smile with one of her own. "I'm having the most wonderful morning, and I wanted to come down and share it with you."

Inga glanced about her. "Vy is dis? Drew, did he come back?"

Drew. She hadn't thought about him once since she'd awakened. Now the hearing of his name threatened to steal her joy. But she couldn't let it. Not on this glorious new morning. "No. But my Lord has been visiting with me. He wants me to tell you something."

That brought Rolf's graying head to attention. But he didn't ask the questions she read on his blocklike face. Instead he sat down at the table, looking dubious. "I t'ink maybe you pour me some of dat coffee. Den ve talk."

She couldn't wait. "Yester's eve I was feeling very sad," she said as she brought the pot and two cups to the table for the Bremmers. Again, the loss of Drew threatened to overtake her, and she paused, using the time it took to pour the coffee to dispel her longing.

Neither of them asked what had caused her sadness—they both undoubtedly knew.

"Anyway, yester's eve while I was over at the church cleaning up, I found myself . . . well . . . searching my soul." Crysta sat down across from them. "And between then and this morning, I've come to realize that I've been more of an 'almost Christian,' as the great evangelist George Whitefield preached, than anything else. When Jesus said, 'Thou shalt love the Lord thy God with all thy heart, and with all thy soul, and with all thy mind,' that's what he purely wants from me, not just some lukewarm *liking*."

"*Ja*," Brother Bremmer agreed, his heavy features lifting with enthusiasm. "Love is most important t'ing. Got is love, *und* if ve haf da great love for Got, he is in us. Ain't dat right, Inga?" he asked, looking at his wife.

Inga, her long night braid across her shoulder, nodded with a brief smile, but Crysta could see by the tilt of her freckled face that she was waiting for more.

"And that brings me to why I wanted to talk to you two before Otto got up. I need to make things right with God and with anyone else I've wronged. Although I have not lied to either of you with the spoken word, Brother Rolf," Crysta said, turning to him now, "from the very first I have allowed you to believe something that wasn't true."

Crysta quickly explained that she had not been sent by Professor Hazlett but had merely taken advantage of the situation. Then she embarked on the more difficult part. "And I am still breaking another of the commandments."

Inga leaned forward. "Dis minute?"

"Yes," Crysta confirmed, "I'm afraid so. I'm not honoring my parents. I was supposed to travel home from school to prepare for my wedding. Instead, I ran away. Finding out about the teaching position seemed a godsend to me at the time, because I knew I couldn't marry the man my parents chose for me. Not only do I not love him, but something about him makes me uncomfortable."

"Did you tell dis to your mama?" Inga questioned sternly.

"I wrote her from school. But she said I was being silly, that he was a fine man from one of the best families. Still, I should have gone home, been strong in my resolve to refuse the marriage. Instead, I'm causing them untold grief. Now that I've been responsible for a classroom of children for the past two weeks, I understand a little of how parents might feel if their child were missing. Mine must be—"

"Looking high *und* low for you, girl," Brother Rolf interjected. "*Und* from dem fancy clothes *und* dat horse, dey haf da money to hire da trackers to help. Sooner or later, dey vill come."

"They might not. I plan to write a letter to them, explaining everything . . . that I'm safe and have this wonderful teaching position, and that I'm living with a good Christian family. If I can convince them that I am determined to stay here, mayhap they'll give up the search."

"So," Brother Rolf said, settling back in his chair, "you are telling your mama *und* papa vere you are?"

"No. I'd rather wait until they've gotten more used to the idea."

He grunted. "I t'ink maybe dey still come. I better get mine own letters ready. Da ones to da Eastern towns, asking for da new teacher. Ve can send dem *mit* Jude Bailey. He takes your rented horses *mit* him as far as Knoxville next week. I like you, girl, *und* it varms dis old heart dat you find da new love for Jesus. But," he said, pointing a finger at her and raising his thick brows, "I don't t'ink you be *mit* us much longer."

26

"You've done good, boy," Drew said, patting Smoky's neck as they started up the creek toward Black Bear's village. A muggy late-afternoon haze turned the water to dull shades of moss and pewter.

Seeing Drew, an otter skittered out of a canebrake and slid into the wide stream, making hardly a ripple.

Drew wished the mosquitoes would be as considerate. He slapped at one on his neck, his palm coming away splattered with blood.

For the past nine days, it had been just he and his horse all the long way from Reardon Valley. Except for a quick stop in Boonesboro for extra supplies, he'd made a point of keeping away from the more trafficked trails. Although it was never considered wise to travel alone in Indian country, Smoky was the most alert horse he'd ever owned—good as any dog. If anyone was within a hundred yards of them, those ears turned in that direction and a low whinny came up from the gelding's barrel-like chest.

Drew caught a whiff of wood smoke, then noticed his horse

picking up the pace without being nudged. Smoky had spent as much time as Drew at this village and was eager to reach their destination.

For Drew, though, the zest to arrive had waned. The closer they got, the more he wondered if coming to visit his closest friend and hunting partner was even a good idea. Not only had Drew been in a foul mood since he'd kissed Crystabelle good-bye, he dreaded the thought of having to field questions about her—which he undoubtedly would.

And Black Bear knew him much too well not to guess something was amiss. Still, Bear would be expecting him. The two of them planned to go trapping up the forks of the Missouri River this winter.

The sooner, the better. Or who knew what his muddled mind might take a notion to do? He'd almost turned around and headed back to the valley a hundred times.

Children's laughter and shouting splashed through the trees. Any second he would be riding into the Shawnee hamlet.

Panic took over, and he tried to rein Smoky around, but the stable-bound animal caught the bit in his teeth and ignored Drew.

Despite the long day on the trail, the horse galloped into a wide clearing of cultivated fields and meadows that surrounded the village of about twenty families.

A yellow wolflike dog started barking, and a group of nearly naked boys let the rolling hoop they'd been throwing small spears through fall to the ground unnoticed. They stared at Drew with wide, almost coal black eyes for a short moment before recognizing the white man. They started shouting and waving, and two ran back to where the dome-shaped dwellings began, eager to be the first to announce his arrival.

It was too late to turn back now. Taking a deep breath, Drew steeled himself for the onslaught of greetings.

By the time he reached the outer circle of *wigewas,* the villagers were converging, coming from their summer cook fires or their dwellings or from the big central lodge. Before he'd even dismounted, they were upon him, old and young alike, their brown arms and legs slick and shiny with mosquito-repelling bear grease. He was surrounded by happy grins and a cacophony of the mostly unintelligible Shawnee tongue.

He'd never mastered more than a smattering of their language and could catch only a word here and there. He had memorized one phrase, though, that he used at these times. *"Ne wes hela shamamo, ne-kah-noh.* I am very well, my friend."

Then Drew spotted a couple of tall, darker men with woolly heads making their way through the throng; he was relieved to see that it was Black Bear and his father, Moses. Dressed like the other Indian men, both wore breechclouts and leggings and little else in this summer humidity.

As they broke through to the inner circle, Drew saw the much shorter Josie tucked at Bear's side. She, too, had on Indian garb, though the deerskin shift's fringes reached almost to her wrists and ankles. Very modest by Indian standards. Of the entire gathering, she was the only one not smiling. If anything, her great dark eyes held fear.

Had these people been mistreating her?

After the mandatory hugs and greetings with Bear and Moses, Drew nodded toward their *wigewa.* "Any hope we might talk privately?"

"My pleasure." Bear then lifted his voice and rattled off a string of Shawnee words.

After that, an Indian lad collected Smoky's reins to lead the gelding away, while the other people began to graciously step back to make a path for them, their parting words still friendly but less robust.

Ducking his head, Drew walked through the opening into Moses' bark-covered hut. It had only two sources of light—the uncovered doorway and the smoke hole above. Since Black Bear's mother died a number of years ago, the two had lived on the outer edge of the Indian village without a woman, cooking their own meals and trading with the squaws for their clothing.

Moses had never felt all that comfortable dwelling among the 'heathens,' as he always called them. He was a man without a country, in a manner of speaking, unable to return to his own kind because of their enslavement. Yet he couldn't accept many of the practices of the Shawnee. Still, the Shawnee respected him for his fairness and hunting ability and had allowed him to remain among them for almost twenty years.

"Sit yo'self down, boy," the graying man said, exposing a missing tooth. A few inches shorter than Drew, his shoulders were beginning to round and his lean frame was taking on a stringy look. With Drew's every return to the village, Moses seemed to age a mite more.

It was uncomfortably stuffy inside as Drew knelt down on the nearest buffalo-robe pallet.

Moses sat beside him, and Bear and Josie settled on the pallet across the empty fire pit from him.

"I'm real pleased," Drew said, "to see you two made it back here safe and sound."

Josie's eyes widened even more. "Are you alone?" she asked in a husky rush. "How many of 'em is after us? Is dey still a-lookin'?"

"No, no. Is that what you're worried about?"

"Ain't dat reason enough?" she retorted.

"Well, you can rest easy. Nobody's after you. No one ever was."

Bear wrapped his arm around Josie and hugged her close. "I tol' you, sugardrop. Drew wouldn't let 'em set the dogs on us."

"But I don' understan'. Fo' sure, Miss Crystabelle—"

"Miss Crystabelle," Drew finished for her, "loves you. She wouldn't want harm to come to you."

Pulling away from Bear, Josie sat up straight and stared unbelievingly at Drew.

"Fact is," he added, "Crysta's worries are that you're happy and well, that Bear here didn't drag you off agin your will in the middle of the night."

"I practically had to," Bear said, looking from Drew to the young woman.

"Is dat so?" Moses asked, his voice suddenly stern. "You tol' me she choosed to come with you."

"I did, Papa Moses." Josie smiled, reassuring the older man, and finally Drew saw her charming dimples. "I's just scared o' bein' caught."

Nodding, he grunted his agreement. As a runaway slave himself, Moses would know the terrors.

Josie relaxed against Bear's side again, and he kissed her temple. She smiled at him, a contented smile.

Their loving sentiments tore at Drew. In the space of only two days, they'd met, fallen in love, and vowed to devote the rest of their lives to each other . . . yet he wouldn't even allow himself to admit he loved Crysta—let alone tell her—for fear of being trapped. Fear, he hated to admit, was dictating every decision he made.

Crysta may have been jesting when she'd called him a coward, but that's what he'd become.

Josie's gaze suddenly flew across the space to Drew, as if she'd just remembered they had company. "Mistah Reardon, sir, if you wouldn't mind, I needs to hear about Miss Crysta. Did her pa catch up to her, or did she make it to your valley?"

The questions he dreaded were upon him. Drew corralled his features. "Aye. That she did. She's doin' a real fine job of teachin' at the new school. An' since Crysta's a young female, Brother Rolf insisted she live with him and his wife. The rest of the folks has taken to her, too. She's fittin' in just fine."

A scowl marred Josie's pretty round face. *"Crystabelle? By* herself in a backwoods settlement? She must'a got herself another slave."

"No. She's all alone." Confessing that Crysta was alone sent a twinge of guilt to Drew's heart.

"But dat gal cain't even get dressed by herself!"

Laughter burst from Drew as the comical sight of Crysta's first attempt flashed through his mind.

After a moment, Josie began giggling right along with him.

Bear and Moses exchanged confused frowns. Obviously neither understood the cause of their amusement.

Drew pulled himself together. "All of Crystabelle's day gowns required a second person to button and lace 'em up. It proved quite a problem for her the first mornin' after Bear and Josie disappeared." Another smile would not be stopped . . . Crysta coming into the inn's dining room, half buttoned and her hair falling down . . . those long silky strands catching fire wherever light touched them.

"And?" Bear prompted.

"And," he recouped, "Crystabelle promptly walked across the street and bought herself a homespun lace-front day gown."

"Crystabelle in homespun?" Dimples dented Josie's cheeks again. "I declare."

"She was determined to keep goin' with or without you. And you know how stubborn she can get when she sets her mind on somethin'."

"You seen dat in her, too?"

Josie's question piqued Bear's interest. "Got to know her right well, did ya?"

"Speakin' of gettin' to know someone," Drew countered, fleeing Bear's trap, "Brother Rolf is just as interested in Josie's welfare as you are in Crysta's. He told me to make sure you two was hitched proper in the sight of God. You are married, ain'tcha?"

Josie stiffened. *"Course we is.* Papa Moses said all da holy church words and we jumped da broom. Then Bear writed our names in da Bible."

"I knew you'd do everything right. That's what I told Brother Rolf and Crystabelle." *Blast*, he'd brought the conversation back to Crysta again. "What's for supper?" he asked, quickly changing the subject. "I'm hungry as a whole pack of wolves."

"Walk with me a spell?" Black Bear asked Drew, rising from the reed mat he'd been sitting on outside their hut. They'd just finished their meal of venison stewed with fresh squash and corn. "I needs to stretch mah legs."

Drew knew it was just a polite way of getting him alone. And he was just as eager to have a private conversation with Bear. "Sure thing." Coming to his feet, he addressed his hostess. "Josie, you cooked one fine meal."

Still eating, she looked up with a hesitant smile. "I thanks y'all, but I's still tryin' to get da hang o' cookin' Indian-style." She flitted a glance to the iron pot suspended over dying coals by a trio of greenwood poles.

"If you're happy here, Josie, you'll do just fine."

"Oh, I is, I is." She gazed up at Bear as if he were the earth, the moon, and the stars all rolled into one lone man.

And Bear wasn't doing any better as he reflected the same adoration back to her.

"And Papa Moses," she said, turning to the older man, sitting Indian-fashion a few feet away, "he helps me a lot, too. He's 'most as glad to have me here as Joshua."

"Dat's right," Moses grunted, still chewing on a tough piece of meat. Then he added good-naturedly, "We 'bout decided on keepin' her, even if she ain't no good at scrapin' hides."

In the deepening dusk, Drew followed Bear out of the village and into the woods. The crickets and the katydids had started their nightly screeching and the lightning bugs their flashing—sights and sounds as familiar as summer itself. But a wildcat's scream echoing from the next hollow was something he no longer heard east of Nashville.

Bear found a quiet spot beside the creek that Drew knew fed into the Whitewater, a tributary that, in turn, poured into the Ohio just below the white man's settlement of Cincinnati—Cincinnati, a place that less than a generation ago had been home to one of the largest Shawnee towns.

Bear sat on a log that had fallen halfway into the stream. An eddy of whirling ripples was caught in a crutch of the downed tree. Several small sticks spun in it, bumping into each other and bouncing away.

Drew picked a fairly flat rock to sit on, where he could watch the action while there was still enough light.

"Won't be long 'fore everything dis side o' da Mississip is gonna be overrun by white folks." Bear reiterated the statement Drew had made so many times the past couple of years.

"I know," Drew agreed as he picked up a stone and tossed it at the floating sticks.

"Now dat I seen some for m'self what lays t'other side o' da mountains, I understand what you been tellin' me. And I knows what we gotta do. I been talkin' to the chiefs. Next spring we's all packin' up an' movin' 'cross da big river. Maybe go up the Missouri aways, where you an' me talked about trappin' dis winter."

"That's the thing to do, 'cause there ain't no stoppin' the white folks. You 'n' me, we oughta head on out there right now, scout out a likely spot," Drew said, his spirits lifting for the first time since he'd left Crystabelle. "Supposed to be mostly Mandans up that way. The Frenchies say they're purty friendly."

"I cain't just up an' leave Josie. I thought you'd know that, Drew. Ever'thing's queer to her here, and 'sides, it ain't fittin' for a man to leave his wife da first year dey's married. It says so right in the Bible."

"Really? I don't recall that."

"Well, it says purty much da same thing. Says a man ain't supposed to go off to war dat first year. An' goin' out 'mongst da hostiles is just as dangerous."

Drew leveled his gaze on Bear in the near darkness. His friend must be plumb gone on Josie if he'd even twist the Scriptures into an excuse. And if that's the way of it, Drew wasn't about to hang around here the rest of the summer, watching those two lovebirds mooning over each other. Every time they hugged or kissed, he'd see in them, as clear as day, the yearning for Crysta he was trying to banish—Crysta, and the way she'd melted into his arms when he'd kissed her—her lips soft, seeking . . . the hurt and confusion in her eyes when he, the coward, rode away.

No. He couldn't stay here. Tomorrow morning he'd be riding on out at first light.

27

Crysta closed the Bible on the thirteenth chapter of First Corinthians. She gazed up past the surrounding dogwood trees to the boughs of a fragrant pine to listen to the chirping of a pair of sparrows.

A few branches below, a gray squirrel peeked at Crysta from around the dark bark of the trunk . . . in this quiet haven she'd been coming to since she confessed everything to Rolf and Inga.

"Thank you, Lord," she prayed as she sat on the three-legged stool she'd brought with her, "that the Bremmers live the love you speak about in Corinthians."

It had been three weeks to the day since she first told the Bremmers about herself, and as far as she knew they had graciously kept the information of her being a runaway bride to themselves. And their many kindnesses hadn't stopped there. Every evening Brother Rolf took the time to study the Scriptures with her, to answer the steady stream of questions brought on by her new and powerful hunger to learn more about Jesus.

Although she took advantage of their hospitality in that area, in all other things she was doing her best not to. She'd made a point of rising early every day to help Inga with the morning chores before coming to this secret spot. Of course, this hideaway wasn't nearly as lovely as Drew's glen, but it was within bell-ringing distance of the kitchen door. And, besides, even if the glen had been handy, it would only be a reminder of the day she and Drew almost kissed there . . . the week before he did kiss her, then left her standing alone as he rode out of her life.

Still, she could never hate him. The sorrow his leaving inflicted had brought her to the joy of the Lord—that same joy her sorrow threatened to steal every time she thought about him.

Quickly she rose. Picking up the stool, she started toward the back of the house, not allowing herself any more thoughts of him.

Just as Crysta reached the clearing, she saw a wagon and a team of horses pull alongside the house. The family she'd promised to sit with in church today then later join for dinner had arrived early, most likely to visit with the Bremmers. From what Inga had said, the Smiths were not only their closest neighbors but their closest friends, along with the Reardons.

Crysta, dressed in her gauzy yellow-and-white attire, was easily spotted by the visitors. The parents and their young daughter waved.

She returned the greeting before climbing over a split-rail meadow fence, careful not to snag her skirt on a splinter. This day gown would have to last her for the rest of the summer Sundays. She'd worn it for the last several services and intended to continue doing so despite her trunks of other clothes—she refused to flaunt her extensive wardrobe before women with so much less.

As Crysta crossed the cow pasture, the Smiths' child scrambled down the wagon wheel and came running toward her, looking like the flowers of the meadow in floral calico. "Miss Amherst! Miss Amherst! We're here!"

Laughing, Crysta shouted back at the delicate-featured girl who had legs as long as any colt's. "I see that!" Crysta had grown to love all her students this past month, but Liza was a particular joy. And this past week, she'd grown even more exuberant—her mother, after nine childless years, would be having a baby any day now.

Mr. Smith, a hulking man who would one day rival Brother Rolf's bulk, helped his wife from the wagon as if she were made of glass instead of flesh and bone and baby. His love for her and the expected little one was evident for all to see.

Crysta's melancholy returned momentarily—along with envy. Shaking off the mood, she reminded herself of the years the couple had waited for a second child, which allowed the Lord to fill her with gladness for them.

Then Liza slammed into her. "Guess what! Guess what!" the child cried, looking up at her with those large, down-slanted brown eyes that always seemed sad even when she laughed or was excited as she now was. "Guess!"

"Let's see," Crysta said, hugging her close. "I'm to sit with you in church and have dinner with you."

"*There's more.* Newcomb Auburn is coming for dinner, too." Her eyes were firefly bright. "Don't you think he's the handsomest fella in the valley? I'm gonna marry up with him soon as I'm old enough."

Crysta's own enthusiasm plummeted. She'd thought that for one Sunday she wouldn't have to be polite to some bachelor brother or oldest son. But it was not to be. Not with every wife in the valley intent on marrying her off. She could think of no good answer for the chatty child's question. Crysta reverted to Liza's last statement. "Don't you think Mr. Auburn is a bit old for you?"

"I'll be nine in January. And he told me I'm even purtier than my mama."

"La, that is a high compliment." Crysta caught Liza's hand.

"Come along. Let's go see if Mistress Bremmer has a cookie or two hidden out somewhere."

"Do you like flowers, Miss Amherst?" Newcomb Auburn asked with hopeful enthusiasm as the two rode into the Smiths' yard ahead of the family's wagon-and-farm team.

"Doesn't everyone?" she asked, her irritation with the rather thin young man barely in check. Not only had he wangled a dinner invitation out of the Smiths, but he'd taken it upon himself to have her horse saddled and waiting when Crysta came out of church. He no doubt had every intention of accompanying her home as well.

"I reckon. But you see, I purty much got my own house built, an' I been thinkin' on puttin' flower boxes at my windows like the ones here at the Smiths' and them at Brother Rolf's. Did I tell you my house is stone on the bottom half and real milled wood on the top?" The fine-boned fellow swung down from his mount. "Me an' Pa's the only masons twixt here an' Nashville. We traded two chimney jobs for the wood with a fellow what's puttin' up a sawmill."

Actually, for this side of the mountains, the details he related were quite impressive. Crysta hadn't seen a single dwelling of milled wood anywhere.

"Gonna get me some paint, too, next time we get back to Nashville." He reached up for her with hands that, for their slenderness, looked as if they'd picked up many a rough stone. "What color would a young lady like yourself be partial to?"

She hesitated to respond as she came down into his arms. This was not a question she felt comfortable answering, since he obviously hoped to entice her into living in this new home.

He did have a rather pleasing face, as Liza had pointed out, but he assumed too much, holding on to Crysta's waist beyond necessity, gazing at her with intent hazel eyes. "I was thinkin' maybe the color yellow like your dress."

She pushed back from him, forcing him to let go or appear ungentlemanly. Turning to the wagon that had come to a halt alongside her, she glanced up at the three Smiths sitting on the bench seat. "What hue do you think Mr. Auburn should paint his house?"

Liza sprang to her feet and crawled past her father to the edge. "Is that so, Newcomb? You're gonna have a painted house? I ain't never seen one! Make it pink, Newcomb. Pink like azaleas." She stepped out onto the wheel and thrust out her arms. "Here, Newcomb! Catch me!" she yelled and dove straight for him in a rainbow flash of calico.

Auburn had to scramble to catch the live, squealing cannonball.

Liza clasped her arms around Auburn's neck as if she intended to stay right with him.

That pleased Crysta immensely. The young man needed something else to concentrate on for a while.

As big, sandy-haired Mr. Smith had done earlier this morning, he helped his pregnant wife down with great care, setting her feet gently on the ground. He then turned to Mr. Auburn. "Newy, bring the horses on around to the barn. We'll water 'em 'fore we go in for dinner."

"An' you come along with me," Mistress Smith said to Crysta with that same sad-eyed smile her daughter had.

"What can I do to help with dinner?" Crysta asked, relieved to see her latest, most persistent suitor gather up the reins of the two mounts.

With Liza still perched on his arm, he ambled away with their host.

Coming into the Smith house, Crysta's attention was immediately caught by the fact that, though the rest of the furniture was simply made, their dining-room table and chairs had been carved by craftsmen . . . not the rarer cherrywood of the set at the Clay house, but still, the grainier oak had its charm.

"Ah, you noticed my table," her hostess said, coming alongside Crysta in a simple but generously gathered and high-waisted day gown of cool blue dimity. "My family gave us the set as our weddin' gift. Kenny toted it all the way over the mountains for me, and there wasn't no easy wagon road back then. That's how important it was to us. You see, my mama always said a family is built around the dinner table." Her expression warmed as she put her hands on her ripe belly. "An' in a few days we'll have another chair to fill."

"I couldn't be happier for you." Crysta glanced back at the table, already set with dishes of earthenware. The only difference from the Bremmers' dishes was a cobalt blue border. "I'd never given a thought to families and the dinner table. But it makes perfect sense. The table's the gathering place where the family prays together and talks about the happenings of the day. At least, that's what I've noticed since I came here. Until I was twelve, my brothers and I were fed at an earlier hour than when my parents dined." Small wonder, Crysta now realized, that her closest bond had always been with her brothers, not her parents. Before she started dwelling on whether or not her family had received the letter she'd sent a few weeks ago, she said, "Tell me what I can do to help with the meal. I'm not the most efficient person around the kitchen, but I'm learning."

Mistress Smith chuckled lightly as she moved awkwardly toward a worktable near the hearth that was loaded with napkin-covered food. "That's what Inga told me. But she says you're tryin' hard, specially with the bakin' you been doin' for the young'uns. With all them goodies you bring to the school, it's easy to see why they've taken to you so."

"And I love all of them. Even the Dagget twins, for all their pranks. One of them brought a garter snake to school last week to scare the girls. But Otto disposed of it for me before someone stomped the poor thing to death."

"Those twins are real good at pranks. Liza come home and tol'" me all about it." From a hook beside the worktable, she removed a full apron. "Here. You don't wanna mess up that purty dress."

"Oh, thank you, Mistress Smith."

"Please call me Betsy. Ever'body does."

There was something in Betsy Smith's gentle lilting voice and those naturally sympathetic eyes that removed all the awkwardness of a first visit. She was someone a person could talk plainly to. "Speaking of my dress," Crysta began as she thrust her arms through the cross straps of the sackcloth apron, "I've noticed that the young unmarried misses don't smile at me or come up to talk at church anymore. I can't help wondering if it's because the bachelors have turned their attentions to me because of my clothes."

"This needs to go to the table," Betsy said, her brows stitched in thought as she handed Crysta a platter of fried chicken. "I hope you don't mind cold meat. It's a mite hot and sticky to start a fire in the middle of the day." She picked up a plate of sliced raw vegetables. "I'm sure you're right about the fellas. They always got to check out any new miss what moves to the neighborhood. But with them fancy clothes and your purty face, you're purely too much competition for the other gals."

"That's what I was afraid of. But I have what I hope is a solution. I've counted four marriageable young women, so I was thinking of giving each of them one of my day gowns to alter for themselves. And, of course, the bonnets to match."

"Oh my, that *is* generous. To be able to give away that many purty outfits, you must have a treasure trove of clothes."

"Far more than I need. But I don't quite know how to go about approaching the girls—I don't want to offend them, have them thinking they would be accepting charity."

"I figure if it's handled right, they'll be pleased as punch," Betsy said with enthusiasm as she placed the cut vegetables on the table beside the fried chicken. It was obvious where Liza got her cheery disposition. "How about I invite them over here for a little tea party. Tell 'em you could use some hard cash, that you'd be willin' to sell a few dresses for, say, two bits apiece; then it would be like they was buyin' 'em."

"La, that's a splendid idea!" Crysta said as they walked back for more food. It wouldn't quite be an outright gift. "And thank you so much for your kind offer."

"No, I thank you. Most folks what come west of the mountains don't bring much in the way of fancies. Them frocks'll make them gals feel real special. But don't forget to save the purtiest for yourself." Then Betsy grinned. "A bride always wants to look her best on her wedding day."

Little Liza came running through the doorway. She stopped in her tracks. "Are you gettin' married, Miss Amherst? Delia Clay said you was marryin' up with her pa. But Otto said she was lyin'. Are you?"

"No, dear. A woman who weds a farmer leads a very, very busy life. I would have to give up teaching at the school, and I would miss all of you too much to do that. Maybe I'll think about marrying in a few years, after another schoolteacher moves to the valley."

Liza's eyes widened. "They ain't never gonna be another teacher like you. Ever'body says so. Promise me. Don't marry till I'm all growed an' gone."

"It's not your place to ask someone to make that kind of promise," Betsy reprimanded in her airy voice. "None of us knows what blessin's the Lord may have waitin' for us tomorrow or next week, let alone years down the road. Now, go back outside and wash the horse smell off your hands."

"And, besides," Betsy continued, leveling a knowing smile on Crysta after the child disappeared out the door, "for all we know, Drew Reardon might bring his handsome self back here any day now. Even a fool could see that skittery buck was as taken with you as you was with him."

"I never—," Crysta started to protest. But from the intuitive woman's expression, it was obvious Betsy had either been talking about her with Inga or had simply seen right through her.

Betsy patted Crysta's arm as she passed by. "No, you ain't done or said nothin'. But love's the hardest thing on God's green earth to hide." Betsy pulled a pitcher of fruit punch from a sawdust-filled cooler and handed it to Crysta. "And even if Drew don't come back, don't you let one of them young bucks around here talk you into settlin' for anything less. If you're meant to marry, the good Lord has some fella picked out who's just perfect for you, like Kenny is for me. I hope it's a man here in these parts, but if it ain't, you just wait on the Lord. He'll let you know who it is."

Those were the very thoughts Crysta had had this morning in her quiet place. As if God himself were repeating it so she wouldn't forget. Pitcher in hand, she caught hold of Betsy and gave her a resounding hug. "Thank you. You don't know how much I needed to hear that."

Just then, Betsy's own big fella walked in with Newcomb Auburn.

No longer the least irritated with the younger man, Crysta turned and smiled at them both. How could she be perturbed when the Lord was taking such good care of her?

28

Drew lazed beneath a crusty-barked cottonwood, watching the ferry cross from the eastern bank of the wide Tennessee. The raft inched slowly toward him, pulled along by a thick rope looped to a mule-driven wheel at the far bank. Loaded down with half a dozen men and horses, the crossing would take extra time—plenty of time to rest himself and ol' Smoky in the noonday shade.

He lay back on the cool grass and closed his eyes.

The return trip across the water would be quicker, since he and Smoky would be the only passengers.

He was getting used to being alone. Just him and his horse for weeks now. First, going north across the Ohio River to Black Bear's village. Then when he'd started for Cincinnati to see if he could hook up with another partner, his guilt over deserting Crysta had gotten the best of him. There had been no way he could go trapping or trading this winter until he made sure Crystabelle's pa wasn't going to catch up to her.

Drew had had one piece of luck, though, when he'd run across

Grady Jessup on the Nashville trail. From the Reardon Valley man, he'd learned that Crysta was still safe, freeing him from the treacherous task of riding in and seeing her face-to-face. So he'd ridden past the valley cutoff instead of heading home as he had planned. Still . . . the first ten miles past that point on the trail had been the hardest he had travelled since he left her the first time.

Now his task was simple. He was retracing their steps back to North Carolina. He'd learn whether Mr. Amherst had even tracked her as far as Salem. If not, Drew would feel free to go on his way.

But if Mr. Amherst was still scouring the countryside for his daughter . . . well, Drew would cross that bridge if and when he reached it.

Something made a loud splash in the water. Opening his eyes, Drew sat up. He saw that nothing was near enough to have made the noise. Then a huge catfish leapt from the water after a beetle and belly flopped down again, missing its snack.

The thought of fried fish sent a pang of hunger to his stomach. Maybe the tavern up the road would be serving fish this eve. But for now . . .

Drew eased up to his feet and sauntered to his tethered horse, where he retrieved some jerky. Not as tasty as catfish, but it would do.

He glanced back at the ferry and saw that it would land in a minute or so. He noticed that the men aboard were heavily armed with braces of pistols in their waistbands and rifles scabbarded on their mounts—a hunting party of some sort. Because of the lack of pack animals to haul their kills, Drew surmised they were headed into Indian territory.

Lord, he prayed, *I sure do hope they're not plannin' to stir up trouble. This is the first year in a long time there ain't been no trouble anywhere this side of the mountains. Even up north.* He looked heavenward. *And I'd like it to stay that way.*

When the raft nudged into the bank, the group hurried to debark.

Drew stayed back as they unloaded their horses, giving them plenty of room. Seconds later, the men were mounted and riding up the bank at a clod-flying gallop.

"Anyone else 'sides you a-waitin'?" asked the husky lad in charge of the raft.

"No," Drew said, still watching the riders as he brought Smoky forward. "Most folks is smarter'n me and that bunch, layin' low in this heat."

Shucking off his floppy hat, the kid pulled a bandana from his shirt pocket and wiped the sweat from his brow. "Hope you're right. Sun sure beats down on a fella out there on the water. They say it's pert'near September, so I reckon this heat won't last too much longer." He beckoned Drew with his hat. "Let's get on back. I got some cider coolin' in the water on the other side."

No sooner had Drew coaxed Smoky onto the log raft than the lad used his red-print kerchief to signal across the river to the mule driver.

The ferry lurched and began floating away from the bank. The kid then picked up a long pole he used to deflect debris coming down the river and took his place near the wrist-thick rope threading through an iron ring.

"Any other news," Drew asked, "'sides the fact it's almost September?" Folks working along the main roads always knew everything first. "Heard anything about statehood for Tennessee?"

"Nay. My Grampa don't think they're gonna give it to us this year." Narrowing his eyes, the lad studied Drew a second. "You look familiar. Didn't you come through here two, three months ago?"

"Aye. We was comin' back from Carolina."

"Whereabouts you live? Out Nashville way?"

"About three days short of there. Place called Reardon Valley."

"You don't say . . ." The kid glanced back to the shore they'd just departed. "That's where that pack is headed. They're lookin' for some rich runaway bride."

Crysta.

Drew wheeled around, then caught himself before he dove for shore.

What a fool he'd been not to question those men. "Can you get this raft goin' in the other direction?"

"You mean go back?"

"Aye. I'll give you four bits."

"I guess I can try. But only if I can get Grampa to notice. He's half blind and hard a hearin'." The lad pulled out his bandana and started waving it back and forth.

On the distant shore, the old man never looked up from where he sat on a stump, lazily snapping a whip over the mules' backs.

Drew started shouting and waving his arms.

The kid helped out.

Still the lad's grandfather never turned their way.

There wasn't time for this. Drew pulled his rifle from its sheath as he unsnagged the string to his powder horn. Bracing himself against the lapping current, he uncorked and poured powder into his flashpan then, raising the barrel skyward, pulled the trigger.

That got the old man's attention. And after a few of the kid's hand signals, he lumbered to his feet and reversed the direction the mules were trudging.

"Did ya forget somethin' back there?" the lad asked.

"More or less."

More or less. Those had been the first words he ever used to tease Crysta. He had to beat those men to the valley, warn her. He could not fail.

Then what?

Drew concentrated on the kid again. "Did they say anything else?" Pulling some coins from a small pouch tucked inside his shirt, he handed an entire dollar to the lad. "Tell me everything they said."

The kid looked greedily at the coin, then bit it just to make sure it was real, before giving Drew a crooked-toothed smile. "I only talked to one of 'em. He said he hired on with the girl's pa in Virginy back in June. And he's been ridin' with him and her betrothed ever since."

"Since June? And they're just now gettin' to here?"

"Seems they been on a big wild-goose chase. They been all the way down to Savannah in Georgia. From what he said, the gal rented some horses overmountain in Salem-town an' told the owner she was goin' thataway. Wasn't till some fella from Knoxville brought the horses back that them fellas found out where she really went."

"Speakin' of horses, I need a couple of swift ones. Tell me quick, who's got the fastest mounts west of the river?"

"Don't forget to practice your letters now, you hear?"

Otto's reminder almost brought tears to Crysta's eyes as he slapped the rump of the last child-stacked horse to leave school. In six short weeks, he'd gone from being the Dagget twins' cohort to a responsible young man, right before her eyes.

Today's class had been the final session for the next month or so. As she and Otto saw the children off, she already missed them.

But it was harvesttime. The students would not return until after all the fields in the valley were harvested and the cash crops floating downriver to Nashville. Every able body would be helping. Even some who weren't quite so able, she mused as she watched the youngest of the three riders, the child's skirts all bunched around her as she clung to her older sister. They rode an old plow nag, which would also be put to work again.

Realizing she and Otto were merely standing in the dusty road gawking, she whirled around. "Time to finish up. Everything goes back to the teacher's cabin."

Otto caught up to her. "You want me to bust down the tables for you first?" He referred to the cumbersome contraptions of boards nailed across barrelheads. "They won't take up so much room that way."

"Why don't you go ask your father? He'll know better if he has a use for them during the fall recess."

While the big-footed lad ran down the road to the smithy, Crysta gathered up an armload of books and carried them out back to the cabin that would have been hers had she been a man.

The last thought brought on a grin and a chuckle. The Crystabelle who first started overmountain to Tennessee would have insisted on living in that cabin, demanding those rights Miss Wollstonecraft had written about. And if she had, she would have missed living with the boisterous, loving Bremmers, not to mention having the benefit of their monitoring the bachelors who "happened by" two or three evenings every single week.

Now, as she glanced around the one-room cabin, she envisioned a much different purpose for it . . . a partition for a storeroom on one side and on the other, shelves built for her books and hopefully books donated by neighbors. A start to a lending library . . . *if* she were allowed to stay.

Since the day Rolf sent his letters of inquiry to cities in the East asking for interested teachers to respond, he'd not spoken another word on the subject.

After six weeks, he should agree that not only was no one coming after her, but there'd scarcely been time for his letters to reach many of their destinations—surely not enough for replies. Besides, from what Brother Rolf said, the postrider who brought mail by here on his way to Nashville did so only once every two or three months.

She took an encouraging breath. The valley's men would surely let her remain through the winter, even if Brother Rolf told them how she came to be here. She truly felt the Lord had brought her here for not only herself but also for the children of these families.

As Crysta stacked the second load of writing supplies into hinge-lidded boxes, Rolf and Otto shuffled through the doorway toting a table.

"Ve chust bring dem over today," Brother Rolf said as they set it down against the back wall. "Ve can decide vat to do *mit* da tables later."

As he lumbered around to follow Otto out for the next one, Crysta stopped him. "Brother Rolf, I would like to take this opportunity to thank you for the tremendous help you and Otto have been here at the school. I, for one, think our first session was an unequivocal success. And I also want to thank you for making me feel such a blessed part of your family. You have no idea how much I treasure that. I spent most of my last four years away at school. And even when I was home, well, just let me say, it wasn't anything like being here with all of us pulling together."

Brother Rolf's big arms reached out and folded her into a fatherly hug. Then he set her at arm's length, peering down at her with those sharp blue eyes. "You are goot girl, Crystabelle." Then he glanced out the door in the direction Otto had gone before returning his attention to her. "I haf somet'ing to say to you, too. Me *und* Inga talked, *und* ve decide if you don't vant to tell nobody you are da runavay bride, den ve not say anyt'ing either. If your papa does not come to get you before vinter, da teaching job is yours."

Crysta flung her arms around his thick neck. "Truly? You mean it?"

"*Ja, ja.*" He sounded almost embarrassed as he pulled her away. "Unless you'd rather . . ."

"Rather what?" Was he going to ask her to tell the other people?

"I been meaning to tell you—Baxter Clay come by da odder day to haf da shoes put on his horse *und* . . ." He hesitated.

"Yes, I know," she prompted. "He rode in with his children."

"Vell," Rolf said, drawing out the word, "he says he is coming by dis evening, if dat is all right *mit* me. He vant to ask you to marry him."

Crysta stepped back. "Oh, dear. I've been so careful not to give any of the men the notion that I'm interested in them."

Brother Rolf shrugged. "You haf to understand, he is not da carefree young buck like da odders. He needs a vife in da vorst vay. He already gives more time dan he can spare to come courting you."

"But—"

Brother Rolf placed a stilling finger to her lips. "He says he is villing to let you teach school until you haf a baby of your own."

"But I don't love him. I feel sorry for him and his children, but I don't love him."

Holding her in a steady stare, he nodded. "Inga, she does not luf me ven her folks first give her to me. But I chust keep on lufing her till she luf me back."

But what if she didn't learn to care for Baxter Clay? Betsy Smith's advice slammed through her brain. *Don't settle for less than love. Don't settle.* "I'm pleased for you and Inga. But that doesn't always happen. My father's sister never has come to love her husband. Now he spends all his free time in Williamsburg, and Aunt Charlotte mostly keeps herself shut away in her room."

Brother Rolf huffed out a breath. "Do vat you vill. But I t'ink you bedder go be alone *und* pray about dis before da poor man comes. You listen to da Lord long *und* hard before you refuse him."

Crysta didn't want to disappoint Brother Rolf, but as he walked out of the cabin, all she could think about was Betsy Smith and the baby boy she'd borne last week. How they'd all laughed over its lusty cry when Crysta had accompanied the Bremmers for a visit.

But most of all, she remembered the tender glances that had passed between Betsy and her husband.

Don't settle. Don't.

Crysta clutched her hands together as she started for the entrance. She would pray as she promised, but at the moment, the last thing she wanted was a marriage proposal from Mr. Clay.

Just as she reached the doorway, Brother Rolf turned back to her.

Had he left some point in Clay's favor unsaid?

"Looks like Baxter is already here. Dere is two horses tied outside da house. He probably brings his *kinder mit* him." The stout man brought forth what Crysta thought was a thoroughly misplaced chuckle. "I bet he t'inks you vill not be able to say no *mit* his *kinder* standing dere. You take all da time you need to pray. I vill keep him busy till you come."

Steeling herself for a most difficult situation, Crysta looked past Brother Rolf. And frowned. "That's not the kids' horse."

The slamming of the Bremmers' front door diverted Crysta's attention to the porch. Then she saw the visitor. Tall, lean, broad-shouldered, and blond. Ike? Noah? She stepped past Rolf for a better view.

Spotting Crysta, the man hurried toward her. It wasn't either of the older Reardon brothers. *It was Drew!*

She stopped breathing. He'd come back. He was back!

Reaching her in a mad rush, he grabbed her arms. "Crysta. Thank God, I got to you first. Your pa . . . men . . . they're comin'. Can't be more'n o' couple hours behind me."

29

Crystabelle stared back at Drew, her dazed gaze locked onto his, reminding him of a deer's the instant after it had been shot. "Please don't say that."

He felt her starting to sink and tightened his grip on her arms. "It's true. I passed the search party on the road when they stopped for the night. I rode in the darkness for several extra hours to put more distance between them an' me."

"But how do you know it's my father?"

"And your betrothed," he added, wishing he'd taken a closer look at the men in the group. "A ferry operator told me about 'em. Said they'd been all the way to Georgia lookin' for you. The others looked like seasoned slavers."

"Oh my . . ." Her eyes rolled backward.

"*Crystabelle.*" He gave her a shake. "This is no time to faint."

Her attention focused on him again. "Yes." She inhaled deeply. "Absolutely. I'll need to pack as much as I can carry. And saddle my horse. Oh, but I do wish I'd traded my sidesaddle for a man's. How far behind did you say they were?"

Drew cringed at the thought that he'd ever left Crystabelle to face this probability by herself . . . her riding off, a beautiful woman alone, with a single-minded tracking party racing after her.

Brother Rolf stepped close and placed a hand on Crysta's shoulder, saying what Drew should have said. "You need to stop *und* pray about dis. Running avay only delays da problem."

Drew was fully aware of the truth of that, since he'd done that very thing only to come face-to-face with the consequences at the ferry crossing. "Crysta, I know you'll think this strange comin' from me, but Brother Rolf is right. These are very determined men."

"It's been almost three months since I ran away. I can't believe Papa would stay gone from the plantation this long, or from Mama, just to search for me." Her voice, which had been close to a whine, now hardened as she hiked her chin. "But I can't marry Harland Chastain. I won't. I don't trust him. Though he makes an effort to appear charming, he can be quite ruthless."

If she didn't want to marry this fancy Easterner, Drew would see to it she didn't have to. He had done nothing but think about her situation the whole ride back here. And he'd come up with what seemed the only solid solution. At the thought, his heart started banging against his breastbone. He inhaled a strengthening lungful of air, gaining the courage to say his next words.

Rolf spoke ahead of him. "Remember vat ve vas talking about, Crystabelle? Baxter Clay? He is goot Christian man. Kind to his *kinder und* his livestock. *Und* he come from da same kind of people dat you do. If you marry vit him, your papa cannot give you to da odder man. 'Vat Got has put togedder, let no man put asunder.'"

Crysta stared at the minister, her lips parted.

Watching the play of emotion in her eyes, Drew couldn't believe she was actually considering the idea. He cupped her chin, turned her to face him. "Don't do this to yourself. Don't bury yourself with a widower and four children—unless . . ." He had to know. "Do you love him?"

Her breath caught. "No . . . but—"

"Then don't marry the man," he urged, relief and resolve flowing through him. "Marry me."

"*What?*"

"*Vat?*" Rolf boomed right after.

But the two of them weren't any more shocked than Drew had been this morning when he first hit upon the idea. But the more he'd mulled it over, the more credible it seemed.

Still holding on to Crysta, he started pulling her toward the cabin doorway. "Brother Rolf, would you please excuse us a moment? I'd like to speak to Miss Amherst alone."

As soon as they were out of sight of Brother Rolf, Crysta turned on Drew. "If this is another of your jokes, this is hardly the right time."

"Nay," Drew protested with what looked like absolute sincerity. "I thought it all through on the way here. Don't you see? If we marry, they won't be able to take you back to Virginia. You can go right on teaching like you been doin' this summer."

She reared back her chin. "And you? What would *you* be doing?"

"Me? Why, I'd just go on as I always have. Huntin' and explorin'."

It was all so bizarre. How often in the most secret reaches of her heart had she envisioned Drew Reardon dashing back from the wilds, whisking her off her feet with proclamations of his undying love and assurances that he couldn't live without her. But here he was, proposing marriage just as if it were another of his bargains with her. He was not asking her to marry him because he loved her. He didn't want to make a life with her. He was merely taking it upon himself to come to her rescue one more time. Like the hero he surely must think he is. But this was not merely a rescue. . . . "This would tie us together for life. Surely you've considered that."

Her statement barely fazed him. "It doesn't have to. Not if we don't think of it that way. You told me yourself, you didn't want to become some man's chattel, and, as you know, I don't want to be burdened with chattel of any sort myself."

"Ah, I see." Weeks of romantic illusions disintegrated one by one in Crysta's heart as his personal motive became clear. "If you're no longer a bachelor, your family shan't be able to continue pressuring you to marry." Her "hero" was really quite despicable. With supreme effort, she smoothed her features, not wanting him to suspect her anger or the pain he'd caused her. She affected her most airy tone of voice. "Well, that all sounds so reasonable, so logical. But I'm most pleased to say, I no longer fear marriage. Since I've been living here in the valley, I've seen love and marriage in a new light. I do hope to wed one day to a man I can love and respect as much as he does me. If I married you, that would dash my hopes."

Drew caught her hand. "Not necessarily."

Did he think she was about to flee? She couldn't read his intent expression. A last ember of hope flickered to life again. Perhaps he was going to say more, tell her he loved her, wanted her for his wife. That he'd give up his lust for wandering and stay with her. Almost afraid to hope, yet afraid not to, she braced herself. "What do you mean?"

He paused, dropped her hand. His gaze, becoming somewhat self-conscious, slid away. "As long as we don't live together as man and wife," he said in a strained tone she couldn't quite decipher, "the marriage could be annulled later."

"Annulled . . ."

He made a pitiable attempt at a smile, then shrugged. But it was a rather stiff effort.

Crysta's spirit plummeted to her feet. She was beginning to wonder if she would survive this day of one crushing blow after another. She pushed past Drew. She needed to get out of this room.

264

To breathe, think, get away from his overpowering presence, the nearness of this one she'd so longed to have return to her. But not like this. Never like this. "If you'll excuse me, I must be by myself for a few minutes. I really need to pray. This is too much to sort out without the Lord's guidance."

The second she was out the door, she picked up her skirts and sprinted for her wooded haven.

"Don't stay long," he called after her. "We don't have much time."

Drew watched as she bolted from him, her blue-and-gray-striped skirts flying out behind her. He'd thought that God had been with him in his wild dash to reach her. But was his chore, in reality, only that of message bearer?

What did God truly think of his proposal? Probably no more than what Brother Rolf would think of it. Drew had known better than to present the details of his marriage proposal in front of the minister.

But to have Crystabelle wed Baxter Clay . . . or one of the young whippersnappers here in the valley? That was as unthinkable as having her dragged back to marry a man who frightened her. "Because, God, you know she don't scare easy," he said aloud and started out the door after her. He'd better speak to her again, tell her how much he needed for her to be safe and happy.

"Vere is Crystabelle going?"

Drew had forgotten about Brother Rolf.

The minister hurried toward him from beneath the shade of an elm, where he'd undoubtedly been waiting.

"She said she wanted to go pray."

"Goot. A voman *mit* three men vanting to marry her on da same day has much to pray about. You stay here," he ordered. "Let her be."

Although reluctant to comply, Drew remained where he stood. "Ten minutes. If she's not back in ten minutes, I'm goin' after her."

"In da meantime, I t'ink maybe you need to pray about dis, too. Dat is a fine girl. She is luffing da Lord *mit* all her heart since she come to live *mit* us. Inga *und* me, ve care about her like she is our own daughter."

Drew hated being preached to. "I *have* been prayin'. From the minute I learned that her pa and that man he betrothed her to were on their way here. I am *not* the heathen you take me for."

Brother Rolf's mouth fell open. He lumbered over to Drew and clapped an arm around him. "I know you are da goot man . . . a better man dan you t'ink. I am chust waiting for you to find dat out for yourself." He gave Drew's shoulder a squeeze. "Come *mit* me to da house. Haf a cool glass of buddermilk. Sit down, rest a minute. From da lat'er on your horses, you been ridin' dem hard."

Drew glanced back to where Crysta had disappeared into the trees, then attempted a nonchalant shrug. "I reckon I could use somethin' cool to drink."

As they walked toward the house, Otto slammed out of one of the church outhouses. He spotted them. "Drew! You're back!" The big kid came running toward them. "Are those your horses by the front porch?" he sputtered, catching up. "Where's Smoky? Is he hurt?"

Drew was in no mood to appease Otto's curiosity. "Smoky's fine. I'll ride back and pick him up in a few days."

"Where is he? Where you been?"

"Let da poor man catch his breath," Otto's pa interceded. "Drew needs to cool off."

"Where's Miss Crysta? Does she know Drew's here?"

"*Ja.* She be along in a minute."

She'd better be, Drew thought as he took a last glance in her direction before walking up the Bremmers' porch steps.

"Inga," Brother Rolf called as they filed through the front door and headed toward the kitchen at the rear. "Inga, ve got company."

"Papa, don't you remember? She was riding over to the Smiths' soon as school let out."

Drew breathed a little easier knowing the woman was gone. Inga was not one to mince words, and Drew knew she would've had plenty to say about this business between him and Crysta.

"Otto, run out to da springhouse *und* fetch in da buddermilk. *Und* be kvick!"

Rolf didn't have to hurry him—the flush-faced towhead slammed out at a dead run. The sooner he came back, the sooner he could ask more questions.

Within a couple of minutes, the three were settled on chairs in the shade of the covered porch, tall glasses in hand. Drew took a deep swallow of the refreshing drink, trying to relax. Still, he noticed every creaking porch board, every bird's chirp.

Otto, though, took only one big gulp before he started rattling on again. "You should've hung around here, Drew. There's been so much going on. You wouldn't believe how much this porch has been used lately. For courting, I mean. Mr. Clay's coming by this evening. Ain't he, Papa?" The lad glanced fleetingly at Rolf, sitting between them. "No more'n a day goes by that there ain't some fella parked out here, sweet-talking Miss Crysta. Fact is, for a while they flat quit all the other gals and was just coming here. And do you know what Miss Crysta did about it?"

Drew wasn't sure if he wanted to know.

But Otto didn't wait for his reply. "She gave some of her fancy dresses to the other gals, just so's the fellas would start noticing them again. Didn't do much good, though, cuz there ain't no one purty as Miss Crystabelle, no matter what they wear."

"Sounds like a real entertainin' summer," Drew said out of the barest politeness. It wasn't as if he hadn't known that once he was out of the way, the bachelors would start coming. But Crysta had always maintained she didn't want to marry . . . at least till today.

Did she already have a husband in mind? Someone besides Baxter Clay?

Drew lunged to his feet. "We're runnin' out of time here. I need to get an answer."

"Sit down," Brother Rolf ordered. "It is only five minutes. Check da mantel clock if you don't believe me. It say a quarter past two ven ve come in."

Peering through the open window, Drew saw that the simple oak timekeeper marked 2:21. Reluctantly, he retook his seat. "Four more minutes."

"Then what?" Otto asked. "What's going on?"

Rolf exchanged glances with Drew, then rested his head back against the house's log wall. "I t'ink dis is for Drew to explain."

"There ain't enough time." He couldn't deal with some inquisitive lad. *Not now.* He came to his feet again and strode to the side of the porch where he had a view of the back meadow.

"Is somebody sick? Or hurt?" Otto wasn't giving up.

"Boy, quit badgering da man," his father ordered gruffly. "Drew asked Crystabelle to marry him, *und* he vaits for da answer."

Otto sprang to his feet and rushed to Drew's side. "Is that so? But, Drew, you always said you didn't want to be tied down to some female. That you're a hunter and an explorer."

"Well," Drew practically growled at the kid, "I reckon I talk too much."

Then he saw her.

She emerged from the woods, the gray-and-blue stripes of her dress a subtle contrast against the fading greens of late summer. But her auburn hair caught fire in the sunlight. Her expression, though, he couldn't read at all.

He leapt off the porch to go meet her.

The blasted kid was right behind him.

Miffed, Drew slowed his pace. No sense making a fool of himself, since he wouldn't be able to say much with Otto tagging along. He caught the overeager kid's shirttail, slowing him down, too.

When Crystabelle reached them, she seemed much calmer than when she'd left to go pray. Almost aloof, if the truth be told. Her decision had obviously been made.

Drew couldn't summon the courage to inquire.

Otto didn't have that problem, however, and jumped in with both of his big feet. "Well? What did you decide? Are you going to marry him or not?"

Stiffening, Crysta clasped her hands together and shot Drew an appalled expression.

Still speechless, he only managed a nervous, I-didn't-tell-him roll of the eyes.

Crysta stared at him a moment longer—a pinning stare—then turned to Otto. "I've made a decision. But I'd rather wait until we reach the house. I don't want to have to say this more than once."

30

"Please, could we go inside?" Crysta asked, noting a wagon pulling up to Bailey's store just down the way. "I'd rather not talk about this out here in sight of anyone who rides in." Without waiting for a response, she walked to the front door.

"What is there to talk about?" Otto asked, his youthful square face one of consternation as she passed by him.

Drew hooked an arm in Otto's and practically dragged the boy into the house.

Brother Rolf followed close behind. "Sit in da parlor," he said, pointing to the simple wood chairs and bench, which were softened with cotton pillows of bright prints.

But no one responded. They all stood in the center of the room on the large rag rug and stared at her.

She seemed to be the only calm person in the room, however tentative that composure might be in light of what she was about to say. "Please," she urged, taking one of the chairs positioned around an iron-legged tea table.

Drew claimed the seat next to her, and the Bremmers crowded onto the opposite bench. No one said anything—not even Otto. They just continued to eye her.

The room seemed to shrink. Crysta's hands grew moist, and her cool assurance began to melt. "First," she announced in a breathy voice that she had to pump more air into, "I want to say that I feel the Lord's leading in this decision. So I truly cannot make another."

"*Und* vat is dat, child?" Brother Rolf's heavy features appeared as serious as her own mood. She knew her spiritual well-being was of prime importance to him.

"I am to marry . . ." She turned her attention to Drew, the one who had the right to know her decision first.

There was actually fear in his dove gray eyes. Was he afraid she'd say yes—or no? He leaned forward slightly.

"I shall wed Drew."

He sucked in a breath. Then shot to his feet. "*Now,* Brother Rolf. The wedding needs to be performed at once."

"*Right here, this minute?*" Otto asked, more confused than ever.

Ignoring his son, the frowning minister glanced from Drew to Crysta. "Is it sure in your heart dat Andrew Reardon is da goot Lord's choice for you?"

Crysta rose and moved to Drew's side, taking his arm. "The Lord didn't audibly speak the words to me. But, strangely enough, that was the only answer that gave me peace."

"I surely do hope you interpret Got's vill da right vay." Brother Rolf still sounded dubious.

"*She did,*" Drew retorted with force. "Now, please say the words, and let's get the certificate signed and stamped."

Otto stepped into the fray. "Ain't we even gonna wait for Mama?"

Crysta couldn't help but take pity on the perplexed lad. She brushed aside a hank of hair drooping over one of his eyes.

"Dearest Otto, my father is coming here this very afternoon to take me back to Virginia. If I do not marry Drew before he arrives, I'll be forced to go with him."

Bafflement still clouded Otto's sky blue eyes. "Once your papa hears about what a fine school you and me made, I'll bet he won't make you go."

"As wonderful as our school is," Crysta replied in a placating tone, "I'm afraid that will be of little consequence to him. You see, he has promised me to someone in marriage. He and his friend, Mr. Chastain, have signed an agreement. Money and lands have changed hands."

"And," Drew added with finality, "Chastain is with her pa."

"Oh." Otto nodded. No more explanations were needed.

"Vell, best ve get on *mit* dis in all haste den." Brother Rolf walked to the mantel and picked up his Bible. "Andrew, take Crystabelle's hand . . . *if* you two are sure. *Und* Otto, you be da vitness."

Before Crysta even had a chance to check her hair in a mirror, she found herself facing Drew, both her hands folded within his . . . her hands, which had been clammy mere moments ago, now icy. It was as if the blood had drained from her entire body.

Was her decision truly from God? Or merely her own willful desire? She glanced up at Drew and saw he was gazing at her.

Squeezing her hands gently, he offered that crooked grin of his and nodded.

That small sign of assurance infused her with courage, and the peace she'd felt while praying descended upon her again. Everything would be fine. Just fine.

Drew still had a problem believing he was standing here, the bridegroom, as Brother Rolf recited the wedding ritual, and that he'd said "I do" in the appropriate place. Promising to cherish Crysta, however, took no effort at all.

The minister now came to Crysta's vows. "Do you, Crystabelle Amherst, promise to love, honor, and obey, for better or worse, richer or poorer, in sickness and in health, till death do you part?"

Drew held his breath. She wasn't being asked to cherish, but to honor and *obey*. That one word could bring a halt to this vital proceeding. No matter what the two of them had agreed upon, he knew how that would stick in her craw.

She gazed up at him, and for the first time since he'd arrived, he saw her cheeks plump in a bit of a smile. She either recognized the humor in the moment or saw his panic. Regardless, she answered, "I do."

Releasing his pent-up breath, Drew tried to return her smile, but he was too full of emotion.

"*Mit* da power vested in me by Got *und* da Territory of Tennessee, I now pronounce you man *und* vife. Andrew, you may kiss da bride."

Kiss the bride? *Kiss the bride.* He was not only being given permission, it was expected. Drew's gaze fell to her lips—full, rosy . . . waiting. *Kiss my bride. . . .*

He gathered her into his arms and for the first time realized he was still in his horse-smelling riding clothes. But from the tenderness in her expression, she didn't seem to mind. Not at all. Heart pounding, he lowered his lips to hers in a breath-stopping, dizzying kiss. He felt the softness of her in his arms . . . Crystabelle . . . beautiful, funny, exciting, stubborn Crystabelle . . . in his arms. . . . She was really his.

Someone clamped a hand on his arm.

"Didn't you say you vas in da hurry?" Brother Rolf asked.

With the greatest of effort, Drew pulled away from Crystabelle. His gaze, though, left those mind-stealing lips more slowly.

For the first time, Brother Rolf looked pleased. Chest puffed out with satisfaction, he wore a big gregarious smile. "Dere is still da marriage certificate to sign *und* stamp *mit* da vax, all legal."

Drew straightened, trying to pull himself together as the words penetrated. "Aye. Yes. A paper to sign." Of its own accord, one of his arms wrapped around Crysta again. "Lead the way."

By the time the certificate was official and tucked inside Drew's shirt, he'd regained his senses enough to remember that an armed party of six would be riding down on them before nightfall. "Crysta, while I go saddle your horse, run upstairs and pack enough clothes for a few days."

Her eyes flared wide. "I thought we weren't going to run."

"We're not. But you're my wife now—a Reardon—so naturally you'll be livin' out at our place." *Where,* he reflected inwardly, *I've got two marksmen for brothers, and sisters-in-law who are just about as skilled.*

That moment, that rapturous moment when Drew had kissed Crysta, an even more profound love for him had surged through her. It had kept her feet as light as her heart while she and Drew made haste to depart the Bremmers'. But as they sped their mounts toward the Reardon place, her anxieties resurfaced. Not only would she be facing her father and Harland Chastain, but what would the Reardons, her new family, think about this sudden and unexpected marriage?

Drew, just ahead of her on a fresh roan he borrowed from Rolf, took one last look behind them, then reined his mount onto the heavily wooded Reardon cutoff. Off the main road now, he slowed the broad-chested animal to a walk, allowing Crysta to guide Sheba alongside. Both horses were winded and heaving mightily. They'd been ridden hard, permitted to slow only twice on the four-mile run.

But Crysta knew it couldn't be helped.

Drew turned to her. None of the earlier tenderness remained in his expression. His face had a hard chiseled look to it. "It'll probably be best if you let me do the explaining to my family."

"Of course. Whatever you want." She certainly wasn't opposed to relinquishing that dubious honor.

A slow grin crept along his mouth. *"Whatever you want.* I sure do like the sound of them words."

She knew he was teasing her, and she slid him a coy glance. "Try not to get too used to it." But the light moment quickly passed as she added in all seriousness, "You'll be facing a lot today. All for me. I can't thank you enough for coming back."

Her gratitude seemed to catch him off guard. "I . . . uh . . . let's just take it one minute at a time. See how everything ends up at the close of the day."

And the first of those minutes was soon upon them. As she and Drew rode out of the woods, Ike and Noah, bare-chested, were in the closest field, slashing already harvested cornstalks. They both stopped and stared openmouthed, sickles dangling from their hands.

Drew waved.

The two men gave a nod, then dropped their implements and started jogging for the trio of houses.

Crysta and Drew reached the barnyard well ahead of them. Crysta couldn't help remembering the first time she had come to visit. The same dog barking and shouts of youngsters greeted her now. Only that time she'd been invited, expected.

"Drew!" one of the younger children yelled.

"Miss Amherst!" came from Gracie.

Ike's wife, Annie, her hair tightly bound in a scarf, stepped out of the building where she was making cheese.

Jessica, who looked as if she'd have her baby any day now, pushed herself up from a chair on the porch, where she'd been snapping beans.

Mistress Reardon stepped from behind a row of sheets gently flapping on the clothesline. "Andrew! You've come back!" His mother's rather severe features softened into a joyous smile. She practically ran the distance to her son. Glancing past him, her smile now included Crysta. "I knew he wouldn't stay away. I knew it."

Drew didn't respond as he dismounted. Instead he spoke to the oldest of the children crowding around. "Jacob, would you mind puttin' up the horses and waterin' them for me? They been rode purty hard."

"And why is that?" Annie asked warily, removing the scarf from her golden hair as she approached. She tucked it into her apron pocket. "Considering this is such a hot afternoon."

"That's a good question." Sidestepping the answer, Drew reached up for Crysta.

His gaze locked with hers as she slid from her saddle and down in his arms. The nearness of him brought back the moment they'd kissed, and her attention drifted to his lips.

"Drew! Drew!" One of the little girls tugged on his hunting shirt. "Did you bring me a present?"

The private moment evaporated as he turned from Crysta to pick up Jessica's dark-haired daughter. "I'm sorry, sweet pea, but I haven't been to a store where they keep purty little girl things."

Crysta saw Ike and Noah, their shirts now on, striding in from the field. Akin to Annie's, their expressions were uneasy.

"What's amiss?" Ike asked, not bothering with greetings.

Still toting his niece, Drew reached for Crysta and pulled her close.

Crysta swelled with emotion. When things got tough, Drew was always there for her, even if it meant standing between what she'd done and his family's wrath.

"Well? What is it?" Noah asked, echoing Ike's concern.

Drew set the child on her feet. "I'll come play with you kids in a little while. First I need to talk to your papas."

Crysta saw that she and Drew were now surrounded by all the adult Reardons, and she suddenly wished he hadn't sent the horses to the barn with Jacob.

"Crystabelle has a bit of a problem," Drew began slowly. "When she left Virginia to come here, she rode away from an unwanted betrothal arranged by her family. And, well, I reckon they'll be comin' by here some time this evenin', lookin' to take her back. But she don't wanna go, and I'm seein' to it she don't have to."

"How do you know this?" Jessica asked.

Mistress Reardon's gray eyes hardened. "How long have you been back, Son? Have you been stayin' here in the valley without comin' home to see us?"

"No, Ma." Drew turned to the others. "Look, it's a long story. But right now we need to get prepared. Load our weapons and decide on the best defensive positions."

"What on earth for?" Mistress Reardon glanced hither and yon.

"Because six armed men will be ridin' in here anytime now. Her pa, along with the man she was supposed to marry and four hired men. But they're not takin' her."

Drew's older brothers looked at each other, mouths grim.

His mother moved directly in front of Crysta, wagging her head. "I should've guessed. All them fancy clothes, that expensive horse. Them uppity ways . . . like pieces from a picture puzzle. You're that rich planter Lee Henry Amherst's daughter, ain't you?"

Crysta gasped out loud.

"You didn't know my people come from along the Potomac River, did you?" the older woman continued evenly. "And just who, might I ask, is your intended?"

"Harland Chastain." The name came out scarcely audible.

But it was loud enough. "Harland Chastain," Mistress Reardon repeated so everyone else could hear. "Chastain Tobacco of Stafford County?" She grated out the question, the muscles in her slim jaws knotting.

"Yes."

Drew tightened his hold on Crysta.

His mother's face had gone ashen. She swung her attention to her youngest son. "You knew about this? And you brung that gal here anyway? Brung the wrath of them high-and-mighty folks down on us? How dare you stand there talkin' about guns and shootin', with all my grandchildren smack in harm's way?"

"Your mother's right." Crysta tried to step out of Drew's grip. "I should never have come here."

He pulled her back next to him. "Ma, I reckon I should've started off by tellin' you one important detail here. She ain't Crystabelle Amherst anymore." He looked down at Crysta and winked. "This here's my wife, Mistress Andrew Reardon."

31

"*Married! When?*" Crysta watched Mistress Reardon stagger back as if she'd been struck.

Drew caught his mother's arm to steady her. "This afternoon. Crystabelle and I are man and wife. For better or worse."

A stunned hush followed.

After a moment, Jessica took Crysta's hand and breached the silence. "I'm so pleased to welcome you as my new sister. Aren't we, Annie?"

The taller woman wasn't so quick to agree. Expressionless, she eyed her younger brother-in-law instead. "That so, Drew? You've suddenly decided to grow up? Or do you think of this as just another adventure?"

"Let it go, Annie," her husband said. "What's done is done." Ike then stepped up to Crysta. Capturing her face in his callused hands, he planted a kiss on her forehead. "Welcome to the family."

Much more exuberant, Noah thumped Drew on the back. "Baby brother, you're in for it now."

"He *is not,*" Jessica resoundingly disagreed. "If anyone is in for anything, it's poor Crysta. But don't you worry, dear. Annie and I will make you privy to all the Reardon idiosyncrasies."

"Our idio-what?" Drew teased.

"Idio*cies,*" Annie quipped, getting into the spirit as she gave Drew a hug.

Then they were all laughing and talking at once, and for a moment Crysta felt the joy any bride might at such a welcome . . . until she remembered she wasn't a bride in the truest sense. Theirs was naught but a marriage of convenience. A bargain. A sham.

How could this truly be God's will?

"Andrew," his mother blurted in a loud voice, nose wrinkled, as she held him at arm's length. "You smell like a horse three days dead. Get yourself down to the river and take a bath."

"Not yet," he said as his grin died away. "Not till after the—" he hesitated— "later, Ma."

Ike clapped a hand on Drew's shoulder. "Well, little brother, if you're gonna smell like a horse, we might as well go on out and join 'em. Get the saddles off them lathered-up animals and cool 'em down." He glanced over to Noah. "Comin'?"

The three tall, broad-shouldered brothers walked away toward the barnyard, looking as powerful and capable as any men Crysta had ever seen, and she knew they'd be doing more than tending the horses. They'd be discussing how they were going to handle the imminent confrontation. And a dire realization surfaced: *Violence was in the air.* The threat was not only to her and the Reardon family but to her father and his party as well.

No blood must be allowed to spill because of her rash actions. With that declaration in mind, she started after the men.

Annie caught her arm. "Give them a few minutes to talk. They need to sort things through."

"I'm afraid they'll be doing more than that."

"Believe me when I say this; Ike ain't one to rush headlong into nothin' that might bring on harm."

"Annie speaks the absolute truth," the more literate Jessica concurred, offering Crysta a hand. "Come along. Let's all go rest in the shade and have something refreshing to drink."

Still deeply troubled, Crysta cast an anxious glance after the men before she acquiesced.

It wasn't long before they were settled beneath one of the sycamores on a bedsheet from the clothesline, "to protect Crystabelle's dress from grass stains," Mistress Reardon had said, disregarding the spoiling of her bed linen. The glass of springwater flavored with plum juice was indeed a satisfying treat in the late-afternoon warmth. Still there was a constant awareness, considering neither young mother allowed any of the children to wander far from the tree.

Crysta's thoughts never strayed for more than a few seconds from the men who could be riding in at any time or from the Reardons. The brothers had remained in the barn for only a few minutes before they'd left and headed for Ike's house, with Drew carrying his rifle and brace of pistols. And they'd been in there ever since.

"Wouldn't that be grand, Crystabelle?" Jessica asked, interrupting her musings.

Crysta returned her attention to the expectant mother lounging against the tree trunk, one hand relaxed atop her bulging tummy. "I'm sorry, dear. What did you say?"

Jessica smiled blithely. "Do try to be calm. God will see us through." There was always an air of innocence about her. A pure faith. "I was saying," she continued, "wouldn't it be grand if, after the crops were in next summer, we all took a trip East. Visit all our families. My family lives in Baltimore. They're merchants with a fleet of ships. Perhaps your family knows them—the Hargraves."

"Could be," Crysta replied, only half listening as she again checked the path that led to the road. "Perhaps when my father comes, you could ask him."

"I'd just as soon *not* go visit my folks," Annie said on a flat note. "Pa still hasn't forgiven me for doin' him outta my cows."

"But that's been nigh onto ten years," Mistress Reardon reminded Annie. "Time does have a way of healing old wounds."

Crysta certainly hoped so, for her own sake.

The sun lowered toward the western horizon so slowly, one would think it could take days to set. The children danced around, wallowing on the once-clean sheet, eventually napping . . . as the women sat and chatted and watched the road.

Finally, the older woman struggled to her feet. "Whether your pa comes or not, Crystabelle, these young'uns has got to be fed." Mistress Reardon offered assistance to the expectant mother. "Here, let me help you up."

Coming to her knees, Crysta rose from the ground. But she had no desire to go to Jessica's house. She desperately wanted to find out what the men were planning.

She saw Ike's wife start for her own log home, giving Crysta a ray of hope.

"I'll go help Annie," she said to the two other women.

Walking in the door to the simple log house, Crysta spotted all three men at the big table, making paper cartridges for their rifles. Before them sat a wooden bowl filled with small lead balls, horns of powder, and a stack of paper squares they'd cut from an old broadside. It looked as if they were preparing for war.

Crysta's temples began to throb, and she realized she'd developed a fierce headache.

Seeing her, Drew stopped pouring powder into a paper and came to her. "I pray to God we don't have to use a single one, Crysta. We all are. But we need to be prepared just in case."

"Annie," Ike said, addressing his wife in a commanding tone, "from what Drew figures, the Amherst party should be comin' anytime now." He looked out a side window that had a clear view of their wagon path to the main road. "Soon as you see 'em, I want you to send all the children down into Noah's cellar. Tell 'em to stay there till we come for 'em."

"I was just fixin' to feed 'em our leftovers from dinner."

"Take the food with you over to Noah's. They can eat there."

"What about you?"

Noah got up, moved to the window, and spoke for the men in a quieter tone. "We're not very hungry at the moment. Maybe later when things settle down."

"Crystabelle, you go with Annie," Drew added.

She bristled. "No. I'm sure the other women can take care of supper quite nicely without me. I'm staying here with you." She targeted a glance at each of the men. *"There will be no shooting.* I will have no bloodshed on my account."

"Crysta." Rising, Drew took her by the shoulders. "We don't want trouble any more than you do."

"Believe your husband, Crysta," Ike said. "No man wants to shoot his father-in-law on his wedding day."

"I see riders. They're coming," Noah stated flatly as he wheeled away from the window.

Ike pulled Annie toward the entrance. "Get on over there, and get the kids in the cellar."

"You go with her." Drew pushed Crysta in the same direction.

"No!" She wrenched away from him and ran to check out the side window. Immediately, she recognized her father's big dappled gray stallion at the lead, cantering alongside another rider.

"That's them, all right." Drew was right behind her. He turned her around to face him. "Don't come outside unless I call you." He snatched up his rifle and his pistols. "And stay away from the windows."

Without waiting for her answer, he strode out the open door, closed it behind him, and, to her amazement, walked over to a bench on the porch and sat down as if he didn't have a worry in the world—except, of course, a Pennsylvania rifle lay across his lap and the handguns were right beside him.

His brothers, with two rifles each, positioned themselves inside at the windows on either side of the front door.

Crysta's pulse picked up as she heard the rumble of horse hooves growing louder. A numbing chill coursed through her body as she moved to a spot behind Noah to get a clearer view of the front. *God, help us. Help us all.*

As the search party reined in their mounts in front of his mother's house, Drew had no problem picking out Crysta's betrothed. Although Harland Chastain, a fit man, wore merely a white shirt, gray breeches, and tall black boots, his low-crowned, broad-brimmed hat sported a huge ostrich plume.

Drew also noted that each of the men had a weapon ready, Chastain's a shiny silver-plated dueling pistol.

They had yet to spot Drew in the deep early evening shade of the porch. "Over here, gentlemen," he called as he stood up, his own rifle in hand. "May I be of service?"

The fact that he was also armed was not lost on the riders. Drew saw the tension in their faces as they reined their mounts around and brought them toward Ike's porch. He also noted that Chastain's deep blue eyes were a striking contrast to his black hair. Any woman would think him handsome.

"Reckon I should forewarn you," Drew drawled, trying to appear relaxed as they lined their horses before him. "We been expectin' you."

At the scraping sound behind him, Drew knew his brothers were running the barrels of their rifles out the windows.

"So we're surrounded, are we?" Harland Chastain, Crysta's betrothed, railed. "That would be the work of a degenerate reprobate who kidnaps young helpless maidens. Let's get this dirty business over with. What's your price?"

Drew maintained his steady gaze. "Since you were directed here to find her, you know that accusation ain't true." Drew scanned the others, looking for Crysta's father.

Only one older man was among them, but he looked nothing like Crysta. With silvered and faded red hair, he had a pasty, weathered complexion. But there was some resemblance in the eyes, even though they were a much lighter shade.

"We've been given different accounts," Mr. Amherst said with more restraint than rigid-jawed Chastain. "Where is my daughter? I insist you produce her at once."

"Sorry. I can't do that just yet," Drew said. "Not with so many guns pointing from every direction. One of 'em might go off, accidental-like."

The hired men swiveled in their saddles, looking behind them. Turning back, fear had crept past their rough exteriors.

"Mr. Amherst," Drew said, shifting his attention to the older man, "I'd like to introduce myself. The name's Andrew Reardon, your daughter's legal husband, and I have a marriage certificate to prove it."

"We learned all about your hasty wedding in town," Chastain spat, his gaze narrowing murderously. "It's just a scrap of paper until the marriage is recorded at the courthouse. And I'm not leaving here without it—*and my bride.*"

"Then you just might not be leaving at all."

Slowly, deliberately, Chastain raised the barrel of his pistol and took aim.

Drew did the same.

"*Stop!*" Crysta charged out onto the porch.

"I told you to stay inside," Drew said, not taking his eyes off Chastain.

"And I told you I will not allow people to shoot each other over me," she returned with surprising force.

"Crystabelle, thank God you're alive." Her father looked genuinely relieved. "Tell me, have they harmed you in any way?"

Crysta took a step toward him. "No, Papa, no. I've been shown nothing but kindness from everyone in the valley."

"And I suppose," Chastain sneered, "this one's been kinder than most."

The insinuated insult exploded past Drew's good sense. He lunged forward.

Crysta flung herself in Drew's path and whirled to face him. "Ignore him. Nothing Mr. Chastain says is of the slightest importance."

He could easily have moved her aside, but her words stopped him— words that left his adversary with no real power. Still, it took a moment for Drew to uncoil from his rage.

"Harland." Mr. Amherst had also stiffened, his voice now brittle and commanding. "I think you'd better leave the matter of my daughter to me."

"Thank you, Papa." Crysta's voice took on a gentleness. "I know my running away has caused you terrible distress. I wrote home apologizing for the worry I've caused you. But, Papa, you must understand. I could not turn my entire life over to a man for whom I have no love and, I'm sorry to say, little respect. It's all in the letter. Here in this valley I have found a full and worthwhile life. To give it up would pain me more than I can say."

"And you don't have to," Drew reminded her as he continued to keep close watch on Chastain.

"How do I know you're not being coerced into saying these things?" Crysta's pa asked suspiciously, shifting his attention to Drew.

Drew straightened. "Because, on this very day, I vowed before God that I would love and cherish your daughter . . . with the kind of love that helps, not harms."

Chastain snorted. "What do we have here, a backwoods poet?"

288

"*No,*" Crysta retorted, her voice proud, "a man who under-stands the mercies of the Bible." With renewed purpose, she shifted back to her father. "Papa, I'm living among good Christian people, and I truly love my life here. I would never want to give up teaching the valley's children."

"But, darling, teaching boys is not a fitting pursuit for a well-bred young lady."

"I thank you for the compliment, Papa, but I'm afraid I'm still much too outspoken to ever fit that description. And I'm just as willful as ever."

"Ain't *that* the truth." The words slipped out before Drew could retrieve them.

Not only did Crysta's pa burst out laughing, but so did Ike and Noah and the hired men who'd been observing the whole affair in silence.

Even Crysta saw the humor and let a smile slip.

Everyone but Chastain. He turned on Mr. Amherst. "Are you seriously thinking of allowing your daughter to remain in this backwoods sinkhole?"

Amherst studied Chastain a moment before answering. "Harland, I know our families have been friends for generations, and I would hate to see that friendship come to an end. But it's obvious that whatever else is decided here today, my daughter has no intention of marrying you. I realize you've expended a great deal of time on this search these past two months. As compensa-tion, I will honor my agreement with you concerning Crysta's dowry. As soon as we return home, I will deed to you the acreage and money."

Chastain tilted his head as if he hadn't heard correctly. "You mean . . . ?"

"I mean, Harland, that I would like for you to ride back to the settlement store and wait for me there. Any business you might have had here is concluded." He glanced behind him. "You men go on back with Mr. Chastain. See if you can find us lodging for the night."

Chastain's face darkened. "These men are all witness to what Lee Henry Amherst just said to me. I will receive full and complete redress, or I'll have you hauled into court." A final glower at Crysta's father and he wrenched on the reins of his mount, causing the horse to squeal, before he spurred the animal away at a full gallop.

The other riders followed, but at a much slower pace, grins splattered across their unshaven faces. For all Chastain's good looks and obvious wealth, they seemed quite pleased with his fall from Amherst's favor.

With ever-growing respect, Drew reassessed the older man— this one who'd taken charge and quickly defused what had verged on a deadly gun battle.

Then Lee Henry Amherst swung his full attention on Drew.

32

Mr. Amherst dismounted from his thoroughbred stallion, still looking quite fit for his age with only a bit of a paunch. He never took his eyes off Drew.

An inquisition was surely forthcoming.

Crysta, in front of Drew, started down the steps toward her father, giving Drew a reprieve for a moment or two, anyway. A few feet from Amherst's stern gaze, Crysta's steps faltered and she, too, hesitated.

Was her pa a violent man? Drew understood the disapproval of family—his own had been unhappy with him from the first time he rode out with the long hunter Ethan Yarnell. And that sort of reckless behavior was *never* tolerated from a young maiden. Drew moved up behind her.

Knowing he was near must have bolstered Crysta's courage— she began walking again.

Amherst's forbidding expression caved, and he stretched out his arms to her.

"Papa," came her husky whisper, and she ran headlong into them. "Papa, I'm sorry. I'm so sorry. But I couldn't wed Harland Chastain."

Her pa fiercely hugged her to him, his eyes becoming redder than his hair. "I know, I know. I'm just so relieved you're unharmed. I give you my solemn word, I won't ever force you to marry him. Come home with me, and I'll even send Harland on ahead. We won't have to bother with him during the trip."

She pulled back enough to look up at him. "Papa, you forget. I'm married to Drew Reardon."

Amherst's light hazel gaze glittered stone hard. "I haven't forgotten. But if you leave with me now, that can be easily remedied."

Drew opened his mouth to protest. Then closed it. If she wanted to go with her father, it would be best if she left today. Not prolong the agony.

Crysta looked back at Drew, her autumn gold eyes reaching out to him, searching, digging into his heart. "Papa," she said, turning away again, "I'm just as resolved in my decision to remain here as before. Could we take a walk? I think I can explain more easily if we're alone."

Amherst shot an accusing glance at Drew as if Crysta couldn't speak freely in front of him. "Yes, that's a splendid idea. Mr. Reardon, if you'll excuse us . . ."

Drew hesitated. He didn't trust Amherst either. But as long as the man left his horse behind, he couldn't very well abscond with Crysta, carry her off against her will. Reluctantly, Drew nodded his agreement.

He watched the two stroll toward the fenced meadow, the setting sun casting Crysta's slender figure in its aura. What would he do if he lost her to her father?

Just then, Crystabelle glanced back over her shoulder. With a smile, she mouthed, "Don't worry."

At least, that's what he thought she said . . . hoped she said.

A hand clapped onto his shoulder.

Noah had stepped outside. "She'll be all right, Drew. Don't worry. That's the same courageous young woman who left the luxuries of plantation life behind to come to this wilderness settlement to teach. She's not going anywhere."

"Drew!" his ma hollered. She came in hurried strides from Noah's house two doors down. "Where are they off to?"

Not wanting to broadcast Crysta's business like seeds on the wind, Drew waited until his mother reached him. "Crystabelle thought it would be easier to explain her actions to her pa alone."

Ma harrumphed. "Maybe so. But after that, it's only fittin' that her pa stay for supper—get to know the family. The gals is feedin' the young'uns now, so's we can talk and eat without 'em buttin' in. Now you get on down to that river and take a bath. With soap. And change into somethin' more befittin' a man on his weddin' day."

Drew glanced down at the garb he'd been wearing for almost a week. It was far from a pretty sight. He headed for his mother's cabin next door.

"I'll be movin' some of my things over to Jessica's," his ma said, stepping right along with him, "and puttin' fresh linens on my big bed for the two of you. I know you and Crystabelle will be wantin' your privacy tonight."

"Good bottomland, I see," Crysta's father admitted as they rested their arms on a fence rail. He surveyed the cultivated fields that stretched away from the meadow on both sides.

"Yes," Crysta agreed, glancing at him. He looked far more weathered than she'd ever seen him. And fit. A couple of months in the saddle had done him good. "The people here are very optimistic about this valley. Everyone is looking to its future. And I think the fact that these folks all pooled their money to send for a teacher speaks highly of them."

"I suppose. But it'll be two or three generations before this side of the mountain begins to have the luxuries we in Virginia enjoy. If ever."

"But, Papa, don't you see? The building of it is the thrilling part—watching what you made with your own hands turn into something. Being at the beginning, watching your creation grow and thrive. Papa, the thought of being relegated to a life of sipping apricot tea and embroidering in the parlor with nothing but talk of fashions and inane gossip to fill my days . . . while real life passes me by . . . ? Papa, I just can't do it. When I said my life here had purpose and meaning, I meant it—more than I've ever meant anything."

"Daughter, if your desire is to teach, I'm sure Miss Soulier would be more than happy to let you instruct your own class at her academy."

"That's not remotely the same. Teaching about the latest European fashions or how to set a proper table is trite, indeed, compared to watching a child read his first line in a book . . . the joy on his face . . . knowing that I'm helping him open that first door to an entire world of knowledge. Or assisting some farmer search out the best cure for the ailment of his one and only milk cow. Please say you understand. I love it here."

"But you're my only daughter. How will we survive without you? Hank and Monty? Your mother?"

A bitterness swept in. "You've managed quite nicely for the past four years."

His expression dimmed. "Darling girl, we didn't want to send you away. We were at our wit's end, the way you kept chasing around with your brothers like a wild Indian. It was our duty to see that you, an Amherst miss, be properly educated for your future as a gracious wife and hostess."

Crysta couldn't help smiling. She placed her hand over his freckled one. "Poor Papa. Then and now . . . I never would fit into a mold, would I?"

He smiled then too. "It must be that fiery French blood of your mama's. Like you, she refused to stay in her place, just as her tavern-maid mama refused to before her."

Crysta feigned surprise. "My grandmother was a *serving wench?*"

"It's your mother's deep dark secret," he said on a long, rolling chuckle as if he were remembering something else. "My beautiful wife always felt she had more than enough to live down with her father being a mere ship's captain without bringing up her mother's even humbler beginnings. It is never to be spoken of. Especially in polite society."

"Papa, that's the very sort of nonsense I'm talking about. Mama is more worried about appearances than about living in the truth."

Her father turned to her, took her hands. "Dear child, at the moment I know only two truths. One—after spending almost three months with Harland Chastain, I was only too glad to break off the marriage agreement. The man is conceited, petulant, and vindictive. He doesn't even try to rise above a given situation. I will be heartily glad to rid myself of his oppressive presence. My other truth is that I fear your mother will throttle me if I fail to deliver a marriageable bride to her. She's spent a king's ransom preparing for your wedding and reception."

Crysta burst out laughing. "Throttle you? Not if you tell her of my actual wedding first. She'll die of apoplexy. It was so rushed, I didn't even have time to change out of my work clothes or run a brush through my hair. And you saw what Drew is wearing—deerskin and homespun."

Her father's mouth flattened to a thin line. He obviously did not see the humor. "Trust me, his attire was not lost on me."

"He was on his way east," she defended, "when he discovered that you and your men were headed here. He rode like a madman to reach me before you did. Drew cares that much about my well-being. He can be infuriating at times—he likes to tease even more than Hank and Monty—but if he thinks I'm in any kind of trouble, he's always there to make it right . . . no matter what it costs him." Those last words tore at her heart. Drew always saw that no harm befell her, even if it meant marrying a woman he didn't want to keep.

"I must admit, that sounds quite admirable. But I'm afraid I have a hard time seeing this backwoodsman as the innocent lamb you perceive. Hasn't it ever occurred to you that he might think of you as the rainbow that will lead him to my pot of gold?"

"Never." Crysta took a step back from her father. "You've completely misjudged him. I don't believe he ever gives much thought to money one way or the other. When he left here six weeks ago, he tossed me a bag of coins as if they meant nothing to him. Forty dollars. And in this cash-poor territory, that's a small fortune. For instance, my wage as teacher is only twenty dollars a year plus my keep." Moving nearer, she placed a hand on his sleeve. "Please, Papa, stay for supper. Get to know him. He may not wear the cut of the elegantly dressed or live in a fine manse, but there's a fairness about him and a respect for all of God's creation that's worth any pot of gold. Please, try to see him as I do."

Her father dredged up a sigh from his depths. "Very well, Daughter. I'll try my best."

With a bundle of bathing needs tucked under his arm, Drew escaped down the brushy trail to the river. He knew he should have told his mother not to bother moving out of her bedroom, but he hadn't been able to bring himself to say the words . . . to tell her that this evening's sleeping arrangements would not be those expected of newlyweds. Arrangements he desperately yearned to change.

"I know, God," he muttered. "I know I can't go back on my word to Crysta. And even if she agreed, I know I can't make her my true wife, then go off and leave her."

Drew slowed to a halt. Maybe he'd just pack her up and take her with him. He tilted a glance skyward. "She's a good healthy lass, Lord. She'd hold up."

Drag her into the dangers of the wilds with no womanly comforts? No tight shelter to protect all that beauty from the heat and rain and cold? *And didn't you promise her you wouldn't make her give up her teaching?*

"But, Lord, you know the very idea of hitchin' myself to a plow and ploddin' down row upon endless row is the worst kind of drudgery to me," Drew argued as he pushed passed a spiny vine. "Workin' till my hands are bleedin' and my back's about to break, only to spend the next few months worryin' if it's gonna rain enough for the crop to grow or frettin' cuz it rained too much. All for a paltry few dollars profit . . . if it's a *good* year."

Reaching the riverbank, he dropped his bundle in the crutch of some exposed roots and looked across to the unclaimed wilderness on the other side . . . to the lure of the wonders that awaited him in the great beyond.

Oh, he could tell Crysta he'd give it up for her. That, for her, he would forsake his life's dream. He could probably even convince himself into believing it. But after a season or two? Would he want to stay after that?

He knew the ugly truth. Not even for her could he stay here forever.

Frustration and anger overtook him. He picked up a smooth flat stone to skip across the water. Instead, he threw it with all his might, watching it plunk into the current and sink like his heavy heart.

His eyes began to burn; his throat tightened. He slumped down on a boulder more desolate than he'd ever been in his life. "It's not fair, God. Why did you bring her into my life . . . this one woman I can't have and can't walk away from? Why did you make me love her so much if I can't make her mine?"

Then, as if a wind blew through him, his anger and the very depths of his anguish were swept away, leaving behind an incredible peace . . . as all the pieces of his life suddenly fell into place.

33

"Where's Josie?"

The question surprised Crysta. She'd completely forgotten that queries about the Amherst slave would need answering. Praying for the right words, she took a sip of the plum water Gracie had brought to her and her father on Noah's front porch. Crysta mustered a happy smile. "Didn't I tell you? Josie's on her honeymoon."

"*Honeymoon?* Slaves don't take honeymoons."

"Mine does." Crysta glanced toward the river where Noah had told her Drew had gone to bathe. He certainly was taking a long time.

"If you'll recall, dear child, I own Josie's papers."

With reluctance, Crysta returned her attention to the matter at hand. "After all the years of faithful service to me, putting up with my nonsense, Josie deserves all the pleasure the good Lord will allow in this special time with her new husband. And if you ever contemplate giving me a wedding gift, I would very much like it to be Josie."

"*Wedding gift.* You're actually going to insist upon staying here?"

"Yes, Papa, I am. Josie's papers, will you send them to me?"

"Very well." His agreement sounded grudging. "But I don't like it. I just told you I wasn't going to make it profitable for Drew Reardon to marry an Amherst."

"And you won't be. Just send the document to me, and I'll keep it in a safe place. I'll only bring it out if I'm required to show proof of ownership."

Her father leaned back in his chair and drank down a portion of his beverage, seemingly satisfied. "It's going to be a nice evening," he said. "I think the sticky weather's mostly behind us. And whatever your new family is cooking inside surely smells delicious. I haven't had too many decent meals these past three months."

"Well, you never looked more fit, Papa."

"You think so?" He sat a bit straighter in his chair. "I feel fit. But don't try to change the subject. I know you love Josie, but now that she's your sole responsibility, you must remember that if you spoil her, she'll turn lazy on you. She won't want to do a lick of work after that. And it's plain to see, in this backwoods place, there's more than plenty to do."

Crysta's smile was no longer forced as she thought of Josie's even more primitive conditions. "Papa, Josie and I grew very close in the years we were at the academy. We were all each other had. Then I did a cruel disservice to her. When Josie learned that we were on our way to Tennessee instead of back to the plantation, she was frightened practically witless. Every moment of every day, she was sure you'd catch up to us. And no matter what I told her, she thought you would beat her to death for failing to report to you. Yet she was almost as wary of going with me to the Chastain plantation had I married Harland. She'd heard tales about the harsh treatment there."

"That family's always been known for keeping a tight rope on their slaves." Her father looked as if he were about to say more, but abruptly rose to his feet instead. He stepped toward the edge of the porch and finished his drink.

Crysta stood and followed him, hoping the guilt he must feel for arranging a marriage to a man with less than admirable qualities would soften him toward her own choices. "Papa, I owe Josie this time with her new husband. And more."

"Speaking of husbands, where's yours?"

She gazed out over the cleared land that stretched to the brush and trees fringing the river. Only the four youngest children were in sight. At least a hundred yards away, they played near the path leading down to the water, waiting, she was sure, for their hero to reappear. In the fading light, faint strains of the children's ditty "London Bridge Is Falling Down" reached her ears as the children played the musical game—one she'd seen enacted numerous times by her younger students these past two months.

"Odd, isn't it?" her father remarked. "To be visiting someone's home of an evening, yet there's not a single person to keep us company."

"They're not being rude. Drew's brothers are just tending the animals. They'll be in soon. If you were one of the neighbors, you would've offered to help—just as I would have in the kitchen if I weren't out here visiting with you."

"Surely you would've sent Josie in your place."

"No, Papa. That would be considered rude out here in the backcountry. You see, the real visiting goes on in the kitchen. And with all my extra activity, I, too, feel a whole lot more fit in so many ways. And, Papa, in this simple setting, rid of so much of Virginia's social clutter, I've grown so much closer to the Lord. I've never known such peace and happiness. I just wish you could see the richness of the life I now lead."

"I'm trying, darling. I am trying." His chin notched up. "At last. Your new husband is returning. He probably thought I'd get tired of waiting and leave if he stayed gone long enough."

Following her father's gaze, Crysta saw Drew striding forth, his clean hair undone and falling around his shoulders. A magnificent leonine sight. Her pulse picked up pace.

The children saw Drew, too, and ran to him, laughing and shouting. They surrounded the man, now dressed in a fresh white shirt and breeches that flattered his height and lean breadth. Clasping each other's hands, they locked him in as they circled Drew and sang, "Take the key and lock him up, lock him up, lock him up . . ."

He laughed along with them, despite the fact that Crysta knew the last thing he ever wanted was to be locked up in any way, shape, or form. He tossed his bundle to Ike's Rebecca and caught the two three-year-olds up in his arms as he came up the path, singing the song with them. Obviously, Drew hadn't spotted his audience—his father-in-law and his bride— standing on Noah and Jessica's porch.

"Well, I suppose the man's good with children," her father begrudged as he returned to his seat.

"Aye, that he is," she mused, still watching her new husband from the deep shade of the porch, wondering if his good humor would continue after her father finished with him.

To her disappointment, Drew veered toward his mother's cabin next door.

Just before he and his merry bunch reached it, his mother came outside. "Give me those dirty things," she called as she walked purposefully out to intercept them.

Drew lowered the two little ones to the ground and hauled the surprised woman into a zestful hug with an exaggerated kiss to her cheek.

She looked no less amazed after he released her.

"Your new husband does seem to be in an exuberant mood, doesn't he?" her father, coming up behind her, observed.

"Yes, that he does." Had Drew changed his mind in favor of her and this valley? Did he plan to stay?

Annie stepped out of the open door behind Crysta and her father. "Supper's ready." Then, with her golden braid bouncing against her back, she stepped to the edge of the porch and hollered. "Supper's on! Just the adults this time," she reminded the children. "Rebecca, run tell the men out in the barn."

At that moment, Drew's gaze found Crysta. He looked as thrilled as he was happy . . . as if he'd just spotted his beloved after a long absence.

There was nothing to do but return his tender greeting as she watched him come to her. She also couldn't help having an over-whelming sense of anticipation.

"Come along, folks," Annie urged as she turned back inside. "Drew, see that your father-in-law is seated comfortable."

"My pleasure." Drew continued to grin as if seating her father would truly be his pleasure.

Crysta figured, though, that *comfortable* to Drew meant posi-tioning her father as far away from himself as possible.

But she was wrong. He seated their guest in an honored place at the end, then Crysta to her father's right, and Drew himself to Crysta's right.

Pulling his chair up next to hers, Drew leaned close and whis-pered, "After supper we need to talk. Alone."

She turned to him with a wild mix of feelings. Surely this sudden merry mood boded good news?

As Drew watched his brothers come in and take their places at the table, Mr. Amherst commented, "The food smells delightful. I haven't had a good home-cooked meal in months."

"Sorry it's just a plain ever'day spread," Drew's mother apologized as she settled on the other side of Drew. "Notice was a mite short for a real weddin' supper."

"That it was," Noah laughed at the other end.

Drew noted two low bouquets of his mother's pale roses among a generous array of serving bowls and platters. Undoubtedly young Gracie's contribution to the festive occasion. Then, seeing that Crysta had her hands in her lap, he slipped one of his over them.

She flinched, but only slightly, before turning a palm up to twine her fingers through his. She gave his hand a quick squeeze before removing her hands and bringing them to the surface of the table.

He would have preferred that her hands were still enfolded in his, but her secret gesture was enough.

"Shall we ask God's blessing?" Noah, their host, asked, prompting those gathered to bow their heads. "Almighty God in heaven, we do thank you for this bounty set before us this evening. But most of all, we thank you for a peaceful end to this day. And, Father, I know each of us here wishes a long and happy marriage for this young couple, a union blessed with many children and an earnest desire to follow in your righteous ways. We also thank you that Crystabelle could have at least one member of her family here to share this eventful day in her life."

As several murmured, "Amen," Drew again marveled that a morning that had begun so frantically with his racing across hill and vale to come warn Crysta could end with an exalted peace he'd never known existed. And so much of the exaltation he felt was due to the enchanting woman sitting next to him. He was aware of her every breath, the brush of her fingers as she handed him a serving dish, the rather shy smile, her silence. Others around them were talking, but there was only one person he wanted to speak to, and then, only once they were alone.

"Mr. Reardon . . . *Mr. Reardon.*"

Drew shot a glance up and saw that Crysta's florid-faced father was addressing him. "Yes? May I get you something?"

"Crystabelle tells me that you care very little for money. That you're overly casual with it. I feel rather uncomfortable leaving my daughter with a man who does not keep watch over his livelihood."

"My livelihood . . . and your daughter will always be in safe hands," Drew assured him.

"That's right," his mother piped in. "I've kept Andrew's savings tucked away since he was a lad. Over the years, his trade with the tribes has been quite profitable. Hasn't it, Son?"

"I reckon. But I wouldn't think by Mr. Amherst's standards."

"By anyone's standards," his mother blurted. She looked past him to Amherst. "My son has never been one to waste his earnings on hard drink or gambling."

She was starting to sound like a mother hen coming to the rescue of her chick.

Ike, across from Crysta, jumped in, but in a more casual manner. "There's a lumber mill in Nashville now, so if Crystabelle would prefer to live in a wood-frame house with paint and all the trimmin's, Drew can easily provide that as well as journeyman-crafted furniture to fill it. I assure you, Mr. Amherst, he can provide any comforts she needs."

"That's right," Noah added at the other end. "Soon as the harvest is in, we'll start clearing Drew's land for his house and fields."

It was nice to see his brothers rallying to what they thought was his cause, but their plans were not his. Drew changed the subject. "Mr. Amherst, you must be anxious to get back to your own place after all this time."

"How much land do you have?" the older man asked, unwilling to turn loose of the matter.

"A square mile, more or less. And how much land do you have, sir?"

"A square mile . . . six hundred and forty acres. That's a sizable piece of property for one man to work. I didn't see any slaves on the place. Do you plan to turn my daughter and grandchildren into field hands?"

The man purely was starting to steal the joy of the evening. "No, sir, I don't. I have no intention of clearing my land to plant. I'm leaving it in its natural state. Except for maybe a spot to build a summerhouse in the glen." Drew picked up his fork. His food was getting mighty cold now.

"Andrew," his mother scolded, "surely you don't expect your wife to go traipsin' off into Indian country with you, huntin' and tradin'? I won't hear of it."

"No, Ma." His mother could have gone all evening without saying that.

Mr. Amherst's faded green eyes turned dark beneath his colorless brows. "Just exactly what are you planning, Mr. Reardon? To come to Virginia to live off your wife's rich family?"

Beside Drew, Crysta stiffened. "Papa, that is uncalled for. Living in the East is the last thing Drew would want." She turned to him. "Isn't it?"

Drew surveyed the table. Since he'd just told his family he didn't intend to take up his place farming, they looked none too pleased. Only Jessica, across from his mother, seemed sympathetic. He supposed he didn't have any choice but to speak now, tell them his plan, at least the first part. "For the next year or so, I plan to ask Brother Rolf if he'll let me work with him."

Ike slammed down the mug in his hand, all pretense at calmness gone. "You'd rather be smithin' with Rolf than workin' with your own brothers?"

"Now, Ike," Noah cajoled, "having someone in the family who can work with iron isn't a bad thing."

"Aye," Drew said, "I reckon it would be a handy trade to know.

But I was thinkin' more of exchangin' my labor to study theology with him."

The room dropped into sudden silence.

Ike was the first to find his voice. "Did I hear you right, Drew? You're plannin' on becomin' a minister? You? A *preacher?*"

34

"*Andrew Vickersund Reardon, a minister?*" Ma's jaw went slack. "My baby boy, the pastor of a church?"

"More or less," Drew replied uncomfortably. He knew his news would come as a surprise, but to look at them, one would think he'd just said he was flying to the moon and back again.

He turned to Crysta beside him and was thrilled to see, not shock, but a warm smile and understanding in those beautiful golden eyes.

"I'm so pleased for you." She spoke softly, for him only. "I knew there was something different about you when you came back from the river."

His mother sprang up from the table, looking almost youthful, her face alight. "Do you know how many nights I spent prayin' for you, Andrew? *Years.* That you'd come home, settle down . . . but I can't believe this! Oh my, God purely does answer prayer." She took in a breath so deep, Drew thought she would burst. Tears sprang to her faded gray eyes. Wiping them with her apron, she laughed, then fluttered a hand to dismiss her embarrassment. "Tears . . . can you imagine that? Me, cryin' like a child. Oh my. Would anyone like more coffee?"

"Yes, thank you," Mr. Amherst said as she swung away to the hearth for the pot. The older man eased back in his chair as if he were settling in for the night. "Well, I suppose telling my wife that Crysta has wed a man of the cloth will help to appease her somewhat. It does have a respectable ring to it."

Conversely, Ike's and Noah's narrowed stares clearly reflected their doubt that Drew was serious. But who could blame them? For years, he'd always managed to slip the bonds of farmwork. They most likely thought he'd just come up with a convenient tale to forestall Amherst.

Whatever they thought, Drew prayed they'd keep their doubts to themselves until after the man was gone. Not ask the questions he didn't want to answer until after he'd spoken to Crystabelle.

"Food's gettin' cold," he reminded everyone, then glanced from one brother to the other. "There'll be plenty of time for talk later."

Food. Who could think of food at a time like this? Crysta pushed her meal around on her plate, pretending to eat, but nothing could keep her mind off the man beside her.

Drew was staying! And every day he'd be working within hollering distance of the school. *Dear Lord, never in my most fanciful dreams did I think he'd consider going into service for you. Live for you in such a meaningful way.*

Her mind continued to whirl with what his revelation meant to her. If he truly wanted her for his wife—which she was almost certain he did—they could have the same kind of evenings of Bible discussions that had become the best part of her life with the Bremmers. And she could help him in his calling . . . help him search the Scriptures and the sermons of such great ministers as

310

Jonathan Edwards, George Whitefield, and the Wesleys, for his preaching . . . visit the sick with him, pray with him as she'd heard the Bremmers do at night alone in their room.

It was all so wonderful, she wanted to spring up and shout for joy.

But what was expected of her at the moment was to eat. So much happiness to keep contained. However, there was one thing she could do. While trying to chew a bite of some wild-tasting meat, she slipped her hand under the table and found Drew's.

He caught hold of it, seeming just as ardent to share their private moment as she.

Table conversation after that bypassed Crysta and Drew as it switched to farm talk . . . crop rotation, climate, and soil . . . the market in Europe.

After what seemed forever, Papa pushed back his chair. "Mistress Reardon, you and your daughters do set a fine table. I shan't forget your most gracious hospitality. You all must come visit us at Amherst Farms. Give me the pleasure of repaying your kindness."

"That's a most opportune offer," tiny Jessica said in her soft low voice. At Noah's right, she struggled to her feet. "Just this afternoon, I was speaking of that very thing to your daughter. I thought it would be most companionable if we all journeyed east next summer to visit our families. I haven't seen my relatives in Baltimore for three years now. Crystabelle mentioned that you might know of them. They're merchants in Baltimore. The Hargraves."

"You're a Hargrave? Living here?" Papa blurted before regaining his composure. Then he smiled. "Ah yes. That's where I've seen those unusual eyes. Janie Hargrave . . . God rest her soul . . . yes, indeed. Do come. I'll invite your family for a visit, and we'll make a splendid party of it."

Crysta couldn't help smiling. Her father had now found an enticing advantage to her marriage—the familial ear of a tobacco buyer. He would go home now much more satisfied, even touting the fact that his daughter had made a beneficial match for herself and the family.

"Again, I thank you all," he continued. "But I must be off. If I stay here much longer, my men will think you Reardons are holding *me* hostage this time." His attention then fell upon Crysta. "Walk out with me, Daughter. You, too, Andrew."

As Crysta and her father strolled out into the darkness, Drew turned back. "Sir, I'd better light a lantern to see you on your way."

Reaching the bottom of the steps, she accompanied her father toward his horse hitched two doors down in front of Annie and Noah's house.

He took her hand. "You do know it's going to be very hard to leave you here in such humble surroundings. But the young Hargrave matron does seem quite content. Perhaps it's not as dreadful a circumstance as I imagine."

"Dearest Papa, leaving me here with your blessing is the greatest gift you could bestow upon me." Rising to her toes, she kissed him on the cheek. "Truly, I've never been happier in my life." Realizing how very deeply she meant that, her heart swelled as another conviction pulsed through her. Drew would be asking her to be his true wife this very night.

She saw him coming then, a lantern swinging in his hand. Drew, so tall and stalwart, stopped next to her.

"Well, I suppose this is farewell," Papa sighed. "A father-in-law isn't exactly the most welcome guest on one's honeymoon now, is he?"

That crooked smile appeared, and Drew shrugged. "Not that I'd ever mention it."

Pressing his lips together, Papa nodded. This was a hard moment for him. "Very well, I'll leave. But only if I have your promise that you'll bring my daughter home for a visit next summer."

"You have my word, sir."

Papa pulled her into one last fierce hug, then, wheeling away, was mounted and riding forth. The lantern Drew had placed in his hand cast a wide glowing circle that soon disappeared into the woods.

"Walk with me." Drew tucked Crysta's hand in the crook of his arm and started toward the meadow.

The moment had come. He would be saying the words she yearned to hear.

"I meant what I said when I told my family that I'd be staying here to study with Brother Rolf." He stopped in the deeper shadows of one of the sycamores and faced her, folding her hand within both of his.

She felt a bit of a tremor but couldn't tell if it came from her or him. He seemed so much closer in the darkness. It took a moment to regather her senses enough to reply. "I know you spoke from your heart. Since you came walking back from the river, all the worries of this hectic day have been gone from your face."

"You know me that well, do you?" Though she couldn't quite make out that mischievous smile, it was present in his voice.

"Aye, that I do," she returned in a tease, then sobered. When his mother had asked him if he planned to be a pastor, he'd used that evasive line—the one he'd used on Crysta several times before. *More or less*. "At least I hope I know you."

"Crystabelle." The smile had vanished from his voice. "There is more I need to tell you. It must be said before we can speak of anything else. Our heavenly Father has not asked me to be a minister out of the same mold as Brother Rolf. My years in the wilderness trading with the Indians has been for me what you might call an apprenticeship."

What was Drew trying to tell her? "Please," she said, pulling him into the light of a three-quarter moon. "I need to see your face. What do you mean?"

He sucked in a breath. "Though I wasn't aware of it until today,

I feel the Lord has been preparing me for a mission. To go among the tribes with the message of hope and mercy. Something I pray they'll come to rely on in the coming years. I'm afraid their future is a bleak one. Since they fought against the Americans during both wars—first for the French and then the English—destroying so many of the frontier settlements, our people are afraid to trust them. And with so many folks losing family to the Indians, hatred runs deep. Despite the teachings of Jesus. With each year one tribe or another is pushed farther west, farther away from their hunting grounds. I haven't had much of a chance to tell you about Black Bear and Josie, but their Shawnee village will be moving west up the Missouri River next spring. When I'm prepared, I'll begin there, see if I can help Bear and his pa to reach them with the good news of Jesus."

"I see." Crysta had tried to listen with an open mind, to praise God for the work Drew would be doing to further the kingdom, but it was as if the earth had dropped away from her. She had completely misread the situation. Drew's plan to go exploring the wilds really hadn't changed at all. It had merely been delayed for a time. His original intent was the same as ever—to leave her behind. Pulling every bit of her will together, she resolved not to let him know how devastated she was.

"Don't leave me just hangin' here. What do you say?"

About abandoning her again? And asking her blessing to boot? There was no end to this man's gall. "What would you have me say? Going up the Missouri is all you talked about when you were here. You said you were going, and, well, it seems you are." She whirled away while she still had her pride.

"Wait. Please." He caught her arm. "What I'm tryin' to say is I want you to come with me."

She stared in shock. "*With* you? *Me*? Crystabelle Amherst of Miss Soulier's Academy for Young Ladies? Spoiled, pampered belle of Virginia? You want me to trek off into the savage wilds?"

"You've come a long way from that shallow female, Crystabelle *Reardon,*" he argued gently. "Besides, you already proved what a quick learner you are." He rushed on, holding on to both her arms now as if she might try to escape. "And you told me yourself you're a tomboy. You like to put on men's clothes and ride free as the wind. And you've shown how brave and coolheaded you are when you have to be. I'll teach you the rest . . . what I know of the Indian tongue, how to do things their way. Not only that—when we get there, you'd have Josie for company. You could start a school right there in their village, teach anyone who's interested to read the Bible and—"

She touched her fingers to his lips, hushing the fervent outpouring. "Andrew Reardon, is this your roundabout way of asking me to be your wife? Your *true* wife?"

"Aye, I reckon it is." His voice, husky and deep now, flowed over her like warm honey. "I know I promised you the marriage would be in name only. But I'm askin' you to reconsider. You have no idea how much I love you. I loved you somethin' awful before, but since I came back from the river . . . it's the kind of love that wouldn't ever let me leave here without you again. The kind that causes my chest to knot at just the thought of you sayin' no."

Crysta couldn't believe that a day that had brought so many concerns and fears could turn into one where the man she loved so completely had asked her to be his wife . . . not once, but twice. And this time, his true and forever wife.

"Crysta, please say yes. I know you always wanted to be free. But I promise you something even better. A life filled with love and adventure beyond anything you ever dreamt."

She smiled. "My life's been one adventure after another since the first day we met. And now that you're offering adventure *and* love, how could a young miss resist?"

"I'm gonna take that as a yes," Drew said, hauling her into his arms. His hand cupped the back of her head as he lowered his mouth toward hers.

Then abruptly he pulled back. "There's one more thing."

"*What now?*" Could there be anything so important it couldn't possibly wait?

"It's those blasted pins. I've been wantin' to see your hair all down and flowing around you since the first day we met." He started plucking at them.

"That's it? You stopped because of some silly old pins?" Crysta shoved his hands out of the way and ripped the remaining ones out, letting them and her combs fly where they may until her hair came down in a wild tumble. "It's done. And now, Drew, I expect you to thoroughly, passionately—"

And that he did. With his fingers tangled in her hair, her arms twining his neck, their mouths explored wonders that had been awaiting them all along . . . those first rapturous discoveries of a bride and her bridegroom.

And the adventure had just begun.

A Note from the Author

Dear Reader,

The cares of the world crowded in much more than usual during the writing of this novel. I had so many other obligations tugging at me that when I was three chapters from the end of the book I found that I'd written myself into a corner. Despite the fact that Drew and Crystabelle were deeply attracted to each other, their goals were too different for me to bring them together logically for a satisfying romantic ending . . . or so I thought.

I'd had a particularly trying day with several other situations becoming critical all at once. That night while I was praying, I felt completely overwhelmed with no way to successfully work my way through all those diverse problems. I was feeling sorry for myself and asking God, "Why me?" What had I done to deserve to be so oppressed—me, who always tries to do the right thing, the righteous thing. And not only could I not fix things, but, I wailed, "I don't even have an ending for my novel, and it's due in a couple of weeks!"

Then a few Bible verses came to mind, and I was shown very clearly that while I might have asked God to take my problems, I had not actually "put my money where my mouth is" and handed them over to him. When I truly did that, I was finally able to regain the peace to fall asleep.

The next morning I was awakened by a surprising idea for the end of the novel. Had the first of my "insurmountable" problems been solved? Being a bit of a Doubting Thomas, I told God that particular ending wouldn't work.

Nonetheless, curiosity pulled me out of bed and sent me leafing through the manuscript. And, lo and behold, the ending *did* work, beautifully. I could hardly believe the entire novel had been pointed in that direction all along without my noticing. And not only did God solve that dilemma, but my other problems also started working out in unexpected ways . . . blessed proofs that our heavenly Father surely is an awesome God.

I will always have a special affection for this novel, this reminder that I must not pray about something and then continue to fret over it as if the problem were still mine to solve. As Jesus says in Mark 11:24, "Listen to me! You can pray for anything, and if you believe, you will have it." I must never again forget that my whole-hearted faith in his absolute power equals pure joy and peace beyond understanding.

I do hope you enjoyed and were inspired by this novel and the rest of the trilogy as much as I was while writing about the Reardon brothers.

Blessings to you and yours,

Dianna Crawford

About the Author

Dianna Crawford lives in southern California with her husband, Byron, and the youngest of their four daughters. Although she loves writing historical fiction, her most gratifying blessings are her husband of nearly forty years, her daughters, and her grandchildren. Aside from writing, Dianna is active in her church's children's ministries and in a Christian organization that counsels mothers-to-be, offering alternatives to abortion.

Dianna's first novel was published in 1992 under the pen name Elaine Crawford. Written for the general market, the book became a best-seller and was nominated for Best First Book by the Romance Writers of America. Three more novels and several novellas followed under that pen name.

Dianna much prefers writing Christian historical fiction, because our wonderful Christian heritage is commonly diluted or distorted—if not completely deleted—from most historical fiction, nonfiction, and textbooks. She felt very blessed when she and Sally

Laity were given the opportunity to coauthor the Freedom's Holy Light series for Tyndale House. The books center on fictional characters who are woven into many of the real-life adventures and miracles that took place during the American Revolution.

The Freedom's Holy Light series consists of *The Gathering Dawn, The Kindled Flame, The Tempering Blaze, The Fires of Freedom, The Embers of Hope,* and *The Torch of Triumph.* Dianna has also authored two HeartQuest novellas, which appear in the anthologies *A Victorian Christmas Tea* and *With This Ring.* She is the coauthor with Rachel Druten of the novel *Out of the Darkness* (Heartsong Presents). Her HeartQuest series, The Reardon Brothers, consists of *Freedom's Promise, Freedom's Hope,* and *Freedom's Belle.*

Dianna welcomes letters from readers written to her at P.O. Box 80176, Bakersfield, CA 93301.

HEART QUEST

Current HeartQuest Releases

- *Magnolia*, Ginny Aiken
- *Lark*, Ginny Aiken
- *A Bouquet of Love*, Ginny Aiken, Ranee McCollum, Jeri Odell, and Debra White Smith
- *Dream Vacation*, Ginny Aiken, Jeri Odell, and Elizabeth White
- *Reunited*, Judy Baer, Jeri Odell, Jan Duffy, and Peggy Stoks
- *Sweet Delights*, Terri Blackstock, Elizabeth White, and Ranee McCollum
- *Awakening Mercy*, Angela Benson
- *Faith*, Lori Copeland
- *Hope*, Lori Copeland
- *June*, Lori Copeland
- *Glory*, Lori Copeland
- *With This Ring*, Lori Copeland, Dianna Crawford, Ginny Aiken, and Catherine Palmer
- *Freedom's Promise*, Dianna Crawford
- *Freedom's Hope*, Dianna Crawford
- *Freedom's Belle*, Dianna Crawford

- *Prairie Rose*, Catherine Palmer
- *Prairie Fire*, Catherine Palmer
- *Prairie Storm*, Catherine Palmer
- *Prairie Christmas*, Catherine Palmer, Elizabeth White, and Peggy Stoks
- *Finders Keepers*, Catherine Palmer
- *Hide and Seek*, Catherine Palmer
- *A Kiss of Adventure*, Catherine Palmer (original title: *The Treasure of Timbuktu*)
- *A Whisper of Danger*, Catherine Palmer (original title: *The Treasure of Zanzibar*)
- *A Touch of Betrayal*, Catherine Palmer
- *A Victorian Christmas Cottage*, Catherine Palmer, Debra White Smith, Jeri Odell, and Peggy Stoks
- *A Victorian Christmas Quilt*, Catherine Palmer, Debra White Smith, Ginny Aiken, and Peggy Stoks
- *A Victorian Christmas Tea*, Catherine Palmer, Dianna Crawford, Peggy Stoks, and Katherine Chute
- *Olivia's Touch*, Peggy Stoks

Coming Soon (Summer 2001)

- *Camellia*, Ginny Aiken
- *Romy's Walk*, Peggy Stoks

Other Great Tyndale House Fiction

HEART
QUEST®

HeartQuest Books by Dianna Crawford

Freedom's Promise—For the first time in Annie McGregor's life, she's free. *Free!* Her years of servitude drawing to a close, Annie hears there's a man in town looking for settlers to accompany him across the mountains into Tennessee country. Could this be the answer to her prayers?

Isaac Reardon is on a mission to claim his betrothed—along with a preacher and a small group of settlers—and return to the beautiful home he has carved from the rugged wilderness. He is devastated to learn of his intended wife's betrayal. And now to make matters worse, he's confronted with a hard-headed, irresistible young woman who is determined to accompany his wagon train—without a man of her own to protect her!

Together, Annie and Ike fight perilous mountain passages, menacing outlaws, and a rebellious companion. And as they do, both are shocked to discover their growing attraction, which threatens to destroy the dream of freedom for which they have risked their very lives.

Book 1 in The Reardon Brothers series.

Freedom's Hope—Jessica Whitman lives for one hope: Reaching her mother's family, the distinguished Hargraves of Baltimore, far from the clutches of her drunken father.

Noah Reardon, bitter over a broken betrothal, wants nothing to do with people. So why is he captivated by the intriguing Jessica? Despite himself, Noah reluctantly offers his protection to this feisty young woman.

Together Noah and Jessica discover a shared passion for truth, for integrity, for the very ideals upon which their new nation was founded. Noah is tempted to make the biggest mistake of his life—giving his heart to a woman who doesn't share his faith. Then a shocking discovery about Jessica's family threatens to shatter her hope. As they struggle to understand God's plan, both Noah and Jessica learn who truly offers hope for each tomorrow.

Book 2 in The Reardon Brothers series.

A Daddy for Christmas—One stormy Christmas Eve on the coast of Maine, the prayers of a young widow's child are answered in a most unusual manner. This novella by Dianna Crawford appears in the anthology *A Victorian Christmas Tea*.

Something New—An arranged marriage awaits Rachel in San Francisco. But her discovery on the voyage from the Old Country threatens to change everything. This novella by Dianna Crawford appears in the anthology *With This Ring*.